NAGUIB MAHFOUZ

The Beggar
The Thief and the Dogs
Autumn Quail

—————

Naguib Mahfouz was born in 1911 in the crowded Cairo district of Gamaliyya, an area on which he has drawn heavily for the setting of many of his novels. He worked in various government ministries until his retirement in 1972. He began writing at the age of seventeen, and his first novel was published in 1939. Since then he has written over thirty novels and more than a hundred short stories. Today Naguib Mahfouz lives in the Cairo suburb of Agouza with his wife and two daughters.

The Beggar

The Thief and the Dogs

Autumn Quail

The Beggar
The Thief and the Dogs
Autumn Quail

NAGUIB MAHFOUZ

ANCHOR BOOKS
A DIVISION OF RANDOM HOUSE, INC.
NEW YORK

AN ANCHOR ORIGINAL, DECEMBER 2000

These three works, originally published in Arabic in 1961, 1962, and 1965,
as *Al-Liss wa-al-Kilāb, Al-Summan Wal-Kharif,* and *Al-Shahhādh*
Copyright © by Naguib Mahfouz, were originally published separately in
English translations in 1984, 1985, and 1986 by The American University
in Cairo Press, Cairo, Egypt. *The Beggar* was translated by
Kristin Walker Henry and Nariman Khales Naili al-Warraki.
The Thief and the Dogs was translated by Trevor Le Gassick and
M. M. Badawi and revised by John Rodenbeck. *Autumn Quail*
was translated by Roger Allen and revised by John Rodenbeck.

Library of Congress Cataloging-in-Publication Data

Mahfuz, Najib, 1911-
[Novels. English. Selections]
The beggar ; The thief and the dogs ; Autumn quail / Naguib Mahfouz.
p. cm.
ISBN 0-385-49835-7 (trade paper)
1. Maòfàò, Najâb, 1911—Translation into English. I. Title: Beggar ;
The thief and the dogs ; Autumn quail. II. Title: Thief and the dogs.
III. Title: Autumn quail. IV. Title.
PJ7846.A46 A2 2000
892.7'36—dc21   00-040145
www.anchorbooks.com

Printed in the United States of America
10 9 8 7 6 5 4 3 2 1

CONTENTS

The Beggar

"The trouble with most modern Arabic literature," I have frequently heard Western editors complain, "is that it's always about politics." The complaint itself is interesting, not only in what it presumes to be important but also in the historical attitude it implies toward even Western literature, in which from the ancient Greeks onward politics has been a central subject during every period—except perhaps the Dark Ages. What would the Dante of the *Inferno* or the Shakespeare of the Histories make of this complaint, for example, not to mention Milton, whose Council in Pandemonium remains our finest description of a Cabinet debate? What, for that matter, would a V. S. Naipaul or a Gabriel García Márquez have to say? One suspects that in this instance, as in so many others, special rules of some sort have been devised for application to Arabs only.

The Beggar is an ironic case in point, since few Western readers coming to it or to Mahfouz for the first time are likely to understand that it, too, like "most modern Arabic literature," is a political book. First published in 1965, when Mahfouz was in his mid-fifties, it belongs to a remarkable series of novels (*The Children of Gebelawi, The Thief and the Dogs, Autumn Quail, The Path, Small Talk on the Nile*, and *Miramar*) in which he tried to assess the impact of political change upon the country he had known before the Revolution of July 1952.

Though his famous Cairo Trilogy was published between 1954 and 1957, Mahfouz had in fact composed its last words in 1952, then stopped writing for more than five years. "The world I had made it my mission to describe," he told Philip Stewart, one of his translators, "had disappeared." When a new work—*The Children of Gebelawi*—finally appeared in 1959, it created a scandal, not only because of its subject matter but also because of its technique, which represented a complete abandonment of the old-fashioned descriptive novel. Making allegorical use of religious history, it suggested that the new regime would ultimately not be much different from the old ones; and did so with a passionate, darting intelligence that seemed to have turned political disappointment—even despair—into a new freedom of expression.

Despair is the keynote of the series of six novels that followed, which ended with the debacle of the Six-Day War in 1967. Omar, the protagonist of *The Beggar,* belongs to the class and the generation that should have provided Egypt with leadership, but have instead been deprived of any significant function. His old classmates Mustapha and Othman, who are in some sense his alter egos, suggest the dangers of either accommodation or opposition, while Omar himself suggests one of the causes of their irrelevance: failure to care enough at the right time. Their liberal secularism, the central motif in Egyptian higher culture for the previous hundred years, of which they represent a kind of culmination, has simply been shelved as an operative ideal, though it may survive as an irrepressible yearning. It thus finds indirect expression, necessarily inadequate, as sex or poetry, though even in a Voltairean garden one can never be saved by such longings.

The Beggar then is a complex and passionate outcry against irrelevance and against what is likely to follow—alienation. Surely it is about things that matter; and matter in places other than the Arab world.

JOHN RODENBECK

The Beggar

White clouds floated in the blue expanse overlooking a vast green land where cows grazed serenely. Nothing indicated what country it was. In the foreground a child, mounted on a wooden horse, gazed toward the horizon, a mysterious semi-smile in his eyes. Omar wondered idly who did the painting as he sat alone in the waiting room. It was almost time for the appointment he'd made ten days earlier. The table in the middle of the room was strewn with newspapers and magazines; dangling over the edge was the photo of a woman accused of kidnapping children. He turned back to amuse himself with the painting—a pasture, cows, a child, the horizon. Although the painting had little value apart from its ornamental gold frame, he liked the searching child, the tranquil cows. But Omar's condition was worsening, his eyelids were heavy and his heartbeats sluggish. There the child looks at the horizon, and how tightly it grips the earth, closes in upon the earth from any angle you observe it. What an infinite prison.

Why the wooden horse, why the cows so full of tranquillity? Steady footsteps sounded in the hall outside, and then the male nurse appeared at the door, saying, "Come in, please."

Would his old school friend recognize him after a quarter of a century? He entered the office of the distinguished physician. There he stood, smiling, a dark slender man with kinky hair and glowing eyes. He had hardly changed from their days in the school courtyard. The corner of his mouth had the same ironic turn, suggesting his old gaiety and sharp wit.

"Welcome, Omar. You've changed, but for the better!"

"I didn't think you'd remember me."

They shook hands warmly.

"What a giant you are! You were always very tall but now that you've put on weight you've become enormous," he said, raising his head to Omar.

Omar smiled with pleasure and repeated, "I really didn't think you'd remember me."

"But I don't forget anyone, so how could I forget you?"

It was a gracious welcome from one in his position. After all, a distinguished physician is widely renowned; who hears of the lawyer other than those with legal cases?

The physician laughed while surveying him and said, "You really have put on weight. You look like a business tycoon from the past, nothing missing except the cigar!"

A grin appeared on Omar's dark, full face. Slightly abashed, he settled his glasses in place while raising his thick eyebrows.

"I'm happy to meet you again, Doctor."

"And I you, though the occasion of seeing me is not usually pleasant."

He returned to his desk, which was piled with books, papers, and various instruments and gestured to Omar to take a seat.

"Let's leave our reminiscences until after we've reassured ourselves about your health." He opened his case book and started to write. "Name: Omar al-Hamzawi. Profession: Lawyer. Age?" The physician laughed, saying in anticipation, "Don't worry, we're in the same predicament."

"Forty-five."

"Remember what a difference in age a month seemed when we were in school? But now, who cares? Any history of special illness in the family?"

"None, unless you consider high blood pressure after sixty extraordinary."

The physician folded his arms and said seriously, "Let's hear what you've got."

Omar stroked his thick black hair, in which the first strands of white were discernible, and said, "I don't believe I'm ill in the usual sense."

The physician regarded him attentively.

"I mean I don't have the usual symptoms . . ."

"Yes."

"But I feel a strange lethargy."

"Is that all?"

"I think so."

"Perhaps it's overwork."

"I'm not sure that's the answer."

"Of course not. Otherwise you wouldn't have honored me with your visit."

"In fact, I no longer feel any desire to work at all."

"Go on."

"It's not fatigue. I suppose I could still work, but I have no desire to, no desire at all. I've left the work to the assistant lawyer in my office and postponed all my own cases for the past month . . ."

"Haven't you thought of taking a vacation?"

Omar continued as though he hadn't heard. "Very often I'm sick of life, people, even the family. The situation seemed too serious to keep silent."

"Then the problem is not . . ."

"The problem is very serious. I don't want to think, to move, or to feel. Everything is disintegrating and dying. My hope in coming here was to find some physical cause."

The physician remarked with a smile, "If only we could solve our most serious problems with a pill after eating or a spoonful of medicine before sleeping."

They proceeded into the examination room. Omar took off his clothes and lay down on the medical cot. The physician followed the usual procedure. He looked at Omar's outstretched tongue, then pressed up his eyelids and examined his eyes, took his blood pressure, then measured his breathing with the stethoscope. Omar breathed deeply, coughed, and said "Ah" once from the throat, again from the chest, and glanced furtively at the physician's face without reading anything. The elegant fingers then tapped on his chest and on his back and pressed with more force on his abdomen. The examination over, the physician returned to his office, where Omar joined him a few minutes later. He finished looking at the results of the urine analysis taken earlier, rubbed his hands, smiled broadly, and said, "My dear lawyer, there's absolutely nothing."

The nostrils of his long, sharp nose dilated and his face flushed. "Nothing at all?"

"At all," the physician affirmed, but added cautiously, "I'm afraid the problem may be more serious." Then he laughed. "Though it's not a case which can be exaggerated to double the fees!"

Omar laughed while looking at him expectantly.

"Well, then," the doctor stressed, "you should know that it's nothing but . . ."

Omar asked uneasily, "Is the psychiatric ward my fate, then?"

"Neither a psychiatric nor any other kind of ward."

"Really?"

"Yes. You've got a bourgeois disease, if I may use the term our newspapers are so fond of. You're not sick," he continued more slowly, "but I see the first signs of something more than a disease. You've come at the appropriate time. When did the lethargy appear?"

"Two months ago, perhaps a bit earlier, but for the last month it's been agonizing."

"Let me describe your life as I see it. You're a successful, wealthy man. You've virtually forgotten how to walk. You eat the best food, drink good wine, and have overburdened yourself with work to the point of exhaustion. Your mind is preoccupied with your clients' cases and your own holdings. Anxiety about the future of your work and your financial situation has got the better of you."

Omar gave a slight laugh and said, "That's the picture, in general, but now I've lost interest in everything."

"Well, there's nothing wrong with you for the time being, but the enemy lurks on the border."

"Like Israel?"

"And if we don't take care, serious danger may overwhelm us."

"We're getting to the point."

"Be moderate in your eating, drink less, stick to regular exercise such as walking, and there'll be no grounds for fear."

Omar waited, thinking, but the doctor said no more. "Aren't you going to write me a prescription?"

"No. You're not a villager who needs a superfluous prescription to be convinced of my importance. The real cure is in your hands alone."

"I'll be my old self again?"

"And better . . . In spite of my heavy load of work at the university and the hospital and clinic, I walk every day for at least a half hour and I watch my diet."

"I've never felt the advance of years."

"Old age is a disease which you won't feel as long as you follow a sensible regime. There are youths of over sixty. The important thing is to understand life."

"To understand life?"

"I'm not speaking philosophically, of course."

"But your treatment of me is based on some sort of philosophy. Hasn't it ever occurred to you to question the meaning of your life?"

The physician laughed loudly and said, "I have no time for that. As long as I serve those in need each hour, what meaning does the question have?" Then he advised, with friendly concern, "Take a vacation."

"My vacation is usually so interrupted that the summer months hardly seem more than one prolonged weekend."

"No, take a real vacation, practice the new regime, and you'll be on the road to recovery."

"Perhaps."

"Trust in God. You've been given a warning from nature. Listen to it. You should lose forty pounds, but gradually, and without strain."

Omar pressed his hands on his knees and leaned forward in preparation to leave, but the doctor responded quickly, "Wait, you're the last visitor today, so let's sit together a while."

Omar sat back in his seat smiling. "Dr. Hamid Sabri, I know what you want—to bury a quarter of a century and laugh again from the depths of your heart."

"Ah, the days of the past."

"Actually, Doctor, all periods except 'now' have their appeal."

"You're right. Memory is one thing, the experience another."

"So it all passes and scatters without meaning."

"Our love of life gives meaning."

"How I've detested life these last days!"

"And now you're searching for your lost love. Tell me, do you remember those days of politics, demonstrations, and dreams of Utopia?"

"Of course, but those too have passed and are not held in much esteem these days."

"Even so, a great dream was realized. I mean the socialist state."

"Yes . . ."

The doctor smiled. "You're a man of many faces: the fervent socialist, the great lawyer, but the face I remember most vividly is that of Omar the poet."

Omar dissembled his sudden agitation with a wan smile. "That's unfortunate."

"You've abandoned poetry?"

"Of course."

"But, as I remember, you published a collection of poems."

He lowered his eyes so that the doctor wouldn't see his tension and discontent. "Childhood play, nothing more."

"Some of my physician colleagues have given up medicine for the sake of poetry."

The memory disturbed his consciousness like ill-omened weather. He wished the doctor would drop the subject.

"I remember one of our friends was Mustapha al-Minyawi. What was it we called him?"

"Little Baldy. We're still very close friends. He's now a prominent journalist and writes for radio and television."

"My wife is a great fan of his. He was an enthusiastic socialist like you, but the most committed of all, without question, was Othman Khalil."

Omar's face clouded as memory hammered at him. He murmured, "He's in jail."

"Yes, he's spent a long time in jail. Wasn't he your classmate in the Faculty of Law?"

"We graduated in the same year, Mustapha, Othman, and I. I don't really like the past."

The physician said decisively, "So take an interest in the future." Then, looking at his watch: "From now on you're the doctor."

In the waiting room, Omar raised his eyes once again to the picture. The child was still riding his wooden horse, gazing at the horizon. Was it this which prompted his mysterious smile? The horizon still closed in upon the earth. What did the beams of starlight traveling millions of light-years perceive? There are questions which no doctor can answer.

Outside the building he climbed into his black Cadillac, which floated away from the square like a bark on the Nile.

T W O

The faces peered at him expectantly even before they'd exchanged greetings. Their concern was sincere, and he was troubled by his dissatisfaction, the bitterness which spoiled the remaining affection. Behind them the balcony overlooked the Nile. He focused on his wife's thick neck above her white collar and on her fleshy cheeks. She stood as the pillar of faith and virtue. Her green eyes were pouched in fat, but her smile was innocent and affectionate as she said, "My heart tells me all is well."

Mustapha al-Minyawi stood beside her in his sharkskin suit, his slender build overshadowed by her sturdiness. His pale oval face, lackluster eyes, and bald head were turned toward Omar.

"Tell us about our old school friend. What did he say? Did he recognize you?"

Buthayna stood with her elbow leaning on the shoulder of a bronze statue, the statue of a woman stretching out her arms in welcome. Her green eyes looked at her father expectantly. She had the fine figure of her mother when she was fourteen, but it seemed unlikely that she would grow obese with the years, that she would allow fat to mar her beauty. As was often the case, the glance in her eyes expressed an unspoken communication. Jamila, her younger sister, played with her teddy bear between two armchairs, oblivious of his arrival.

They all sat down and he said calmly, "Nothing."

Zeinab exclaimed gratefully, "Thank God. How many times did I say that you only needed rest?"

Her complacency exasperated him. Pointing to his wife, he said to Mustapha, "The responsibility is hers." And he repeated the charge after summarizing the doctor's remarks.

Mustapha said gleefully, "This is no more than play therapy!" But then he added ruefully, "Except for food and drinking. Curse them."

Why should he curse them? He's not the one affected. The one who sets out on the mysterious voyage, perplexed by love and dissatisfaction, unable to speak to himself in a suitable language, what is *he* to do? Omar said to Mustapha, "Dr. Hamid asked about Baldy." After the burst of laughter had subsided, he added, "And congratulations on winning his wife's admiration."

Mustapha grinned boyishly, displaying his white teeth. "Thanks to the radio and TV, I've developed into a plague, striking those with weak resistance."

Omar reflected about his other friend in jail. Ennui dulls even the sensitive conscience. Omar had been in the heat of danger, but his friend had not confessed. In spite of torture, he had not confessed. Now he'd melted into the darkness as though he'd never existed, while Omar grew sick with luxury, and his wife had become the exemplary symbol of the kitchen and the bank. Ask yourself whether the Nile beneath us doesn't despair.

"Papa, should we get ready to travel?"

"We'll have a great time. I'm going to teach your sister to swim as I once taught you."

"Away to the life buoys."

Here is your mother resembling a giant life buoy. How oppressive the horizon is. Freedom is hidden somewhere beyond it and no hope remains except a troubled conscience.

"Unfortunately my wife prefers the beach at Ras el Bar, and someone like me never gets a vacation unless he's stricken with cancer."

Jamila raised her head from her teddy bear, asking, "When will we leave, Papa?"

Mustapha was a monument to his love and marriage; counselor, helper, and witness. Every day he proved anew his friendship to Omar and the family. As yet he knew nothing of the waters which drifted in the river's depths.

"The doctor reminded me of my poetical youth!"

Mustapha laughed. "It seems he hasn't heard of my recent dramatic masterpieces."

"I wish I'd told him of your experiences with art."

"I wonder if the great physician believes in art."

"His wife is fond of you. Isn't that enough?"

"Then she's fond of watermelon seeds and popcorn."

Zeinab, who'd been watching the servant through the arched doorway, then said, "Let's go in to dinner."

Omar announced that he would restrict himself to a chicken breast, fruit, and one glass of whiskey, to which Mustapha replied, "How about the caviar? Do I consume it alone?" Then he proceeded to give the description of

Churchill's breakfast which appeared in one of the newspapers during his visit to Cyprus. Although Omar hesitated a bit at the beginning of the meal, he soon ate and drank without restraint. Zeinab likewise couldn't resist temptation and drank a whole bottle of beer. Buthayna ate with moderation, a perversity in the eyes of her mother.

Mustapha remarked, "Food offers a better explanation of human behavior than sex does."

Omar forgot himself for the first time, exclaiming merrily, "It seems you've got chickenitis!"

After dinner they sat together for half an hour, then Jamila was taken to bed and Buthayna and her mother went to visit friends in the same building. So Omar and Mustapha were left alone on the large balcony, a bottle of whiskey and an ice bucket on the glass-topped table between them. Not a movement stirred the trees and the lamps were covered with a veil of sand. The Nile appeared through the gaps of the treetops, silent, pale, devoid of life and meaning. Mustapha drank alone and muttered despairingly, "One hand on its own does not clap."

Omar said, lighting a cigarette, "It's awful weather, and nothing pleases me anymore."

Mustapha laughed. "I remember you couldn't stand me at one time."

Omar disregarded the interruption. "I'm afraid my attitude toward work will continue indefinitely."

"If you stick to your diet and exercise, you won't indulge in despair and let Buthayna down."

"I'm going to drink another glass."

"Okay, but you'll have to be stricter in Alexandria."

"What do you mean, I couldn't stand you? You're a liar like most of those who practice your profession."

"You were disgusted with me at the time of my great commitment to art."

"I was undergoing an agonizing conflict within myself."

"Yes, you were battling a secret urge which you suppressed cruelly, and my commitment must have been alarming to you."

"But I never despised you; I found in you simply a tortured conscience."

"I respected your conflict and forgave you, determined to keep you and art." Then Mustapha laughed and said, "You must have been reassured when I decided to forsake art. Here I am, selling watermelon seeds and popcorn via the mass media, while you scale the summit of the legal profession in Al-Azhar Square."

Repeated memories as stifling as the summer heat and the perennial dust revolve in a closed cycle. The child imagines he's riding a genuine horse. "He was exasperated, he is exasperated, be exasperated, so he is exasperated, she is exasperated, and the plural is they are exasperated."

"Diet and sports."

"You're a riot."

"Amusement is my mission in life, and the plural is amusements. Art had meaning in the past, but science intruded and destroyed its significance."

"I deserted art without being influenced by science."

"Why did you give it up, then?"

He's as aggravating as the summer heat. The night lacked personality and merriment. There was noise in the street. How clever he is, posing questions to which he knows the answer. "Let me ask you the reason."

"You told me at the time you wanted to live well and succeed."

"So why did you ask the question?"

A look of recognition flickered in the eyes dulled by a past illness.

"You yourself didn't give up art for the sake of science alone."

"Enlighten me further."

"You couldn't create art that measured up to science."

Mustapha laughed with an abandon bestowed by the whiskey and said, "Escape is always partly caused by failure, but believe me, science has robbed art of everything. In science you find the rapture of poetry, the ecstasy of religion, and the aspirations of philosophy. All that is left to art is amusement. One day it will be no more than a bridal ornament worn during the honeymoon."

"This marvelous indictment springs from a revenge against art rather than a love of science."

"Read the astronomy, physics, or other science texts, recall whatever plays and collections of poetry you wish, and note the sense of shame which overwhelms you."

"Similar to my feelings when I think of legal cases and the law."

"It's only the feeling of the artist out of step with time."

Omar yawned, then said, "Damn it, I smell something serious in the air, and I have the horrible feeling that a building is going to be demolished."

Mustapha filled a new glass and said, "We won't let the building be demolished."

Omar leaned toward him and asked, "What do you think is wrong with me?"

"Exhaustion, monotony, and time."

"Will diet and sports be enough?"

"More than enough, rest assured."

THREE

From now on you're the doctor and you're free. Freedom of action is a type of creativity, even while you're struggling against the appetites. If we say that man was not created to gorge himself with food, then with the liberation of the stomach the spirit is free to soar. Thus the clouds grow limpid and the August storms thunder. But how oppressive are the crowds, the humidity, and the smell of sweat. The exercise exhausted you and your feet ached as though you were learning how to walk for the first time. Eyes stared as the giant slowed his steps and, overcome by fatigue, sat down on the nearest bench on the Corniche. After a quarter of a century's blindness, you looked at people again. Thus had the shore witnessed the birth of Adam and Eve, but no one knows who will emerge from paradise. As a tall, thin youth, the son of a petty employee, he'd walked the length and breadth of Cairo without complaint, and generations of his ancestors had bruised their feet struggling with the land and had collapsed in the end from fatigue. Soon the past will emerge from prison, and existence will become more of a torment.

"Othman, why are you looking at me like that?"

"Don't you want to play ball?"

"I don't like sports."

"Nothing except poetry?"

Where can one escape your piercing glance? What's the use of arguing with you? You know that poetry is my life and that the coupling of two lines begets a melody which makes the wings of heaven dance.

"Isn't that so, Mustapha?"

The balding adolescent stated, "Existence itself is nothing but a composition of art."

One day Othman in a state of revelation proclaimed, "I found the magic solution to all our problems." Trembling with fervor, we raced up the heights of Utopia. The poetry meters were disrupted by convulsive explosions. We agreed that our souls were worthless. We proposed a gravitational force, other than Newton's, around which the living and dead revolved in an imaginary balance; none rising above or falling beneath the others. But when other forces opposed us, we preferred comfort to failure and thus the giant climbed with extraordinary speed from a Ford to a Packard until he settled in the end in a Cadillac and was on the verge of drowning in a quagmire of fat.

The umbrellas with their tassels touching each other formed a huge multicolored dome under which seminude bodies reclined. The pungent smell of perspiration dispersed in the bracing sea air under a sun which had renounced its tyranny. Buthayna stood smiling, a slim wet figure with red arms and legs, her hair shoved under a blue nylon cap. He himself was almost naked, the bushy black hair of his chest exposed to the sun. Jamila was sitting between his legs building a sand pyramid. Zeinab reclined on a leather chaise longue stitching rose petals on an embroidery frame, her healthy bulk and swelling breasts inviting the stares of imbecilic adolescents.

Dear Mustapha,

I read your weekly review of the arts. It was superb—both witty and provocative. You say you're a mere vendor of melon seeds and popcorn, but your inherent discernment and your long experience as a serious critic are evident. Even in jest you write with style. Thanks for your letter inquiring about us, but it was distressingly brief. You probably consider letters secondary to your articles, but I'm in urgent need of a long talk. Zeinab is well. She sends you her regards and reminds you of the medicine she'd asked you to get from one of your colleagues traveling abroad. I think her intestinal problems are simple, but she's fond of medicine, as you know. Buthayna is happy—how I wish I could read her mind—but the happiest of us all is certainly Jamila, who as yet understands nothing. You'd be amazed at the progress I've made—I've lost fifteen pounds, walked thousands of kilometers, sacrificed tons of meat, fish roe, butter, and eggs. Having stuffed myself to death for so long, I yearn for food. Since I find no one to talk to in your absence, I often talk to myself. Zeinab's speech is too sober, though why sober speech should annoy me these days I don't know. I met a madman on the road about a kilometer before the Glim beach. He assails those who pass by raising his hand in the manner of our leaders and delivering obscure speeches. He's the only one whose conversation I've enjoyed. He accosted me, saying, "Didn't I tell you?" I replied with concern, "Yes, indeed." "But what's the use? Tomorrow the city will be full of flounder and you won't find space for one foot." "The municipality should . . ." He interrupted me sharply. "The municipality won't do anything. They'll welcome it as an encouragement to tourism and it will increase to such fantastic proportions that the inhabitants will be forced to leave and the Agricultural Road will be packed with lines of emigrants and in spite of all this the price of fish will continue to rise. . . ."

I wish I could have read his mind, too. His language was no less strange than mathematical equations and we reasonable men are lost between the two. We who live in the corporeal, mundane realm know neither the pleasure of madness nor the marvels of equations. With all that, I remain the father of a happy family. Witness us as I confide in Buthayna while Jamila attacks us with sand. Our house in Glim is very comfortable. My craving for whiskey is increasing noticeably. Yesterday while we were in the beach cabin, we overheard our neighbor say that the apartment buildings would be nationalized. Zeinab blanched and looked at me, appealing for help, so I said, "We have a lot of money." She asked, "Can the money be rescued?" "We've taken out various insurance policies against fate." She began questioning me anxiously, "How do we know that . . . ?" But I interrupted her. "Then for God's sake how did you get so fat?" She exclaimed, "In your youth you were just like them. You talked about nothing but socialism, and it is still in your blood." Then she asked me again to remind you about the medicine. Mustapha, I don't care about anything. Nothing concerns me, honestly. I don't know what has happened to me. All that matters is that we resume our chats, our grand, meaningless chats. By chance I overheard a conversation between two lovers in the dark.

The man said, "Dear, it's becoming very dangerous." The woman replied, "This means you don't love me." "But you know very well that I love you." "You're speaking reasonably, which means that you no longer love me." "Can't you see I'm a grown man with responsibilities?" "Just say you don't love me anymore." "We'll destroy ourselves and our homes." "Will you stop preaching?" "You have your husband and daughter; I have my wife and children." "Didn't I say you don't love me anymore?" she said. "But I do love you." "Then don't remind me of anything but love."

I left imagining the delicious scandal and laughing at the woman's daring and the man's consternation. But they reminded me of an old friend called love. God, what a long time has passed without love! All that is left are mummified memories. How I'd like to sneak into the heart of a lover. As you know, Zeinab has been my only love; but that was more than twenty years ago, and what I remember of that affair are events and situations rather than the feelings and agitations. I remember I told you one day, "Her eyes slay me," but you never forsook me in my insanity. However, the memory of insanity is not like insanity itself—the feverish thoughts, volcanic heart, and sleepless nights. Agony lifted me to poetic ecstasies. Tears streamed from my eyes and I approached heaven. But these are no more than mummified memories. Here I am struggling to lose weight and I see in dear Zeinab only a statue of family unity and constructive work. Honestly, I've lost interest in everything. Let them take the three apartment buildings and the revenues. I won't claim that the principles which once nearly landed us in jail along with Othman make it easy to accept, for those days of strife are themselves no more than pallid memories. I don't know what has happened to me or changed me. Rejoice, dear friend, for while I grow healthy in body, I'm approaching an exquisite madness. May you be so lucky.

"Don't forget to write him about the medicine."

"I haven't, dear."

How sweet you are, Buthayna. Your budding breasts are proof of the world's good taste. Perhaps I'm an old conservative, for I've let your mother take over your instruction about the facts of life. It's regrettable that you know nothing about life, that I've kept you enclosed like a little canary in your school bus. What lies behind your dreamy look? Despite the frankness of our talks, haven't you withheld certain secrets from me? Are you affected by the scent of these bare bodies, by the flirtations exchanged among the waves? God, let society conform with her thoughts and deeds so that she won't be exposed to evil. He said to her as she was sitting with her bare legs stretched under his beach chair, "We haven't had such a good time together before."

"It's your fault."

"I've stayed in the office all my life for your sake alone."

She leaned back on her elbows, exposing her stomach and chest to the sun, which shone in the clear sky while one lonely white cloud floated above the curve of the bay. Her mother said without raising her head from her embroidery, "Tell him that his health is now more important than anything else."

"More important than the building nationalizations?"

She answered defiantly, "Even than the building nationalizations."

He remarked factually, "Social conformity is a fine thing."

She said nothing. A pretty girl strutted in front of them and the glance he caught from her delighted his senses like the scent of jasmine.

"When I return to normal, I'll have to develop a philosophy of life which allows true happiness."

"God help us."

"God wishes us to be concerned about the welfare of all." He glanced at her teasingly, then said, "But how would God respond to supplication in this case?"

She understood the implication, but withheld comment. He forgot the subject and turned to other thoughts. Although he felt lighter and more energetic, a nagging exasperation remained—the flies, his work, and his wife. One day Buthayna will be preoccupied by someone other than you, as will Jamila, who now builds pyramids in the sand. For God's sake, what do you want? Why does silence reign amid all the clamor? Why do you have the foreboding of fantastic perils? You hear the distressing sound of links snapping and feel that your footing is shaking so violently that your teeth will fall out. In the end you'll lose all your weight and float in space. Hold fast to things and regard them carefully, for soon their forms will disappear and no one will heed you. The waves are destroying Jamila's sand pyramid and the wind blows away the newspapers in which truth is relegated to the obituary sections. The client says to you, "I want to entrust my case to the Master." How ludicrous! Honorable counselors. All that's left for us is to work in the national circus.

"Why are you so distracted, dear?"

"It's nothing."

"Are you really all right?"

"I think so."

"Judging from experience, I think you're in need of care."

"We must respect experience."

"Shall I tell you the cook's opinion?"

"Does the cook have an opinion?"

"She said that the man who's satisfied and successful is vulnerable to the evil eye."

"And you believe that?"

"Of course not, but sometimes confusion drives us to seek any explanation."

"So all you have to do is consult an exorcist."

"Sarcasm was not in your nature before."

He said, smiling, "A little sarcasm doesn't do any harm."

"Let's forget it, dear."

On their way home, she detained him briefly as the two girls walked ahead. "I have some good news for you."

He looked at her with secret despair.

"I discovered something unexpected in Buthayna."

"Other than what you discovered last year?"

"Yes. She's a poet, Omar."

He raised his thick eyebrows in surprise.

"I'd noticed her absorption in writing and that she'd tear up what she'd worked on only to start it again. At last she confided to me that she writes poetry, so I laughed and told her. . . ."

Zeinab hesitated, so he asked, "What did you tell her?"

"I told her that you also started out as a poet."

He frowned and asked, "Didn't you tell her how I ended up?"

"But it's lovely for a girl her age to write poetry."

"It is."

"You must read her poetry and give her some advice."

"If my advice had any value it would have benefited me!"

"You're pleased with the news?"

"Very much so."

F O U R

His sudden happiness gave way to an agitation, alarming in its intensity, a feeling he had not known for the last twenty years. Buthayna, wearing a printed blouse and brown tapered pants, came at his beckoning to the balcony overlooking the sea.

"I wanted to invite you to watch the sunset with me," he said as she sat down in front of him.

She seemed on the verge of excusing herself, for, as he knew, this was the time she went out with her mother and sister for a late-afternoon stroll on the Corniche, so he said, "You'll join them soon. Poets should enjoy the sunset."

He noticed her cheeks redden, and smiled.

"But . . . but I'm not a poet!"

"But you write poetry."

"How do I know it's poetry?"

"I'll judge after looking at it."

"No," she said, timid and apprehensive.

"There's no secret between us. I'm proud of you."

"It's just silly scribblings."

"I'll love even your silly scribblings."

She lowered her eyes submissively, her long curving eye-lashes nearly brushing her cheeks.

"Buthayna," he said with sudden concern, "tell me why you turned to poetry."

"I don't know."

"You do so well in science. What prompted you to turn to poetry?"

Frowning, she made an effort to remember. "The school readings. I enjoyed them very much, Papa."

"So do many people."

"I was more strongly affected, I think."

"Have you read any other poetry?"

"I've read some collections."

"Collections?"

She laughed. "I borrowed them from your library."

"Really?"

"And I know that you're a poet, too."

The remark pained him but he dissimulated gaiety. "No, no, I'm not a poet. It was a childhood pastime."

"You certainly were a poet. Anyway, I was strongly tempted by poetry."

You suggest the theater, my friend, but I'm a poet. I find myself caught in a whirlpool from which there's no escape except through poetry, for poetry is the very aim of my existence. Without it, what would we do with the love which surrounds us like air, the secret feelings which burn us like fire, the universe which oppresses us without mercy? Don't be supercilious about poetry, my friend.

"Tell me more."

She continued, regaining her usual courage. "It's as though I'm searching for tunes in the air."

"A nice sentiment, Buthayna, and poetry is fine as long as it doesn't spoil life. . . ."

"What do you mean, Papa?"

"I mean your studies and your future. But it is time to look at your poems."

She brought him a silver-colored notebook. With love and anxiety he opened the pages, but as he began to read, the year 1935 intervened tauntingly, that year of agony, secret schemes, wild hopes, and dreams of Utopia spurred by Othman's declaration that he had found the ideal solution. It was evident that his little girl, the bud which had not yet flowered, was in love. Who is this glorious being, whose breath is the clouds, whose mirror is the sun, and for whom the tree branches sway in yearning? Why should we be upset when our children travel the path we once took? What would his father think if he could hear him talking to his granddaughter about love?

"This is really poetry."

Her eyes shone with joy as she exclaimed, "Really?"

"Lovely poetry."

"You're only trying to encourage me, Papa."

"No, it's the truth." Then he asked her, smiling, "But who is he?"

The spark of enthusiasm died down in her eyes and she asked, rather disappointed, "Who?"

"Who is it you're addressing in these lyrics?" Then he said more forcefully, "Come, there are no secrets between us."

She answered enigmatically, "No one."

"It seems I'm no longer the father confidant."

"I mean it's not a human being."

"One of the angels?"

"Nor one of the angels."

"What is it, then—a dream—a symbol?"

In evident confusion, she replied, "Perhaps it is the final purpose of all things."

He wiped the perspiration from his forehead and arms and, making a valiant effort to remove any trace of jest or sarcasm from his tone, said seriously, "Then you are enamored of the secret of existence."

She said nervously, "That's quite possible, Papa."

We're fools to think of ourselves as stranger than others. "And what brought all this about?"

"I don't know . . . It's difficult to say, but your poems first pointed the way."

Omar laughed mechanically, saying, "A family conspiracy! Your mother knew what you were up to all along and showed you that stuff which you call poetry."

"But it's wonderful poetry, and so inspired."

He laughed loudly, attracting the attention of the organ grinder below him on the Corniche who was filling the air with his jarring tones.

"At last I've found an admirer! But it wasn't poetry, just a feverish delusion. Fortunately I got over it in time."

"While it makes me ecstatic!"

"So poetry is your beloved."

"As it is yours."

It was, but is no longer, and my heart feels the deprivation. Between the stars lie emptiness and darkness and millions of light-years.

"What is your advice, Papa?"

"All I can say is, do as you wish."

She asked gaily, "When will you take up poetry again?"

"For God's sake, let me get back to the office first!"

"I'm surprised that you could give it up so easily."

He said, smiling diffidently, "It was simply a frivolous . . ."

"But your collection of poems, Papa."

"I once thought I'd continue."

"I'm asking what made you stop."

He smiled sarcastically, but then a sudden desire to be frank prompted him to confess, "No one listened to my songs."

The silence hurt you, but Mustapha urged, "Perseverance and patience," and Othman said, "Write for the Revolution and you'll have thousands of listeners."

You were beset by privation and oppressed by the silence. Poetry could not sustain you. One day Mustapha announced happily that the Tali'a troupe had accepted his play. The silence became more oppressive. Samson fell asleep before he could destroy the temple.

Buthayna asked, "Do there have to be listeners, Papa?"

He reached over and stroked a lock of her black hair. "Why rescue the secret of existence from silence, only to be greeted by silence?" Then he added gently, "Don't you want people to listen to your poems?"

"Of course, but I'll keep on anyway."

"Fine, you're braver than your father, that's all."

"You can return to poetry if you want."

"The talent has died completely."

"I don't believe it. In my mind you will always be a poet."

What has poetry to do with this hulking body, with the preoccupation with legal cases, the construction of apartment buildings, and gluttony to the point of illness? Even Mustapha slumped on the couch one day as if he were declining visibly into old age.

"What wasted effort," he said.

You replied with concern, "But the Tali'a troupe welcomes your plays, and they're excellent works."

He gestured with his hand in deprecation. "I have to reconsider my life as you have."

"You've always counseled perseverance and patience."

He laughed harshly. "You can't ignore the public."

"You'd like to start out again as a lawyer?"

"Law died even before art. In fact, the concept of art changed without our realizing it. The era of art has ended, and the art of our age is simply diversion, the only art possible in an age of science. Science has taken over all fields except the circus."

"Really, we're all going to pieces, one after the other."

"Say rather that we've grown up, and regard your success in life as an exemplary case. I think that amusement is a splendid objective for the world-weary people of the twentieth century. What we consider real art is only the light coming from a star which died millions of years ago. So we'd better grow up and pay the clowns the respect they deserve."

"It seems to me that philosophy has destroyed art."

"Rather science has destroyed both philosophy and art. So let's amuse ourselves without reserve, with the innocence of children and the intelligence of men—light stories and raucous laughter and nonsensical pictures—and let's renounce delusions of grandeur, and the exalted throne of science, and be content with popular acclaim and the material rewards."

That both pleased me and saddened me. I suffered from conflicting emotions and recollected in dismay the one still in prison.

"Dear Baldy" applies the balsam of consolation to your

failure with surprising skill. In the future he'll strive on a lower level for the force you once had. While you, who once searched for the secret of existence, have turned into a wealthy lawyer sinking in gluttony.

"If science is what you imagine, what are we but intruders on the periphery of life?"

"We're successful men with a secret burden of sorrow; it's unwise to open the wounds."

"We belong, in fact, to a bygone age."

"For God's sake, don't open the wounds."

"Scientists are strong through their allegiance to the truth, but our strength derives from money which loses its legality day by day."

"So I say that death represents the one true hope in human life."

Omar looked gently at his daughter's green eyes and said, "Buthayna, is it unreasonable to ask you not to give up your scientific studies?"

"No, I won't, but poetry will still be the most beautiful thing in my life."

"Let it be. I won't dispute that. But you can be a poet and at the same time an engineer, for example."

"You seem to be preoccupied with my future!"

"Of course! I don't want you to wake up one day to find yourself in the Stone Age while everyone around you is in the age of science."

"But poetry—"

He interrupted. "I won't contradict you, dear. My friend Mustapha finds poetry, religion, and philosophy in science, but I won't argue that position. I'm pleased and proud of you."

The large red disk of the sun was sinking, its force and vitality absorbed by the unknown. The eye could gaze easily at it now, as at the water. Rosy dunes of clouds pressed around it.

Do you really want to know my secret, Mustapha? In the agony of failure, I sought power, that evil which we'd wanted to abolish. But you already know this secret.

F I V E

In the fading glow of the sun, she looked sedate, even elegant. In spite of her extraordinary rotundity, the exasperating evidence of indulgence, she retained a winsome beauty. Her serious green eyes still had their charm, but they were now the eyes of a stranger. She was the wife of another man, the man of yesterday who hadn't known listlessness or fatigue, who had forgotten himself. How was she related to this man, the invalid without an illness, who avoided starches and liquor and who scrutinized the humid air for warnings of undefined peril? The two sisters are ahead; Jamila walks along the stone wall of the Corniche while Buthayna, on the street below, leads her by the hand. They are on the road between Glim and Sidi Bishr, where the crowds are a bit thinner. Buthayna attracted many glances and many murmured comments. Although indistinguishable, their meaning was clear enough. Omar smiled to himself. In a few years you'll be a grandfather, and life will go on, but where to? He watched the last of the sunset in the clear, pallid sky until only a sliver remained on the horizon.

He remarked, "The ancients used to ask where the sun disappeared to. We no longer question."

Zeinab looked at the sun for a moment, then said, "How marvelous to have ended the question!"

Rational answers strangle you to provocation. Sensible behavior annoys you unreasonably. How grand it would be if the sea turned violent, drove away those who loitered on the shore, incited the pedestrians on the Corniche to commit unimaginable follies, sent the casino flying above the clouds, and shattered the familiar images forever. So the heart throbs in the brain and the reptiles dance with the birds.

The two girls stopped in front of the San Stefano cinema, then resumed walking. Suddenly Zeinab put her arm through his and whispered imploringly, "Omar, what's wrong?"

He glanced with a smile at those around him. "So much flirtation!"

"That's nothing new. . . . What's wrong?"

He said, intent on ignoring her question, "There's a lot Buthayna doesn't know. I was thinking of that when I—"

She interrupted him impatiently. "I know what I'm doing. She's an unusually sensitive girl, but you're escaping."

Your soul longs for escape, the magic key at the bottom of a well.

"I'm escaping?"

"You know what I mean, so confess."

"To which crime?"

"That you're no longer yourself."

How we need a violent storm to wash away this cloying humidity.

"Only in body are you among us. Sometimes I'm so sad I could die."

"But as you can see, I'm following the regime rigorously."

"I'm wondering what's behind this change. Your behavior makes me question it again."

"But we diagnosed the condition thoroughly."

"Yes, but is there anything in particular which disturbs you?"

"Nothing."

"I must believe you."

"But apparently you don't, completely."

"I thought maybe something in your office or at the court had disturbed you. You're sensitive, but able to hide your feelings well."

"I went to the doctor only because I couldn't find a tangible cause."

"You haven't told me how it all started."

"I talked to you so often about that."

"Only about the results, but how precisely did it start?"

A reckless impulse drives you to confess. "It's difficult to establish when or how the change began, but I remember meeting with one of the litigants of Soliman Pasha's estate. The man said, 'I'm grateful, Counselor. You've grasped the details of the situation superbly. Your fame is well deserved. I have great hopes of winning the case.'

"I replied, 'So do I.'

"He laughed contentedly and I felt a sudden, inexplicable wave of anger. 'Suppose you win the case today and possess the land only to have it confiscated tomorrow by the government?' He answered disparagingly, 'All that matters is that we win the case. Don't we live our lives knowing that our fate rests with God?' I had to admit the validity of his argument, but my head began to spin and everything seemed to disappear."

She glanced at him with surprise, and said, "That was the reason?"

"No, I don't know an exact reason, but I was undergoing a subtle, persistent change; thus I was agitated unreasonably by the man's words, words repeated by millions of others every day without any effect."

"Of course you can only think about death as men of wisdom do."

"I wonder how wise men regard death."

"Well, fortunately, that's known." She looked at him inquiringly. "And after that you hated work."

"No . . . no, I can't say that. It may have been earlier, or later."

"I'm so depressed that I can hardly discuss it with you."

"Are you so concerned about the work?"

"I care only about you."

A case is postponed, another, then a third. You spend the day glued to your chair, legs stretched under the desk, chain smoking and staring vacantly at the ceiling.

"I'm tired of walking," she said.

"But generally you walk twice this distance."

She lowered her eyes. "It's my turn to confess. I may be pregnant."

His stomach sank and he yearned more sharply for the magic key of escape. "But," he murmured.

She said calmly, "Dear, God's will is stronger than any of our designs." Then she added, pressing his arm, "And you've not been blessed with your crown prince!"

As they walked back home, a coquettish smile played in

her eyes. He said to himself that a bit of liquor would dissipate the languor so he could feign the role of lover, as he feigned marriage and health.

He woke up early, after a few hours of sleep, to the thudding of the waves in the dark, silent morning. Zeinab was sound asleep, satiated, her lips parted in a soft, steady snore and her hair disheveled. And you despair. It's as though you were doomed to thwart yourself. I don't love her anymore. After long years of love, shared life, and loyal memories, not a grain of love remains. Pray that it's just a symptom of the disease which will disappear with recovery, but now I don't love her. This is the most bitter disillusionment. You hear her snoring and feel no sympathy or tenderness. You look at her and only wonder what brought you together, who imposed this damned parody.

"Mustapha, there's the girl."

"The one leaving the church?"

"That's the one. She's wearing black in mourning for her uncle. How pretty she is."

"But her religion."

"I no longer care about those obstacles."

I told her how pleased I was that she'd condescended to meet me. In the public garden, Omar al-Hamzawi, the lawyer, had introduced himself, while she responded with a barely audible murmur, "Kamelia Fouad." Dearest, our love is stronger than all else. Nothing can stand in our way. She answered with a sigh, "I don't know."

Mustapha laughed at all the commotion, saying, "I've known you forever, and you've always sought trouble. A tempest at your house, a more violent one at hers. I'm spinning between the two."

Then what a marvelous attitude he'd had later when,

raising his glass of whiskey, he'd said, "Congratulations to both of you. The past is buried, but she's sacrificed much more than you. Beliefs are apt to tyrannize even those who've deserted them. To your health, Zeinab. To yours, Omar."*

He took you aside and, completely drunk, began to expostulate. "Don't forget the bad times ahead, but never forget love. Remember that she has no other family in the world now. She's been cut from the tree, and has no one but you."

I married a woman of great vitality and charm, a model student of the nuns, refined to the letter. She seemed to be a born businesswoman, with an unflagging zeal for work and a shrewd eye for investment. In her era, you rose from nothing to great eminence and wealth, and in the warmth of her love, you found consolation for wasted effort, for failure, and for poetry.

Still sleeping, she rolled over on her face. Her nightgown slid up, exposing the naked lower half of her body. He slipped from the bed and went out to the balcony, shutting the door behind him. Enveloped by the murky air, he watched the waves racing madly toward the shore and the spray flying against the cabanas. Flocks of clouds had spread across the pale dome of the sky, fogging up the early-morning weather. No feet yet walked the ground. Your spirit was unreceptive and the air did not refresh you. How long will you wait for deliverance? If only he could ask Mustapha about the meaning of the contradictions.

---

*Kamelia converted to Islam and changed her name to that of the Prophet Mohammed's daughter, Zeinab. By marrying Omar, she also cut herself off from her family.

He's a great resource of ideas, even if he only sells popcorn and pumpkin seeds now. Does Zeinab have a role only after work? One of the waves rose to an extraordinary height, shattered in tons of foam, then spread out defeated, giving up the ghost.

Dear God, Zeinab and work are the same. This malady which turns me from work is what turns me from Zeinab, for she is the hidden force, she is its symbol. She is wealth, success, and finally illness. And because I'm sick of these things, I'm disgusted with myself, or rather because I'm disgusted with myself, all else sickens me. But who does Zeinab have apart from me? Last night was a bitter experience. Love shrank and withered, and all that remained was a quickening of the pulse, a rise in blood pressure, and stomach contractions chasing each other in a horrible loneliness; the loneliness of the wave absorbed by the sand, which never returns to the sea. She sings songs of love, while I'm mute; she's the pursuer while I'm the fugitive; she loves while I hate; she's pregnant while I'm sterile; she's sensitive, perspicacious while I'm stupid. She said you're unusually quiet. I said it's simply that my voice is unheard. I said, "Suppose you win the property settlement today and tomorrow the government confiscates the land?" to which he replied, "Don't we live our lives knowing that our fate rests with God?" Even in alienation, the wave rises insanely, shatters in foam, then gives up the ghost. The grave of sleep swallows you, but still you don't rest, your brain still chases phantoms. You even consider seeing the doctor again, admitting that you've changed unaccountably. What do I want, what am I after? Knowledge has no importance, neither have the legal affairs of my clients, the addition of a few hundred pounds to my account, the blessings of a happy home, and the reading of the daily headlines. So why not take a trip in space? Ride the light waves, for their speed is fixed, the only fixed thing in the constantly changing, insanely reeling universe.

The first spacemen have arrived, selling microbes, selling lies.

S I X

At the end of August, the family returned to Cairo. The view of Al-Azhar Square on his way to work the first day was upsetting. It remained a depressing thoroughfare, unchanged since his departure. He was warmly welcomed at the office, especially by Mahmoud Fahmi, his assistant, and the files were soon brought out, the postponed cases and those under review. September had its sticky days, but a gentle breeze had arisen and the early mornings were shaded by the suggestions of white clouds. Mustapha embraced him at length. They stood face to face, Omar towering above his friend, whose bald head, tilted back, was spotlighted by the silver lamp.

He said, sitting on the leather couch before the desk, "You're as slender as a gazelle. Bravo."

He took out a cigarette from the box—a wooden box ornamented with mother-of-pearl which played a tune when opened—lit it, then continued. "I often thought of visiting you in Alexandria, but family obligations called me to Ras el Bar. Apart from that, I was tied up in preparing a new radio serial."

Omar looked at the case files, then at his friend's eyes, pleading for an encouraging word. He smiled enigmatically, then finally said, "I worked without stop this morning."

Mustapha breathed a sigh of relief, but then Omar murmured, "But . . ."

Mustapha inquired anxiously, "But?"

"Honestly, I've regained no desire to work."

An uneasy silence prevailed. Mustapha exhaled the cigarette smoke with a tense expression, then suggested, "Maybe you should have taken more rest."

"Let's stop kidding ourselves. The problem is more serious than that."

Then he lit a cigarette in turn and continued to the echo of new tunes. "The problem is more serious, for it's not only work which has become unbearable. This illness is consuming other things, far more precious than work—my wife, for instance."

"Zeinab?"

He said with something like shame, "I don't know how to put it, but sadly enough, I can't bear her now. My house is no longer the happy abode."

"But Buthayna and Jamila are part of it."

"Fortunately they don't need me . . ."

Mustapha frowned and blinked his round, filmy eyes. In his inquisitive glance was a sorrowful, pressing desire to solve the riddle. "But someone of your intelligence can discover the secret."

He said, smiling bitterly, "Maybe the universe in its eternal, monotonous revolving is the primary cause."

"I'm sure you're exaggerating, at least as far as Zeinab is concerned."

"It's the appalling truth."

He asked with solicitude, "What's to happen in this state of affairs?"

"I live, questioning all the time, but with no answer."

"By now, you must be convinced, at least, that you're going through some sort of psychological crisis."

"Call it what you wish, but what is it, what do I want, what should I do?"

"You're too sensible to be plagued by questions. Probe your hidden desires, look into your dreams. There are things you want to run away from, but where to?"

"That's it. Where?"

"You must find the answer."

"Tell me, what makes *you* stick to work and marriage?"

Because the question seemed somehow funny, he smiled, but the sober atmosphere quickly dispelled his gaiety. "My attachment to my wife is based on reality and on habit. My work is a means of livelihood. Besides, I'm happy with my audience, I'm happy with the hundreds of letters I get from them each week. Acceptance by the public is gratifying, even if it means selling popcorn and watermelon seeds."

"I have neither public, nor reality, nor habit."

Mustapha paused a while and then said, "In fact, you've been extraordinarily successful in your work and your wife worships you, so you're left with nothing to fight for."

Omar smiled sarcastically. "Should I pray God for failure and adultery?"

"If it would help you regain some interest in life!"

Each retreated into himself and the tense silence carried ominous forebodings.

Omar spoke. "It sometimes consoles me that I hate myself just as much." He squashed his cigarette butt in the ashtray impatiently. "My work, Zeinab, and myself are really all one thing, and this is what I want to escape from."

Mustapha looked at him quizzically. "An old dream is enticing you?"

He hesitated before confiding, "Buthayna wrote some poems."

"Buthayna!"

"I read them, and while we were discussing them, I felt a strange yearning for the old books I'd deserted twenty years ago."

"Ah, how often I've thought that would happen."

"Hold on. Yes, a certain sensation crept into my sluggish brain and I began searching for lost tunes. I even asked myself whether it might be possible to start again. But it was just a fleeting sensation which soon disappeared."

"You retreated quickly."

"No. I went back to reading, and jotted down a few words, but it came to nothing. One evening when I was at the cinema, I saw a beautiful face and felt the same sensation."

"Is sensation what you're after?"

"Sensation or intoxication—the creature within me revived all at once and I believed it to be my aim, rather than work, family, or wealth. This strange, mysterious intoxication appeared as the sole victory among a series of defeats. It alone can vanquish doubt, apathy, and bitterness."

Mustapha looked at him steadily, his chin resting on his hand, and asked, "You wish to bid love a final farewell?"

He said, rather vexed, "So you think it's a symptom of middle age. However, this is easily cured when the respectable husband rushes off to the nightclub or marries a new wife. And maybe I, too, will run after a different woman. But what aggravates me is more serious than that."

Mustapha couldn't refrain from laughing. "Is it really a strange intoxication or simply a philosophical justification for adultery?" he asked.

"Don't laugh at me. You were once in a pretty bad way yourself."

A smile spread on his face as he looked into his memories. "Yes," he said, "I was starting to write a new play when suddenly I lost my grip. Art shattered in fragments, disintegrated into dust in my hands. So I exchanged it for another type of art, one which has given happiness to millions of our citizens."

"Well, I've missed the way. I turned from art to a profession which is also dying. Law and art both belong to the past. I can't master the new art, as you have done, and like you, I failed to study science. How can I find the lost ecstasy of creation? Life is short and I can't forget the vertigo caused by the fellow's words: 'Don't we live our lives knowing that our fate rests with God?'"

"Does the idea of death disturb you?"

"No, but it urges me to taste the secret of life."

"As you found it in the movie theater?"

He doesn't know of your walks through the streets and squares of Alexandria, yearning for a face which promised the long-sought ecstasy, of your lingering under the trees by the stream which swayed with the cries of your burning emotions. The mad giant searching for his lost mind beneath the damp grass.

He referred to these times at some length, speaking with a solemnity befitting the mysterious and strange. "Those nights I was not an animal moved by lust, but I was suffering and in despair."

SEVEN

"I can't help wanting you more every time we meet.
The flame leaps higher with each heartbeat."

"A passionate song. Who's the singer?"

"Margaret. The star of the New Paris."

The crescent-shaped garden which bordered the dance floor was cooled by the autumn breeze. The music came from a stage set inside red walls and lit from within.

"She looks English."

"That's what the owner of the nightclub claims, but what passes for English in the nightclubs could easily be something else."

The fine lines of her face, a certain look in her eyes, the lightness of her movement—perhaps it was the harmony of all these which evoked something of the long-sought ecstasy.

"I envy your expertise in these forbidden pleasures."

"Just part of my job as editor of the magazine's art section!"

"Bravo . . . You said her name is Margaret."

He answered laughing, "Or twenty pounds a night, not counting the liquor."

The gentle autumn breeze carried greetings from an unknown world, a world not inhabited by just one mind, a world whose four corners lay behind the darkness of the cypress trees.

"I'm in a mood where anything could happen."

"But don't drink more than one glass!"

"The first thing is to invite her to the table."

Mustapha went to look for the waiter. The fragrance of lilies spread in the air, and in the intervals of silence, the whispering of the branches was audible. He was eager to enter his life of fantasy. Strange shapes of human beings passed before his eyes and he said to himself in apology that all this was the effect of illness.

Margaret approached the table, swaying in her dark evening gown, and greeted them with a smile which displayed her perfect set of teeth. The waiter, her shadow, stood a few feet away.

"Champagne," Omar ordered.

You first drank it on your wedding night. It was a cheap brand, a joint present from Mustapha and Othman. What would the prisoners do if struck with an epidemic of your strange disease?

Mustapha's greeting indicated that he had known the woman previously. "Margaret," he said, "we both admired your voice, and my friend is quite taken with you. It seems that every time you meet . . ." He winked, laughing. "He's a prominent lawyer, but I hope you won't need him in any professional capacity."

Her mouth spread in a soundless laugh, and she said, "I

always need someone to defend me. Isn't that the case with women in general?"

Omar summoned forth a gift for flattery which had lain dormant for many years. "Except for those with your beauty and voice."

Mustapha said, with a cunning blink of his filmy eyes, "He started out as a poet, you know, but he hasn't yet reached the standard of 'I can't help wanting you more.'"

Inspecting Omar, Margaret said cautiously, "A poet . . . but he looks so sedate!"

Omar responded, "That's why I gave it up so quickly."

"So now he regards beauty as a treatment which will cure him of the strange illness he's been suffering from recently."

The champagne bottle popped open and the bubbles raced into their glasses.

"That means I'm some sort of medicine?"

Mustapha followed quickly with a smile. "Yes, why not, of the sort that one takes before sleep."

"Don't rush things. The cure doesn't come as easily as you think."

Omar asked her to dance. Out on the floor, with his arm around her waist and the fragrance of her perfume quickening his senses, he savored the night. The humidity had relented, and the trees, alight with red and white lamps, seemed to have bloomed.

"May it be a happy acquaintance."

"You're as charming as you are tall."

"You're not short yourself."

"But your sharp eyes frighten me."

"They're shining only from joy, but I'm not much of a dancer. I've almost forgotten how."

"Don't you see you're too tall to be a good dancer?"

"When my friend invited me to the New Paris he said I'd like what I'd find."

"Really."

Lying comes so easily in the autumn. Mustapha was clapping for them as they returned to their seats. Omar's face glowed with a boyish happiness, and for a moment, bewitched by the night's charms, he was restored to his lost youth. She touched the ring of his left hand, murmuring, "Married . . . really, you married men don't give the bachelors a chance."

Mustapha said, laughing, "You two are getting along famously. I bet you'll go out together tonight."

"You've lost the bet."

"Why, my dear Margaret? A lawyer like our friend won't tolerate delay."

"Then he must learn."

"Conventions be damned!"

Omar said gently, "In any case, my car's at your disposal to take you wherever you'd like."

When she got into the car with him, he was elated. "Where to?"

"Athens Hotel."

"Have you seen the pyramids after midnight?"

"It's a dark night without any moon."

He headed in the direction of the pyramids. "Civilization has robbed us of the beauty of darkness."

"But—"

He said reassuringly, "I'm a lawyer, not a playboy, or a highway bandit."

His heart had not stirred like this since the rendezvous in the Jardin des Familles. He could hardly remember Zeinab's youthful face and hadn't really looked at their wedding picture for the past ten years. You, Margaret, are everything and nothing. With the desperation of a fugitive, I knock at the gate of the enchanted city.

"Under this open sky by the pyramids, great events took place."

She lifted his arm from around her neck, saying, "Please don't add to those events."

He pressed her hand in gratitude nonetheless.

"It's best that we don't stop," she said. "Don't you see how strong the wind is?"

"We're well protected inside."

How dense the darkness is around us. If only its density could shut out the world, obliterating everything before the weary eye so that the heart alone might see, might gaze on the blazing star of ecstasy. It approaches now like the rays of dawn. Your soul seems to shun everything in its thirst for love, in its love for love, in its yearning for the first ecstasy of creation and for a refuge in the wellsprings of life.

"Why don't we spend the night here?"

"Be sensible. Please take me back."

"You've never heard of what goes on at night at the pyramids?"

"Tell me about it tomorrow."

He leaned toward her and they exchanged a kiss; but then she restrained him, pleading, "I said tomorrow."

He kissed her cheek lightly, signaling retreat, and started moving the car over the sand.

"Please don't be angry."

"I yield to the eternal conditions."

"Eternal?"

"I mean the feminine conditions."

"Actually, I'm tired."

"So am I, but I'll arrange the right place for us."

"Wait till we meet again."

"I'll start setting things up."

"Wait a little."

"I have a feeling that we'll stay together."

"Yes," she said, looking ahead at the road.

It was nearly dawn when he returned home, and as he rode the elevator, he remembered how his father used to rebuke him for his late-night escapades. Entering the bedroom, he saw Zeinab sitting on the dresser stool, looking at him with dulled and saddened eyes.

He said quietly, "You should have been asleep."

She spread her hands in despair. "This is the third night."

Undressing, he said distantly, "It was unavoidable."

She asked him more sharply, "Home upsets you?"

"No, but it's true, I am disturbed."

"And how have you spent your nights?"

"No place in particular, at the movies, at coffeehouses, roaming around in the car."

"And I'm here with all kinds of ideas running through my head."

"While you should be sound asleep."

"I'll grow ill in the end."

"Follow my advice."

She sighed deeply. "You treat me with such deadly coldness."

There's no doubt of that. The man you know has shed his skin and now he runs panting after a mysterious call, leaving behind him a trail of dust, all the joys of yesterday, all his Utopian dreams, even the girl whose youthful beauty held such promise in store when church bells rang.

Infatuated, you once looked into those green eyes and said, "Love is fearless."

She murmured, clinging to you, "But my family."

"I'm your family, I'm your world. The Day of Judgment will come before I desert you."

Today your life hangs on a cheap song.

Sleep, Zeinab, for your sake and mine.

———————

Another woman stood on the red stage, singing,

*"I can't help wanting you more every time we meet.
The flame leaps higher with each heartbeat."*

He leaned over to Mustapha. "Where's Margaret?" he asked.

Mustapha got up to inquire, then returned saying, "An unpleasant surprise."

"What is it?"

"She's gone."

"Where?"

"Abroad."

"Did this happen unexpectedly?"

Mustapha brushed his hand disdainfully. "Let's look for someone else."

EIGHT

This act of faithlessness set off a reaction twice as intense and he felt he was in a desperate race with insanity. In the end those swaying branches would speak. Mustapha asked, "Do you really think this is the remedy?"

"Maybe. It's the only thing that's helped so far."

He stopped the car in front of the Capri Club and said as they were getting out, "I've tried so many things, as you know, to no avail. I did feel a heartthrob with Margaret. Passing illusion that she was, the heartthrob was real."

They sat under a trellis roofing. In the dim light, the people sitting at the other tables appeared to be phantoms.

Mustapha remarked, "The manager of this club is a friend of yours," and indicated a man standing at the far end of the stage. He was a short barrel of a man, with a fleshy white face and heavy jowls puffed up like a waterskin. His heavy-lidded eyes peered drowsily yet they had a certain mischievous tilt. When he saw Mustapha he moved toward them with surprising speed for one so heavy. Omar recognized him as a former client for whom he'd won two cases. The man shook their hands warmly, then sat down, saying, "Omar Bey, this is a pleasant surprise." He ordered whiskey and went on. "I never dreamed you'd stop by here, but after all, those who work hard deserve to play."

Mustapha interrupted with a decisive voice. "Let's dispense with the formalities, Mr. Yazbeck." As the manager looked at them warily, Mustapha laughed. "It's as you suspected. The time has come to return the good services of your lawyer."

"Omar Bey?"

"I thought of asking you to recommend a suitable girl for him."

The man smiled broadly and said, "A refined and beautiful girl . . . of good family."

"I'm speaking about love, not marriage!"

"It's up to him, sir."

"Do you have any such cultivated lovelies?"

He waved his small, soft hand in deprecation and said proudly, "Capri's main attraction."

He went on to elaborate, still glancing at Omar a bit skeptically. "She was a student at the Drama Institute, but wasn't a success at acting. She loves to dance, though, and has created a sensation at the Capri."

"Warda!"

"None other."

Mustapha said apologetically, "I didn't think of her because of her height, which would naturally discourage me."

Yazbeck gestured grandiosely toward the stage, where the musicians had started playing an Oriental dance. A storm of applause greeted the dancer, a magnificent statuesque woman with wide-set languid eyes and a high forehead which gave her face a certain aristocratic distinction.

Mustapha murmured, "Marvelous."

Yazbeck said jestingly, "You're immune to such delightful temptations . . ."

"I'm self-sufficient. It's a pastime enjoyed by the best of husbands."

Omar smiled, remembering how Mustapha once said that he couldn't betray his wife since he wasn't able to make love with anyone else. Then he drifted away from the voices around him as he followed the movements of the lovely body, lithe in spite of her height. He loved her smile as he loved the cypress tree. Yazbeck's outstretched hand, bidding them goodbye, drew him back to awareness. After the man had gone, Mustapha looked at him seriously and cautioned, "The raptures of love are seldom found in nightclubs."

Omar muttered sarcastically, "He who strives will be rewarded."

"You know whenever I see Zeinab now my conscience bothers me."

He said scornfully, "These pains are more severe than the luxury of conscience."

Mustapha pointed out the problems involved in such affairs, but Omar interjected, "In the feminine sex, I seem to see life on two feet."

Warda walked directly toward them, without pretense of delay, her wide, gray eyes glancing steadily at Omar.

The scent of the jasmine flowers she wore in her bracelet diffused in the air. Shaking his hand, she exclaimed happily, "At last I've found a man I don't have to look at from above!"

She sat down between the two men and flicked her hand so that the jasmine spilled onto the red tablecloth. The champagne came and bubbled forth. Warda seemed composed, but there was a look in her gray eyes that cautioned against haste. She exchanged a smile of familiarity with Mustapha and listened to the accustomed praise of her dancing and beauty. Throughout, she continued looking at Omar with respect, while he searched her gray eyes for some clue, some answer to his unsatisfied longings. I came not because I loved but in order to love. The complexion is clear, the scent pleasant, and the long eyelashes alluring.

"So you're the famous lawyer?"

"That's of little importance unless you have problems."

"My problems can't be solved through the law courts, unfortunately."

"Why unfortunately?"

"They might have been solved by you."

Mustapha said, laughing, "He's trustworthy, both in court and outside it."

He noticed her long neck surrounded by a simple pearl strand, the bare spread of her chest, the healthy passion expressed in her full, colored lips and flowing from her eyes, and felt his being throb with a strange and unbounded desire, like the mysterious yearnings which assailed him in the late hours of the night. He wished to address the depths, and to have the depths speak to

him without an intermediary, but if the long-sought
ecstasy eluded him, he would find a substitute in the firebrand of sex, the convulsive climax which consumes
the wine of life and all its dreams in one gulp. He
was delirious with longing, anticipation, the titillation
of adventure, the effect of abandoned drinking, the
scent of jasmine pressed under his glass, Warda's encouraging glance, a star blinking through a gap in the trellis.
As the club showed signs of closing, he said, "Shall we
go?"

Mustapha said his farewells and left.

Warda was impressed by the sight of his Cadillac, an
elegant little coupe de ville. "Where's your home?" he
asked.

"It's out of the question. Don't you have a place?"

"With a wife and two daughters."

"Then take me home as those without homes do."

He drove out to the desert by the pyramids, racing
madly, seeking the shelter of the open sky as he had with
Margaret. The half-moon was sinking toward the west. He
reached toward her and gave her a light, artful kiss as a
start. Then they exchanged a long kiss, incited by passions
as old as the moon.

She sighed, whispering. "This is nice."

He pressed her against him with a fervor which
stretched into the solitudes of the desert. His fingers
entwined in her hair, which was lit by moonbeams, and he
said in a strange, breathless voice, "When the dawn
comes."

With his cheek pressed against hers, they gazed at the
sleepy moon, on a level with their eyes, and followed its
languid beams on the sand. Its beams would die, leav-

ing the heart still thirsting. No power on earth can preserve this godly moment, a moment which has conferred a secret meaning to the universe. You stand on its threshold, with your hand stretched out imploringly toward the darkness, the horizon, and the depths where the moon has fallen. A firebrand seems to burn in your chest as the dawn breaks forth and fears of bankruptcy and want recede.

"Are you a dreamer?" she asked.

"No, I'm realistic to the point of illness."

She laughed. "But you're not a woman beater."

"I don't beat men either."

"That's good."

Pressing her closer, he said, "But at one time, I was about to kill."

"Because of a woman?"

"No."

"Don't talk of such things in the moonlight."

"In the end I decided to kill myself."

"In my presence?"

"In your arms."

"In the moonlight?"

"Now the moon is disappearing."

When he returned home and switched on the bedroom light, Zeinab opened her lifeless eyes. As he greeted her indifferently, she said tensely, "It's almost dawn."

"So?"

She sat on the bed, her eyelids swollen, looking tormented and desperate.

"I haven't heard this tone from you in all the years we've been married."

He put on his pajamas in silence and she cried out, "I've never heard anything like it."

He muttered resignedly, "Illness is like that."

"How can I bear such a life?"

"My days are spoiled. Don't spoil the nights."

"The girls are asking questions."

"Well, let's face the situation with a certain amount of wisdom."

She buried her face against the wall. "If only I had some place to go."

He turned off the light and lay down, closing his eyes. Soon, the first movements of the morning would be heard, and tears would be shed next to him, while betrayal gnawed beneath like an insect. Only a few moments remained before this existence would die. She's cut off from the tree and no longer has anyone but you. It's strange that you should be filled with such determination. Tonight's ecstasy is as erratic as a bolt of lightning. How can it fill the emptiness of life?

On Friday he sought out Buthayna on the balcony while she was watering the flowerpots. He smiled somewhat bashfully, but she welcomed him by racing over and presenting her cheek to be kissed. In spite of her happy glow, he detected in her evasive glance a faint reprimand.

"I've missed you very much," she said.

He bit the inside of his lip and said, "I'm sorry, but I'm determined to get well, and just need a bit of forbearance."

She turned back to the flowerpots, and he asked, "Are you okay?"

"Yes," she said, then added after a pause, "But Mama's not."

"That's understandable. But things will change. Just be patient."

She pointed out a jasmine bud, still barely visible, and exclaimed happily, "The first jasmine. It's very small but the scent is strong. Shall I pick it for you?"

How strange it seems, going to work every day in an office which had become so alien and meaningless. When would he have the courage to close it down?

The head clerk remarked, "Every day we lose another case. I've become almost inactive."

In fact, he'd left the burden of work almost entirely to others and did very little supervising or reviewing anymore. Gloomy eyes stared at him from the walls in the stagnant, musty air. His creative energies were spent outside now in setting up the flat in Soliman Pasha Square.

"I'm glad we're setting up our own place," he said to Warda. "We can't go to the pyramids in winter."

She asked, swinging her shoulders to a jazz beat under the trellis of the Capri, "When winter comes, will you still be interested in our affair?"

He raised his glass of champagne. "To a permanent affair." Yazbeck was standing in the distance, the grand master of ceremonies. Omar returned his smile and said, taking Warda's hand, "I owe a lot to him."

"He's nice and better than most of his sort, but greedy, as you'd expect."

"But I'm a champagne customer."

She frowned slightly. "It's extravagant to come here every night."

He beamed, murmuring, "Your concern is encouraging."

She embraced him with her eyes, and said, "Haven't the pyramids already witnessed that?"

"Yes, love, and for me it's not just an affair as I said, but . . ."

She urged silence with a press of her hand. "Don't name it. Isn't it better that it names itself?"

"You're so lovely, it drives me mad."

"I have no confidence in words, since I was originally an actress."

"And a lady through and through."

"Thank you, but you know most people have a low opinion of the art. For that reason I left my family. It's just as well I have no brother or father."

He thought for a moment, then said, "Certainly acting would be better than dancing at the Capri."

"I didn't have the proper devotion to it, and they said I had no talent. Dancing was my real love all along, so it was the Capri, and the rest followed, inevitably. . . ."

He said with warmth, "But you have a heart of gold."

"That I've never heard before."

He commissioned a couple of men to work on the new flat—the furniture, the bar, the objets d'art and decor. And soon the place was quite beautifully set up. Apart from the bedroom, dining room, and entrance hall, there was an

Oriental room which recaptured the fantasies of *A Thousand and One Nights*. He spent without limit, as though ridding himself of a painful financial tumor. He followed Mustapha's amazed eyes as he toured the place, and when they finally met his glance, said, "Instead of reprimanding me, talk to me about the meaning of life."

"Life!"

"I'll knock the deaf walls at every spot until the voice inside betrays the hidden treasure."

Mustapha shrugged resignedly and said, "There is a certain beauty in the madness."

"The last few days have given me a taste for life I've never had before. Nothing else matters."

Mustapha said, smiling, "Yazbeck's uneasiness proves the girl's loyalty."

"She's loyal and honest or else the greatest of actresses."

"But she's a failure as an actress."

The apartment overwhelmed her when she entered it the first time. She exclaimed in admiration, "You really do have champagne taste, but you've been too extravagant."

He gave her a light kiss and said, "This is our little nest."

"I don't want to burden you or give you any false impressions about me."

"If I didn't know the real Warda, I wouldn't have made any effort."

She laughed coquettishly. "You're alone responsible for your understanding."

"And the pyramids?"

"Just because we shriek when fire burns us doesn't mean shrieking is in our nature."

He stretched out on the divan, saying, "Mustapha tells me Yazbeck is upset."

"I refused to go out with anyone else. He can jump in the lake."

"And stay there indefinitely."

"I'll restrict my work at the Capri to dancing."

"You're so sweet."

"It's hot today. I'm going to take a shower in the new bathroom."

He changed from his street clothes into a gallabiyya, for that, he decided, was more in keeping with the Oriental room than pajamas. Looking contentedly around the elegant place, he reflected that happiness was enough to cure him; he could let up on the regime. A sudden lightheartedness prompted him to ask in a booming voice, "What's the shower water up to?"

Her voice responded behind the bathroom door, "Something very impolite!" The door opened, she darted past him, wrapped in a towel, and shot into the bedroom. He closed his eyes in contentment. May this nest repeat the ecstasies of the pyramids, and what he now holds in his hands, may it satisfy her longings. For its sake he has tread on other hearts and learned recklessness and cruelty. May she not vanish as Margaret did. Your colleague, the great lawyer, said to you in your office, "You look too dapper these days for a successful, hardworking lawyer."

You laughed. "Less so for a happy lawyer."

He glanced at him with misgiving, the brazen lover, then quickly changed the conversation to politics, his favorite subject. "So, what are people doing these days?" he asked.

Uninterested in politics, you answered, "Searching madly for ecstasy."

He didn't understand. He's a womanizer, but you're not. You're neither brazen nor frivolous, but who distinguishes between the slayer and the worshipper, or believes you're building a temple from the wreckage?

The bedroom door opened halfway, and her head appeared. "Making up is tedious. I'm dying for a kiss."

He rushed over to her and held her cheeks between his hands, pressing her mouth closed, and as he kissed her, he savored the fragrance of her soap, the scent of her skin. "Shall I come in?" he whispered.

Laughing, she pushed him away and said, "Don't be primitive."

He reclined again on the divan, and looked at the radio-television console in front of him. In a playful mood, he got up and turned both of them on at once and was assaulted by a discussion of juvenile crimes running simultaneously with "Listener's Request." He turned them off, but still feeling playful, went to the bedroom door and knocked. "Hi," the voice called.

"I love you."

"With all my heart."

"What do you want most in life?"

"Love."

He continued in a playful tone. "Have you ever thought of the meaning of life?"

"It has no meaning apart from love."

"Have you finished making yourself up?"

"Just a minute more."

He persisted. "Doesn't it bother you, love, that we play while the world around us is serious?"

She laughed exuberantly. "Don't you see that it's we who are serious while the world around us plays?"

"Where do you get such eloquence?"

"After a while you'll learn the secret."

When the night is spent and the relentless dawn overtakes us, you'll return inevitably to the dreary room where there is no music, no ecstasy, where sad eyes and a wall of stone will close upon you. Then the chords of somber wisdom will ring out with reproaches as harsh as the dust of a sandstorm. Make your reply as resolute and final as your aversion.

"Don't disturb me." Deafen your ears to all words. "I said, don't disturb me. This is the way I am, today, tomorrow, and every day. . . . Accept matters as they are, and leave our daughter out of the quarrel." "There is no point in arguing, I'll do as I please." And don't back down if Buthayna asks why you've changed. "Think what you want, I'm too bored by it all to make excuses."

The door opened and Warda emerged in all her splendor. "What do you think of me, sweetheart?"

He looked at her dazzled, and murmured, "Let me be a sentence never uttered by a tongue before."

T E N

She sat facing him on the balcony that Friday, their holi-day, and he reflected uneasily that he'd hardly seen her the past week. The rays of the sun crossed her lap and her legs and sparkled on the Nile beneath them. It was strange that he couldn't remember her as a child, whether she was a devil like Jamila. Now she's a beautiful girl, intelligent, studious, refined, poetic. Her resemblance to her mother as a girl he preferred to forget.

"You're too serious for a poet!"

Jamila, who'd been standing at the entrance to the bal-cony, shouted defiantly, "A poet!"

He shook his finger at her, then turned to Buthayna, whose serious expression showed signs of displeasure. "You're too thin, and your sister's too fat. What do the two of you eat?"

Jamila shouted, "She eats."

Umm Mohammed, the maid, carried off the protesting Jamila.

"Mama's unwell," Buthayna said.

"Mama's all right. Tell me about you."

"There's nothing much to say, but Mama's not all right."

The chase never stops in this house. And you, Buthayna, does nothing concern you but poetry, math, and chemistry? Is God alone your lover?

"You don't like to talk about Mama?"

"She no longer understands my illness."

Their eyes met for a moment; then, defeated, he turned to look at the Nile.

"But the doctor, Papa."

He interrupted her gently, trying to hide his exasperation. "I'm the doctor, no one else."

"I'm sorry, but you've taught me to be open with you."

"Of course."

Suddenly a shrill little voice shouted, "Course!" He held the little girl's arm until Umm Mohammed took her away again.

"Have we caused you irritation?"

"God forbid. But we tend to escape when we're disturbed within ourselves."

"She cries a lot and that's very painful."

"You must convince her that she's mistaken."

She said, playing with the bracelet of her gold watch, "But you treat her differently now. You told her very harshly you'd do as you pleased."

"She told you that, too?"

"I'm the only one she can complain to."

Depressed, he muttered, "It was just anger, as you know."

"Anyway, she's willing to help you as much as she can."

"There's nothing she can do."

She hesitated a moment, then said, "Mightn't she think . . ."

"Isn't it better for us to go over your latest poems?"

"There's nothing new."

"But your lover still inspires you."

"Maybe she thinks . . . well, you know."

"She even lets you in on her ridiculous fears."

"It makes me very sad."

Lighting a cigarette, he said, "Ridiculous illusions."

She said anxiously, "I'll believe you. You've always been a model of truth. Are they merely illusions?"

You're backed into a corner. "Your mother has upset you too much."

"Say that they're just illusions."

He glanced at her reproachfully, but she avoided his eyes. Looking at the Nile, she asked, "There's no other woman?"

"A woman!" the shrill little voice returned.

This time he pulled her onto his lap as though seeking her protection and started roughhousing with her, the only way to deal with the little imp. But Buthayna continued her worrying. "I want an answer, Papa."

"What do you think of your father?"

"I believe you, so speak. Please, for my sake, speak."

In bitter despair, he said, "There's nothing."

Her face brightened while his heart sank. Her eyes shone with victorious relief but the world scowled. Autumn was in the air, a tinge of yellow had spread over the treetops, and flocks of white clouds were reflected in the gray water. The emptiness was filled with silent tunes, sad and delicate, and weary questions with hard answers. His lie expanded until it threatened him with annihilation.

In the depths of despair, he went to visit Mustapha at his office. After a futile discussion, Mustapha concluded, "I've gone along with you and helped, hoping that you'd realize the futility of this venture, but you're drowned."

He sighed. "You don't realize I'm living the art I always longed to create."

Mustapha finished the page he was writing, then sent it down to the press. "I've often thought the crisis you're suffering resulted from suppressed art."

He rejected the idea with a shake of his head, then said, "No, it's not art, but it may be what we turn to art in search of."

Mustapha paused a minute, then said, "If we were scientists, spending twenty years of our lives searching for an equation, perhaps we'd be invulnerable to despair."

Shaking his head sorrowfully, he said, "My misfortune may be that I'm searching for an equation without scientific qualifications."

Mustapha laughed. "And since there's no revelation in our age, people like you can only go begging."

Begging, day and night in aimless reading, in futile poetry, in pagan prayers in the nightclub halls, in stirring the deaf heart through infernal adventures.

Mustapha spoke about Zeinab and said that she was suffering, both from his desertion and from the effects of her pregnancy. She must be in a bad way. You've become so hard-hearted, yet you're prepared to be magnanimous if she'd only free you from the shackles of this dead love.

"Yes, Zeinab, there is another woman, since you insist on knowing."

Disgust has sprouted in a fetid swamp choked with traditional platitudes and household management. What wealth and success you've attained offer no comfort, for all is consumed by decay. Your soul is sealed in a putrid jar like an aborted fetus, your heart suffocated by apathy and by grimy ashes. The flowers of life, withered and fallen, will come to rest on the garbage heap.

"Weep all you like, you'll have to accept things as they are."

Disaffection has killed everything. A few questions have tumbled the very foundations of life. I said to him, "Suppose you win the case today and the government confiscates your land tomorrow?" to which he replied, "Don't we live our lives knowing that our fate rests with God?"

He was in his office, dawdling over a memorandum, when the office boy announced Mr. Yazbeck. The man walked in, his paunch bulging in front of him, greeted Omar with a bow, and sat down.

"Since I was passing through Al-Azhar Square, I thought I'd drop by for a visit."

Omar said with a sarcastic smile, "You'd come from the far ends of the earth for Warda's sake, wouldn't you?"

"My dear counselor, you know that my garden is full of roses."

"Fine, so don't talk about Warda."

He smiled broadly and said, "It would be foolish to think I could get around you, but let's try to bridge the distance between us as directly as possible."

"Yes?"

His eyelids lowered and he said seriously, "Warda's been neglecting her duties."

"She has duties other than dancing?"

"You didn't honor us with your presence that night, sir, just to watch Warda dance."

"So?"

"So I said I'd complain to the great man himself."

Omar frowned but remained silent. Yazbeck continued. "Business is business, sir, and I don't like . . ."

He interrupted curtly. "Do whatever you think is in your interest."

"I don't want to anger you . . ."

"But I'm excusing you in advance."

The man bowed his head gratefully. "And I promise I'll take her back to work if you tire of her in the future."

"That day will never come, Mr. Yazbeck."

"I wish you happiness, *mon chéri*."

Yazbeck was about to get up, but Omar, overcome by a sudden absurd impulse, detained him. "Tell me, Mr. Yazbeck, what meaning does life hold for you?"

The man raised his eyebrows in surprise, then, reading the seriousness of Omar's expression, answered, "Life is life. . . . "

"Are you happy?"

"Praise the Lord. . . . Sometimes business is slow, sometimes the club is disturbed by a love affair like Warda's, but the carnival goes on. . . ."

"So you live knowing your fate rests with God?"

"That's undeniable, of course. But I have a beautiful house, a good wife, a son studying chemistry in Switzerland who's going to settle there."

He smiled. "Do you believe in God?"

The man replied in astonishment, "Naturally. What an odd question."

"Then tell me what He is."

He laughed openly, for the strange questions had removed all ceremony. "Will your infatuation for Warda last long?"

"Of course."

"Couldn't it . . . ?"

He interrupted. "If you tell me what God is, I promise I'll let you have her immediately!"

The man rose, bowed once more, and said on his way out, "I'm always at your service."

ELEVEN

He kissed her with fervent gratitude. "I know it's a great sacrifice to quit your job."

Her wide eyes shone with tears. "For your sake."

The Oriental room exuded the breath of love. He'd never dreamed he would love her so intensely. She withdrew a dark blue box from the pocket of her robe and handed it to him shyly—a gift of golden cuff links.

He exclaimed, as though he'd never owned gold before, "Sweetheart!"

"The cuff links, you can see, have two hearts."

"Because your heart is made of gold, as I told you."

Running her fingers through his thick black hair, she asked, "Why did you bring all your clothes with you today?"

His face clouded, and he said in a voice devoid of tenderness, "I've left home for good."

She exclaimed in astonishment, "No!"

"It's the only solution."

"But I told you, I don't want to cause you any trouble."

"Let's not talk about it."

The room's atmosphere in the silence of dawn was electric. She looked at him with angry and desperate eyes, her makeup smudged with all the tears she'd shed. How ravaged by anger is a face which had remained placid for twenty years.

"You should train yourself to accept the facts."

"While you stain your honor with a prostitute."

"Your voice will wake everyone up."

"Look at the lipstick on your handkerchief. How disgusting!"

Overcome by anger, he shouted, "What of it?"

"Your daughter is of marriageable age."

"I'm ridding myself of death."

"Aren't you ashamed? I'm ashamed for you."

His anger increasing, he replied, "Accepting death is even more shameful."

Her head dropped as she wept. "Twenty years without knowing your filth," she said in a choked voice.

He said insanely, "So, let it be the end."

"I'll wander around aimlessly."

"No, this is your home; so stay. I'll go."

You threw yourself on a chair in the living room, your eyes closed with pain. Hearing a noise, you raised your head and found Buthayna standing before you, pale-faced and still drowsy-eyed with sleep.

The atmosphere was charged with guilt and reproach as you gazed at each other in silence. You remembered the disgraceful lie, and in all your life had never felt so ashamed.

"I'm sorry, Buthayna, for upsetting you."

The compressed lips revealed her wounded pride. "There's no use talking," she said, then reverted to silence, succumbing to the burden which had fallen upon her.

"Your mother will remain in the house, provided with every comfort."

He prayed to God that she wouldn't cry. "It's distressing," he murmured, "but I'm ridding my soul of something more serious."

She looked sadly into his eyes. "But you told me there was nothing."

His face burning, he sighed. "The truth was inappropriate."

"Why?"

"Let's preserve what love there is between us."

You left, unable to meet her glance again until she pardons you.

Warda commented, "You'll regret your decision."

"No, I can't stand the hypocrisy anymore."

She said anxiously, "I'm so afraid that I'll fail to make you happy."

"But I am happy, really."

And so he applied himself to happiness and shunned all disturbing thoughts. Anticipating resistance from Mustapha, he accosted him. "I'm happy. Does that displease you? I even feel some poetic stirrings."

He also became more receptive to work, though he was still reluctant to accept cases. His work breaks were spent talking to her on the phone, and at the end of the day, he would rush back to his nest and she would welcome him with a shining face. They usually stayed in the Oriental room, but sometimes they'd go out to the distant parts of Cairo, to the rendezvous of lovers; sometimes they'd take night excursions to Fayum or to the rest house on the Desert Road. When she learned that his poetical aspirations of the past were again seeking expression, she encouraged him with superb recitations of her own. As a student at the Drama Institute, she'd memorized Shawki's plays, and many love poems as well.

He said to her admiringly, "Your love of poetry is wonderful."

She urged him to start writing again, but he was reluctant. "Isn't it better to live poetry than to write it?"

One day she remarked, "You haven't asked me about my past."

Giving her a kiss, he answered, "When we're in love, we accept everything on faith. There's no need to ask questions."

But she wanted to talk about her past. "My father was an English teacher, a wonderful teacher, the sort that students never forget. If he'd been alive when I decided to enter the Drama Institute, he would have given me his blessings and encouragement. But my mother's a very pious, narrow-minded woman. I entered the Institute against her wishes, and when I decided to take up dancing, she was furious. So were my uncles, on both sides. It ended in our cutting off relations. I deserted my family."

"And how did you manage on your own?"

"I lived in the house of one of my actress friends."

He fondled her soft hand and asked, "Have you always loved dancing?"

"Yes, I loved to dance, but I had aspirations of being an actress. I tried, and failed, and so ended up as I started, as a dancer."

He asked, disturbed, "Did Yazbeck bully you?"

"Actually, he's kinder than the others, and I knew what working in a nightclub entailed."

"You're my first and last love," he said fervently, pressing her to him in gratitude. Then he asked, "Why didn't you return to your mother after you'd failed in acting?"

"It was too late. I have my pride, and failure only intensified it."

Failure! The curse that never ends. It's awful that no one listens to your songs, that your love for the secret of existence dies, so that existence itself loses all mystery. Sighs of lament will one day destroy everything.

The office witnessed sober visits from his uncle, a justice, and from his only sister. They besought him not to marry "the dancer" and his uncle observed, "If this relationship continues, you won't be considered for the justiceship."

He said rather abruptly, "I haven't striven for it or wanted it."

He defended his happiness fiercely, with all the force of despair which had seized him. He seemed so childishly gay and innocent that Mustapha remarked, laughing, "Now tell us about the meaning of life."

Omar laughed loudly. "That question nags at us only when our hearts are empty. . . . A full vessel doesn't produce hollow sounds. Ecstasy is fulfillment, so I can only hope that love will bring everlasting ecstasy."

"Sometimes I pity you, other times I envy you." Omar's eyes shone triumphantly as Mustapha continued. "As fast as I speed through life, now and then the old sense of failure, buried deep in my heart, returns—perhaps on one of the dusty days of the sandstorm season, and I'm bedeviled by questions about life's meaning, but I soon repress them, like shameful memories."

A wintry wind rattled the windows of the office and the

late afternoon faded into night. Mustapha's bald head would now brave the cold. He went on. "Why do we ask? Religious conviction provided meaning. Now we try to fill the void with the verifications of natural law. Yesterday, frustrated and dissatisfied, I asserted that my artistic commentaries were meaningful, that my past and present radio programs were meaningful, that my television plays were meaningful, and so I had no right to question."

"What a hero you are!"

He continued enumerating his achievements. "The way I made love to my wife last night was so fantastic that I suggested to the editor that it be written up as 'The Artistic Event of the Week.' My son Omar, unfortunately named after you, has become a sulky adolescent, as mad about soccer as we once were about overturning the world."

He overturned the world and landed in jail. But someday he'd get out, in a few years, and astonished glances would be exchanged. Let others worry about it.

Mustapha remarked in a more serious vein, "The editor suggested that I give a lecture to the employees on socialist consciousness."

"In what capacity?"

"In my capacity as an old socialist!"

"You accepted, of course?"

"Of course, but I wonder, with the state so intent on applying its progressive ideals, isn't it better for us to be concerned with our own private affairs?"

"Such as selling popcorn and watermelon seeds and wondering about the meaning of life?"

"Or falling in love to find the ecstasy of fulfillment."

"Or growing ill without cause."

They smoked in silence, then Omar asked suddenly, "How are they?"

Mustapha smiled. "Zeinab is fine, back to normal, though exhausted by her pregnancy. But there's something you should know."

Omar showed signs of interest.

"She's thinking of looking for work after the delivery."

He made a gesture of annoyance as Mustapha continued. "As a translator, for example. I'm afraid that she'll leave home one day."

"But it's her home."

Mustapha looked at him sarcastically. "Buthayna's immersed in her studies, and Jamila has almost forgotten you."

He lowered his eyes, disconcerted.

"And I fulfill my duty by criticizing you relentlessly in the bitterest terms."

Omar laughed. "You old hypocrite."

"My wife, on her part, never ceases attacking you."

"Of course, of course."

"I often defend you when we're alone and attribute your behavior to a 'severe psychological illness,' reassuring her at the same time that it's not infectious!"

T W E L V E

No one excelled Warda in the art of love. Mad about her man and their little nest, she devoted herself completely to the service of love and to performing all its tasks. Omar would look around the place, smell the roses in the vase, listen to the music in the Oriental room, and would feel he was in paradise. Though she asked nothing of him, he would urge her occasionally to buy clothes and other things. She tried to keep her weight down by taking walks and watching her diet, and urged him also to be careful about his eating and drinking. He felt that she'd become a part of his personality and that she clung to him as her last hope. In the long winter nights they withdrew into themselves and stayed in the Oriental room until late at night, and between kisses and embraces talked endlessly about the past, present, and future, about truth and fantasy, reality and dreams, and were it not for the closed porch overlooking the square, the winter storms and rain showers would never have disturbed them at all. When conversation was exhausted, the silence that fell was one of mutual

88 / Naguib Mahfouz

understanding, security, and comfort. But at times he was overcome by his fantasies, some of them laughable, others more disturbing. He was alarmed by one particular vision: the collision of two cars at a crossroad, a middle-aged gentleman tossed in the air.

"Where are you?" the gentle voice whispered.

He answered, a bit ashamed, "It's nothing."

She put her arm around his neck. "It must be something important."

He shook his head. After a moment's silence she probed again. "Why wouldn't Buthayna and Jamila visit you in your office?"

He was thinking of what a strange house the spider builds to hunt flies. "Buthayna didn't want to."

"She knew of your wish?"

"Mustapha conveyed it to her."

"You haven't talked to me about it."

"It's not important."

"Whatever concerns you is important to me."

They began to watch television more. It helped in forestalling the strange fantasies. Mustapha rang them up one day to ask how they were. She invited him to drop by, and so he began visiting them. He asked Omar how his poetry was progressing.

"He does write," Warda replied

Omar protested, "It's an abortion."

"Happiness is more important than poetry," Mustapha said consolingly.

He was on the verge of asking, "But what is happiness?" but the concern, so evident in Mustapha's gray eyes, deterred him. Mustapha and the radio and the television rescued them from repetitious talk. And then there were his fantasies, "Oh God!" He saw himself as a magician, entertaining the people with his miraculous powers. He would cause the opera house to vanish in the blink of an eye, as the astonished crowds looked on, and then, to exclamations of wonder, suddenly restore it. Dear God, how much we need such potions of magic. As he gazed at her dreamily, she asked, "Why don't you invite some friends over to pass the time?"

He said quietly, "I have no friends besides Mustapha."

She seemed unconvinced, so he explained, "I don't consider colleagues and acquaintances friends."

So she arranged, on her own, for them to go out more often, to the theater and the cinema, even to the night-clubs.

"Isn't this better," she said, "than staying alone by ourselves at home?"

He nodded in agreement.

She reproached him. "This is the first time you've been unflattering!"

Too late, he tried to make amends. "I simply meant to compliment you for arranging these outings."

"I'll never tire of your company."

"Nor I of yours, believe me."

He was annoyed at his inattentiveness. Dear God, what's happening? Mustapha, at any rate, was clearly impressed by his happiness, and remarked one day as they were sitting together in his office, "Tell me about love. In the end you may persuade me to adopt a new philosophy of life."

Omar saw the glint of maliciousness in his eyes. Ignoring the question, he asked, "Have I become so unimportant to Buthayna?"

"You know she's idealistic and proud, but in her heart she adores you."

"Hasn't she missed me, the traitor?"

"She'll see you again one day, but for God's sake tell me about this romance of yours."

"As strong as ever!" he said defiantly.

"A political declaration?"

"You have no right to probe the secrets of the heart, you hypocrite!"

Mustapha laughed at length, and said, "Let me describe the situation as I see it. Those delightful conversations are dwindling, the games are losing their charm, inadvertently you drink more."

"Drop dead."

How awful. Warda was the perfect lover and beautiful as well. Dear God, how can ecstasy be aroused again and the dead poetry revived? How dark the late afternoon of winter.

They went one night to the New Paris and suddenly Margaret appeared on the stage. His heart raced, remembering the past, but with a great effort of will, he controlled his nerves.

She sang:

*"I can't help wanting you more every time we meet.
The flame leaps higher with each heartbeat."*

Warda whispered, "How true."

One glance exchanged between you and Margaret would be a giveaway. So they left at his suggestion, and drove aimlessly in the cold night through the empty roads. There's no need to be agitated, no reason to be. But her sudden return gave impetus to his vexation. You'll stand at the edge of the abyss again, prey to the forces of destruction summoned forth by despair.

He called Warda from the office to tell her he'd been invited to a party in honor of a colleague recently appointed justice. He went to the New Paris and listened to Margaret sing while he waited. What brought me here, and why so quickly? What am I looking for? Is it all over with Warda?

Margaret came to the table, along with the champagne. Her face glowing, she said, "I'm sorry I had to leave so unexpectedly."

"Unexpectedly?"

"I received a cable from abroad."

He studied her, marveling at the force of her attraction. He asked her to leave with him, but she answered, "Not tonight."

He tried to control his impatience. "When?"

"Perhaps tomorrow."

When he returned to the nest, around one o'clock that night, Warda was sitting in the Oriental room. He kissed her and asked, as he'd once asked Zeinab, "You're still awake?"

She said reprovingly, "Of course!"

She looked at him for a while, then remarked, "I hope you haven't overeaten or drunk too much."

Later as he was lying in his pajamas on the couch, she crept over to him and pressed her lips to his, but he felt no stirrings of desire. "Let it be an innocent night," he said to himself.

She called him at work the next day, but unable to think of any excuse, he made no mention of his plans to be absent. He went off to the New Paris congratulating himself on his indifference. The red lights transformed Margaret into a bewitching she-devil, and her slender neck and rich voice thrilled him.

Spanish lamps hung from a ceiling covered with paintings of nude women. How can ecstasy filter into such a place, filled with cigarette smoke and the odor of wine? Peering behind a huge pillar, he saw a couple embracing as if in the throes of death.

Could Warda be uprooted so easily from his soul, as if only an artificial flower? Why are we reminded of death so insistently, whatever we do? Who can affirm that these drunken souls really exist?

They raced out to the pyramids in his car. "The night's cold," she objected. He turned on the heater, but she kept on. "Why don't we go to your home?"

"I have no home."

He stopped the car in the darkness. A heavy bank of clouds covered the sky. "Not a star in sight," he said happily.

He pressed her to his chest with desperate force. She whispered breathlessly, "The darkness is frightening."

He silenced her with a kiss, then said, "Now is not the time for fear."

How wonderful her touch was, yet in itself it meant nothing. To touch life's secrets is all that matters. Their words were lost in sighs, the silent language of the night; a song of harmony seemed to herald a better life, and their intermingled breaths warmed a heart stricken with cold. The darkness was free of peering eyes. The heart could relax and rejoice triumphantly. He sighed with the fullness of pleasure, he sighed with relaxation, but then, dear God, he sighed with weariness and distress. He looked into the black night and wondered where ecstasy was. Where had Margaret gone?

He returned to the nest discontented. She faced him with rigid features, he smiled in greeting, and they remained standing for an uncomfortable minute. Then he flung himself on the couch, saying, "I'm sorry."

"There is no need to invent excuses." She walked back and forth across the room, and then sat in a chair near him.

"It's been clear to me that you've needed a change."

"Things aren't that simple."

Unable to control her anxiety, she said, "I'm not going to conduct a cross-examination. Just one simple question. Have we failed?"

He answered truthfully, but wearily. "No one can match you. I'm sure of that."

She looked off into space. "Were you with a woman?"

He hesitated a moment before answering, "To tell you the truth, I'm not yet cured of the illness."

She spoke sharply for the first time. "An illness whose only cure is a woman!" Then she resumed her calm tone. "All I can offer you is love, so if you refuse it, all will end." She observed his silence with a kind of desperation, and then went on. "Fickle passions in the young can be cured; in wise men like you they can't."

His eyes wandered hopelessly around the room. "Am I insane?"

"Oddly enough, your personality doesn't seem unstable."

"But I'm accused of insanity because of my behavior."

She burst out, "If you mean living with me, then go back to your wife."

"I have no wife."

"Then I'll go. My situation's easier than your wife's since I can always get a job and a place to stay."

Her words stung him, almost causing him to shout, "Go!" but instead he stretched out his legs and closed his eyes.

"So you were with a woman?"

He answered with annoyance, "You know."

"Who?"

"A woman."

"But who is she?"

"It doesn't matter."

"You knew her before knowing me?"

"We'd met casually."

"Do you love her?"

"No."

"Then why did you go out with her?"

He shrugged.

"Maybe you felt a sudden desire?"

"Maybe."

"Do you always give in to your desire?"

"Not always."

"When?"

He was getting vexed. "When I feel ill."

"Are you a womanizer?"

"No."

"Weren't you in love with me?"

"Yes, certainly."

"But no longer?"

"I love you, but the illness is starting again."

She said impatiently, "I've been noticing a change in you for the last few days."

"Since the illness set in."

"The illness . . . the illness!" she shouted with exasperation, then asked, her expression distorted, "Are you going to meet her again?"

"I don't know."

"Do you enjoy torturing me?"

He blew out a breath. "A rest break, please."

He took Margaret one cold, starry night to the rest house on the Desert Road, and on the way back she said tenderly, "Wouldn't it be better to have a place of our own?"

"No . . ." he said vaguely, having decided there was no point in continuing with her.

Displeased with his answer, she said coldly, "I really don't enjoy affairs in parked cars."

He drove her back to the hotel without saying another word.

The ecstasy of love fades and the frenzy of sex is too ephemeral to have any effect. What can we do when we find no food to satisfy our hunger? You'll be swept into the tornado and annihilated. There is no way to bring back stability after it has died.

A brunette dancer at the New Paris attracted him with her gaiety and lithe body, so he went after her. He saw Margaret on the stage, returned her smile, then invited the brunette to his table. To Margaret it must have seemed a clumsy ploy in the game of love, but in the storm he'd lost all sense of humor. The brunette left with him, enticed by money. It didn't really make things better, but he thought his heart stirred slightly as she laughed. If his heart didn't stir, it would die. Poetry, wine, love—none of them could call forth the elusive ecstasy.

Every night he picked up a woman, from one club or another, sometimes from the streets. At the Capri he sat with a dancer named Muna. Yazbeck rushed over to greet him, exhibiting obvious pleasure. It angered Omar, for he saw it as a kind of death notice of his frustrated hopes.

"My good man. Did . . . ?"

Omar looked at him sternly and left with Muna. As he pressed her to him, he trembled with an unaccountable urge to kill her. He imagined himself ripping open her chest with a knife, and suddenly finding what he'd been looking for all along. Killing is the complement of creation, the completion of the silent, mysterious cycle.

"What's wrong?" Muna whispered.

He awoke, startled. "Nothing, just the dark."

"But there's no one around."

He raced the car at such a speed that she grasped his arm and threatened to scream. Later, as he was undressing, he felt that the end was coming—the answer to his search—insanity or death. Warda sat on the bed. "I'm going away," she said.

He answered gently, "I feel responsible for you."

"I don't want anything." After a moment's silence, she spoke again. "What's sad is that I've really loved you."

He said wearily, "But you're not patient with me."

"My patience is at an end."

He felt such revulsion toward her in his soul that he didn't comment.

Finding no trace of her when he returned the next night, he smiled in relief and lay down in his suit on the divan to enjoy the silent, empty flat. Every night he brought a new woman to it.

Mustapha laughed and said, "Hail to the greatest Don Juan on the African continent."

Omar smiled lamely as Mustapha continued. "It's no secret anymore. Several of my colleagues have spoken about you. The news has also reached your cronies at the club. They wonder what's the story behind your rejuvenation."

He said with distaste, "Honestly, I hate women."

"That's obvious!" Then he continued more seriously. "Empty your heart of what's troubling you so you can settle down, once and for all."

In the spring it was a relief to sit outdoors in the nightclub gardens, rather than in the closed halls. But the agitation remained, and he was exhausted by his dreams. Occasionally he found solace in reading, especially the poems of India and Persia.

His nighttime adventures took him once more to the Capri. As he sat under the trellis, sipping his drink and receiving the spring breeze, Warda appeared again on the stage. He felt no emotion, surprise, agitation, or pleasure. In autumn it had started. Ecstasy, love, then aversion; when will the grieved heart smash these vicious cycles? When will it break through the barrier of no return? She sees him, then continues dancing, while Yazbeck steals worried glances. He felt no determination. But after the show, noticing Warda not far from him, he invited her to his table. She approached with a smile, as though nothing had happened. He ordered the usual—the drink which had earned him renown in the clubs—and said with sincerity, "I'm really sorry, Warda."

Smiling enigmatically, she said, "You shouldn't regret what has passed." Then gaily: "And the experience of love is precious even if it brings suffering."

He said, biting his lip, "I'm not well."

She whispered, "Then let's pray to God for your recovery."

He felt the glances of the other women who'd gone with

him, night after night. As Warda smiled, he muttered, "I didn't desire them."

She raised her eyebrows.

"I knew them all, without exception, but there was never any desire."

"Then why?"

"Hoping the divine moment would unlock the answer."

She said resentfully, "How cruel you were. You men don't believe in love unless we disbelieve in it."

"Perhaps, but that's not my problem."

The scent of orange blossoms drifting from the dark fields suggested secret worlds of delight. Feeling suddenly light and unfettered, he asked her fervently, "Tell me, Warda, why do you live?"

She shrugged her shoulders and finished her drink, but when he repeated the question, he was so clearly in earnest that she replied, "Does that question have any meaning?"

"It doesn't hurt to ask it once in a while."

"I live, that's all."

"I'm waiting for a better answer."

She thought a moment, then said, "I love to dance, and to be admired, and I hope to find true love."

"To you, then, life means love."

"Why not?"

"After loving once, weren't you disillusioned?"

She said with annoyance, "That may be true of others."

"And as for you?"

"No."

"How many times have you loved?"

"I told you once . . ."

He interrupted her. "What you told me once doesn't matter; let's discuss things openly now."

"Your violent nature is getting the better of you."

"Don't you want to talk?"

"I've said all that I . . ."

He sighed, then continued feverishly. "And God, what do you think of Him?"

She looked at him distrustfully, but he entreated, "Please answer me, Warda."

"I believe in Him."

"With certainty?"

"Of course."

"How does such certainty arise?"

"It exists, that's all."

"Do you think about Him often?"

Her laugh was a bit forced. "When in need or adversity."

"And other than that?"

She said sharply, "You love to torture others, don't you?"

He stayed in the club till 3 A.M. and then raced out in the car to the Pyramids Road. Going out alone that night, he reflected, was an interesting development. He parked the car along the side of the deserted road and got out. The darkness, unrelieved by ground lights, was peculiarly dense, unlike any night he could remember. The earth and space itself seemed to have disappeared and he was lost in blackness. Raising his head to the gigantic dome overhead, he was assaulted by thousands of stars, alone, in clusters, and in constellations. A gentle breeze blew, dry and refreshing, harmonizing the parts of the universe. The desert sands, clothed in darkness, hid the whispers, as numberless as the grains, of past generations—their hopes, their suffering, and all their last questions. There's no pain without a cause, something told him, and somewhere this enchanted, ephemeral moment will endure. Here I am, beseeching the silence to utter, for if that happened, all would change. If only the sands would loosen their hidden powers, and liberate me from this oppressive impotence. What prevents me from shouting, knowing that no echo will reverberate? He leaned against the car and gazed for a long time at the horizon. Slowly it changed as the darkness relented and a line appeared, diffusing a strange luminosity like a fragrance or a secret. Then it grew more pronounced, sending forth waves of light and splendor. His heart danced with an intoxicated joy, and his fears and miseries were swept away. His eyes seemed drawn out of their very sockets by the marvelous light, but he kept his head raised with unyielding determination. A delirious, entrancing happiness overwhelmed him, a dance of joy which embraced all earth's creatures. All his limbs were alive, all his senses intoxicated. Doubts, fears, and hardships were buried. He was shadowed by a strange, heavy certitude, one of peace and contentment, and a sense of confidence, never felt before, that he would achieve what he wanted. But he was raised above all desire, the earth fell beneath him like a handful of dust, and he wanted nothing. I don't ask for health, peace, security, glory, or old age. Let the end come now, for this is my best moment.

The delirium had left him panting, his body twisted crazily toward the horizon. He took a deep breath, as if trying to regain his strength after a stiff race, and felt a creeping sensation from afar, from the depths of his being, pulling him earthward. He tried to fight it, or delay it, but in vain. It was as deep-rooted as fate, as sly as a fox, as ironic as death. He revived with a sigh to the waves of sadness and the laughing lights.

He returned to the car and drove off. Looking at the road dispiritedly, he said, as if addressing someone else,

"This is ecstasy." He paused before continuing. "Certainly, without argumentation or logic." Then in a more forceful voice: "Breaths of the unknown, whispers of the secret." Accelerating the car, he asked, "Isn't it worth giving up everything for its sake?"

FOURTEEN

The ringing of the telephone in the empty nest awakened him. He picked up the receiver and heard Mustapha's voice. "Where were you all night?" When he didn't answer, the voice went on. "Zeinab has gone to the hospital."

There was a moment of incomprehension before he recalled that he was a husband, and a father with more of fatherhood in store. In the waiting room he found Buthayna, Mustapha, and Aliyyat, his wife, a staid, strong-willed matron in her forties, on the short side, plump, and with a round face and features. When it was Buthayna's turn to greet him, she held out her hand with lowered eyes, to hide her agitation.

"She's in the delivery room," Mustapha said, "and everything is going normally."

As he was about to enter, Aliyyat detained him. "I was just with her, and I'm going in again right now."

"Shouldn't I go in too?"

Mustapha said, "It's better to avoid any sudden excitement."

It was only a short while before Aliyyat returned and with a beaming face announced to Omar, "Congratulations. You've got your crown prince and Zeinab is being taken to her room."

He sat down beside Buthayna, looking at her tenderly, and placed his hand on hers without a word. In her shyness she let it rest there for a while, then gently withdrew it.

Mustapha followed these motions, and said, "Fortunately hospitals are places where feuds are buried."

Hiding his disappointment at the withdrawal of her hand, he asked, "When did she get here?"

"Around midnight."

While he and Warda, animated by champagne, were having their discussion.

"And you don't go to school?"

"Of course not, she came with her mother."

"Thank you, Aliyyat, thank you very much."

"You're welcome," she said, leaving for Zeinab's room.

"By dawn, she was very tired," Mustapha remarked.

Ah, dawn in the desert and the glimpse of a perfect, eternal ecstasy. But where is it? Mustapha excused himself to go catch some sleep. The two of them, he and Buthayna, remained waiting. Sensitive to the awkwardness of the situation, he said in a conciliatory tone, "You haven't slept, Buthayna?"

She shook her head, looking at the beige carpet in the hall.

"Don't you want to talk to me?"

Fearful of a showdown, she asked, "What can I say?"

"Anything. Whatever is on your mind. I'm your father and your friend. Our relationship cannot be severed."

She remained silent, obviously touched.

"Don't we agree about that?"

She nodded, and her lips moved in assent.

"You're angry, which is understandable. But whatever the problem is, it doesn't affect you directly. Your alienation from me is unbearable. I've invited you to visit me repeatedly. Why have you never come?"

"I couldn't."

"Did anyone prevent you?"

"No, but I was so sad."

"Was your sadness greater than our love?"

She said bitterly, "You never once came to see us."

"That wasn't possible. But you should have come when I repeated the invitation so often. Your refusal only made matters worse."

She tried to steel herself against the tears that were threatening. "Grief prevented me."

"That's too bad. Passivity is a trait I don't like, and I needed you after I'd left." Then he smiled to ease the tension of the situation, and said, "Enough. There's no time for reprimands now." He patted her shoulder and asked, "How's the poetry?"

She smiled freely for the first time.

He said enthusiastically, "You know we may be closer to each other today than we've ever been before."

"What do you mean?"

"It seems we're both drawn to the same source."

She turned her green eyes to him, seeking clarification.

"I've been reading poetry again and have been trying my hand at it."

"Really?"

"Abortive attempts."

"Why is that?"

"I don't know. Maybe the dust is too thick to be shaken off at once. Maybe the crisis resists poetry."

"The crisis?"

"I mean my illness."

She smiled, looking at the ground.

"Don't you believe me?"

"I always believe you."

Her words cut him, but he said, "You must believe me, in spite of that one lie. It was a necessary lie, but it will never be repeated. My illness is real."

"You haven't yet discovered what it is?"

He thought a moment, then said, "Suffering—the only cure is patience."

She said compassionately, "Which you don't find with us?"

He stated quietly, "I'm living alone."

She looked at him with astonishment.

"Alone, believe me."

"But . . ."

"Alone now."

She responded with an urgency which gratified him. "Why haven't you come back, Papa?"

He kissed her flushed cheek. "Maybe it's best to remain this way."

"No." She held his hand and repeated, "No."

Aliyyat returned to tell him he could see Zeinab. As he entered the room, he saw her lying in bed covered from the neck down with a white sheet. Her face was very pale, drained of vitality, and her eyes were half closed. He felt sympathy, respect, and a certain regret. Here she is, able to create, while all his efforts have failed. He murmured in embarrassment, "Thank God, it all went well."

She smiled faintly.

"Congratulations. You've produced a crown prince."

He sat there, feeling awkward, until rescued by the arrival of Aliyyat and Buthayna. Aliyyat helped relieve the tension with her jokes and anecdotes, and after a while the baby was wheeled in on his cot. They uncovered his face, a red ball of flesh with rubbery features. It was hard to believe it would ever fall into shape, let alone an acceptable one. But he was reassured by his previous experiences of fatherhood—indeed, the subject of one of them was leaning over the cot right now, her green eyes peering at the baby with amazement and tenderness. He felt nothing in particular toward the baby but knew that he would grow to love him as he should. The child's neutral, rather startled look was enough for the moment. If you'd been able to express yourself, I would have asked you about your feelings, and your memories of the world from which you've just come.

"Have you chosen a name for him?" asked Aliyyat.

"Samir," Buthayna answered.

Samir, the companion and entertainer. May his name protect him from grief.

Aliyyat said pointedly, "Let's hope his upbringing will be in the hands of both parents."

He'd glided along the brink of creation, yet there was no intimation of change. He felt as alienated as ever. The newborn child had not bridged the gap between Zeinab and himself. He began wondering how long he'd have to sit there, the object of their glances and curiosity.

As lunchtime approached, he took his leave. Buthayna followed him outside, and her usual openness with him was apparent as she said, "Papa, you won't remain alone . . ."

He really didn't need the empty flat anymore now that he was dreaming of a new kind of solitude. "What do you want?" he asked submissively.

"I want you to come back."

Kissing her cheek, he said, "On condition that you won't get fed up with me."

Her face beaming, she took his arm and walked with him to the outer door.

FIFTEEN

He returned home, unchanged, feeling neither love nor hatred for Zeinab. But the disappearance of hatred signified the disappearance of Zeinab herself, the victory of his advancing exile over her world.

"We must accept this ordeal courageously," he told her.

And indeed she appeared brave, even deserting his bed. Touched by her attitude, he commended her. "You're a model of patience."

He refrained from his futile night adventures, and was able to find pleasure in his children. But as he watched the Nile flowing incessantly under the balcony, he yearned for the peace of that desert dawn. He spent his nights in his room, reading and meditating, then at daybreak he would return to the balcony, look at the horizon, and wonder: Where is peace? The poems of the Arabs, the Persians, and the Indians are full of secrets, but where is happiness? Why do you feel so depressed within these patient walls, why this uneasy feeling that you're only a guest, soon to depart?

"Thank God," Mustapha said. "Everything is back to normal."

He replied angrily, "Nothing is back to normal."

Mustapha avoided arguing out of kindness, but Omar would not let up. "I have not returned home; I have not returned to work."

"But my dear friend . . ."

"And no one knows what changes the next hour has in store."

One afternoon the door of his office opened suddenly and a man entered. He was of medium stature, with a shaved head and a large, pale face. His nose and hands were strong, and his amber eyes had a sharp glint. Omar looked at him incredulously for a moment, then stood up and exclaimed in a trembling voice, "Othman Khalil!"

They embraced and then sat down facing each other on the two chairs in front of the desk. Unable to control his excitement, Omar kept on repeating his greetings, congratulations, and blessings, while Othman smiled, as though he didn't know what to say. Then there was a short pause and they exchanged glances. Fantasies mingled with memory, but in the depths of his being Omar felt a certain misgiving, a certain premonition of fear. So often he'd envisioned the meeting and had dealt with it in his imagination, yet it had now come as a surprise. He'd lost track of time and everything else recently—he knew that the prison term would not have ended yet, but hadn't realized that three-quarters of it had already passed. In his present psychological state, he was not ready for the meeting. A man reenters this world from prison; another man leaves this world for an unknown universe.

"It's been such a long time."

Othman smiled.

"You were never absent for an hour from our minds. And here you are, determined to live a normal life again."

He said in a rich, guttural voice, "You haven't changed in appearance, but your health is not up to par."

Omar was pleased that he'd noticed. "Yes, I've suffered a strange crisis. But, please, let's not talk about me. I want to listen to what you have to say."

Othman waited until the servant had brought in a Coca-Cola and a coffee, then said, "Years and years have passed. The day is as detestable as the year; the year as trivial as the day. But I'm not going to reminisce about prison life."

"I understand, I'm sorry . . . but when did you get out?"

"Two weeks ago."

"Why haven't you come before now?"

"I went straight to the village, where I came down with influenza. When I recovered, I returned to Cairo."

There's no use in trying to escape. Your sense of guilt increases by the moment. "It tortured us that we couldn't visit you."

Othman said with an expressionless face, "Any visitors other than family members would have been arrested."

"We longed for reassurance about you."

"We were badly treated in the beginning, but after the Revolution, of course, things changed."

Omar winced.

"If we were thrown into hell, I believe we'd get used to it eventually and to its fiery minions."

He yielded to his sense of guilt. "It would have been more just if we'd gone with you to jail."

Othman was sarcastically, "It was the law, not justice, which threw me in jail."

He murmured submissively, "In any case, we owe you our freedom, perhaps even our lives."

"Wouldn't you have done the same thing if you'd been arrested and I'd gotten away?"

Embarrassed and ashamed, Omar remained silent.

Othman continued bitterly. "Here I am, back in the world again in my mid-fifties."

Omar tried to console him. "You're still young and have a long life ahead of you."

"And behind me an experience more bitter than despair."

He said sadly, "We lived outside the bars without, I'm afraid, accomplishing anything important."

Othman protested, "Don't say that. Don't rob me of my only consolation."

The sense of dread returned, and a feeling that he was a corpse, lying forgotten on the earth's surface.

"We practiced our professions, married, had children, but I feel I have nothing to reap but dust. You must excuse me, I have no right to talk about myself."

"But we are two integral halves."

The past is over, and the reckoning is hard. Othman had boasted in the basement of Mustapha al-Minyawi's house, "Our cell is an unbreakable fist of iron. We work for humanity as a whole, not for one country alone. We propose a human nation, a world of tomorrow founded on revolution and science."

After he'd been chosen by lot, he'd said, "I'm glad. Mustapha's nervous and you're a newlywed. Tomorrow a bomb will be thrown on those pigs. They've sucked our blood long enough."

"The planning was perfect. If a stray bullet hadn't hit your leg, they'd never have caught you."

"True. What did you do, you and Mustapha?"

"We stayed up till morning, feeling miserable."

He laughed briefly. "Weren't you afraid that I'd confess?"

"Mustapha urged me to flee with him; then we thought of hiding. We went through a few miserable days. But you proved to be superhuman. We were and remain nothing."

As a man gets used to hell, he gets used to the sacrifice of others. However disgusting the rat is, the sight of him in his cage is pitiable.

Othman alluded to the assistance his parents had received from Omar before their death. Omar seemed not to want to listen, so he went on. "I don't want to lament the past, for I chose my fate, fully conscious of what I was doing. But now you must tell me what's been happening in the world."

Omar said enigmatically, looking for an escape, "Let the future be our main concern."

"The future? . . . Yes, I'll have to dust off my law degree."

"My office is at your disposal."

"Excellent. The authorities have no objection to my practicing."

"Then why not start right away?"

"Many thanks . . . but tell me what's been happening."

He doesn't want to budge. How strange, it's as though you'd never been associated with him, as though you'd never wanted this meeting at all. You share nothing but a dead history, and he arouses in you only feelings of guilt, fear, and self-contempt. He hasn't yet discovered that philosophical works have replaced the socialist tracts in your library. Here he sits obstructing you like fate while you try to flee from your people and from the world.

Tiring of the silence, Othman coaxed, "Tell me about our friends."

"Oh, they're all gone their own ways. I haven't kept up with any of them except Mustapha al-Minyawi."

"And what have you all done?"

How distasteful is this calling to account.

"Actually the years that followed your arrest were characterized by so much violence and terrorism that we had to resort to silence. Then each of us became involved in his work, we grew older, the Revolution broke out, and the old world collapsed."

Othman rested his broad chin on his hand, and his eyes gleamed coldly. Perhaps he was lamenting the lost years. What an unpleasant situation! How often the thought of it had disturbed his sleep like a nightmare. He said, "I often asked myself why, yes why, and it seemed to me that life was a revolting swindle. The feet that kicked in my head belonged to the very people for whose sake I went to prison. Were cowardice and folly, then, what life was all about? But this wasn't true of the ants and other creatures. I won't prolong the speech. In the end I regained my faith."

"How unfortunate."

"I rediscovered my faith hewing rocks under the sun. I affirmed to myself that my life had not been wasted, that millions of unknown victims since the time of our forebears, the apes, have raised man to a lofty position."

Omar bowed his head in respectful agreement, as Othman continued in an agitated voice. "It's stupid to get caught up in a sick past while the future rises before us, a million times stronger than our cowardice."

He looked for some means of escape from the onrush. "In any case, the corrupt world of the past has been destroyed by a genuine revolution, so one of your dreams has been realized."

How morose and sullen his face has grown. Here you

are, swallowing defeat in an area which doesn't interest you at all. Doesn't he realize you no longer care about anything?

Othman said ruefully, "If you hadn't rushed into hiding, you wouldn't have lost the field."

"We had neither power nor any followers among the people to speak of. If, by some miracle, we'd succeeded, continents would have risen to destroy us."

"It's unfortunate that the ill only think of disease."

"Do you think it is reasonable for them it ignore it?"

"No, it's mad, not reasonable, but haven't you realized how much the world owes to madness?"

He said mildly, "In any case, the Revolution has occurred, and is going in the direction of genuine socialism." Othman scrutinized him closely, and Omar didn't like what he saw in his expression. "Though it didn't touch the heads of capitalists like me, it imposed a just tax." He concluded lamely. "Believe me, I'm not a slave of anything. Let them all go to hell."

Othman smiled. "Be frank with me, my dear friend. Are you a true believer as you once were?"

Put on the spot, Omar thought for a while. "I was until the Revolution broke out, then I felt reassured, began losing interest in politics, and turned in another direction."

"Another direction?"

He said hesitantly, "Mustapha is fond of describing it as an irrepressible nostalgia for my artistic past."

Othman asked impatiently, "And is there any contradiction between art and principle?"

Annoyed and perplexed, he answered, "It's not that simple."

Othman despaired. "I understand only that you're not what you were."

So Zeinab and Warda have remarked. "I admit you shouldn't concern yourself with me." Then he said more positively, "What's important now is to start a new life, in compensation for the past."

"I'm afraid I won't find anything that can really compensate for the past."

"My office is at your disposal, with all that you need to get started."

"I don't know how to thank you."

"It's far less than you deserve. I will always be indebted to you." Then in a voice quite free of constraint, he suggested, "No doubt you're longing to see Zeinab, the family, and Mustapha. Let's all have dinner at home tonight."

SIXTEEN

The dinner party was as rich in memories as it was in food and drink. Zeinab pressed his hand in welcome, her eyes brimming with tears, and Mustapha gave him a warm hug. It was the first time he'd seen Aliyyat. As he sat next to Buthayna at the table, he remarked with surprise that she was the picture of her mother as a girl.

"I can't possibly taste all of them!" he said as the appetizers were offered. Then he turned to Buthayna. "They told you I was an old friend, but that is only a partial truth. Actually, I'm an old friend who's just gotten out of prison."

She smiled, taking it as a joke.

"It's true. I'm an old friend and a veteran prisoner."

At this point, Zeinab intervened. "Then she should know that you're a political hero, not merely a prisoner."

Buthayna looked at him with astonishment.

"Hero. Criminal. The words are interchangeable."

Omar said to her, "Othman is an old friend, and now a colleague in the firm. I'll tell you his story another time.

But you already know something about the political prisoners . . ."

"Did the King imprison you?" Buthayna asked.

As the houseboy was placing a slice of turkey and some peas on his plate, he said, "No, the whole society did."

"What had you done?"

When he didn't answer, Mustapha laughed. "He was a socialist prematurely." Then he added with a wink, "And he was fond of playing with bombs."

The green eyes widened, and Zeinab stepped in again, trying tactfully to change the subject. "Buthayna is a poet."

Othman looked at Omar and smiled. "Poetry is hereditary in this family."

Mustapha warned him, "Her poems are paeans of praise to the Divine Spirit!"

Restraining the urge to say something sarcastic, he commented politely, "I hope to have the good fortune to hear some of your poems."

Omar managed to hide his restlessness and maintain the appearance of calm. He took a stuffed pigeon, reflecting that if it had flown better, it wouldn't have been eaten, and followed with pleasure the conversation between Buthayna and Othman. Suddenly the girl asked, "How could you endure prison life?"

"I endured it because I had no choice, and I came to be known for my good conduct. It seems that we only misbehave in society." He laughed. "Actually, prisons are not without their advantages. Life among prisoners is classless, something we'd like to achieve in the world outside."

"I don't understand a thing!"

"You'll understand my words if I'm able to understand your poetry."

"Have you read Papa's poems?"

"Of course."

"Did you like them?"

Omar protested. "For God's sake, you'll never finish dinner if you don't stop talking."

But Othman continued, obviously enjoying her conversation. "Will you study literature in the university?"

"Science."

"Bravo, but why science when writing poetry is your main interest?"

Zeinab said proudly. "She excels in science."

Buthayna explained, "Papa's enthusiastic about studying science."

Othman looked at Omar quizzically, then said to Buthayna, "One day you'll realize science is the great hope."

"But I won't give up poetry."

"And why should you?"

"How many years did you spend in prison?"

"About twenty."

He laughed at her astonished expression. "And yet I knew a man who did not want to leave jail. Every time the date of release drew near, he'd commit another small crime, just to prolong his imprisonment."

"What a crazy way to behave."

"How often people behave in crazy ways."

"Don't you want him to eat?" Omar reproached her.

Othman and Buthayna continued their conversation after they'd all adjourned to the parlor for coffee. But around ten o'clock, at Mustapha's suggestion, the three men went out to the balcony, and the women moved to the living room.

Othman wanted to know what Mustapha had done

with his life, so he gave him a frank, rather jaded account and concluded by asking, "What are your thoughts, now that you've heard what our situation is?"

Othman replied, a bit apathetic and sullen after Buthayna's disappearance, "I'll have to get started as a lawyer, first of all."

"Yes, but I'm asking what's going on in your head."

"I'll have to study the conditions . . ."

"As you should, but our old position is no longer really valid."

"It is valid," he said defiantly.

"I mean that the state is now socialist. Isn't that enough?"

Omar looked in silence at the flowing river and at the reflections of lamplight on the surface. A crescent moon was visible on the horizon.

Othman said bitterly, "Just because you have changed doesn't mean truth has changed."

"We haven't changed so much as developed."

"Backward."

"The country has certainly gone forward."

"Maybe, but you've gone backward."

Omar was still looking at the moon as Mustapha said jokingly, "Aren't you satisfied with what you've already sacrificed of your life?"

"Truth is never satisfied."

"My dear friend, it's not your responsibility alone."

"Man shoulders the burden of humanity as a whole, or else he's nothing."

Mustapha laughed. "If I can't shoulder the burden of Mustapha, how could I take on humanity as a whole?"

"How pathetic ... I can't believe how degenerate you've both become."

Mustapha couldn't take the conversation seriously, but, pointing to Omar, he said, "Let Omar be, for he's going through a bad time. A revulsion from work, success, and the family."

Othman looked inquiringly at Omar, but his head was still turned toward the Nile.

"As if he's searching for his soul," Mustapha observed.

Othman frowned. "Wasn't it he who lost it?" Then he sighed. "So it's all ended in philosophical meditations."

Mustapha went on, trying to restrain his mirth. "I've often felt that he wanted to revive his dormant impulse to write, and he continues to try. But he dreams sometimes of a strange ecstasy."

"Can you be more explicit?"

Omar turned toward them. "Drop the subject and just consider it an illness."

Othman looked at him sharply and murmured, "Perhaps it really is a disease, for you've lost your old vigor."

Mustapha said, "Or he's searching for the meaning of his existence."

"When we're aware of our responsibility toward the masses, the search for a personal meaning becomes quite insignificant."

Omar asked with irritation, "Do you think the question will die when the dictatorship of the proletariat is established?"

"But it hasn't been established yet." He looked from one of them to the other. "Scientists search for the secret of life and death through knowledge, not through illness."

"And if I'm not a scientist?"

"At least you shouldn't throw the dust of wailing and lamentation in the faces of the workers."

Mustapha said, "You're hurling some strong language at our friend at a time when he really is in pain."

"I'm sorry, and I'm afraid I'll have to remain sorry indefinitely."

Omar asked, "Won't the heart come to our rescue if we're not scientists?"

"The heart is a pump operating through the arteries and veins. To see it as a means of apprehending the truth is sheer fantasy. Honestly, I'm beginning to understand you. You're looking for ecstasy, or perhaps for something called absolute truth, but because you lack any effective method, you turn to the heart as the rock of salvation. But it is only a rock, and with it you'll recede to the depths of prehistory. Your life will have been wasted. Even my life, spent behind prison bars, has not been sacrificed for nothing. But your life will be. You'll never attain any truth worth speaking of except through reason, science, and work."

He hadn't witnessed the desert sunrise, or felt the ecstasy which gives assurance without proof. The world had not been cast, like a handful of dust, beneath his feet.

Mustapha said, "I believe in science and reason, but I have in my hands a *kasida** which Omar wrote just before renouncing poetry for good. In it, he declares his revolt against reason."

Controlling himself, Othman said, "I'd like to hear it."

Omar was about to protest, but Mustapha had already unfolded the paper, and begun to read:

*An ancient Arabic form of poetry.

*"Because I neither played in the wind
Nor lived on the equator*

*Nothing charmed me but sleeplessness
And a tree which doesn't bend to the storm
And a building which doesn't shake."*

A heavy silence reigned until Othman spoke. "I didn't understand any of it."

Omar said, "And I didn't say it was poetry, just hallucinations while I was in a morbid frame of mind."

Mustapha observed, "But modern art in general breathes this spirit of rebellion."

Othman said disdainfully, "It's the whimper of a dying order."

"Perhaps that's true," Mustapha said, "but speaking as a veteran artist, I see an artistic crisis as well, the crisis of an artist who is fed up with his subject matter and searching for a new form."

"Why should he be fed up with the subject matter?"

"Because whatever subject he hits upon is hackneyed."

"But the artist confers his own spirit on the subject which makes it new to a certain extent."

"This no longer suffices in our era of radical revolutions. Science has ascended the throne and the artist finds himself among the banished entourage. However much he wanted to penetrate the lofty realm, his ignorance and inability prevented him, and so he joined the Angry Young Men, turned to the anti-novel and to the theater of the absurd. While scientists were compelling admiration through their incomprehensible equations, the silly artists strove to impress by producing obscure, strange, and abnormal effects. If you can't attract the public's attention with your profound thoughts, try running naked through Opera Square."

Othman laughed loudly for the first time.

"Therefore I've chosen the simplest and most honest route, and become a clown."

Why get involved, Omar concluded, in discussing matters of no concern to him?

SEVENTEEN

The dawn was speechless. On the banks of the Nile, on the balcony, even in the desert, the dawn was speechless. And nothing but a broken memory bore witness to its ever having spoken. There's no point in continuing to look upward, burning the heart out, listening to its cries of yearning reverberate hopelessly in the heavens. The nagging rhymes, Margaret's golden hair, Warda's gray eyes, and the image of Zeinab leaving church. What are they but pale ghosts wandering in a hollow head? Mustapha laughs, tolling the death of hope, while Othman rages like a prophet of nihilism. I've spoken to the chairs, the walls, the stars, and the darkness; I've argued with the void, I've flirted with something which doesn't yet exist, until I finally found comfort in the prospect of my complete annihilation. Everything has been demeaned, the very laws that rule the universe have been discredited, predicting even the sunrise is impossible. After this how can I peruse the case files or discuss the household budget?

I said to the four walls of my room, "What a mistake it was to accept this truce and return home."

And I told the cat who was rubbing against my leg, "Your word is my command. I'll leave this refuge, so full of emotions which disturb and inhibit."

No diversions were left, other than dancing on the peak of the pyramid, plunging from a bridge into the depths of the Nile, or breakfasting nude at the Hilton. Rome was set aflame by desperate passions, not by Nero. They cause the earth to quake, the volcanoes to erupt.

Warda spoke on the telephone. "I wonder whether you've forgotten my voice."

He answered listlessly, "Hello, Warda."

"Won't you visit us even once a year?"

"No, but I'm at your service if you need anything."

"I'm speaking to you from the heart."

"The heart," he scoffed, "is a pump."

He sought relief from distress by speeding like a madman to the outskirts of Cairo, and further on to Fayum, Tanta, and Alexandria. Often he would leave Cairo in the morning and return the next day, having roamed around all night. He might go into a grocer's for a drink or doze off briefly at a café, or he might join a funeral procession, honoring some unknown deceased, and when he returned at dawn, overcome by fatigue, he would sleep right in the car or on the banks of the Nile.

He went back to the office one day and found Othman zealously working away.

"Where have you been these past days?" the man asked.

He looked at him disparagingly. "Innumerable places."

"You must be tired. I wonder what's going on in your head."

His distress had freed him of self-consciousness and fear, even in confronting Othman. "I'm thinking of exploding the atom, or murdering if that fails, or committing suicide at the very least."

Othman laughed. "But your office."

"You've been with me long enough to understand me."

"Tell me what you plan to do."

He said decisively, "It's time to do something I've never done before—that is, to do nothing."

"You must be joking."

"I've never been more serious."

Omar's stern expression caused Othman to change his tone. "Have you consulted your doctor?"

"I won't consult anyone on something of which he's ignorant."

An oppressive silence fell. "And you, are you confining your energies to the practice of law?" Omar finally asked.

"Yes, but I haven't stopped thinking."

"So, you'll become once more a menace to the country's security."

Othman smiled. "I can't claim that honor yet."

Really, this buzzing going on around him made it impossible to listen to the silence. He would have to leave, and his nerves were so on edge, he could no longer trust himself to keep silent about confidential matters. So he told Zeinab that he would give her power of attorney over his property, and leave his associates in charge of the office. He was determined, he said, to rid himself of distractions, to remove the burden of the world from his shoulders. She should consider it a disease, whether she understood it or not. In any case, he wanted to withdraw into himself. There was no woman involved, she must believe him. And it was not a mere whim; rather his illness had reached crisis proportions. If any cure existed, it lay in the path he'd chosen.

She implored him, her eyes reflecting the pain of the successive blows she'd received. "We've let you alone. If you can't stand your work, then leave it. If your artistic urges are so strong, then follow them. But don't desert us, for the sake of your children."

Her words affected him, but he said there was no use in trying to put off a decision as unavoidable as fate. "I've had long talks with Mustapha. It hurt me that you've confided in him what you've hidden from us, but I suppose in your present condition, you're not to be blamed. Forgive me for not understanding this search for the meaning of your existence. I don't see why it involves leaving your work and your family, disregarding your future. Why don't you consult your doctor again?"

"That's why I haven't been open with you."

"But illness isn't shameful."

"You think I'm insane."

She sobbed convulsively, but he remained resolute, "The solution I've chosen is best for us all."

"All right, then, leave until you've regained your health, but then return."

"It's best to reconcile ourselves to a permanent absence." He continued as she wept. "If I don't do that, I'll go mad or commit suicide."

She stood up, saying, "Buthayna's not a child. You must listen to her."

"Don't make the torment any worse," he shouted.

He could imagine what was being said about his "illness," but what difference did it make? Perhaps the diagnosis was even true. He talked to the animals and objects around him, and held discussions with extinct creatures. Sometimes when he was racing along in the car, the solid earth would explode into fragments, then disintegrate into a vast network of atoms, and, trembling uncontrollably, he'd have to stop. Sometimes as he was gazing at the Nile or at a tree it would come alive, the image would assume features which indicated feelings and awareness, and he'd imagine that it peered at him warily, that it questioned his existence in comparison with its own, so much more ancient and immutable. What did it all indicate? What did his desertion of work, family, and friends signify? Ah, he'd have to be on guard or else he'd find himself driven to the insane asylum.

Mustapha and Othman came to see him, at the urging of Zeinab, he realized. Mustapha's laughter failed to ease the tension. Omar himself barely murmured a greeting, but when the whiskey was brought out, he took a drink in their honor. They looked at him awkwardly, revealing the concern they'd striven to conceal. Zeinab then came out to greet the men, and commented as she was leaving, "We were such a happy family, he was the best of men, then suddenly everything fell apart."

Her words made it impossible to avoid the subject any longer. "Is what we've heard true?" Mustapha asked.

He didn't answer, but his determined expression was sufficient confirmation.

"So, you're leaving."

"Ycs," he said sharply.

"Where?"

"Somewhere."

"But where?"

He remained silent. The place, stretching on to infinity, was still a prison. Mustapha was stupid to use words without meaning.

"So now it's our turn to be thrown on the garbage heap."

"Yesterday Buthayna cried, but that was the only answer she got."

"Is it the end of our relationship with you?" Mustapha asked fearfully.

"It's the end of my relationship with everything."

"I'll mourn with all my heart and soul."

"What I've suffered is worse."

"And to what end?" Mustapha asked.

"To ram my head against the rock," he answered bitterly.

"I don't understand," said Othman.

Mustapha continued, "Whatever it is, stay among us."

"I must go."

Othman said, his eyes fixed on Omar, "Shouldn't you consult the doctor?"

"I'm not in need of anyone," he replied sharply.

"You're an intact organism which shouldn't be destroyed to no purpose."

"In reality, I'm nothing."

"Can't a man think while he's among other people?"

"I don't care about thinking."

"What will you do, then?"

He said with annoyance, "We don't understand each other at all."

"But I'm sure that you're driving yourself to ruin."

"Rather, it's you who are on the way to ruin."

"Well, if ruin is unavoidable, isn't it better to go down together?"

He brushed the remark aside. "I won't look back."

"In fact, you're running after nothing."

Is the ecstasy of the dawn nothing? Does truth then lie in nothingness? When will the torture end?

"Imagine if all the intelligent men in this world followed your example," Othman said.

"Let the intelligent men concern themselves with the world."

"But you're one of them."

He wiped his forehead, then thrust his fist toward the ground. "Trample my mind under your feet," he said disdainfully.

Othman asked sadly, "What's the use in arguing?"

"It's futile, for tomorrow you won't see me."

Mustapha sighed. "I don't believe a word of what's been said."

He answered, his eyes on the ground, "It's best for you to forget that I ever existed."

"It's too hard to bear," Mustapha said.

Othman's face hardened with suppressed grief, while Omar assumed a mask of indifference. As he gazed at them, their figures disintegrated into two groups of atoms, effacing their individuality, but the conflict he felt showed that his love for them, as for his family, was still rooted in his heart, causing him more anguish than he could bear. How his soul longed for the moment of victory, the moment of complete liberation!

EIGHTEEN

When your heart achieves its desire, you will have transcended the confines of time and space. But you still feel oppressed in this cottage, in the midst of a grassy lawn surrounded by a fence lined with cypress trees. And you await the day when the cypresses and all they enclose will disappear, the day when the plants will no longer whisper of the night's sorrows, the day when the scuttling of the cockroaches and the croaking of the frogs will fall silent, the day when memory will lose its tyranny and you'll merge into nothingness. Then the chants of India and Persia will no longer echo and the rosy beams of ecstasy will fall directly upon you. That precious, hard-won ecstasy of dawn will draw you with all the force of the unknown into heaven's dome, where your heart will awake while the bodily senses sleep.

Buthayna stood in front of him, like a graceful cypress, and turned her green eyes to the garden, to the canal running between the acacia trees, and to the fields stretching beyond. "For the sake of this?" she asked reproachfully.

Affected by her presence, you stroked the wavy locks of her hair and murmured, "For the sake of nothingness."

"Aren't you afraid of loneliness in this empty place?"

You whispered in her ear, "I was oppressed by loneliness in the midst of the crowds."

She retreated a step. "Yesterday, Othman said . . ."

He interrupted her gently. "My girl, haven't you realized yet that I'm deaf?"

She left the garden through the wooden gate in the ivy-covered fence and vanished from sight. I sighed wearily and opened my eyes to the dark. This dream could only mean that I've not yet escaped the call of life. However often I think of you during my waking hours, these weird fantasies mock my sleep.

———

Mustapha embraced you affectionately and then peered sadly into your eyes. You noticed that on his bald pate there now grew a heavy black shank of hair and couldn't help remarking, "Congratulations. How did you manage to grow it?"

He answered with unaccustomed seriousness. "I recited the 'All-Merciful Sura' at dawn."

You were astonished. "When did you find your way to God?"

"When you departed from the world for this place."

"Why did you come?"

"To tell you that Zeinab is working with the energy of ten men."

"God help her!"

He looked around at the house, the garden, and the fields. "What an ideal love nest or artist's retreat this place is!"

Nonplussed, you said, "So you're still the jester!"

He sighed. "For us children of the Stone Age, jesting is the only recourse, but I see you've become infatuated with despair."

I backed off, saying, "Haven't you realized that my senses are dead?"

He shrugged his shoulders and climbed up a cypress tree until he'd overtaken the current moon high above the horizon. His bald head glimmering in the moonlight, he shook a bell in his hand, and as it rang, insects of all sorts came to the tree and proceeded to dance in a circle around it.

I sighed wearily and opened my eyes to the dark. This dream could only mean that I've not yet escaped the call of life. However often I think of you during my waking hours, these weird fantasies mock my sleep.

Yesterday as I was roaming around the garden, reciting the poetry of Majnun, I suddenly heard a gruff voice coming from behind the northern wall where the canal runs.

"Hey, man, where's the door?"

Peering over, I saw Othman perched on a motorcycle. Little flags, the sort used by people of the village for decoration on feast days, embellished the handlebars and wheels.

"Don't come in," I said peremptorily.

"Haven't you witnessed the miracle?" he exclaimed. "I've crossed the surface of the canal by motorcycle."

"I don't believe in miracles."

He laughed loudly. "But we live in an age of miracles."

I retreated a step. "What do you want?"

He said augustly, "I've come as the family delegate."

"I have no family."

"Don't you know of the miracle? New branches of your family have appeared on all five continents. Wouldn't you like to return to that remarkable mixture of platinum and coal?"

I defied him. "Aren't you aware that our real family is nothingness?"

"I'm going to chase you with a pack of trained dogs," he said menacingly.

As the motorcycle roared and the dogs yelped, I sighed wearily and opened my eyes to the darkness. This dream could only mean that I've not yet escaped. However often I think of you during my waking hours, these weird fantasies mock . . .

———

I stayed up all night in the garden, alone in the darkness with the stars shining overhead in the dome. I asked them when my desires would be fulfilled, and shouting so that the atoms of the cypress tree shook, reprimanded both everything and nothingness.

"I want to see," I said, gazing at one of the stars.

"Then look," it whispered.

I looked and found only emptiness. This is not the vision I've yearned to see.

"Look," it whispered.

The darkness lifted from the figure of a naked man. He was savage in appearance with shoulder-length hair and held a stone club in readiness to fight. Suddenly a wild beast sprang upon him. It was an unrecognizable species; though it resembled a crocodile, it stood on four legs and had the face of a bull. A bloody battle ensued between them, but in the end the beast was vanquished and the man staggered away. Blood splotched his face and chest and flowed from his arms, yet pain did not prevent him from smiling.

But this is not the image I've yearned to see, as you well know.

"Look," it whispered.

The darkness faded, revealing an open space in the forest at the bottom of a mountain. Mountain men armed with stones rushed into the clearing and were opposed by men of the forest, equally fierce, equally ready for the kill. They fought ferociously. The flowing blood and frenzied screams so frightened the wild animals that they fled for refuge in the canals, in the treetops, and up the mountains. Eventually the forest men were routed, killed, or taken prisoner, and the mountain men made merry.

Nor is this the image I've yearned to see.

"Look," it whispered.

I saw nothing at first, but then a sudden surge of happiness filled my heart, a sudden sense of victory. I remembered the glowing sensation which preceded the other revelation, that dawn in the desert, and I was sure that ecstasy was approaching, and that the bridegroom's face would break forth as the music played. The darkness lifted from a scene which gradually became clearer and more distinct and my heart throbbed as it never had before. I saw a bouquet, not of roses, but of human faces, and I was stunned when I recognized them—the faces of Zeinab, Buthayna, Samir, Jamila, Othman, Mustapha, and Warda. Suddenly my fervor abated and I felt bitter disappointment in its place. This is not the vision I've yearned to see. You know that very well. Where is it, where is it? But the vision held fast and only grew sharper with time. Then the figures played tricks. Zeinab and Warda exchanged heads. Othman had Mustapha's bald pate, while Mustapha looked at me with Othman's eyes. All at once Samir slid to the ground, and putting on Othman's head in place of his own, started crawling toward me. Frightened, I tried to escape this hybrid of Samir and Othman, but the faster I ran, the faster he pursued me. I jumped over the garden fence, but like a cricket, he cleared it with a hop. I ran alongside the canal, but like a stubborn bull, he followed in my tracks. Out of breath, my muscles aching with fatigue, and my head in a spin, I collapsed to the ground, and as I lay face down on the damp grass, I heard the feet of the creature coming closer and closer.

The devil has played havoc with the dream. Ecstasy has become a curse, and paradise a stage for fools. I lay there submissively, no longer trying to resist, then raised my head slightly to look around. A willow recited a line of poetry, a cow approached and stated she was giving up the milk business in order to study chemistry, a spotted snake crept forward, darted out his poisonous fang, then proceeded to dance merrily. A fox stood upright, guarding the chickens, a choir of beetles sang an angelic hymn, and a scorpion confronted me, wearing a nurse's uniform.

I sighed wearily and opened my eyes to the darkness. This dream could only mean that . . . However often I think of you during my waking hours . . .

I lay on the grass, gazing up at the trees which swayed in the darkness, and resolved to wait as long as necessary. Suddenly I heard steps approach and a voice whisper, "Good evening, Omar."

A ghost loomed up beside me. Another dream, and yet I fail to perceive anything.

"I'd almost lost hope of finding you. Why are you lying here? Aren't you afraid of the damp?"

He sat down on the grass and stretched his hand toward me. I ignored it.

"Haven't you recognized me yet? Have you forgotten my voice?"

I groaned. "When will the devil let me rest in peace?"

"What are you saying, Omar? For God's sake, talk to me, for I'm very upset."

"Who are you?"

"How strange! I'm Othman Khalil!"

"What do you want?"

"It's Othman, don't you understand? What I should have avoided has happened, and now I'm being chased."

I felt him with my hand. "But this is not Samir's body. What guise have you come in this time?"

"Samir? . . . You frighten me!"

"But you won't frighten me. I won't go tearing off like a madman."

He touched me, "Talk to me, for God's sake, as a friend. Don't make me despair of you!"

"What does that matter?"

"Listen, Omar, I'm in a bad situation. They're looking for me everywhere. If they catch me I'll die."

"So it's you who's running away this time."

"I'm going to hide at your place until it's safe to run."

I asked sadly, "How did the devil know I was here?"

"We've known your whereabouts all along—not a hard thing for a journalist like Mustapha to track down. He often comes around here, asking the peasants who bring your food to keep an eye on you. We didn't want to disturb you."

I groaned. "It's they who've blocked his face from me."

"During the past year and a half we haven't once disturbed you."

"I don't care even if Samir's head has been replaced by yours."

He sighed sorrowfully. "What's happened to you? No, I refuse to believe that you haven't recognized me yet."

"You can believe it or not."

"Pay attention to me, Omar, I have some startling news for you. I've married Buthayna."

"Let the devil go ahead and play his tricks."

He stuck his face in front of mine. "In spite of the difference in age, we got married, for we love one another, and now in her belly a new life throbs, my son, your grandson!"

"As you have been both my son and my enemy!"

"Hasn't this incredible news awakened you?"

"Like the snake who darts out his fang and dances."

"What a pity!"

"That's what I always say, but no one replies."

He patted my shoulder. "Come back down to earth. I've escaped just in time. They're combing the place for me now; they've searched your office and may try to implicate you. Go back, clear yourself, and look after your family. They're in great need of you. Buthayna's expecting a child and will never see me again . . ."

"And I have never seen him."

"Don't you want to understand?"

"I die a score of deaths every day in order to understand, but still I've not understood."

"Can't you understand that I'm married to your daughter and that I must hide or else die?"

"Run until you drop from fatigue, then you'll hear the beetles sing."

"How awful!"

"Yes, it's awful."

He shook me and said angrily, "Wake up. This is not the time for hallucinations. I must make you understand before I leave."

"Go. Don't sully the purity of my dreams."

"How wretched! What have you done to yourself?"

"The devil is giving up on me."

"You must wake up. Your family is in danger. If suspicion falls on you, they'll be exposed to all sorts of abuse. I don't fear for myself, I'm resigned to my own downfall, but you must get back to your family."

"Go back to hell where you belong."

Exasperated, he shook me once more. "I must run and you must go back."

"Stay, if you'd care to witness my victory."

He shook his head sadly. "What a fool you are. You've wasted all your ability searching for something that doesn't exist."

"When will you realize that you don't exist?"

The man stood up. "I now attest that I've despaired of you, though the word 'despair' has been eliminated from my dictionary."

"There, the devil has given up . . ."

The specter retreated into the darkness, saying sadly, "Farewell, old comrade-in-arms."

The night was still once more, but suddenly the moon returned. "They've come. God knows how they found me so soon."

He ran through the garden toward the western wall, but soon fell back, shouting frantically, "I'm surrounded."

He ran to the cottage while I gazed up at the stars. But my peace was disturbed by a voice which shouted, "Give yourself up, Othman Khalil. Give up. You're surrounded on all sides."

There was no answer. I turned my eyes in the direction of the voice, but saw nothing in the darkness. "The devil persists in playing tricks, but I'm not surrounded. On the contrary, I'm free."

Voices came from all around the fence and gradually drew closer. One of them barked out, "Resistance is useless, meaningless."

The man in hiding didn't answer.

"There's meaning in everything," I murmured.

Suddenly the beam of a searchlight flooded the house with light. A noose was tightening around the place. "Give up, Othman," the voice shouted. "Come on out with your hands up."

"When will these infernal voices leave me alone?" I sighed.

But the dreadful voice persisted. "Don't you see that resistance is futile?"

"Nothing in this world is futile," I whispered.

The running footsteps and yelling voices went around to the back of the house. A specter lunged out onto the front porch, then screamed.

"It's over, he's been caught . . . it's all over."

I whispered, "Nothing has an end."

Other specters now ran from the garden toward the house. One of them tripped over my leg and shouted as he fell, "Watch out! There are others."

A shot rang out and I moaned. It felt like a real pain rather than a dream confounded by the devil.

I sighed wearily and opened my eyes. This dream could only mean that I've not yet escaped. Why is it I think of you whenever I'm awake, yet these delusions mock my sleep? But wait. Where am I? Where are the stars, the grass, and the cypress trees? I'm riding in a car, lying on a stretcher, on the edge of which a man is perched. On the other side of the car, Othman sits in silence between two men. I must still be dreaming, but the pain in my shoulder causes me to moan.

"The bullet fractured his collarbone, but it's only a superficial wound. He's in no danger."

What is the meaning of this dream, where is it taking

me? When will the pain in my shoulder ease up? When will the devil and his follies be put to flight? When will the world disappear from my dreams? I moaned in spite of myself.

"Be patient a little longer," a voice said.

I answered defiantly, "Disappear, so I can see the stars."

"You're going to be all right."

I said stubbornly, "I'll be all right when I succeed in vanquishing you."

"Calm down. The doctor will see you right away."

"I don't need anyone."

"Don't tire yourself by talking."

I said insistently, "The willow tree talks, snakes dance, and beetles sing."

He went on talking to himself in a low voice. He shut his eyes, but the pain persisted. When would he see the vision? Hadn't he deserted the world for its sake?

————

He had the feeling that his heart was beating in reality, not in a dream, and that he was returning to the world.

He found himself trying to remember a line of poetry. When had he read it? Who was the poet?

The line reverberated in his consciousness with a strange clarity: *"If you really wanted me, why did you desert me?"*

Translated from the Arabic by Kristin Walker Henry
and Nariman Khales Naili al-Warraki.

The Thief and the Dogs

———

FOREWORD

No writer of the modern Arab world has enjoyed a success in literature to approach that of Naguib Mahfouz. His work has become appreciated as a voluminous and sharply focused reflection of the Egyptian experience through the turbulent changes of the twentieth century. His fame within the Middle East is consequently unrivaled and the importance of his score of published works has been widely noted abroad. Many of his stories have previously appeared in English and other foreign languages and he has received honorary awards and degrees from Denmark, France, and the Soviet Union. His achievements are all the more extraordinary for his having remained employed full-time for over thirty years in various departments of the Egyptian civil service in which he reached administrative positions of importance before his retirement in 1972.

The work of Mahfouz, then, reveals many of the changes of aspiration and orientation of Egyptian intellectuals over the span of his lifetime. In the thirties, a time when Mahfouz was emerging from Cairo University with a degree in philosophy, Egyptians were struggling for equilibrium between the contradictory pulls of pride in Islam or in ancient Egypt. Their dilemma was compounded by their awareness of the attitude of foreigners toward their national heritage. They witnessed every day in the streets of Cairo the enthusiasm of archaeologists and tourists for the treasures of their ancient tombs and pyramids but they also knew of the glories of their religious, architectural, cultural, and, above all, language heritage from Islam and the Arabs. And they were only too aware of the disdain of foreigners for the state of their contemporary government and society.

Mahfouz's dilemma in orientation lasted, however, only for the thirties, during which he composed a rather strange medley of short stories dealing with the life of his own time and several works on the ancient history of his country. He translated an English text on ancient Egypt and wrote three historical novels depicting aspects of the lives and times of the pharaohs. In them his particular concern was for the relationships between rulers and the people and the uprising of the Egyptians against the Hyksos invaders, subjects of obvious interest to his readers critical of the despotic Egyptian monarchy under King Farouk, himself dominated by the strong British presence in the country. By the early forties, however, Mahfouz had abandoned his plan of constructing a massive series of novels based on ancient history and almost all his work since has related specifically to the Egypt that he has himself witnessed.

In that middle period of his work, then, he wrote a series of novels, first published obscurely and later to achieve great and continuing popularity, that dealt both with his own milieu, the Muslim middle-class of Cairo, and with that of the colorful characters of the conservative quarters of the ancient city. These were followed by his Cairo Trilogy, which caused a literary sensation in the late fifties and consequently drew attention back to his earlier works. A voluminous work, the Trilogy presents a detailed panorama of the life experiences of three generations of a Cairo merchant-class family over the turbulent first half of this century. It is a fascinating study of the social, political, religious, and philosophical strains experienced by his countrymen at that time of fast transition and the consequent effects on their personal relationships.

Following the 1952 Revolution of General Naguib and Colonel Nasser, Mahfouz wrote nothing for seven years. His 1959 *Awlad Haritna* (translated as *Children of Gebelawi*) was serialized in the daily newspaper *Al-Ahram* and never since republished in Egypt. It is a pessimistic portrayal in allegorical form of man's struggle for comprehension and solution of the problems of his existence. Discouraged by the furor the novel caused in traditional and religious circles, Mahfouz again refrained from writing for some time, until his publication of his present novel, *The Thief and the Dogs,* in 1961. This was well received and was followed by a stream of fine novels in the sixties that detailed with delicacy and great courage the crisis of identity and conscience suffered by Egyptian intellectuals during that period of pervasive malaise and dissatisfaction.

His more recent works, following the 1967 war with Israel, have been circumspect and philosophical and he has favored the short story and the short play for expression of his frequently allegorical themes. However, *Al-Hubb Tahta al-Matar (Love in the Rain)* published in mid-1973 in book form only, without serialization in the widely read daily press, contrasted (and by implication criticized) the free and at times immoral life which continued in Cairo with the soldiers' endless waiting, in discomfort and fear of death, for the inevitable renewal of warfare with Israel.

The present novel, then, was first published in 1961 and both its subject treatment and style marked distinct changes from Mahfouz's earlier work. This is a psychological novel, impressionist rather than realist; it moves with the speed and economy of a detective story. Here Mahfouz uses the stream-of-consciousness technique for the first time to show the mental anguish of his central figure consumed by bitterness and a desire for revenge against the individuals and the society who have corrupted and betrayed him and brought about his inevitable damnation. It is a masterly work, swiftly giving the reader a keenly accurate vision of the workings of a sick and embittered mind doomed to self-destruction. And as he inevitably comes to the protagonist's disillusionment and despair, the reader gains intimate and authentic impressions of the values and structures of Egyptian society of the period.

TREVOR LE GASSICK

The Thief and the Dogs

ONE

Once more he breathed the air of freedom. But there was stifling dust in the air, almost unbearable heat, and no one was waiting for him; nothing but his blue suit and gym shoes.

As the prison gate and its unconfessable miseries receded, the world—streets belabored by the sun, careening cars, crowds of people moving or still—returned.

No one smiled or seemed happy. But who of these people could have suffered more than he had, with four years lost, taken from him by betrayal? And the hour was coming when he would confront them, when his rage would explode and burn, when those who had betrayed him would despair unto death, when treachery would pay for what it had done.

Nabawiyya. Ilish. Your two names merge in my mind. For years you will have been thinking about this day, never imagining, all the while, that the gates would ever actually open. You'll be watching now, but I won't fall into the trap. At the right moment, instead, I'll strike like Fate.

And Sana? What about Sana?

As the thought of her crossed his mind, the heat and the dust, the hatred and pain all disappeared, leaving only love to glow across a soul as clear as a rain-washed sky.

I wonder how much the little one even knows about her father? Nothing, I suppose. No more than this road does, these passersby or this molten air.

She had never been out of his thoughts, where bit by bit she'd taken shape, like an image in a dream, for four long years. Would luck now give him some decent place to live, where such love could be equally shared, where he could take joy in being a winner again, where what Nabawiyya Ilish had done would be no more than a memory, odious, but almost forgotten?

You must pull together all the cunning you possess, to culminate in a blow as powerful as your endurance behind prison walls. Here is a man—a man who can dive like a fish, fly like a hawk, scale walls like a rat, pierce solid doors like a bullet!

How will he look when he first sees you? How will his eyes meet yours? Have you forgotten, Ilish, how you used to rub against my legs like a dog? It was me, wasn't it, who taught you how to stand on your own two feet, who made a man of a cigarette-butt cadger? You've forgotten, Ilish, and you're not the only one: She's forgotten, too, that woman who sprang from filth, from vermin, from treachery and infidelity.

Through all this darkness only your face, Sana, smiles. When we meet I'll know how I stand. In a little while, as soon as I've covered the length of this road, gone past all these gloomy arcades, where people used to have fun. Onward and upward. But not to glory. I swear I hate you all.

The bars have shut down and only the side streets are open, where plots are hatched. From time to time he has to cross over a hole in the pavement set there like a snare and the wheels of streetcars growl and shriek like abuse. *Confused cries seem to seep from the curbside garbage. (I swear I hate you all.) Houses of temptation, their windows beckoning even when eyeless, walls scowling where plaster has fallen. And that strange lane, al-Sayrafi Lane, which brings back dark memories. Where the thief stole, then vanished, whisked away. (Woe to the traitors.) Where police who'd staked out the area had slithered in to surround you.*

The same little street where a year before you'd been carrying home flour to make sweetmeats for the Feast, that woman walking in front of you, carrying Sana in her swaddling clothes. Glorious days—how real they were, no one knows—the Feast, love, parenthood, crime. All mixed up with this spot.

The great mosques and, beyond them, the Citadel against the clear sky, then the road flowing into the square, where the green park lies under the hot sun and a dry breeze blows, refreshing despite the heat—the Citadel square, with all its burning recollections.

What's important now is to make your face relax, to pour a little cold water over your feelings, to appear friendly and conciliatory, to play the planned role well. He crossed the middle of the square, entered Imam Way, and walked along it until he came close to the three-story house at the end, where two little streets joined the main road. *This social visit will tell you what they've got up their sleeves. So study the road carefully, and what's on it. Those shops, for instance, where the men are staring at you, cowering like mice.*

"Said Mahran!" said a voice behind him. "How marvelous!"

He let the man catch up with him; they said hello to each other, hiding their real feelings under mutual grins. *So the bastard has friends. He'll know right away what all these greetings are about. You're probably peeking at us through the shutters now, Ilish, hiding like a woman.*

"I thank you, Mr. Bayaza."

People came up to them from the shops on both sides of the street; voices were loud and warm in congratulation and Said found himself surrounded by a crowd— his enemy's friends, no doubt—who tried to outdo one another in cordiality.

"Thank God you're back safe and sound."

"All of us, your close friends, are overjoyed!"

"We all said we wished you'd be released on the anniversary of the Revolution."

"I thank God and you, gentlemen," he said, staring at them with his brown, almond-shaped eyes.

Bayaza patted him on the shoulder. "Come into the shop and have a cold drink to celebrate."

"Later," he said quietly. "When I'm back."

"Back?"

One man shouts, directing his voice to the second story of the house: "Mr. Ilish! Mr. Ilish, come down and congratulate Said Mahran!" *No need to warn him, you black beetle! I've come in broad daylight. I know you've been watching.*

"Back from what?" said Bayaza.

"There's some business I have to settle."

"With whom?" said Bayaza.

"Have you forgotten I'm a father? And that my little girl's with Ilish?"

"No. But there's a solution to every disagreement. In the sacred law."

"And it's best to reach an understanding," said someone else.

"Said, you're fresh out of prison," a third man added in a conciliatory tone. "A wise man learns his lesson."

"Who said I'm here for anything other than to reach an understanding?"

On the second story of the building a window opened, Ilish leaned out, and they all looked up at him tensely. Before a word could be said, a big man wearing a striped garment and police boots came from the front door of the house. Said recognized Hasaballah, the detective, and pretended to be surprised.

"Don't get excited. I have come only to reach an amicable settlement," he said with feeling.

The detective came up and patted him all over, searching with practiced speed and skill. "Shut up, you cunning bastard. What did you say you wanted?"

"I've come to reach an understanding about the future of my daughter."

"As if you knew what understanding meant!"

"I do indeed, for my daughter's sake."

"You can always go to court."

Ilish shouted from above, "Let him come up. Come up all of you. You're all welcome." *Rally them round you, coward. I've only come to test the strength of your fortifications. When your hour arrives, neither detective nor walls will do you any good.*

They all crowded into a sitting room and planted themselves in sofas and chairs. The windows were opened: flies rushed in with the light. Cigarette burns had made black spots in the sky-blue carpet and from a large photograph on the wall Ilish, holding a thick stick with both his hands, stared out on the room. The detective sat next to Said and began to play with his worry beads.

Ilish Sidra came into the room, a loose garment swelling round his barrel-like body, his fat round face buttressed by a square chin. His huge nose had a broken bridge. "Thank the Lord you're back safe and sound!" he said, as if he had nothing to fear. But no one spoke, anxious looks passed back and forth, and the atmosphere was tense until Ilish continued: "What's over is done with, these things happen every day; unhappiness can occur, and old friendships often break up. But only shameful deeds can shame a man."

Conscious that his eyes were glittering, that he was slim and strong, Said felt like a tiger crouched to spring on an elephant. He found himself repeating Ilish's words: "Only shameful deeds can shame a man." Many eyes stared back at him; the detective's fingers stopped playing with his beads; realizing what was passing in their minds, he added as an afterthought, "I agree with every word you say."

"Come to the point," the detective broke in, "and stop beating about the bush."

"Which point?" Said said innocently.

"There's only one point to discuss, and that's your daughter."

And what about my wife and my fortune, you mangy dogs! I'll show you. Just wait. How I'd like to see now the look you'll have in your eyes. It would give me respect for beetles, scorpions, and worms, you vermin. Damn the man who lets himself be carried away by the melodious voice of woman. But Said nodded in agreement.

One of the sycophants said, "Your daughter is in safe hands with her mother. According to the law a six-year-old girl should stay with her mother. If you like, I could bring her to visit you every week."

Said raised his voice deliberately, so that he could be heard outside the room: "According to the law she should be in my custody. In view of the various circumstances."

"What do you mean?" Ilish said, suddenly angry.

"Arguing will only give you a headache," said the detective, trying to placate him.

"I have committed no crime. It was partly fate and circumstances, partly my sense of duty and decency that drove me to do what I did. And I did it partly for the sake of the little girl."

A sense of duty and decency, indeed, you snake! Double treachery, betrayal, and infidelity! Oh for the sledgehammer and the ax and the gallows rope! I wonder how Sana looks now. "I did not leave her in need," Said said, as calmly as he could. "She had my money, and plenty of it."

"You mean your loot," the detective roared, "the existence of which you denied in court!"

"All right, call it what you like. But where has it gone?"

"There wasn't a penny, believe me, friends!" Ilish protested loudly, "She was in a terrible predicament. I just did my duty."

"Then how have you been able to live in such comfort," Said challenged, "and spend so generously on others?"

"Are you God, that you should call me to account?"

"Peace, peace, shame the devil, Said," said one of Ilish's friends.

"I know you inside out, Said," the detective said slowly. "I can read your thoughts better than anyone. You will only destroy yourself. Just stick to the subject of the girl. That's the best thing for you."

Said looked down to hide his eyes, then smiled and said, in a tone of resignation, "You're quite right, Officer."

"I know you inside out. But I'll go along with you. Out of consideration for the people here. Bring the girl, someone. Wouldn't it be better to find out first what she thinks?"

"What do you mean, Officer?"

"Said, I know you. You don't want the girl. And you can't keep her, because you'll have difficulty enough finding some accommodation for yourself. But it's only fair and kind to let you see her. Bring in the girl."

Bring in her mother, you mean. How I wish our eyes could meet, so I might behold one of the secrets of hell! Oh for the ax and the sledgehammer!

Ilish went to fetch the girl. At the sound of returning footsteps Said's heart began to beat almost painfully, and as he stared at the door, he bit the inside of his lips, anticipation and tenderness stifling all his rage.

After what seemed a thousand years, the girl appeared. She looked surprised. She was wearing a smart white frock and white open slippers that showed henna-dyed toes. She gazed at him, her face dark, her black hair flowing over her forehead, while his soul devoured her. Bewildered, she looked around at all the other faces, then particularly at his, which was staring so intently. He was unable to take his eyes off her. As she felt herself being pushed toward him, she planted her feet on the carpet and leaned backward away from him. And suddenly he felt crushed by a sense of total loss.

It was as if, in spite of her almond-shaped eyes, her long face, and her slender, aquiline nose, she was not his own daughter. Where were the instinctive ties of blood and soul? Were they, too, treacherous, deceptive? And how could he, even so, resist the almost overwhelming desire to hug her to him forever?

"This is your father, child," said the detective impatiently.

"Shake hands with Daddy," said Ilish, his face impassive.

She's like a mouse. What's she afraid of? Doesn't she know how much I love her? He stretched out his hand toward her, but instead of being able to say anything he had a fit of choking and had to swallow hard, managing only to smile at her tenderly, invitingly.

"No!" said Sana. She backed away, trying to steal out of the room, but a man standing behind stopped her. "Mommy!" she cried, but the man pushed her gently and said, "Shake hands with Daddy." Everyone looked on with malicious interest.

Said knew now that prison lashings had not been as cruel as he used to think. "Come to me, Sana," he pleaded, unable to bear her refusal any longer, half standing and drawing closer to her.

"No!" she shouted.

"I am your daddy." She raised her eyes to Ilish Sidra in bewilderment, but Said repeated emphatically, "I am your daddy, come to me." She shrank back even further. He pulled her toward him almost forcibly. Then she screamed, and as he drew her closer, she fought back, crying. He leaned forward to kiss her, disregarding his failure and disappointment, but his lips caught only a whirling arm. "I'm your daddy. Don't be afraid. I'm your dad." The scent on her hair filled his mind with the memory of her mother; he felt his face go hard. The child struggled and wept more violently, and finally the detective intervened: "Easy, easy, the child does not know you."

Defeated, Said let her run away. "I will take her," he said angrily, sitting bolt upright.

A moment of silence passed, at the end of which Bayaza said, "Calm yourself first."

"She must come back to me."

"Let the judge decide that," the detective said sharply, then turned questioningly to Ilish. "Yes?"

"It has nothing to do with me. Her mother will never give her up, except in compliance with the law."

"Just as I pointed out at the beginning. There's no more to be said. It's up to a court of law."

Said felt that if once given vent, his rage would be unrestrainable and therefore with supreme effort he managed to keep it under control, reminding himself of things he had almost forgotten. "Yes, the court of law," he said as calmly as he could.

"And as you can see, the girl is being very well looked after," said Bayaza.

"First find yourself an honest job," the detective said with an ironic smile.

Able now to control himself, Said said, "Yes, of course. All that's quite correct. No need to be upset. I'll reconsider the whole affair. The best thing would be to forget the past and start looking for a job to provide a suitable home for the child when the time comes."

During the surprised silence that followed this speech, glances were exchanged, some incredulous, some perhaps not. The detective gathered his worry beads into his fist and asked, "Are we finished now?"

"Yes," Said answered. "I only want my books."

"Your books?"

"Yes."

"Most of them have been lost by Sana," Ilish said

loudly, "but I'll bring you whatever is left." He disappeared for a few minutes and returned carrying a modest pile of books, which he deposited in the middle of the room.

Said leafed through them, picking up one volume after another. "Yes," he remarked sadly, "most of them have been lost."

"How did you acquire all this learning?" the detective said with a laugh, rising to signal the end of the meeting. "Did you steal reading matter as well?"

They all grinned except Said, who went out carrying his books.

TWO

He looked at the door, open as it always used to be, as he walked up Jabal Road toward it. Here, enclosed by ridges of the Muqattam hill, was the Darrasa quarter, the scene of so many pleasant memories. The sandy ground was dotted with animals, teeming with children. Said gazed delightedly at the little girls panting from both emotion and exhaustion. Men lolled around him in the shade of the hill, away from the declining sun.

At the threshold of the open door he paused, trying to remember when he'd crossed it last. The simplicity of the house, which could hardly be different from those of Adam's day, was striking. At the left corner of the big, open courtyard stood a tall palm tree with a crooked top; to the right an entrance corridor led by an open door—in this strange house no door was ever closed—to a single room. His heart beat fast, carrying him back to a distant, gentle time of childhood, dreams, a loving father, and his own innocent yearning. He recalled the men filling the courtyard, swaying with their chanting, God's praise echoing from the depths of their hearts. "Look and listen, learn and open your heart," his father used to say. Besides a joy like the joy of Paradise that was aroused in him by faith and dreams, there had also been the joy of singing and green tea. He wondered how Ali al-Junaydi was.

From inside the room he could hear a man concluding his prayers. Said smiled, slipped in carrying his books, and saw the Sheikh sitting cross-legged on the prayer carpet, absorbed in quiet recitation. The old room had hardly changed. The rush mats had been replaced by new ones, thanks to his disciples, but the Sheikh's sleeping mattress still lay close to the western wall, pierced by a window through which the rays of the declining sun were pouring down at Said's feet. The other walls of the room were half covered with rows of books on shelves. The odor of incense lingered as if it were the same he remembered, never dissipated, from years ago. Putting down his load of books, he approached the Sheikh.

"Peace be upon you, my lord and master."

Having completed his recitation, the Sheikh raised his head, disclosing a face that was emaciated but radiant with overflowing vitality, framed by a white beard like a halo, and surmounted by a white skullcap that nestled in thick locks of hair showing silvery at his temples. The Sheikh scrutinized him with eyes that had been viewing this world for eighty years and indeed had glimpsed the next, eyes that had not lost their appeal, acuteness, or charm. Said found himself bending over his hand to kiss it, suppressing tears of nostalgia for his father, his boyish hopes, the innocent purity of the distant past.

"Peace and God's compassion be upon you," said the Sheikh in a voice like Time.

What had his father's voice been like? He could see his

father's face and his lips moving, and tried to make his eyes do the service of ears, but the voice had gone. And the disciples, the men chanting the mystical *dhikr,* "O master, the Prophet is at your gate!"—where were they now?

He sat down cross-legged on the rush mat before the Sheikh. "I am sitting without asking your permission," he said. "I remember that you prefer that." He sensed that the Sheikh was smiling, though on those lips concealed amidst the whiteness, no smile was visible. Did the Sheikh remember him? "Forgive my coming to your house like this. But there's nowhere else in the world for me to go."

The Sheikh's head drooped to his breast. "You seek the walls, not the heart," he whispered.

Said was baffled; not knowing what to say, he sighed, then quietly remarked, "I got out of jail today."

"Jail?" said the Sheikh, his eyes closed.

"Yes. You haven't seen me for more than ten years, and during that time strange things have happened to me. You've probably heard about them from some of your disciples who know me."

"Because I hear much I can hardly hear anything."

"In any case, I didn't want to meet you under false pretenses, so I'm telling you I got out of jail only today."

The Sheikh slowly shook his head, then, opening his eyes, said, "You have not come from jail." The voice was sorrowful.

Said smiled. This was the language of old times again, where words had a double meaning.

"Master, every jail is tolerable, except the government jail."

The Sheikh glanced at him with clear and lucid eyes, then muttered, "He says every jail is tolerable except the government jail."

Said smiled again, though he'd almost given up hope of being able to communicate, and asked, "Do you remember me?"

"Your concern is the present hour."

Fairly certain that he was remembered, Said asked for reassurance: "And do you remember my father, Mr. Mahran, God have mercy upon his soul?"

"May God have mercy upon all of us."

"What wonderful days those were!"

"Say that, if you can, about the present."

"But . . ."

"God have mercy upon us all."

"I was saying, I just got out of jail today."

The Sheikh nodded his head, showing sudden vigor. "And as he was impaled on the stake he smiled and said, 'It was God's will that I should meet Him thus.'"

My father could understand you. But me you turned away from, treating me as if you were turning me out of your house. And even so I've come back here, of my own accord, to this atmosphere of incense and disquiet, because a man so desolate, with no roof over his head, cannot do otherwise.

"Master, I have come to you now when my own daughter has rejected me."

The Sheikh sighed. "God reveals His secrets to His tiniest creatures!"

"I thought that if God had granted you long life, I would find your door open."

"And the door of Heaven? How have you found that?"

"But there is nowhere on earth for me to go. And my own daughter has rejected me."

"How like you she is!"

"In what way, Master?"

"You seek a roof, not an answer."

Said rested his head with its short, wiry hair on his dark, thin hand, and said, "My father used to seek you out when he was in trouble, so I found myself . . ."

"You seek a roof and nothing else."

Convinced that the Sheikh knew who he was, Said felt uneasy but did not know why. "It's not only a roof," he said. "I want more than that. I would like to ask God to be pleased with me."

The Sheikh replied as if intoning. "The celestial Lady said, 'Aren't you ashamed to ask for His good pleasure while you are not well pleased with Him?'"

The open space outside resounded with the braying of a donkey, which ended in a throaty rattle like a sob. Somewhere a harsh voice was singing, "Where have luck and good fortune gone?" He remembered once when his father had caught him singing "I Give You Three Guesses": his father had punched him gently and said, "Is this an appropriate song on our way to the blessed Sheikh?" He remembered how, in the midst of the chanting, his father had reeled in ecstasy, his eyes swimming, his voice hoarse, sweat pouring down his face, while he himself sat at the foot of the palm tree, watching the disciples by the light of a lantern, nibbling a fruit, rapt in curious bliss. All that was before he'd felt the first scalding drop of the draught of love.

The Sheikh's eyes were closed now, as if he were asleep, and Said had become so adjusted to the setting and atmosphere that he could no longer smell the incense. It occurred to him that habit is the root of laziness, boredom, and death, that habit had been responsible for his sufferings, the treachery, the ingratitude, and the waste of his life's hard toil. "Are the *dhikr* meetings still held here?" he asked, attempting to rouse the Sheikh.

But the Sheikh gave no answer. Even more uneasy now, Said asked a further question: "Aren't you going to welcome me here?"

The Sheikh opened his eyes and said, "Weak are the seeker and the sought."

"But you are the master of the house."

"The Owner of the house welcomes you," the Sheikh said, suddenly jovial, "as He welcomes every creature and every thing." Encouraged, Said smiled, but the Sheikh added, as if it were an afterthought, "As for me, I am master of nothing."

The sunlight on the rush mat had retreated to the wall.

"In any case," said Said, "this house is my real home, as it always was a home for my father and for every supplicant. You, my Master, deserve all our gratitude."

"'Lord, you know how incapable I am of doing You justice in thanking you, so please thank yourself on my account!' Thus spake one of the grateful."

"I am in need of a kind word," Said pleaded.

"Do not tell lies." The Sheikh spoke gently, then bowed his head, his beard fanning out over his chest, and seemed lost in thought.

Said waited, then shifted backward to rest against one of the bookshelves, where for several minutes he sat contemplating the fine-looking old man, until finally impatience made him ask, "Is there anything I could do for you?"

The Sheikh did not bother to respond and a period of silence followed, during which Said watched a line of ants nimbly crawling along a fold in the mat. Suddenly the Sheikh said, "Take a copy of the Koran and read."

A little confused, Said explained apologetically, "I just got out of jail today, and I have not performed the prayer ablutions."

"Wash yourself now and read."

"My own daughter has rejected me. She was scared of me, as if I was the devil. And before that her mother was unfaithful to me."

"Wash and read," replied the Sheikh gently.

"She committed adultery with one of my men, a layabout, a mere pupil of mine, utterly servile. She applied for divorce on grounds of my imprisonment and went and married him."

"Wash and read."

"And he took everything I owned, the money and the jewelry. He's a big man now, and all the local crooks have become followers and cronies of his."

"Wash and read."

"It wasn't thanks to any sweat by the police that I was arrested." Said went on, the veins in his forehead pulsing with anger. "No, it wasn't. I was sure of my safety, as usual. It was that dog who betrayed me, in collusion with her. Then disaster followed disaster until finally my daughter rejected me."

"Wash and read the verses: 'Say to them: if you love God, then follow me and God will love you' and 'I have chosen thee for Myself.' Also repeat the words: 'Love is acceptance, which means obeying His commands and refraining from what He has prohibited and contentment with what He decrees and ordains.'"

I could see my father listening and nodding his head with pleasure, looking at me with a smile as if saying: "Listen and learn." I had been happy then, hoping no one could see me, so I could climb the palm tree or throw up a stone to bring down a date, singing to myself along with those chanting men. Then one evening when I'd come back to the students' hostel in Giza I saw her coming towards me, holding a basket, pretty and charming, all the joys of heaven and torments of hell that I was fated to experience hidden within her.

What had it been about the chanting I'd liked, when they recited: "As soon as He appeared the beacon of faith shone" and: "I saw the crescent moon and the face of the beloved"? But the sun is not yet set. The last golden thread is receding from the window. A long night is waiting for me, the first night of freedom. I am alone with my freedom, or rather I'm in the company of the Sheikh, who is lost in heaven, repeating words that cannot be understood by someone approaching hell. What other refuge have I?

THREE

Flipping eagerly through the pages of *Al-Zahra* until he found Rauf Ilwan's column, Said began to read while still only a few yards from the house where he'd spent the night, the house of Sheikh Ali al-Junaydi. But what was it that seemed to be inspiring Ilwan now? Said found only comments on women's fashions, on loudspeakers, and a reply to a complaint by an anonymous wife. Diverting enough, but what had become of the Rauf Ilwan he'd known? Said thought of the good old days at the students' hostel, and particularly of the wonderful enthusiasm that had radiated from a young peasant with shabby clothes, a big heart, and a direct and glittering style of writing. What was it that had happened in the world? What lay behind these strange and mysterious events? Did things happen that were similar to what took place in al-Sayrafi Lane? And how about Nabawiyya and Ilish and that dear little girl who rejected her father? I must see him, he thought. The Sheikh has given me a mat to sleep on, but I need money. *I must begin life afresh, Mr. Ilwan, and for that purpose you are no less important than Sheikh Ali. You are, in fact, the most important thing I have in this insecure world.*

He walked on until he reached the *Zahra* offices in Maarif Square, an enormous building, where his first thought was that it would be very difficult to break into. The rows of cars surrounding it were like guards around a prison; the rumble of printing presses behind the grilles of the basement windows was like the low hum of men sleeping in a dormitory. He joined the stream of people entering the building, presented himself at the information desk, and asked in his deep "public" voice for Mr. Rauf Ilwan. Staring back with some displeasure at the bold, almost impudent look in his eyes, the reception clerk snapped, "Fourth floor." Said made for the elevator at once, joining people among whom he looked rather out of place in his blue suit and gym shoes, the oddness emphasized by the glaring eyes on either side of his long aquiline nose. A girl caught his eye, which made him curse his ex-wife and her lover under his breath, promising them destruction.

From the corridor of the fourth floor he slipped into the secretary's office before an attendant had time to intercept him and found himself in a large rectangular room with one glass wall overlooking the street, but no place to sit. He heard the secretary on the telephone, telling someone that Mr. Rauf was at a meeting with the editor-in-chief and would not be back for at least two hours. Feeling alien and out of place, Said poised himself with bravado, staring at the other people in the room almost defiantly, remembering a time when he would have fixed his gaze on people like them as if he wished to cut their throats. What were such people like nowadays? he wondered.

Rauf was now a very important man, it seemed, a great

man, as great as this room. It isn't a suitable place for reunion of old friends. Rauf won't be able to behave naturally here. There was a time when he'd been nothing more than a scribbler with the magazine *Al-Nadhir,* tucked away in Sharia Muhammad Ali, a poor writer whose voice rang with demands for freedom. *I wonder what you're like now, Rauf? Will he have changed, like you, Nabawiyya? Will he disown me, as Sana has done? No, I must banish these evil thoughts. He's still a friend and mentor, a sword of freedom ever drawn, and he'll always be like that, despite this impressiveness, this plush office suite, and those puzzling articles. If this citadel will not allow me to embrace you, Rauf, I'll have to look in the telephone directory and find your home address.*

Seated on the damp grass along the riverbank beside Sharia al-Nil, he waited. He waited even longer near a tree silhouetted by the light of an electric lamp. The crescent moon had gone down early, leaving stars to glitter in a sky profoundly black, and a soft breeze blew, distilled from the breath of the night after a day of stunning, searing summer. There he sat, with his arms clasped around his knees and his back to the river, his eyes fixed on villa number 18.

What a palace, he thought. It was open on three sides, and an extensive garden lay on the fourth. The trees stood around the white body of the building like whispering figures. A scene like this felt familiar, full of reminders of the good living he'd once enjoyed. How had Rauf managed it? And in such a short time! Not even thieves could dream of owning a thing like this. *I never used to look at a villa like this except when I was making plans to break into it. Is there really any hope of finding friendship in such a place now? You are indeed a mystery, Rauf Ilwan, and you must be made to reveal your secret.*

Wasn't it strange that Ilwan rhymed with Mahran? And that that dog Ilish should grab and wallow in the fruits of my lifetime's labor?

When a car stopped in front of the villa gate he sprang to his feet. As the porter opened the gate he darted across the road and stood before the car, bending a little so the driver could see him. When the man inside apparently failed to recognize him in the dark, Said roared, "Mr. Rauf, I am Said Mahran." The man put his head close to the open window of the car and repeated his name, in obvious surprise, his low voice carefully modulated. Said could not read Rauf's expression, but the tone of voice was encouraging. After a moment of silence and inaction, the car door opened and Said heard him say, "Get in."

A good beginning, he thought. Rauf Ilwan was the same man he knew, despite the glass-filled office suite and the lovely villa. The car went down a drive that curved like the shape of a violin, toward a flight of steps leading to the main entrance of the house.

"How are you, Said? When did you get out?"

"Yesterday."

"Yesterday?"

"Yes, I should have come to see you, but I had some things I had to attend to and I needed rest, so I spent the night at Sheikh Ali al-Junaydi's. Remember him?"

"Sure. Your late father's Sheikh. I watched his meetings with you lots of times." They left the car and went into the reception hall.

"They were fun, weren't they?"

"Yes, and I used to get a big kick out of their singing."

A servant switched on the chandelier, and Said's eyes were dazzled by its size, its multitude of upturned bulbs, its stars and crescents. The light that spread throughout the room was caught in mirrors at the corners, reflecting the brilliance. Objets d'art on gilt stands were displayed as if they had been salvaged from the obscurity of history for that sole purpose. The ceiling, he saw, was richly decorated, while all around him comfortable chairs and cushions were casually disposed among vividly patterned carpets. His eyes rested last on the face of Maître Ilwan, now round and full, a face he had loved, whose features he had long ago learned by heart, having gazed at it so often while listening to Rauf speak; and stealing occasional glances at the objets d'art, Said went on examining that face while a servant drew back curtains and opened French windows to the veranda overlooking the garden, letting a breeze heavy with the perfume of blossomy trees flow into the room.

The mixture of light and scent was distracting, but Said observed that Ilwan's face had become cowlike in its fullness, and that despite his apparent friendliness and courtesy, there was something chilly about him, as well as an unfamiliar and rather disturbing suavity, a quality that could only have come from a touch of blue blood, despite Rauf's flat nose and heavy jaw. What refuge would be left if this only surviving support also collapsed?

Rauf sat near the French windows to the veranda on a sofa that was arranged with three easy chairs in a square around a luminous pillar adorned with mythological figures. Said sat down, without hesitation and without showing his anxiety.

Ilwan stretched out his long legs. "Did you look for me at the paper?"

"Yes, but I saw it wasn't a suitable place for us to meet."

Rauf laughed, showing teeth stained black at the gums.

"The office is like a whirlpool, in constant motion. Have you been waiting long here?"

"A lifetime!"

Rauf laughed again. "There was a time no doubt when you were quite familiar with this street?"

"Of course." Said, too, laughed. "My business transactions with my clients here made their premises unforgettable. The villa of Fadil Hasanayn Pasha, for instance, where my visit netted a thousand pounds, or the one that belongs to the film star Kawakib, where I got a pair of superb diamond earrings."

The servant came in pushing a trolley laden with a bottle, two glasses, a pretty little violet-colored ice bucket, a dish of apples arranged in a pyramid, plates with hors d'oeuvres, and a silver water jug.

Rauf gestured to the servant to withdraw, filled two glasses himself and offered one to Said, raising the other: "To freedom." While Said emptied his glass in one gulp, Rauf took a sip and then said, "And how is your daughter? Oh, I forgot to ask you—why did you spend the night at Sheikh Ali's?"

He doesn't know what happened, thought Said, but he still remembers my daughter. And he gave Rauf a cold-blooded account of his misfortunes.

"So yesterday I paid a visit to al-Sayrafi Lane," he concluded. "There I found a detective waiting for me, as I'd expected, and my daughter disowned me and screamed in my face." He helped himself to another whiskey.

"This is a sad story. But your daughter isn't to blame. She can't remember you now. Later on she'll grow to know and love you."

"I have no faith left in all her sex."

"That's how you feel now. But tomorrow, who knows

how you'll feel? You'll change your opinion of your own accord. That's the way of the world."

The telephone rang. Rauf rose, picked up the receiver and listened for a moment. His face began to beam and he carried the telephone outside to the veranda, while Said's sharp eyes registered everything. It must be a woman. A smile like that, strolling into the dark, could only mean a woman. He wondered if Ilwan was still unmarried. Though they sat there cozily drinking and chatting, Said now sensed that this meeting would be exceedingly difficult to repeat. The feeling was unaccountable, like the whispered premonition of some still undiagnosed cancerous growth, but he trusted it, relying on instinct. A resident now in one of those streets that Said had only visited as a burglar, this man after all, may have felt obliged to welcome him, having actually changed so much that only a shadow of the old self remained. When Said heard Rauf's sudden laugh resounding on the veranda, he felt even less reassured. Calmly, however, he took an apple and began to munch it, pondering the extent to which his whole life had been no more than the mere acting out of ideas that had come from that man now chuckling into a telephone. What if Rauf should prove to have betrayed those ideas?

He would then have to pay dearly for it. On that score there was not the slightest doubt.

Rauf Ilwan came in from the veranda, replaced the telephone, and sat down looking extremely pleased. "So. Congratulations on your freedom. Being free is precious indeed. It more than makes up for losing anything else, no matter how valuable." Helping himself to a slice of pastrami, Said nodded in agreement, but without real interest in what had just been said. "And now you've come out of prison to find a new world," Rauf went on, refilling both glasses while Said wolfed down the hors d'oeuvres.

Glancing at his companion, Said caught a look of disgust, quickly covered by a smile. You must be mad to think he was sincere in welcoming you. This is only superficial courtesy—doing the right thing—and will evaporate. Every kind of treachery pales beside this; what a void would then swallow up the entire world!

Rauf stretched his hand to a cigarette box, adorned with Chinese characters, placed in a hollow in the illuminated pillar. "My dear Said," he said, taking a cigarette, "everything that used to spoil life's pleasures for us has now completely disappeared."

"The news astounded us in prison," Said said, his mouth full of food. "Who could have predicted such things?" He looked at Rauf, smiling. "No class war now?"

"Let there be a truce! Every struggle has its proper field of battle."

"And this magnificent drawing room," said Said, looking around him, "is like a parade ground." He saw a cold look in his companion's eyes and regretted the words instantly. Why can't your tongue ever learn to be polite?

"What do you mean?" Rauf's voice was icy.

"I mean it's a model of sophisticated taste and—"

"Don't try to be evasive," said Rauf with narrowed eyes. "Out with it. I understand you perfectly, I know you better than anybody else."

Said attempted a disarming laugh, then said, "I meant no harm at all."

"Never forget that I live by the sweat of my brow."

"I haven't doubted that for a moment. Please don't be angry."

Rauf puffed hard on his cigarette but made no further comment.

Aware that he ought to stop eating, Said said apologetically, "I haven't quite got over the atmosphere of prison. I need some time to recover my good manners and learn polite conversation. Apart from the fact that my head's still spinning from that strange meeting, when my own daughter rejected me."

Rauf's Mephistophelean eyebrows lifted in what looked like silent forgiveness. When he saw Said's gaze wander from his face to the food, as if asking permission to resume eating, he said quite calmly, "Help yourself."

Said attacked the rest of the dishes without hesitation, as if nothing had happened, until he'd wiped them clean. At this point Rauf said, a little quickly, as if he wished to end the meeting, "Things must now change completely. Have you thought about your future?"

Said lit a cigarette. "My past hasn't yet allowed me to consider the future."

"It occurs to me that there are more women in the world than men. So you mustn't let the infidelity of one lone female bother you. As for your daughter, she'll get to know you and love you one day. The important thing now is to look for a job."

Said eyed a statue of a Chinese god, a perfect embodiment of dignity and repose. "I learned tailoring in prison."

"So you want to set up a tailoring shop?" said Rauf with surprise.

"Certainly not," Said replied quietly.

"What then?"

Said looked at him. "In my whole life I've mastered only one trade."

"You're going back to burglary?" Rauf seemed almost alarmed.

"It's most rewarding, as you know."

"As I know! How the hell do I know?"

"Why are you so angry?" Said gave him a surprised look. "I meant: as you know from my past. Isn't that so?"

Rauf lowered his eyes as if trying to assess the sincerity of Said's remark, clearly unable to maintain his bonhomie and looking for a way to end the meeting. "Listen, Said. Things are no longer what they used to be. In the past you were both a thief and my friend, for reasons you well know. Now the situation has changed. If you go back to burglary you'll be a thief and nothing else."

Dashed by Rauf's unaccommodating frankness, Said sprang to his feet. Then he stifled his agitation, sat down again, and said quietly, "All right. Name a job that's suitable for me."

"Any job, no matter what. You do the talking. I'll listen."

"I would be happy," Said began, without obvious irony, "to work as a journalist on your paper. I'm a well-educated man and an old disciple of yours. Under your supervision I've read countless books, and you often testified to my intelligence."

Rauf shook his head impatiently, his thick black hair glistening in the brilliant light. "This is no time for joking. You've never been a writer, and you got out of jail only yesterday. This fooling around is wasting my time."

"So I have to choose something menial?"

"No job is menial, as long as it's honest."

Said felt utterly reckless. He ran his eyes quickly over the smart drawing room, then said bitterly, "How mar-

velous it is for the rich to recommend poverty to us."
Rauf's reaction was to look at his watch.

"I am sure I have taken too much of your time," Said
said quietly.

"Yes," said Rauf, with all the blank directness of a July
sun. "I'm loaded with work!"

"Thanks for your kindness and hospitality and for the
supper," Said said, standing up.

Rauf took out his wallet and handed him two five-
pound notes. "Take these to tide you over. Please forgive
me for saying I'm overloaded with work. You'll seldom
find me free as I was tonight."

Said smiled, took the bank notes, shook his hand
warmly, and wished him well: "May God increase your
good fortune."

FOUR

So *this is the real Rauf Ilwan, the naked reality—a partial corpse not even decently underground. The other Rauf Ilwan has gone, disappeared, like yesterday, like the first day in the history of man—like Nabawiyya's love or Ilish's loyalty. I must not be deceived by appearances. His kind words are cunning, his smiles no more than a curl of the lips, his generosity a defensive flick of the fingers, and only a sense of guilt moved him to let me cross the threshold of his house. You made me and now you reject me: Your ideas create their embodiment in my person and then you simply change them, leaving me lost—rootless, worthless, without hope—a betrayal so vile that if the whole Muqattam hill toppled over and buried it, I still would not be satisfied.*

I wonder if you ever admit, even to yourself, that you betrayed me. Maybe you've deceived yourself as much as you try to deceive others. Hasn't your conscience bothered you even in the dark? I wish I could penetrate your soul as easily as I've penetrated your house, that house of mirrors and objets d'art, but I suppose I'd find nothing but betrayal there: Nabawiyya disguised as Rauf, Rauf disguised as Nabawiyya, or Ilish Sidra in place of both—and betrayal would cry out to me that it was the lowest crime on earth. Their eyes behind my back must have traded anxious looks throbbing with lust, which carried them in a current crawling like death, like a cat creeping on its belly toward a bewildered sparrow. When their chance came, the last remnants of decency and indecision disappeared, so that in a corner of the lane, even in my own house, Ilish Sidra finally said, "I'll tell the police. We'll get rid of him," and the child's mother was silent—the tongue that so often and so profusely told me, "I love you, the best man in the world," was silent. And I found myself surrounded by police in Al-Sayrafi Lane—though until then demons themselves with all their wiles had failed to trap me—their kicks and punches raining down on me.

You're just the same, Rauf—I don't know which of you is the most treacherous—except that your guilt is greater because of your intelligence and the past association between us: You pushed me into jail, while you leapt free, into that palace of lights and mirrors. You've forgotten your wise sayings about palaces and hovels, haven't you? I will never forget.

At the Abbas Bridge, sitting on a stone bench, he became aware for the first time of where he was.

"It's best to do it now," he said in a loud voice, as if addressing the dark, "before he's had time to get over the shock." I can't hold back, he thought. My profession will always be mine, a just and legitimate trade, especially when it's directed against its own philosopher. There'll be space enough in the world to hide after I've punished the bastards. If I could live without a past, ignoring

183 / The Thief and the Dogs

Nabawiyya, Ilish, and Rauf, I'd be relieved of a great weight, a burden; I'd feel readier to secure an easy life and a lot further from the rope. But unless I settle my account with them, life will have no taste, because I shall not forget the past. For the simple reason that in my mind it's not a past, but the here and now. Tonight's adventure will be the best beginning for my program of action. And it'll be a rich venture indeed.

The Nile flowed in black waves slashed sidelong by arrows of light from the reflected streetlamps along its banks. The silence was soothing and total.

At the approach of dawn, as the stars drew closer to earth, Said rose from his seat, stretched, and began to walk slowly back along the bank toward the place from which he'd come, avoiding the few still-lit lamps, slowing his steps even more when the house came in sight. Examining the street, the terrain, the walls of the big houses as well as the riverbank, his eyes finally came to rest on the sleeping villa, guarded on all sides by trees like ghostly figures, where treachery dozed in a fine unmerited tranquillity. *It's going to be a rich venture, indeed, and one to give an emphatic reply to the treachery of a lifetime.*

He crossed the street casually without a movement to either right or left, without looking wary. Then followed the hedge down a side street, scanning carefully ahead. When he was sure the street was empty he dodged into the hedge, forcing his way in amidst the jasmine and violets, and stood motionless: If there was a dog in the house—other than its owner, of course—it would now fill the universe with barking.

But not a whisper came out of the silence.

Rauf, your pupil is coming, to relieve you of a few worldly goods.

He climbed the hedge nimbly, his expert limbs agile as an ape's, undeterred by the thick, intertwining branches, the heavy foliage and flowers. Gripping the railings, he heaved his body up over the sharp-pointed spikes, then lowered himself until his legs caught the branches inside the garden. Here he clung for a while regaining his breath, studying the terrain: a jungle of bushes, trees, and dark shadows. *I'll have to climb up to the roof and find a way to get in and down. I have no tools, no flashlight, no good knowledge of the house: Nabawiyya hasn't been here before me pretending to work as a washerwoman or a maid; she's busy now with Ilish Sidra.*

Scowling in the dark, trying to chase these thoughts from his mind, he dropped lightly to the ground. Crawling up to the villa on all fours, he felt his way along a wall until he found a drainpipe. Then, gripping it like an acrobat, he began to climb toward the roof. Partway up he spotted an open window, just out of reach, and decided to try it. He steered one foot to the window ledge, and shifted his hands, one at a time, to grip a cornice. Finally, when he could stand with his whole weight, he slid inside, finding himself in what he guessed was the kitchen. The dense darkness was disturbing and he groped for the door. The darkness would be even thicker inside, but where else could he find Rauf's wallet or some of his objets d'art? He had to go on.

Slipping through the door, feeling along the wall with his hands, he had covered a considerable distance, almost deterred by the darkness, when he felt a slight draft touch his face. Wondering where it could come from, he turned a corner and crept along the smooth wall, his arm stretched out, feeling ahead with his fingers. Suddenly they brushed some dangling beads, which rustled slightly as he touched them, making him start. A curtain. He must now be near his goal. He thought of the box of matches in his pocket, but instead of reaching for it he made a quiet little opening for himself in the hanging beads and slipped through, bringing the curtain back into position behind him, slowly, to avoid making any sound. He took one step forward and bumped some object, perhaps a chair, which he edged away from, raising his head to look for a night light. All he could see was a darkness that weighed down upon him like a nightmare. For a moment he thought again of lighting a match.

Suddenly he was assailed by light. It shone all around him, so powerful that it struck him with the force of a blow, making him shut his eyes. When he opened them again, Rauf Ilwan was standing only a couple of yards from him, wearing a long dressing gown, which made him look like a giant, one hand tensed in a pocket, as if he was clutching a weapon. The cold look in his eyes, his tightly closed lips, chilled Said to the core; nothing but deep hatred, hostility. The silence was suffocating, claustrophobic, denser than the walls of a prison. Abd Rabbuh the jailer would soon be jeering: "Back already?"

"Should we call the police?" someone behind him said curtly. Said turned around and saw three servants standing in a row. "Wait outside," said Rauf, breaking the silence.

As the door opened and closed Said observed that it was made of wood in arabesque designs, its upper panel inlaid with an inscription, probably a proverb or a Koranic verse. He turned to face Rauf.

"It was idiotic of you to try your tricks on me; I know

you. I can read you like an open book." Speechless, help-less, and resigned, still recovering from the shock of sur-prise, Said had nevertheless an instinctive sense that he would not be handed back to the custody from which he'd been set free the day before. "I've been waiting for you, fully prepared. In fact, I even drew up your plan of action. I'd hoped my expectation would be disappointed. But evi-dently no mistrust in you can prove groundless." Said lowered his eyes for a moment and became aware of the patterned parquet beneath the wax on the floor. Then he looked up, saying nothing. "It's no use. You'll always be worthless and you'll die a worthless death. The best thing I can do now is hand you over to the police." Said blinked, gulped, and lowered his eyes again.

"What have you come for?" Rauf demanded angrily. "You treat me as an enemy. You've forgotten my kindness, my charity. You feel nothing but malice and envy. I know your thoughts, as clearly as I know your actions."

His eyes still wandering over the floor, Said muttered, "I feel dizzy. Peculiar. It's been like that ever since I got out of jail."

"Liar! Don't try to deceive me. You thought I'd become one of the rich I used to attack. And with that in mind you wished to treat me—"

"It's not true."

"Then why did you break into my house? Why do you want to rob me?"

"I don't know," Said said, after a moment's hesitation. "I'm not in my proper state of mind. But you don't believe me."

"Of course I don't. You know you're lying. My good advice didn't persuade you. Your envy and arrogance were aroused, so you rushed in headlong as always, like a madman. Suit yourself, do what you like, but you'll find your-self in jail again."

"Please forgive me. My mind's the way it was in prison, the way it was even before that."

"There's no forgiving you. I can read your thoughts, everything that passes through your mind. I can see exactly what you think of me. And now it's time I delivered you to the police."

"Please don't."

"No? Don't you deserve it?"

"Yes, I do, but please don't."

"If I set eyes on you again," Rauf bellowed, "I'll squash you like an insect." Thus dismissed, Said was about to make a quick exit, but Rauf stopped him with a shout: "Give me back the money." Frozen for a second, Said slipped his hand into his pocket and brought out the two bank notes. Rauf took them and said, "Don't ever show me your face again."

Said walked back to the banks of the Nile, hardly believing his escape, though relief was spoiled by a sense of defeat, and now in the damp breath of early daybreak, he wondered how he could have failed to take careful note of the room where he'd been caught, how all he'd noticed had been its decorated door and its waxed parquet. But the dawn shed dewy compassion, giving momentary solace for the loss of everything, even the two bank notes, and he surrendered to it. Raising his head to the sky, he found himself awed by the dazzling brilliance of the stars at this hour just before sunrise.

They stared at him incredulously, then everyone in the café rose at once to meet him. Led by the proprietor and his waiter, uttering a variety of colorful expressions of welcome, they formed a circle around him, embraced him, kissing him on the cheeks. Said Mahran shook hands with each of them, saying politely, "Thanks, Mr. Tarzan. Thanks, friends."

"When was it?"

"Day before yesterday."

"There was supposed to be an amnesty. We were keeping our fingers crossed."

"Thank God I'm out."

"And the rest of the boys?"

"They're all well; their turn will come."

They excitedly exchanged news for a while, until Tarzan, the proprietor, led Said to his own sofa, asking the other men to go back to their places, and the café was quiet again. Nothing had changed. Said felt he'd left it only yesterday. The round room with its brass fittings, the wooden chairs with their straw seats, were just the way they used to be. A handful of customers, some of whom he recognized, sat sipping tea and making deals. Through the open door and out the big window opposite you could see the wasteland stretching into the distance, its thick darkness unrelieved by a single glimmer of light. Its impressive silence broken only by occasional laughter borne in on the dry and refreshing breeze—forceful and clean, like the desert itself—that blew between the window and the door.

Said took the glass of tea from the waiter, raised it to his lips without waiting for it to cool, then turned to the proprietor. "How's business these days?"

Tarzan curled his lower lip. "There aren't many men you can rely on nowadays," he said contemptuously.

"What do you mean? That's too bad."

"They're all lazy, like bureaucrats!"

Said grunted sympathetically. "At least a lazy man is better than a traitor. It was thanks to a traitor I had to go to jail, Mr. Tarzan."

"Really? You don't say!"

Said stared at him surprised. "Didn't you hear the story, then?" When Tarzan shook his head sympathetically, Said whispered in his ear, "I need a good revolver."

"If there's anything you need, I'm at your service."

Said patted him on the shoulder gratefully, then began to ask, with some embarrassment, "But I haven't—"

Tarzan interrupted, placing a thick finger on Said's lips, and said, "You don't need to apologize ever to anyone!"

Said savored the rest of his tea, then walked to the window and stood there, a strong, slim, straight-backed figure of medium height, and let the breeze belly out his jacket, gazing into the pitch-dark wasteland that stretched away ahead of him. The stars overhead looked like grains of sand; and the café felt like an island in the midst of an ocean, or an airplane alone in the sky. Behind him, at the foot of the small hill on which the café stood, lighted cigarettes moved like nearer stars in the hands of those who sat there in the dark seeking fresh air. On the horizon to the west, the lights of Abbasiyya seemed very far away, their distance making one understand how deeply in the desert this café had been placed.

As Said stared out the window, he became aware of the voices of the men who sat outside, sprawled around the hill, enjoying the desert breeze—the waiter was going down to them now, carrying a water pipe with glowing coals, from which sparks flew upward with a crackling noise—their lively conversations punctuated by bursts of laughter. He heard the voice of one young man, obviously enjoying a discussion, say, "Show me a single place on earth where there's any security."

Another one disagreed. "Here where we're sitting, for instance. Aren't we enjoying peace and security now?"

"You see, you say 'now.' There's the calamity."

"But why do we curse our anxiety and fears? In the end don't they save us the trouble of thinking about the future?"

"So you're an enemy of peace and tranquillity."

"When all you have to think about is the hangman's rope around your neck, it's natural enough to fear tranquillity."

"Well, that's a private matter—you can settle it between yourself and the hangman."

"You're chattering away happily because here you're protected by the desert and the dark. But you'll have to go back to the city sometime soon. So what's the use?"

"The real tragedy is that our enemy is at the same time our friend."

"On the contrary, it's that our friend is also our enemy."

"No. It's that we're cowards. Why don't we admit it?"

"Maybe we are cowards. But how can you be brave in this age?"

"Courage is courage."

"And death is death."

"And darkness and the desert are all these things."

What a conversation! What did they mean? Somehow they're giving expression to my own situation, in a manner as shapeless and strange as the mysteries of that night. There was a time when I had youth, energy, and conviction too—the time when I got arms for the national cause and not for the sake of murder. On the other side of this very hill, young men, shabby, but pure in heart, used to train for battle. And their leader was the present inhabitant of villa number 18. Training himself, training others, spelling out words of wisdom. "Said Mahran," he used to say to me, "a revolver is more important than a loaf of bread. It's more important than the Sufi sessions you keep rushing off to the way your father did." One evening he asked me, "What does a man need in this country, Said?" and without waiting for an answer he said, "He needs a gun and a book: the gun will take care of the past, the book is for the future. Therefore you must train and read." I can still recall his face that night in the students' hostel, his guffaws of laughter, his words: "So you have stolen. You've actually dared to steal. Bravo! Using theft to relieve the exploiters of some of their guilt is absolutely legitimate, Said. Don't ever doubt it."

This open wasteland had borne witness to Said's own

skill. Didn't it used to be said that he was Death Incarnate, that his shot never missed? He closed his eyes, relaxing, enjoying the fresh air, until suddenly he felt a hand on his shoulder. And looking around, he saw Tarzan, holding out to him a revolver in his other hand.

"May it be fire for your enemy, God willing," Tarzan said to him.

Said took it. "How much is it, Mr. Tarzan?" he said, inspecting the bolt action.

"It's a present from me"

"No, thank you, I can't accept that. All I ask is that you give me some time until I can afford to pay you."

"How many bullets do you need?"

They walked back to Tarzan's sofa. As they passed the open doorway, they heard a woman's laughter ringing outside. Tarzan chuckled. "It's Nur, remember her?"

Said looked into the darkness, but could see nothing. "Does she still come here?" he asked.

"Sometimes. She'll be pleased to see you."

"Has she caught anybody?"

"Of course. This time it's the son of the owner of a candy factory." They sat down and Tarzan called the waiter over. "Tell Nur—tactfully—to come here."

It would be nice to see her, to see what time had done to her. She'd hoped to gain his love, but failed. What love he'd had had been the exclusive property of that other, unfaithful woman. He'd been made of stone. There's nothing more heartbreaking than loving someone like that. It had been like a nightingale singing to a rock, a breeze caressing sharp-pointed spikes. Even the presents she'd given he used to give away—to Nabawiyya or Ilish. He patted the gun in his pocket and clenched his teeth.

Nur appeared at the entrance. Unprepared, she stopped

in amazement as soon as she saw Said, remaining a few steps away from him. He smiled at her, but looked closely. She'd grown thinner, her face was disguised by heavy makeup, and she was wearing a sexy frock that not only showed her arms and legs but was fitted so tightly to her body that it might have been stretched rubber. What it advertised was that she'd given up all claims to self-respect. So did her bobbed hair, ruffled by the breeze. She ran to him.

"Thank God you're safe," she said, as their hands met, giggling a little to hide her emotion, squeezing him and Tarzan.

"How are you, Nur?" he asked.

"As you can see," Tarzan said for her with a smile, "she's all light, like her name."

"I'm fine," she said. "And you? You look very healthy. But what's wrong with your eyes? They remind me of how you used to look when you were angry."

"What do you mean?" he said with a grin.

"I don't know, it's hard to describe. Your eyes turn a sort of red and your lips start twitching!"

Said laughed. Then, with a touch of sadness, he said, "I suppose your friend will be coming soon to take you back?"

"Oh, he's dead drunk," she said, shaking her head, tossing the hair from her eyes.

"In any case, you're tied to him."

"Would you like me," she said with a sly smile, "to bury him in the sand?"

"No, not tonight. We'll meet again later. I'm told he's a real catch," he added, with a look of interest that did not escape her.

"He sure is. We'll go in his car to the Martyr's Tomb. He likes open spaces."

So he likes open spaces. Over near the Martyr's Tomb.

Her eyelashes fluttered, showing a pretty confusion that increased as her gaze met his. "You see," she said with a pout, "you never think of me."

"It's not true," he said. "You're very dear to me."

"You're only thinking about that poor fish."

Said smiled. "He forms a part of my thinking of you."

"I'll be ruined if they find out," she said with sudden seriousness. "His father's an influential man and he comes from a powerful family. Do you need money?"

"What I really need is a car," he said, standing up. "Try to be completely natural with him," he went on, gently pinching one of her cheeks. "Nothing will happen to frighten you and no one will suspect you. I'm not a kid. When this is done we'll see a lot more of each other than you ever thought possible."

SIX

He knew this stretch of ground. Avoiding the road next to the barracks, he set out across the desert to reach the Martyr's Tomb in the shortest time possible, heading for it as if he had a compass built into his head. As soon as he saw the tomb's big dome in the starlight he began looking for the spot where the car would be tucked away. Walking around the tomb, he scanned the ground as sharply as he could, but it was only when he reached its southern wall that the shape at a little distance became visible. He made for it without another thought, keeping his head low, crouching as he came closer to the car, until he could hear through the silence the sounds of love being made in whispers. *There'll be terror, now, he told himself, in the middle of pleasure, and joy will suddenly vanish, but it's no fault of yours: chaos and confusion envelop us all like the vault of the sky. Didn't Rauf Ilwan used to say that our intentions were good but we lacked order or discipline?*

The breathing inside the car had turned to panting.

Almost crawling on his hands and knees, Said crept up until he could touch the door handle. He tightened his grip on the handle, and yanked open the door, shouting, "Don't move!"

Two people cried out in shocked surprise and a pair of heads stared at him in terror. He waved the gun and said, "Don't move or I'll shoot. Get out."

"I beg you," said Nur's voice.

Another voice, throaty, as if strained through sand and gravel, said, "What—what is it you want, please?"

"Get out."

Nur threw herself out of the car, clutching her clothes in one hand, followed by the young man, who stumbled as he struggled to insert his feet in his trousers. Said thrust the gun so menacingly close that the young man began to plead. "No. No. Please don't shoot," he said almost tearfully.

"The money," Said growled.

"In my jacket. In the car."

Said shoved Nur back to the car. "You get in."

Groaning with pain, she climbed in. "Please let me go. For God's sake let me go," she stammered.

"Give me the jacket." He snatched it from her, removed the wallet, and threw the jacket in the man's face. "You have exactly one minute to save your skin." While the young man bolted off in the dark like a comet, Said flung himself into the driver's seat and switched on the engine. The car shot forward with a roar.

"I was really scared," Nur said as she dressed, "as if I hadn't really been expecting you."

"Let's have a drink," he said as soon as they reached the road, still hurtling forward. She handed him a bottle and he took a swig. He handed it back to her and she did the same.

"Poor man, his knees were shaking," she said.

"You're very kindhearted. As for me, I don't particularly like factory owners."

"You don't like anybody, that's a fact," she said, sitting up and looking ahead. Said didn't feel like trying to charm her and said nothing.

"They'll see me with you!" she squealed when she saw that the car was approaching Abbasiyya. The same thought had occurred to him, so he turned off into a side street that led toward Darrasa and drove a little slower.

"I went to Tarzan's café to get a gun and try to arrange something with an old friend, a taxi driver. But now look how luck has sent me this car!"

"Don't you think I'm always useful?"

"Always. And you were fantastic, too. Why don't you go on the stage?"

"In the beginning I was really scared."

"But later?"

"I hope I was convincing, so he won't suspect me."

"He was so out of his mind with fear he wasn't capable of suspecting anything."

"Why do you need a gun and a car?" she asked, putting her head close to his.

"They're the tools of the trade."

"Heaven! When did you get out of jail?"

"The day before yesterday."

"And you're already thinking of doing that again?"

"Have you ever found it easy to change your job?"

Staring ahead at the dark road, visible only in the car's headlights, Nur made no reply. At the turn, the hill of the

Muqattam loomed nearer, like a chunk of the night more solid than the rest.

"Do you realize how sad I was," she said softly, "when I heard you'd been sent up?"

"No. How sad?"

"When will you stop being sarcastic?" She sounded a little annoyed.

"But I'm dead serious. And absolutely certain of the sincerity of your affection."

"You have no heart."

"They've got it locked up in prison, according to regulations!"

"You were heartless long before you ever went to jail."

Why does she harp on the subject of affection? She should talk to that treacherous woman, and the dogs, and the little girl who rejected me. "One day we'll succeed in finding it," he said.

"Where will you stay tonight? Does your wife know where you are?"

"I don't think so."

"Are you going home, then?"

"I don't think so. Not tonight, in any case."

"Come to my place."

"Do you live alone?"

"Yes, in Sharia Najm al-Din beyond the cemetery at Bab el-Nasr."

"Number?"

"There's only one house on the street; it's over a sackcloth store and right behind it is the cemetery."

"What a great location!" Said laughed.

Nur laughed, too. "No one knows me there and no one's ever visited me. You'll find it on the top floor." She waited for his reply, but he was busy watching the road, which began to narrow between the hill and the houses that came after Sheikh Ali al-Junaydi's place. At the top of Sharia Darrasa he stopped the car and turned toward her.

"This is a good place for you to get out."

"Won't you come with me?"

"I'll come to you later on."

"But where are you going at this hour of night?"

"You go straight to the police station now. Tell them exactly what happened as if you had nothing to do with me and give them a description of a person completely different from me. Say he's fat, fair-skinned, and has an old scar on his right cheek. Tell them I kidnapped you, robbed you, and raped you.

"Raped me?"

"In the desert at Zinhum," he went on, ignoring her exclamation, "and say I threw you out of the car and drove away."

"Are you really coming to see me?"

"Yes, that's a solemn promise. Will you be able to act as well in the police station as you did in the car?"

"I hope so."

"Goodbye, then." And he drove away.

SEVEN

To kill them both—Nabawiyya and Ilish—at the same time would be a triumph. Even better would be to settle with Rauf Ilwan, too, then escape, go abroad if possible. But who'll look after Sana? The thorn in my side. You always act impulsively, Said, without thinking, but you mustn't rush this time; you must wait until you've arranged things, then swoop like an eagle. But there's no point in delay either: you're a hunted man—you became a hunted man as soon as they knew you were coming out—and now, after the car incident, the search will be intensified. Only a few pounds in the wallet of the factory owner's son—another stroke of bad luck. If you don't strike soon everything will collapse. Who'll look after Sana, though? That thorn again. She rejected me but I still love her. Should I spare your unfaithful mother for your sake, then? I must find the answer right away.

He was hovering on foot in the pitch-darkness surrounding the house at the crossroads where two lanes met in Imam Way. The car was parked at the top of the road, back toward the Citadel square. Shops were closed, the road was deserted, and no one seemed to be looking for him: at such an hour every creature took shelter, blind and unsuspecting, in his hole. Said could easily have taken further precautions, but he was not going to be diverted from his purpose, even if it meant Sana's having to live alone all her life. For treachery, Mr. Rauf, is an abomination.

He looked up at the windows of the house, his hand clutching the revolver in his pocket. Treachery is abominable, Ilish, and for the living to enjoy life it is imperative that criminal and vicious elements be eradicated. Keeping close to the wall, he approached the door, then entered the house and cautiously climbed the pitch-dark stairs, passing the first floor, then the second to the third. Right. And there was the flat, the door, snugly closed on the most rotten intentions and desires. If he knocked, who would answer? Would it be Nabawiyya? Was the police detective perhaps lurking somewhere? There was hellfire for them both even if he had to break into the flat. He must act at once. It was not right that Ilish Sidra should stay alive for even one day while Said Mahran was a free man. *You'll get away without a scratch, just as easily as you have scores of times: you can scale an apartment building in seconds, jump unhurt from a third-floor window—even fly if you wish!*

It seems you must knock on the door. But knocking might arouse suspicion, especially at this hour. Nabawiyya would fill the world with her screams, and bring some cowardly fools. That detective, too. So you'd better break the little glass pane in the door.

He'd had the idea in the car on the way here and now he came back to it. He drew his gun and gave the glass one blow through the twisted bars that protected it. As the glass broke and the pieces scattered, it made a noise like a choked-off scream in the silent night. He flattened himself against the wall, next to the door and waited, his heart beating fast and his eyes peering into the darkness of the entrance hall, where the gun was pointed. A man's voice, which he could recognize as Ilish Sidra's despite the throbbing noise in his temples, said, "Who's there?" and a door to the left opened, giving a faint light by which he could just make out the figure of a man approaching cautiously. Said pressed the trigger and the gun roared like a demon in the night. The man cried out and began to fall, but another bullet struck him even before he hit the floor, where he lay like a sack. A woman shrieked for help—Nabawiyya's voice. "Your turn will come! There's no escape from me! I'm the devil himself!" he shouted as he turned to escape, leaping down the stairs so recklessly that he reached the bottom in seconds, where he paused briefly to listen, then slipped out. Once outside he walked away calmly, keeping close to the wall, leaving behind him the sounds of windows opening and voices questioning and vague cries whose words he could not make out. When he reached the place at the top of the road where he'd parked the car, and had pulled open the door to get in, he spotted a policeman running from the square toward Imam Way. Ducking down, he hid on the floor of the car as the policeman ran on past toward the screaming, remaining still until the footsteps sounded far enough away, then he sat up behind the steering wheel and sped off. At the square he slowed down to a normal speed, the din still haunting his senses and settling at last within his nerves. He felt stunned. Confusion pervaded his whole being and he was only half aware of what he did as he drove on. *A murderer! But there's still Rauf Ilwan, the high-class traitor, really much more important and dangerous than Ilish Sidra. A murderer! You are now one of those who commit murder; you have a new identity now and a new destiny! You used to take precious goods—now you take worthless lives!*

Your turn will come, Nabawiyya. There's no escape from me. I'm the devil himself. I've granted you life, thanks to Sana, but I've enclosed you in a punishment greater than death; fear of death, the unrelenting terror. As long as I live you'll never enjoy the taste of peace.

He came down Sharia Muhammad Ali in a stupor, without a thought to where he was going. Many people would now have a murderer on their minds. The murderer must hide. He must take care to avoid the rope and the gallows. *You must never have the executioner asking what your last wish is, Said! Oh no. The government must be made to ask you this question, but on some better occasion!*

When he returned to full awareness he found he'd covered the last stretch of Sharia al-Gaysh and was speeding toward Abbasiyya. Alarmed to find himself unexpectedly returning to a place of danger, he doubled his speed and in a few minutes reached Manshiyyat al-Bakri, where he stopped at the first street branching from the main road, quietly abandoned the car, and walked away without looking left or right, slowly, as if exercising his legs. He felt numbness, then some sort of pain, as if in reaction to the great nervous effort he had made.

Nowhere is safe for you now. Or ever after. And Nur? It would be risky to go to her place tonight, of all nights, what with the investigations and suspicions that are bound to ensue. Darkness must extend from now on to all eternity.

EIGHT

He pushed the Sheikh's door, met no resistance, entered, closed it behind him, and found himself in the open courtyard where the palm tree towered, as if stretched upward into space as high as the watchful stars. What a superb place for hiding, he thought. The Sheikh's room was open at night, just as it was by day. There it stood, pitch-black, as if waiting for his return, and he walked toward it quietly. He heard the voice muttering but could only distinguish the word "Allah," "God!" It went on muttering as if the Sheikh were unaware or perhaps reluctant to acknowledge his presence.

Said withdrew into a corner at the left of the room close to his pile of books and flung himself down on the rush mat, still in his suit and shoes and carrying his revolver. He stretched out his legs, supporting his trunk on the palms of his hands, his head falling back in exhaustion. His head felt like a beehive, but there was nothing he could do.

You wish to recall the sound of the bullet and the screams of Nabawiyya, feeling happy again that you did

206 / Naguib Mahfouz

*not hear Sana scream. You'd better greet the Sheikh, but
your voice is too weak to say "Peace be upon you!" There's
this feeling of helplessness, as if you were drowning. And
you thought you were going to sleep like a log as soon as
your skin touched the floor!*

How the righteous and God-fearing would have shuddered, turned away from him in fright—until recitation of
the name of God had made them less particular, less hard
of heart. When would this strange man go to sleep? But
the strange old man now raised his voice and began to
sing: "In my view, passion is nothing but ingratitude unless
it issues from my witnesses." And in a voice that seemed to
fill the room, he said, "The eyes of their hearts are open,
but those in their heads are closed!" Said smiled in spite of
himself. So that's why he is not aware of my presence. But
then I, too, am not fully aware of my own self.

The call to the dawn prayers rose above the quiet waves
of the night. It reminded him of a night he'd once spent
sleepless until the same call to the dawn prayers, excited
over some special joy promised for the following day. On
that occasion, he'd got up as soon as he heard the call,
happy at release from a night of torment, had looked out
of the window at the blue dawn and the smiling sunrise,
and had rubbed his hands in anticipation of whatever it
was he'd been about to enjoy, something he had since completely forgotten. And therefore he loved the dawn, which
he associated with the singing of the prayer call, the deep
blue sky, the smile of the approaching sunrise, and that
unremembered joy.

It was dawn now, but his exhaustion was so great he
could not move, not even to shift his revolver. The Sheikh
rose to perform his prayers. Showing no awareness of
Said's presence, he lit the oil lamp, spread out the prayer

mat, took up his position on it, then suddenly asked, "Aren't you going to perform the dawn prayers?"

Said was so tired he was incapable of giving an answer, and no sooner had the Sheikh begun his prayers than he dropped off to sleep.

He dreamt that he was in jail, being whipped despite his good conduct, screaming shamelessly, but not offering any resistance. They gave him milk to drink. Suddenly he saw little Sana lashing Rauf Ilwan with a whip at the bottom of a staircase. He heard the sound of a Koranic recitation and had the impression that someone had died, but then he found himself, a wanted man, somehow involved in a car chase! The car he was driving was incapable of speed—there was something wrong with its engine—and he had to begin shooting in every direction. Suddenly, Rauf Ilwan appeared from the radio in the dashboard, grabbed his wrist before Said was able to kill him, and tightened his grip so mercilessly that he was able to snatch the revolver. At this point Said Mahran said to him, "Kill me if you wish, but my daughter is innocent. It wasn't she who whipped you at the bottom of the staircase. It was her mother, Nabawiyya, at the instigation of Ilish Sidra." Escaping his pursuers, Said then slipped into the circle of Sufi chanters gathered around Sheikh al-Junaydi, but the Sheikh denied him. "Who are you?" he asked. "How did you come to be with us?" He told him he was Said Mahran, son of Amm Mahran, his old disciple, and reminded him of the old days, but the Sheikh demanded his identity card. Said was surprised and objected that a Sufi disciple didn't need an identity card, that in the eyes of the mystical order the righteous and the sinner were alike. When the Sheikh replied that he did not like the righteous and wanted to see Said's identity card to make sure that

Said was really a sinner, Said handed him the revolver, explaining that every missing bullet meant a murder, but the Sheikh insisted on seeing his card; the government instructions, he said, were stringent on this point. Said was astounded: why did the government interfere with the affairs of the order? he asked. The Sheikh informed him that it had all resulted from a suggestion by their great authority Rauf Ilwan, who had been nominated for the post of Supreme Sheikh. Stunned with amazement for the third time, Said protested that Rauf was nothing but a traitor who had only criminal thoughts, and the Sheikh retorted that that was why he'd been recommended for this responsible position. He added that Rauf had promised to offer a new exegesis of the Holy Koran, giving all possible interpretations, so as to benefit each man according to his purchasing power; the money this beneficent move would bring in would be invested in setting up clubs for shooting, hunting, and committing suicide. Said declared that he was prepared to act as treasurer for the new Exegesis Administration and that Rauf Ilwan would no doubt testify to his integrity as one of his brightest former pupils. At that point the Sheikh intoned the opening chapter of the Koran, lanterns were suspended from the trunk of the palm tree, and a reciter chanted, "Blessed be ye, O people of Egypt, our lord Husayn is now yours."

When he opened his eyes the whole world looked red, empty and meaningless. The Sheikh sat in repose, everything about him, from his loose garment to his skullcap and beard, a shiny white, and at Said's first movement the Sheikh turned his gaze on him. Said sat up hurriedly and looked apologetic, assailed by memories that rushed into his mind like roaring flames.

"It is now late afternoon," said the Sheikh, "and you haven't had a bite of food."

Said looked first at the hole in the wall, then at the Sheikh, and muttered absentmindedly, "Late afternoon!"

"Yes. I thought to myself: Let him sleep. God presents His gifts as His will alone decides."

Said was suddenly troubled. He wondered if anybody had seen him asleep there all day. "I was aware of many people coming in while I was asleep," he lied.

"You were aware of nothing. But one man brought me my lunch, another came to sweep the place, water the cactus, tend the palm tree, and get the courtyard ready for God's loving worshippers."

"What time are they coming?" he said, a little worried.

"At sunset. When did you arrive?"

"At dawn."

The Sheikh sat silent for a while, stroking his beard, then said, "You are very wretched, my son!"

"Why?" said Said, anxious to know the answer.

"You've had a long sleep, but you know no rest. Just like a child laid under the fire of the blazing sun. Your burning heart yearns for shade, yet continues forward under the fire of the sun. Haven't you learned to walk yet?"

Said rubbed his bloodshot almond-shaped eyes. "It's a disturbing thought, to be seen asleep by others."

"The world is unaware of him who is unaware of it," the Sheikh replied, showing no concern.

Said's hand passed lightly over the pocket where he kept the revolver. He wondered what the Sheikh would do if he were to point his gun at him. Would his maddening composure be shaken?

"Are you hungry?" the Sheikh asked.

"No."

"If it is true that man can be poor in God, so is it true man can be rich in Him," the Sheikh went on, his eyes almost smiling.

If, that is, the first proposition is indeed true! thought Said. "Well then, Master," he said lightly, "what would you have done if you'd been afflicted with a wife like mine and if your daughter had rejected you as mine has me?"

A look of pity appeared in the old man's clear eyes. "God's slave is owned by God alone!"

Cut off your tongue before it betrays you and confesses your crime! You wish to tell him everything. He probably doesn't need to be told. He may even have seen you fire the gun. And he may be able to see much more than that.

A voice outside the window hawked *The Sphinx*. Said got up at once, walked to the window, called the newspaper boy, handed him a small coin, and returned with the paper to where he'd been sitting, forgetting all about the Sheikh, his eyes riveted to a huge black headline: "Dastardly Murder in the Citadel Quarter!" He devoured the lines beneath in a flash, not understanding anything. Was this another murder? His own picture was there and so were pictures of Nabawiyya and Ilish Sidra, but who was that bloodstained man? His own life story was staring at him, too, sensational doings blown in every direction like dust in a whirlwind—the story of a man who came out of prison to find his wife married to one of his underlings. But who was the bloodstained man? How had his bullet entered this stranger's chest? This victim was someone else, and Said was seeing him for the first time in his life. *You'd better start reading again.*

The same day he'd visited them with the detective and

Ilish's friends, Ilish Sidra and Nabawiyya had moved out of their flat and another family had moved in, so the voice he'd heard had not been Ilish Sidra's nor had the screams been Nabawiyya's. The body was that of one Shaban Husayn, the new tenant, who'd worked in a haberdashery in Sharia Muhammad Ali. Said Mahran had come to murder his wife and his old friend, but had killed the new tenant instead. A neighbor testified that he'd seen Said Mahran leaving the house after the murder and that he'd shouted for the police but his voice had been lost in the din that had filled the entire street.

A failure. It was insane. And pointless. The rope would be after him now, while Ilish sat safe and secure. The truth was as clear as the bottom of an open tomb.

He tore his eyes away from the paper and found the Sheikh staring through the window at the sky, smiling. The smile, for some reason or other, frightened Said: he wished he could stand at the window and look at exactly the same bit of sky the Sheikh was looking at so he could see what it was that made him smile. But the wish was unfulfilled.

Let the Sheikh smile and keep his secret, he thought. Before long the disciples would be here and some of them who'd seen the picture in the paper might recognize him; thousands and thousands would be gaping at his picture now, in a mixture of terror and titillation. Said's life was finished, spent to no purpose; he was a hunted man and would be to the end of his days; he was alone, and would have to beware of even his own reflection in a mirror—alive but without real life. Like a mummy. He'd have to flee like a rat from one hole to another, threatened by poison, cats, and the clubs of disgusted human beings, suffering all this while his enemies kicked up their heels.

The Sheikh turned to him, saying gently, "You are tired. Go and wash your face."

"Yes," Said said irritably, folding up the paper. "I'll go—and relieve you of the sight of my face."

With even greater gentleness, the Sheikh said, "This is your home."

"True, but why shouldn't I have another place of shelter?"

The Sheikh bowed his head, replying, "If you had another you would never have come to me."

You must go up the hill and stay there until dark. Avoid the light. Shelter in the dark. Hell, it's all a waste of time. You've killed Shaban Husayn. I wonder who you are, Shaban. We never knew each other. Did you have children? Did you ever imagine that one day you would be killed for no reason—that you'd be killed because Nabawiyya Sulayman married Ilish Sidra? That you'd be killed in error but Ilish, Nabawiyya, and Rauf would not be killed in justice? I, the murderer, understand nothing. Not even Sheikh Ali al-Jumaydi himself can understand anything. I've tried to solve part of the riddle, but have only succeeded in unearthing an even greater one. He sighed aloud.

"How tired you are," said the Sheikh.

"And it is your world that makes me tired!"

"That is what we sing of sometimes," the Sheikh said placidly.

Said rose, then said, as he was about to go, "Farewell, my Master."

"Utterly meaningless words, whatever you intend by them," the Sheikh remonstrated. "Say rather: until we meet again."

NINE

God it's dark! I'd be better off like a bat. Why is that smell of hot fat seeping out from under some door at this hour of the night? When will Nur be back? Will she come alone? And can I stay in her flat long enough to be forgotten? You might perhaps be thinking you've got rid of me forever now, Rauf! But with this revolver, if I have any luck, I can do wonderful things. With this revolver I can awake those who are asleep. They're the root of the trouble. They're the ones who've made creatures like Nabawiyya, Ilish, and Rauf Ilwan possible.

There was a sound like footsteps climbing the stairs. When he was sure he heard someone coming, he crouched and looked down through the banisters. A faint light was moving slowly along the wall. The light of a match, he thought. The footsteps came higher, heavy and slow. To let her know he was there and to avoid surprising her, he cleared his throat with a loud rasp.

"Who is it?" she said apprehensively.

Said leaned his head out between the banisters as far as he could and replied in a whisper, "Said Mahran."

She ran the rest of the way up and stopped in front of him out of breath. The match was almost out.

"It's you!" she said, breathless and happy, seizing his arm. "I'm sorry. Have you been waiting long?"

Opening the door to the flat, she led him in by the arm, switched on the light in a bare rectangular hall, then drew him into a reception room, square and somewhat larger, where she rushed to the window and flung it open wide to release the stifling air.

"It was midnight when I got here," he said, flinging himself down on one of two sofas that stood face to face. "I've waited for ages."

She sat down opposite him, moving a pile of scraps of cloth and dress cuttings. "You know what?" she said. "I'd given up hope. I didn't think you'd really come."

Their tired eyes met. "Even after my definite promise?" he said, hiding his frozen feelings with a smile.

She smiled back faintly, without answering. Then she said, "Yesterday they kept questioning me at the police station over and over. They nearly killed me. Where's the car?"

"I thought I'd better dump it somewhere, even though I need it." He took off his jacket and tossed it on the sofa next to him. His brown shirt was caked with sweat and dust. "They'll find it and give it back to its owner, as you'd expect of a government that favors some thieves more than others."

"What did you do with it yesterday?"

"Nothing whatever, in fact. Anyway, you'll know everything at the proper time." He gazed at the open window, took a deep breath, and said, "It must face north. Really fresh air."

"It's open country from here to Bab al-Noor. All around here is the cemetery."

"That's why the air isn't polluted," he said with a grin. *She's looking at you as if she could eat you up, but you only feel bored, annoyed. Why can't you stop brooding over your wounded pride and enjoy her?*

"I'm terribly sorry you had to wait so long on the landing."

"Well, I'm going to be your guest for quite some time," he said, giving her a strange, scrutinizing look.

She lifted her head, raised her chin, and said happily, "Stay here all your life, if you like."

"Until I move over to the neighbors'!" he said with another grin, pointing through the window. She seemed preoccupied. She didn't seem to hear his joke. "Won't your people ask about you?" she said.

"I have no people," he replied, looking down at his gym shoes.

"I mean your wife."

She means pain and fury and wasted bullets! What she wants is to hear a humiliating confession; she'll only find that a locked heart becomes increasingly difficult to unlock. But what is the point of lying when the newspapers are screaming with sensation?

"I said I have no people." *Now you're wondering what my words mean. Your face is beaming with happiness. But I hate this joy. And I can see now that your face has lost whatever bloom it had, particularly under the eyes.*

"Divorced?" she asked.

"Yes. When I was in jail. But let's close the subject," he said, waving his hand impatiently.

"The bitch!" she said angrily. "A man like you deserves to be waited for, even if he's been sent up for life!"

How sly she is! But a man like me doesn't like to be pitied. Beware of sympathy! "The truth is that I neglected her far too much." What a waste for bullets to strike the innocent!

"Anyway, she isn't the kind of woman who deserves you."

True. Neither is any other woman. But Nabawiyya's still full of vitality, while you're hovering on the brink: one puff of wind would be enough to blow you out. You only arouse pity in me. "No one must know I am here."

Laughing, as if sure she possessed him forever, she said, "Don't worry; I'll keep you hidden all right." Then, hopefully, she added, "But you haven't done anything really serious, have you?"

He dismissed the question by shrugging nonchalantly.

She stood up and said, "I'll get some food for you. I do have food and drink. Do you remember how cold you used to be to me?"

"I had no time for love then."

She eyed him reproachfully. "Is anything more important than love? I often wondered if your heart wasn't made of stone. When you went to jail, no one grieved as much as I did."

"That's why I came to you instead of anybody else."

"But you only ran into me by chance," she said with a pout. "You might even have forgotten all about me!"

"Do you think I can't find anywhere else?" he said, framing his face into a scowl.

As if to head off an outburst, she came up close to him and took his cheeks between the palms of her hands. "The guards at the zoo won't let visitors tease the lion. I'd forgotten that. Please forgive me. But your face is burning and your beard is bristly. Why not have a cold shower?" His smile showed her he welcomed the idea. "Off you go to the bathroom, then! When you come out you'll find some food ready. We'll eat in the bedroom, it's much nicer than this room. It looks out over the cemetery, too."

What a lot of graves there are, laid out as far as the eye can see. Their headstones are like hands raised in surrender, though they are beyond being threatened by anything. A city of silence and truth, where success and failure, murderer and victim, come together, where thieves and policemen lie side by side in peace for the first and last time.

Nur's snoring seemed likely to end only when she awoke in late afternoon.

You'll stay in this prison until the police forget you. And will they ever really forget? The graves remind you that death cheats the living. They speak of betrayal; and thus they make you remember Nabawiyya, Ilish, and Rauf, telling you that you yourself are dead, ever since that unseeing bullet was fired.

But you still have bullets of fire.

At the sound of Nur's yawning, loud, like a groan, he turned away from the window shutters toward the bed. Nur was sitting up, naked, her hair disheveled, looking unrested and run-down. But she smiled as she said, "I dreamed you were far away and I was going out of my mind waiting for you."

"That was a dream," he observed grimly. "In fact, you're the one who's going out and I'm the one who'll wait."

She went into the bathroom, emerged again drying her hair; and he followed her hands as they re-created her face in a new form, happy and young. She was, like himself, thirty years old, but she lied outright, hoping to appear younger, adding to the multitude of sins and sillinesses which are openly committed. But theft, unfortunately, was not one of them.

"Don't forget the papers," he reminded her at the door.

When she'd gone he moved into the reception room and flung himself down on one of the sofas. Now he was alone in the full sense of the word, without even his books, which he'd left with Sheikh Ali. He stared up at the cracked white ceiling, a dull echo of the threadbare carpet, killing time. The setting sun flashed through the open window, like a jewel being carried by a flight of doves from one point in time to the next.

Your coldness, Sana, was very disquieting. Like seeing these graves. I don't know if we'll meet again, or where or when. You'll certainly never love me now. Not in this life, so full of badly aimed bullets, desires gone astray. What's left behind is a dangling chain of regrets. The first link was the students' hostel on the road to Giza. Ilish didn't matter much, but Nabawiyya—she'd shaken him, torn him up by the roots. If only a deceit could be as plainly read in the face as fever or an infectious disease! Then beauty would never be false and many a man would be spared the ravages of deception.

That grocery near the students' hostel, where Naba-

wiyya used to come shopping, gripping her bowl. She was always so nicely dressed, much neater than the other servant girls, which was why she'd been known as the "Turkish lady's maid." The rich, proud old Turkish woman, who lived alone at the end of the road, in a house at the center of a big garden, insisted that everyone who worked for her should be good-looking, clean, and well dressed. So Nabawiyya always appeared with her hair neatly combed and plaited in a long pigtail, and wearing slippers. Her peasant's gown flowed around a sprightly and nimble body, and even those not bewitched by her agreed that she was a fine example of country beauty with her dark complexion, her round, full face, her brown eyes, her small chubby nose, and her lips moist with the juices of life. There was a small green tattoo mark on her chin like a beauty spot.

You used to stand at the entrance to the students' hostel and wait for her after work, staring up the street until her fine form with her adorable gait appeared in the distance. As she stepped closer and closer, you'd glow with anticipation. She was like some lovely melody, welcomed wherever she went. As she slipped in among the dozens of women standing at the grocer's, your eyes would follow her, drunk with ecstasy. She'd disappear and emerge again, your desire and curiosity increasing all the time—so did your impulse to do something, no matter what, by word, gesture, or invocation—and she'd move off on her way home, to disappear for the rest of the day and another whole night. And you'd let out a long, bitter sigh and your elation would subside; the birds in the roadside trees would cease their song and a cold autumn breeze would suddenly spring up from nowhere.

But then you notice that her form is reacting to your stare, that she's swaying coquettishly as she walks, and you stand there no longer, but, with your natural impetuosity, hurry after her along the road. Then at the lone palm tree at the edge of the fields you bar her way. She's dumbfounded by your audacity, or pretends to be, and asks you indignantly who you might be. You reply in feigned surprise, "Who might I be? You really ask who I am? Don't you know? I'm known to every inch of your being!"

"I don't like ill-mannered people!" she snaps.

"Neither do I. I'm like you, I hate ill-mannered people. Oh no. On the contrary, I admire good manners, beauty, and gentleness. And all of those things are you! You still don't know who I am? I must carry that basket for you and see you to the door of your house."

"I don't need your help," she says, "and don't ever stand in my way again!" With that she walks away, but with you at her side, encouraged by the faint smile slipping through her pretense of indignation, which you receive like the first cool breeze on a hot and sultry night. Then she had said, "Go back; you must! My mistress sits at the window and if you come one step more she'll see you."

"But I'm a very determined fellow," you reply, "and if you want me to go back, you'll have to come along with me. Just a few steps. Back to the palm tree. You see, I've got to talk to you. And why shouldn't I? Am I not respectable enough?"

She shakes her head vigorously, but, murmuring an angry protest, she does slow down, her neck arched like an angry cat's. She did slow down and I no longer doubt I've won, that Nabawiyya is not indifferent and knows very well how I stand sighing there at the students' hostel. You know that casual stares in the street will become something big in your life, in hers, and in the world at large, too, which would grow larger as a result.

"Till tomorrow, then," you say, stopping there, afraid for her, afraid of the biting tongue of the old Turk who lives like an enigma at the bottom of the street. So you return to the palm tree and climb it, quick as a monkey, out of sheer high spirits, then jump down again, from ten feet up, into a plot of green. Then you go back to the hostel, singing, in your deep voice, like a bull in ecstasy.

And later, when circumstances sent you to al-Zayyat Circus, to work that took you from quarter to quarter, village to village, you feared that "out of sight, out of mind" might well be applied to you and you asked her to marry you. Yes, you asked her to marry you, in the good old legal, traditional Muslim way, standing outside the university that you had—unfairly—been unable to enter, though so many fools did. There was no light in the street or the sky, just a big crescent moon over the horizon. Gazing shyly down at the ground, her forehead reflecting the pale moonlight, she seemed full of happiness. You told her about your good wages, your excellent prospects, and your neat ground-floor flat in Darrasa, on Jabal Road, near Sheikh Ali's house. "You'll get to know the godly Sheikh," you said, "when we marry. And we've got to have the wedding as soon as possible. After all, our love has lasted quite a while already. You'll have to leave the old lady now."

"I'm an orphan, you know. There's only my aunt at Sidi al-Arbain."

"That's fine."

Then you kissed her under the crescent moon. The wedding was so lovely that everyone talked about it ever after.

From Zayyat I got a wedding present of ten pounds. Ilish Sidra seemed absolutely overjoyed at it all, as if it was his own wedding, playing the part of the faithful friend while he was really no friend at all. And the oddest thing of all is that you were taken in by him—you, clever old you, smart enough to scare the devil himself, you the hero and Ilish your willing slave, admiring, flattering, and doing everything to avoid upsetting you, happy to pick up the scraps of your labor, your smartness. You were sure you could have sent him and Nabawiyya off together alone, into the very deserts where our Lord Moses wandered, and that all the time he'd keep seeing you between himself and her and would never step out of line. How could she ever give up a lion and take to a dog? She's rotten to the core, rotten enough to deserve death and damnation. For sightless bullets not to stray, blindly missing their vile and evil targets, and hit innocent people, leaving others torn with remorse and rage and on the verge of insanity. Compelled to forget everything good in life, the way you used to play as a kid in the street, innocent first love, your wedding night, Sana's birth and seeing her little face, hearing her cry, carrying her in your arms for the first time. All the smiles you never counted—how you wish you'd counted them. And how she looked—you wish it was one of the things you've forgotten—when she was frightened, that screaming of hers that shook the ground and made springs and breezes dry up. All the good feelings that ever were.

The shadows are lengthening now. It's getting dark in the room and outside the window. The silence of the graves is more intense, but you can't switch on the light. The flat must look the way it always has when Nur is out. Your eyes will get used to the dark, the way they did to prison and all those ugly faces. And you can't start drink-

ing, either, lest you bump into something or shout out loud. The flat must stay as silent as the grave; even the dead mustn't know you're here. God alone can tell how long you'll have to stay here and how patient in this jail. Just as He alone could tell you'd kill Shaban Husayn and not Ilish Sidra.

Well, you'll have to go out sooner or later, to take a walk in the night, even if only to safe places. But let's postpone that until the police are worn out looking for you. And let's hope to God Shaban Husayn isn't buried in one of these graves here; this run-down quarter could hardly stand the strain of such a painful irony of fate. Just keep cool, keep patient, until Nur comes back. You must not ask when Nur will come back. You'll have to put up with the dark, the silence, and the loneliness—for as long as the world refuses to change its naughty ways. Nur, poor girl, is caught in it, too. What, after all, is her love for you but a bad habit, getting stuck on someone who's already dead of pain and anger, is put off by her affection no less than by her ageing looks, who doesn't really know what to do with her except maybe drink with her, toasting, as it were, defeat and grief, and pity her for her worthy but hopeless efforts. And in the end you can't even forget she's a woman. Like that slinking bitch Nabawiyya, who'll be in mortal fear until the rope's safely installed around your neck or some rotten bullet is lodged in your heart. And the police will tell such lies that you'll be cut off forever from Sana. She'll never even know the truth of your love for her, as if that, too, was just a bullet that went astray.

Sleep came over Said Mahran and he dozed off for a while on the sofa, unaware that he had been dreaming in his sleep until he awoke, to find himself in complete darkness, still alone in Nur's flat in Sharia Najm al-Din, where

Ilish Sidra had not surprised him and had not fired a hail of bullets at him. He had no idea what time it was.

Suddenly he heard the rattle of a key in the lock and then the door being closed. A light in the hallway went on and filtered in above the door. Nur came in smiling, carrying a big parcel. She kissed him and said, "Let's have a feast! I've brought home a restaurant, a delicatessen, and a patisserie all in one!"

"You've been drinking," he said as he kissed her.

"I have to; it's part of my job. I'll take a bath, then come back. Here are the papers for you."

His eyes followed her as she left, then he buried himself in the newspapers, both morning and evening. There was nothing that was news to him, but there was clearly enormous interest in both the crime and its perpetrator, far more than he'd expected, especially in *Al-Zahra*, Rauf Ilwan's paper. It discussed at length his history as a burglar and the list of the exploits revealed at his trial, with stories about the great houses of the rich he had burglarized, comments on his character, his latent insanity, and an analysis of "the criminal boldness that finally led to bloodshed."

What enormous black headlines! Thousands upon thousands must be discussing his crimes at that moment, all amused at Nabawiyya's infidelity and laying bets as to what his fate would be. He was the very center of the news, the man of the hour, and the thought filled him with both apprehension and pride, conflicting emotions that were so intense they almost tore him apart. Meanwhile, so many other thoughts and ideas crowded in confusion into his mind that a kind of intoxication seemed to engulf him. He felt sure he was about to do something truly extraordinary, even miraculous; and he wished he could somehow communicate with all the people outside, to tell them what was making him—there all alone in the silence—burst with emotion, to convince them that he'd win in the end, even if only after death.

He was quite alone, separate from everyone else. They didn't even know, did not comprehend the language of silence and solitude. They didn't understand that they themselves were silent and alone sometimes, and that the mirrors dimly reflecting their own images were in fact deceptive, making them falsely imagine they were seeing people unknown to themselves.

His mind's eye focused on the photograph of Sana with a sense of wonder, and he was deeply moved. Then, in his imagination, he conjured up all their pictures—his own wild-looking self, Nabawiyya, looking like a whore—coming back to the picture of Sana. She was smiling. Yes. Smiling. Because she could not see him and because she knew nothing. He scrutinized her intensely, overwhelmed by the sense that he'd failed, that the night out there through the window was sighing in some kind of sympathetic sadness, desperately wishing he could run away with her to some place known to no one else. He yearned to see her, if only as his last wish on earth before his execution.

He went over to the other sofa to pick up the scissors lying on a pile of pieces of fabric, then returned to snip the picture carefully out of the newspaper. By the time Nur emerged from the bathroom he felt calmer. When she called him, he went into the bedroom, wondering how she could have brought him all those news reports and know nothing of them herself.

She'd spent a lot of money. As he sat by her side on a sofa, facing the food-covered table, his mouth watered, and to show his pleasure he stroked her moist hair and murmured, "You know, there aren't many women like you."

She tied a red scarf around her head and began filling the glasses, smiling at the compliment. To see her sitting there, proud and confident of having him, if only for a while, made him feel somehow glad. She was wearing no makeup over her light brown skin and she looked invigorated from her bath, like a dish of good food, somehow, modest and fresh.

"You can say things like that!" she said, giving him a quizzical stare. "Sometimes I almost think the police know more about kindness than you."

"No, do believe me, I'm happy being with you."

"Truly?"

"Yes. Truly. You're so kind, so good. I don't know why anyone could resist you."

"Wasn't I like that in the old days?"

No easy victory can ever make one forget a bloody defeat! "At that time, I just wasn't an affectionate person."

"And now?"

"Let's have a drink and enjoy ourselves," he said, picking up his glass.

They set about the food and drink with gusto, until she said, "How did you spend your time?"

"Between the shadows and the graves," he said, dipping a piece of meat in tahini. "Do you have any family buried here?"

"No, mine are all buried in al-Balyana, God rest their souls."

Only the sounds of their eating and the clink of glasses and dishes on the tray broke the silence, until Said said, "I'm going to ask you to buy some cloth for me—something suitable for an officer's uniform."

"An army officer?"

"You didn't know I learned tailoring in jail?"

"But why do you want it?" she said uneasily.

"Ah, well, the time has come for me to do my military service."

"Don't you understand I don't want to lose you again?"

"Don't worry about me at all," he said with extraordinary confidence. "If no one had given me away the police would never have caught me."

Nur sighed, still troubled.

"You're not in any danger yourself, are you?" Said asked, grinning, his mouth stuffed with food. "No highwayman's going to waylay you in the desert, right?"

They laughed together, and she leaned over and kissed him full on the lips. Their lips were equally sticky.

"The truth is," she said, "that to live at all we've got to be afraid of nothing."

"Not even death?" Said said, nodding toward the window.

"Listen, I even forget that, too, when time brings me together with someone I love."

Astonished at the strength and tenacity of her affection, Said relaxed and let himself feel a mixture of compassion, respect, and gratitude toward Nur.

A moth overhead made love to a naked light bulb in the dead of the night.

ELEVEN

Not a day passes without the graveyard welcoming new guests. Why, it's as though there's nothing more left to do but crouch behind the shutters watching these endless progressions of death. It's the mourners who deserve one's sympathy, of course. They come in one weeping throng and then they go away drying their tears and conversing, as if while they're here some force stronger than death itself has convinced them to stay alive.

That was how your own parents were buried: your father, Amm Mahran, the kindly concierge of the student's hostel, who died middle-aged after a hard but honest and satisfying life. You helped him in his work from your childhood on. For all the extreme simplicity, even poverty of their lives, the family enjoyed sitting together when the day's work was done, in their ground-floor room at the entrance to the building, where Amm Mahran and his wife would chat together while their child played. His piety made him happy, and the students respected him. The only entertainment he knew was making pilgrimage to the

home of Sheikh Ali al-Junaydi, and it was through your
father that you came to know the house. "Come along,"
he'd say, "and I'll show you how to have more fun than
playing in the fields. You'll see how sweet life can be, what
it's like in an atmosphere of godliness. It'll give you a sense
of peace and contentment, the finest thing you can achieve
in life."

The Sheikh greeted you with that sweet and kindly look
of his. And how enchanted you were by his fine white
beard! "So this is your son you were telling me about," he
said to your father. "There's a lot of intelligence in his eyes.
His heart is as spotless as yours. You'll find he'll turn out,
with God's will, a truly good man." Yes, you really adored
Sheikh Ali al-Junaydi, attracted by the purity in his face
and the love in his eyes. And those songs and chants of his
had delighted you even before your heart was purified by
love.

"Tell this boy what it's his duty to do," your father said
to the Sheikh one day.

The Sheikh had gazed down at you and said, "We continue learning from the cradle to the grave, but at least
start out, Said, by keeping close account of yourself and
making sure that from whatever action you initiate some
good comes to someone."

Yes, you certainly followed his counsel as best you
could, though you only brought it to complete fulfillment
when you took up burglary!

The days passed like dreams. And then your good father
disappeared, suddenly gone, in a way that a boy simply
could not comprehend, and that seemed to baffle even
Sheikh Ali himself. How shocked you were that morning,
shaking your head and rubbing your eyes to clear away the
sleep, awakened by your mother's screams and tears in the

little room at the entrance to the student's hostel! You wept with fear and frustration at your helplessness. That evening, however, Rauf Ilwan, at that time a student in law school, had shown how very capable he was. Yes, he was impressive all right, no matter what the circumstances, and you loved him as you did Sheikh Ali, perhaps even more. It was he who later worked hard to have you—or you and your mother, to be more precise—take over Father's job as custodian for the building. Yes, you took on responsibilities at an early age.

And then your mother died. You almost died yourself during your mother's illness, as Rauf Ilwan must surely remember, from that unforgettable day when she had hemorrhaged and you had rushed her to the nearest hospital, the Sabir Hospital, standing like a castle amidst beautiful grounds, where you found yourself and your mother in a reception hall at an entrance more luxurious than anything you could ever have imagined possible. The entire place seemed forbidding, even hostile, but you were in the direst need of help, immediate help.

As the famous doctor was coming out of a room, they mentioned his name and you raced toward him in your gallabiya and sandals, shouting, "My mother! The blood!"

The man had fixed you in a glassy, disapproving stare and had glanced where your mother was lying, stretched out in her filthy dress on a soft couch, a foreign nurse standing nearby, observing the scene. Then the doctor had simply disappeared, saying nothing. The nurse jabbered something in a language you did not understand, though you sensed she was expressing sympathy for your tragedy. At that point, for all your youth, you flew into a real adult's rage, screaming and cursing in protest, smashing a chair to the floor with a crash, so the veneer wood on its *back broke in pieces. A horde of servants had appeared and you'd soon found yourself and your mother alone in the tree-lined road outside. A month later your mother had died in the Kasr al-Aini Hospital.*

All the time she lay close to death she never released your hand, refusing to take her eyes off you. It was during that long month of illness, however, that you stole for the first time—from the country boy resident in the hostel, who'd accused you without any investigation and was beating you vigorously when Rauf Ilwan turned up and freed you, settling the matter without any further complications. You were a true human being then, Rauf, and you were my teacher, too.

Alone with you Rauf had said quietly, "Don't you worry. The fact is, I consider this theft perfectly justified. Only you'll find the police watching for you, and the judge won't be lenient with you," he'd added ominously with bitter sarcasm, "however convincing your motives, because he, too, will be protecting himself. Isn't it justice," he'd shouted, "that what is taken by theft should be retrieved by theft? Here I am studying, away from home and family, suffering daily from hunger and deprivation!"

Where have all your principles gone now, Rauf? Dead, no doubt, like my father and my mother, and like my wife's fidelity.

You had no alternative but to leave the students' hostel and seek a living somewhere else. So you waited under the lone palm tree at the end of the green plot until Nabawiyya came and you sprang toward her, saying, "Don't be afraid. I must speak to you. I'm leaving to get a better job. I love you. Don't ever forget me. I love you and always will. And I'll prove I can make you happy and give you a respectable home." Yes, those had been times when sorrows could be forgotten, wounds could be healed, and hope could bring forth fruit from adversity.

All you graves out there, immersed in the gloom, don't jeer at my memories!

He sat up on the sofa, still in the dark, addressing Rauf Ilwan just as though he could see him standing in front of him. "You should have agreed to get me a job writing for your newspaper, you scoundrel. I'd have published our mutual reminiscences there, I'd have shut off your false light good and proper." Then he wondered aloud: "How am I going to stand it here in the dark till Nur comes back near dawn?"

Suddenly he was attacked by an irresistible urge to leave the house and take a walk in the dark. In an instant, his resistance crumbled, collapsing like a building ready to give way; soon he was moving stealthily out of the house. He set off toward Sharia Masani and from there turned toward open wasteland.

Leaving his hideout made him all the more conscious of being hunted. He now knew how mice and foxes feel, slipping away on the run. Alone in the dark, he could see the city's lights glimmering in the distance, lying in wait for him. He quaffed his sense of being alone, until it intoxicated him, then walked on, winding up at last in his old seat next to Tarzan in the coffeehouse. The only other person inside apart from the waiter was an arms smuggler, although outside, a little lower down, at the foot of the hill, the sounds of people talking could be heard.

The waiter brought him some tea at once and then Tarzan leaned over. "Don't spend more than one night in the same place," he whispered.

The smuggler added his advice: "Move way up the Nile."

"But I don't know anyone up there," Said objected.

"You know," the smuggler went on, "I've heard many people express their admiration for you."

"And the police?" Tarzan said heatedly. "Do they admire him, too?"

The smuggler laughed so hard that his whole body shook, as if he were mounted on a camel at the gallop. "Nothing impresses the police," he said at last, when he'd recovered his breath.

"Absolutely nothing," agreed Said.

"But what harm is there in stealing from the rich anyway?" the waiter asked with feeling.

Said beamed as if he were receiving a compliment at some public reception in his honor. "Yes," he said, "but the newspapers have tongues longer than a hangman's rope. And what good does being liked by the people do if the police loathe you?"

Suddenly Tarzan got up, moved to the window, stared outside, looking to left and right, then came back. "I thought I saw a face staring in at us," he reported, clearly worried.

Said's eyes glinted as they darted back and forth between window and door and the waiter went outside to investigate.

"You're always seeing things that aren't there," the smuggler said.

Enraged, Tarzan yelled at him, "Shut up, will you! You seem to think a hangman's rope is some sort of a joke!"

Said left the coffeehouse. Clutching the revolver in his pocket, walking off into the open darkness, he looked cautiously around him, listening as he went. His consciousness of fear, of being alone and hunted, was even stronger now and he knew he must not underestimate his enemies, fearful themselves, but so eager to catch him that they would not rest till they saw him a corpse, laid out and still.

As he neared the house in Sharia Najm al-Din he saw light in Nur's window. It gave him a sense of security for the first time since he'd left the coffeehouse. He found her lying down and wanted to caress her, but it was obvious from her face that she was terribly tired. Her eyes were red. Clearly, something was wrong. He sat down at her feet.

"Please tell me what's wrong, Nur," he said.

"I'm worn out," she said weakly. "I've vomited so much I'm exhausted."

"Was it drink?"

"I've been drinking all my life," she said, her eyes brimming with tears.

This was the first time Said had seen her cry and he was deeply moved. "What was the reason, then?" he said.

"They beat me!"

"The police?"

"No, some young louts, probably students, when I asked them to pay the bill."

Said was touched. "Why not wash your face," he said, "and drink some water?"

"A little later. I'm too tired now."

"The dogs!" Said muttered, tenderly caressing her leg.

"The fabric for the uniform," Nur said, pointing to a parcel on the other sofa. He made a gesture with his hand affectionately and in gratitude.

"I can't look very attractive for you tonight," she said almost apologetically.

"It's not your fault. Just wash your face and get some sleep."

Up in the graveyard heights a dog barked and Nur let

out a long, audible sigh. "And she said, 'You have such a rosy future!'" she murmured sadly.

"Who?"

"A fortune-teller. She said there'd be security, peace of mind." Said stared out at the blackness of night piled up outside the window as she went on: "When will that ever be? It's been such a long wait, and all so useless. I have a girlfriend, a little older than me, who always says we'll become just bones or even worse than that, so that even dogs will loathe us." Her voice seemed to come from the very grave and so depressed Said that he could find nothing to say in reply. "Some fortune-teller!" she said. "When is she going to start telling the truth? Where is there any security? I just want to sleep safe and secure, wake up feeling good, and have a quiet, pleasant time. Is that so impossible—for him who raised the Seven Heavens?"

You, too, used to dream of a life like that, but it's all been spent climbing up drainpipes, jumping down from roofs, and being chased in the dark, with badly aimed bullets killing innocent people.

"You need to get some sleep," he told her, thoroughly depressed.

"What I need is a promise," she said. "A promise from the fortune-teller. And that day will come."

"Good."

"You're treating me like a child," she said angrily.

"Never."

"That day really will come!"

T W E L V E

Nur watched him as he tried on the uniform, staring at him in surprised delight, until he'd done up the last button. Then, after a moment or two, she said, "Do be sensible. I couldn't bear to lose you again."

"This was a good idea," Said said, displaying his work and examining his reflection in the mirror. "I suppose I'd better be satisfied with the rank of captain!"

By the next evening, however, she'd heard all about his recent dramatic adventure and seen pictures of him in a copy of a weekly magazine belonging to one of her transient male companions. She broke down in front of him. "You've killed someone!" she said, letting out the words with a wail of despair. "How terrible! Didn't I plead with you?"

"But it happened before we met," he said, caressing her.

She looked away. "You don't love me," she said wanly. "I know that. But at least we could have lived together until you did love me!"

"But we can still do that."

"What's the use," she said, almost crying, "when you've committed murder?"

"We can run away together," Said said with a reassuring grin. "It's easy."

"What are we waiting for, then?"

"For the storm to blow over."

Nur stamped her foot in frustration. "But I've heard that there are troops blocking all the exits from Cairo, as if you were the first murderer ever!"

The newspapers! Said thought. All part of the secret war! But he hid his feelings and showed her only his outward calm. "I'll get away all right," he said, "as soon as I decide to. You'll see." Pretending a sudden rage, he gripped her by the hair and snarled: "Don't you know yet who Said Mahran is? All the papers are talking about him! You still don't believe in him? Listen to me; we'll live together forever. And you'll see what the fortune-teller told you come true!"

Next evening, escaping from his loneliness and hoping for news, he slipped out again to Tarzan's coffeehouse, but as soon as he appeared in the doorway Tarzan hurried over and took him out into the open, some distance off. "Please, don't be angry with me," he said apologetically. "Even my café is no longer safe for you."

"But I thought the storm had died down now," Said said, the darkness hiding his concern.

"No. It's getting worse all the time. Because of the newspapers. Go into hiding. But forget about trying to get out of Cairo for a while."

"Don't the papers have anything to go on about but Said Mahran?"

"They made such a lot of noise to everyone about your past raids that they've got all the government forces in the area stirred up against you." Said got up to leave. "We can meet again—outside the café—anytime you wish," Tarzan remarked as they said goodbye.

So Said went back to his hideout in Nur's house—the solitude, the dark, the waiting—where he suddenly found himself roaring, "It's you, Rauf, you're behind all this!" By this time, all the papers had dropped his case, all except *Al-Zahra*. It was still busy raking up the past, goading the police; by trying so hard to kill him, in fact, it was making a national hero of him. Rauf Ilwan would never rest until the noose was around his neck, and Rauf had all the forces of repression: the law.

And you. Does your ruined life have any meaning at all unless it is to kill your enemies—Ilish Sidra, whereabouts unknown, and Rauf Ilwan, in his mansion of steel? What meaning will there have been to your life if you fail to teach your enemies a lesson? No power on earth will prevent the punishing of the dogs! That's right! No power on earth!

"Rauf Ilwan," Said pleaded aloud, "tell me how it is that time can bring such terrible changes to people!" *Not just a revolutionary student, but revolution personified as a student. Your stirring voice, pitching itself downward toward my ears as I sat at my father's feet in the courtyard of the building, with a force to awaken the very soul. And you'd talk about princes and pashas, transforming those fine gentlemen with your magic into mere thieves. And to see you on Mudiriyya Road, striding out amidst your men you called your equals as they munched their sugarcane in their flowing gallabiyyas, when your voice would reach such a pitch that it seemed to flow right over the field and make the palm tree bow before it—unforgettable. Yes, there was a strange power in you that I found nowhere else, not even in Sheikh Ali al-Junaydi.*

That's how you were, Rauf. To you alone goes the credit for my father's enrolling me in school. You'd roar with delighted laughter at my success. "Do you see now?" you'd say to my father. "You didn't even want him to get an education. Just you look at those eyes of his; he's going to shake things to their foundations!" You taught me to love reading. You discussed everything with me, as if I were your equal. I was one of your listeners—at the foot of the same tree where the history of my love began—and the times themselves were listening to you, too: "The people! Theft! The holy fire! The rich! Hunger! Justice!"

The day you were imprisoned you rose up in my eyes to the very sky, higher still when you protected me the first time I stole, when your remarks about theft gave me back my self-respect. Then there was the time you told me sadly, "There's no real point in isolated theft; there has to be organization." After that I never stopped either reading or robbing. It was you who gave me the names of people who deserved to be robbed, and it was in theft that I found my glory, my honor. And I was generous to many people, Ilish Sidra among them.

Said shouted in anger to the darkened room: "Are you really the same one? The Rauf Ilwan who owns a mansion? You're the fox behind the newspaper campaign. You, too, want to kill me, to murder your conscience and the past as well. But I won't die before I've killed you: you're the number one traitor. What nonsense life would turn out to be if I were myself killed tomorrow—in retribution for murdering a man I didn't even know! If there's going to be any meaning to life—and to death, too—I simply have to kill you. My last outburst of rage at the evil of the world. And all those things lying out there in the graveyard below the window will help me. As for the rest, I'll leave it to Sheikh Ali to solve the riddle."

Just when the call to the dawn prayers was announced he heard the door open and Nur came in carrying some grilled meat, drinks, and newspapers. She seemed quite happy, having apparently forgotten her two days of distress and depression, and her presence dispelled his own gloom and exhaustion, made him ready again to embrace what life had to offer: food, drink, and news. She kissed him and, for the first time, he responded spontaneously, with a sense of gratitude, knowing her now to be the person closest to him for as long as he might live. He wished she'd never leave.

He uncorked a bottle as usual, poured himself a glass, and drank it down in one gulp.

"Why didn't you get some sleep?" Nur said, peering closely at his tired face.

Flipping through the newspapers, he made no reply.

"It must be torture to wait in the dark," she said, feeling sorry for him.

"How are things outside?" he asked, tossing the papers aside.

"Just like always." She undressed down to her slip and Said smelled powder moistened with sweat. "People are talking about you," she went on, "as if you were some storybook hero. But they don't have any idea what torture we go through."

"Most Egyptians neither fear nor dislike thieves," said Said as he bit into a piece of meat. Several minutes passed in silence while they ate, then he added: "But they do have an instinctive dislike for dogs."

"Well," said Nur with a smile, licking her fingertips, "I like dogs."

"I don't mean that kind of dog."

"Yes, I always had one at home until I saw the last one die. That made me cry a lot and so I decided not to have one again."

"That's right," said Said. "If love's going to cause problems, just steer clear of it."

"You don't understand me. Or love me."

"Don't be like that," he said, pleading. "Can't you see the whole world is cruel enough and unjust enough as it is?"

Nur drank until she could hardly sit up. Her real name was Shalabiyya, she confessed. Then she told him tales of the old days in Balyana, of her childhood amid the quiet waters, of her youth and how she'd run away. "And my father was the *umda*," she said proudly, "the village headman."

"You mean the *umda's* servant!" She frowned, but he went on: "Well, that's what you told me first."

Nur laughed so heartily that Said could see bits of parsley caught in her teeth. "Did I really say that?" she asked.

"Yes. And that's what turned Rauf Ilwan into a traitor."

She stared at him uncomprehendingly. "And who's Rauf Ilwan?"

"Don't lie to me," Said snarled. "A man who has to stay in the dark, waiting by himself, a man like that can't stand lies."

A little after midnight, with a quarter-moon shining faintly in the west, Said headed off across the wasteland. A hundred yards or so from the café he stopped, whistled three times, and stood waiting, feeling that he had to strike his blow or else go mad, hoping that Tarzan would have some information at last.

When Tarzan appeared, moving like a wave of darkness, they embraced and Said asked him, "What's new?"

"One of them's finally turned up," the stout man replied, out of breath from walking.

"Who?" Said asked anxiously.

"It's Bayaza," said Tarzan, still gripping his hand, "and he's in my place now, clinching a deal."

"So my waiting wasn't wasted. Do you know which way he's going?"

"He'll go back by Jabal Road."

"Thanks very much indeed, friend."

Said left quickly, making his way east, guided by the faint moonlight to the clump of trees around the wells. He moved on along the south side of the grove until he reached its tip, ending in the sands where the road up the mountain began. There he crouched behind a tree and waited.

A cool breeze sent a whisper through the grove. It was a desolate, lonely spot. Gripping his revolver hard, he pondered the chance that might now be at hand, to bear down on his enemy and achieve his long-awaited goal. And then death, a final resting place. "Ilish Sidra," he said aloud, heard only by the trees as they drank in the breeze, "and then Rauf Ilwan. Both in one night. After that, let come what may."

Tense, impatient, he did not have long to wait for a figure to come hurrying in the dark from the direction of the café toward the tip of the woods. When there was only a yard or two left between the man and the road, Said leaped out, leveling his revolver.

"Stop!" he roared.

The man stopped as if hit by a bolt of electricity, and stared at Said speechless.

"Bayaza, I know where you were, what you've been doing, how much cash you're carrying."

The man's breath came forth in a hiss and his arm made a slight, hesitant movement, a twitch. "The money's for my children," he gasped.

Said slapped him hard across the face, making him blink. "You still don't recognize me, Bayaza, you dog!"

"Who are you? I know your voice, but I can't believe . . ." Bayaza said, then cried out, "Said Mahran!"

"Don't move! The first move you make, you're dead."

"You kill me? Why? We've no reason to be enemies."

"Well, here's one," muttered Said, stretching his hand to reach into the man's clothing, locating the heavy purse, and ripping it loose.

"But that's my money. I'm not your enemy."

"Shut up. I haven't got all I want yet."

"But we're old pals. That's something you should respect."

"If you want to live, tell me where Ilish Sidra is staying."

"I don't know," Bayaza replied emphatically. "No one knows."

Said slapped him again, harder than before. "I'll kill you if you don't tell me where he is," he shouted. "And you won't get your money back until I know you're telling the truth!"

"I don't know. I swear I don't know," Bayaza whispered.

"You liar!"

"I'll swear any oath you like!"

"You're telling me he's disappeared completely, dissolved like salt in water?"

"I really don't know. No one knows. He moved out right after your visit, afraid of what you might do. I'm telling the truth. He moved to Rod al-Farag."

"His address?"

"Wait, Said," he pleaded. "And after Shaban Husayn was killed he took his family away again. He didn't tell anyone where. He was scared, all right, and his wife was, too. And no one knows anything more about them."

"Bayaza!"

"I swear I'm telling the truth!" Said hit him again, and the man groaned with pain and fear. "Why are you beating me, Said? God damn Sidra wherever he may be; is he my brother or my father that I would die on his account?"

At last, and reluctantly, Said believed him and began to lose hope of ever finding his enemy. If only he wasn't a hunted man, wanted for murder, he would bide his time and wait patiently for the proper opportunity! But that misdirected shot of his had struck at the heart of his own most intense desire.

"You're being unfair to me," said Bayaza. When Said did not reply, he went on: "And what about my money? I never harmed you." He held a hand to the side of his face where Said had struck him. "And you've no right to take my money. We used to work together!"

"And you were always one of Sidra's buddies, too."

"Yes, I was his friend and his partner, but that doesn't mean I'm your enemy. I had nothing to do with what he did to you."

The fight was over now and a retreat was the only course. "Well," Said told him, "I'm in need of some cash."

"Take what you like, then," said Bayaza.

Said was satisfied with ten pounds. The other man left, dazed, as if he scarcely believed his escape, and Said found himself alone again in the desert, the light from the moon brighter now and the whispering of the trees harsher. So Ilish Sidra has slipped out of his clutches, escaped his due punishment, rescued his own treacherous self, adding one to the number of scot-free traitors. Rauf, the only hope I have left is in you, that you won't make me lose my life in vain.

FOURTEEN

By the time Said had returned to the flat, dressed in his officer's uniform, and left, it was well after one o'clock. He turned toward Abbasiyya Street, avoiding the lights and forcing himself to walk very naturally, then took a taxi to Gala's Bridge, passing an unpleasant number of policemen en route.

At the dock near the bridge he rented a small rowboat for two hours and promptly set off in it south, toward Rauf Ilwan's house. It was a fine starry night, a cool breeze blowing, the quarter-moon still visible in the clear sky above the trees along the riverbank. Excited, full of energy, Said felt ready to spring into vigorous action. Ilish Sidra's escape was not a defeat, not as long as punishment was about to descend on Rauf Ilwan. For Rauf, after all, personified the highest standard of treachery, from which people like Ilish and Nabawiyya and all the other traitors on earth sought inspiration.

"It's time to settle accounts, Rauf," he said, pulling hard on the oars. "And if anyone but the police stood as judges between us, I'd teach you a lesson in front of everyone. They, the people, everyone—all the people except the real robbers—are on my side, and that's what will console me in my everlasting perdition. I am, in fact, your soul. You've sacrificed me. I lack organization, as you would put it. I now understand many of the things you used to say that I couldn't comprehend then. And the worst of it is that despite this support from millions of people I find myself driven away into dismal isolation, with no one to help. It's senseless, all of it, a waste. No bullet could clear away its absurdity. But at least a bullet will be right, a bloody protest, something to comfort the living and the dead, to let them hold on to their last shred of hope."

At a point opposite the big house, he turned shoreward, rowed in to the bank, jumped out, pulled the boat up after him until its bow was well up on dry land, then climbed the bank up to the road, where, feeling calm and secure in his officer's uniform, he walked away. The road seemed empty and when he got to the house he saw no sign of guards, which both pleased and angered him. The house itself was shrouded in darkness except for a single light at the entrance, convincing him that the owner was not yet back, that forced entry was unnecessary, and that a number of other difficulties had been removed.

Walking quite casually, he turned down the street along the left side of the house and followed it to its end at Sharia Giza, then he turned along Sharia Giza and proceeded to the other street, passing along the right side of the house, until he regained the riverside, examining everything along the way most carefully. Then he made his way over to a patch of ground shaded from the streetlights by a tree, and stood waiting, his eyes fixed on the house, relaxing them only by gazing out from time to time at the dark surface of the river; his thoughts fled to Rauf's treachery, the deception that had crushed his life, the ruin that was facing him, the death blocking his path, all the things that made Rauf's death an absolute necessity. He watched each car with bated breath as it approached.

Finally one of them stopped before the gate of the house, which was promptly opened by the doorkeeper, and Said darted into the street to the left of the house, keeping close to the wall, stopping at a point opposite the entrance, while the car moved slowly down the drive. It came to a halt in front of the entrance, where the light that had been left on illuminated the whole entranceway. Said took out his revolver now and aimed it carefully as the car door opened and Rauf Ilwan got out.

"Rauf!" Said bellowed. As the man turned in shock toward the source of this shout, Said yelled again: "This is Said Mahran! Take that!"

But before he could fire, a shot from within the garden, whistling past him very close, disturbed his aim. He fired and ducked to escape the next shot, then raised his head in desperate determination, took aim, and fired again.

All this happened in an instant. After one more wild, hasty shot, he sped away as fast as he could run toward the river, pushed the boat out into the water, and leapt into it, rowing toward the opposite bank. Unknown sources deep within him released immediate reserves of physical strength, but his thoughts and emotions swirled as though caught in a whirlpool. He seemed to sense shots being fired, voices of people gathering, and a sudden loss of power in some part of his body, but the distance between the riverbanks was small at that point and he reached the other side, quickly leapt ashore, leaving the boat to drift in the water, and climbed up to the street, clutching the gun in his pocket.

Despite his confused emotions, he proceeded carefully and calmly, looking neither to the right nor to the left. Aware of people rushing down to the water's edge behind him, of confused shouts from the direction of a bridge, and a shrill whistle piercing the night air, he expected a pursuer to accost him at any moment, and he was ready to put all his efforts into either bluffing his way out or entering one last battle. Before anything else could happen, however, a taxi cruised by. He hailed it and climbed in; the piercing pain he felt as soon as he sat back on the seat was nothing compared to the relief of being safe again.

He crept up to Nur's flat in complete darkness and stretched out on one of the sofas, still in his uniform. The pain returned now, and he identified its source, a little above his knee, where he put his hand and felt a sticky liquid, with sharper pain. Had he knocked against something? Or was it a bullet, when he'd been behind the wall perhaps, or running? Pressing fingers all around the wound, he determined that it was only a scratch; if it had been a bullet, it must have grazed him without penetrating.

He got up, took off his uniform, felt for his nightshirt on the sofa, and put it on. Then he walked around the flat testing out the leg, remembering how once he'd run down Sharia Muhammad Ali with a bullet lodged in the leg. "Why, you're capable of miracles," he told himself. "You'll get away all right. With a little coffee powder this wound will bind up nicely."

But had he managed to kill Rauf Ilwan? And who had shot at him from inside the garden? *Let's hope you didn't hit some other poor innocent fellow like before. And Rauf must surely have been killed—you never miss, as you used to demonstrate in target practice out in the desert beyond the hill. Yes, now you can write a letter to the papers: "Why I Killed Rauf Ilwan." That will give back the meaning your life has lost: the bullet that killed Rauf Ilwan will at the same time have destroyed your sense of loss, of waste. A world without morals is like a universe without gravity. I want nothing, long for nothing more than to die a death that has some meaning to it.*

Nur came home worn out, carrying food and drink. She kissed him as usual and smiled a greeting, but her eyes suddenly fastened on his uniform trousers. She put her parcel on the sofa, picked them up, and held them out to him.

"There's blood!" she said.

Said noticed it for the first time. "It's just a minor wound," he said, showing her his leg. "I hit it on the door of a taxi."

"You've been out in that uniform for some specific reason! There's no limit to your madness. You'll kill me with worry!"

"A little bit of coffee powder will cure this wound even before the sun rises."

"My soul rises, you mean! You are simply murdering me! Oh, when will this nightmare end?"

In a burst of nervous energy Nur dressed the wound with powdered coffee, then bound it up with a cutting from fabric she was using to make a dress, complaining about her ill-fortune all the time she worked.

"Why don't you take a shower?" said Said. "It'll make you feel good."

"You don't know good from bad," she said, leaving the room.

By the time she came back to the bedroom, he had

already drunk a third of a bottle of wine and his mood and nerves felt much improved.

"Drink up!" he said as she sat down. "After all, I'm here, all right, in a nice safe place, way out of sight of the police."

"I'm really very depressed," Nur whimpered, combing her wet hair.

"Who can determine the future anyway?" he said, taking a swallow.

"Only our own actions can."

"Nothing, absolutely nothing is certain. Except your being with me, and that's something I can't do without."

"So you say now!"

"And I've got more to say. Being with you, after being out there with bullets tearing after me, is like being in Paradise." Her long sigh in response was deep, as if in self-communion at night; and he went on: "You really are very good to me. I want you to know I'm grateful."

"But I'm so worried. All I want is for you to be safe."

"We'll still have our opportunity."

"Escape! Put your mind to how we can escape."

"Yes, I will. But let's wait for the dogs to close their eyes for a while."

"But you go outside so carelessly. You're obsessed with killing your wife and this other man. You won't kill them. But you will bring about your own destruction."

"What did you hear in town?"

"The taxi driver who brought me home was on your side. But he said you'd killed some poor innocent fellow."

Said grunted irritably and forestalled any expression of regret by taking another big swallow, gesturing at Nur to drink, too. She raised the glass to her lips.

"What else did you hear?" he said.

"On the houseboat where I spent the evening one man said you act as a stimulant, a diversion to relieve people's boredom."

"And what did you reply?"

"Nothing at all," Nur said, pouting. "But I do defend you, and you don't look after yourself at all. You don't love me either. But to me you're more precious than my life itself; I've never in my whole life known happiness except in your arms. But you'd rather destroy yourself than love me." She was crying now, the glass still in her hand.

Said put his arm around her. "You'll find me true to my promise," he whispered. "We will escape and live together forever."

FIFTEEN

What enormous headlines and dramatic photos! It was obviously the major news item. Rauf Ilwan had been interviewed and had said that Said Mahran had been a servant in the students' hostel when he'd lived there, that he'd felt very sorry for him, and that later, after his release from prison, Said had visited him to ask for help, so he'd given him some money to start a new life; that Said had tried to rob his house the very same night and that he, Rauf, had caught and scolded him, but let him go out of compassion. And that then Said had come back to kill him!

The papers accused Said of being mad, craving for power and blood: his wife's infidelity had made him lose his mind, they said, and now he was killing at random. Rauf had apparently been untouched, but the unfortunate doorkeeper had fallen. Another poor innocent killed!

"Damnation!" cursed Said as he read the news.

The hue and cry was deafening now.

A huge reward was offered to anyone giving information of his whereabouts, and articles warned people against any sympathy for him. Yes, he thought, you're the top story today, all right. *And you'll be the top story until you're dead. You're a source of fear and fascination—like some freak of nature—and all those people choking with boredom owe their pleasure to you. As for your gun, it's obvious that it will kill only the innocent. You'll be its last victim.*

"Is this madness, then?" he asked himself, choking on the question.

Yes, you always wanted to cause a real stir, even if you were only a clown. Your triumphant raids on the homes of the rich were like wine, intoxicating your pride-filled head. And those words of Rauf that you believed, even though he did not—it was they that really chopped off your head, that killed you dead!

He was alone in the night. There was still some wine in a bottle, which he drank down to the last drop. As he stood in the dark, enveloped in the silence of the neighboring graves, slightly giddy, he began to feel that he would indeed overcome all his difficulties, that he could disdain death. The sound of mysterious music within him delighted him.

"A misdirected bullet has made of me the man of the hour!" he declared to the dark.

Through the window shutters he looked over the cemetery, at the graves lying there quiet in the moonlight.

"Hey, all you judges out there, listen well to me," he said. "I've decided to offer my own defense for myself."

Back in the center of the room he took off his nightshirt. The room was hot, the wine had raised his body heat. His wound throbbed beneath the bandage, but the pain convinced him it was beginning to heal.

"I'm not like the others," he said, staring into the dark,

"who have stood on this stand before. You must give special consideration to the education of the accused. But the truth is, there's no difference between me and you except that I'm on the stand and you're not. And that difference is only incidental, of no real importance at all. But what's truly ridiculous is that the distinguished teacher of the accused is a treacherous scoundrel. You may well be astonished at this fact. It can happen, however, that the cord carrying current to a lamp is dirty, speckled with fly shit."

He turned to a sofa and lay down on it. In the distance he could hear a dog barking. *How can you ever convince your judges, when there is a personal animosity between you and them that has nothing to do with the so-called public welfare? They're kin to the scoundrel after all, whereas there's a whole century of time between you and them. You must then ask the victim to bear witness. You must assert that the treachery has become a silent conspiracy:* "I did not kill the servant of Rauf Ilwan. How could I kill a man I did not know and who didn't know me? Rauf Ilwan's servant was killed because, quite simply, he was the servant of Rauf Ilwan. Yesterday his spirit visited me and I jumped to hide in shame, but he pointed out to me that millions of people are killed by mistake and without due cause."

Yes, these words will glitter; they'll be crowned with a not-guilty verdict. You are sure of what you say. And apart from that, they will believe, deep down, that your profession is lawful, a profession of gentlemen at all times and everywhere, that the truly false values—yes!—are those that value your life in pennies and your death at a thousand pounds. The judge over on the left is winking at you; cheer up!

"I will always seek the head of Rauf Ilwan, even as a

last request from the hangman, even before seeing my daughter. I am forced not to count my life in days. A hunted man only feeds on new excitements, which pour down upon him in the span of his solitude like rain."

The verdict will be no more cruel that Sana's cold shyness toward you. She killed you before the hangman could. And even the sympathy of the millions for you is voiceless, impotent, like the longings of the dead. Will they not forgive the gun its error, when it is their most elevated master?

"Whoever kills me will be killing the millions. I am the hope and the dream, the redemption of cowards; I am good principles, consolation, the tears that recall the weeper to humility. And the declaration that I'm mad must encompass all who are loving. Examine the causes of this insane occasion, then reach your judgment however you wish!"

His dizziness increased.

Then the verdict came down: that he was a great man, truly great in every sense of the word. His greatness might be momentarily shrouded in black, from a community of sympathy with all those graves out there, but the glory of his greatness would live on, even after death. Its fury was blessed by the force that flowed through the roots of plants, the cells of animals, and the hearts of men.

Eventually sleep overtook him, though he only knew it when he awoke to find light filling the room and he saw Nur standing looking down at him. Her eyes were dead tired, her lower lip drooped, and her shoulders slumped. She looked the very picture of despair. He knew in an instant what the trouble was; she'd heard about his latest exploit and it had shocked her deeply.

"You are even more cruel than I imagined," she said. "I

just don't understand you. But for heaven's sake have mercy and kill me, too." He sat up on the sofa, but made no reply. "You're busy thinking how to kill, not how to escape, and you'll be killed, too. Do you imagine you can defeat the whole government, with its troops filling the streets?"

"Sit down and let's discuss it calmly."

"How can I be calm? And what are we to discuss? Everything's over now. Just kill me, too, for mercy's sake!"

"I don't ever want harm to come to you," he said quietly and in a tender tone of voice.

"I'll never believe a word you say. Why do you murder doorkeepers?"

"I didn't mean to harm him!" he said angrily.

"And the other one? Who is this Rauf Ilwan? What is your relationship with him? Was he involved with your wife?"

"What a ridiculous idea," he said, laughing so drily it was like a cough. "No, there are other reasons. He's a traitor, too, but of another sort. I can't explain it all to you."

"But you can torture me to death."

"As I just said, sit down so we can talk calmly."

"You're still in love with your wife, that bitch, but you want to put me through hell all the same."

"Nur," he pleaded, "please don't torture me. I'm terribly depressed."

Nur stopped talking, affected by a distress she could never have seen in him before. "I feel as if the most precious thing in my whole life is about to die," she said at last, sadly.

"That's just your imagination, your fear. Gamblers like me never admit to setbacks. I'll remind you of that sometime."

"When will that be?" she asked quietly.

"Oh, sooner than you think," Said replied, pretending boundless self-confidence.

He leaned toward her and pulled her down by the hand. He pressed his face against hers, his nose filling with the smell of wine and sweat. But he felt no disgust and kissed her with genuine tenderness.

SIXTEEN

Dawn was close, but Nur had not returned—though the waiting and all his worry had exhausted him, bouts of insomnia kept crushing against his brain—and now the warm darkness was splitting apart to reveal one flaming question: Was it possible that the promised reward was having some effect on Nur?

Suspicion had tainted his blood to the last drop now: he had visions of infidelity as pervasive as dust in a windstorm. He remembered how sure he was once that Nabawiyya belonged to him, when in reality she'd probably never loved him at all, even in the days of the lone palm tree at the edge of the field.

But surely Nur would never betray him, never turn him over to the police for the reward. She had no interest now in such financial transactions. She was getting on in life. What she wanted was a sincere emotional relationship with someone. He ought to feel guilty for his suspicious thoughts.

The worry over Nur's absence persisted, nevertheless. It's your hunger, thirst, and all the waiting that's getting you down, he said to himself. *Just like that time you stood waiting beneath the palm tree, waiting for Nabawiyya, and she didn't come. You began prowling around the old Turkish woman's house, biting your fingernails with impatience and so crazy with worry you almost knocked on her door. And what a quiver of joy when she did emerge—a feeling of complete exhilaration, spreading through you, lifting you up to the seventh heaven.*

It had been a time for tears and laughter, of uncontrolled emotion, a time of confidence, a time of boundless joy. Don't think about the palm tree days now. They're gone forever, cut off by blood, bullets, and madness. Think only about what you've got to do now, waiting here, filled with bitterness, in this murderous stifling darkness.

He could only conclude that Nur did not want to come back, did not want to save him from the tortures of solitude in the dark, from hunger and thirst. At the height of a bout of remorse and despair, he at last fell asleep. When he opened his eyes again he saw daylight and felt the heat slipping through the shutters into the closed room. Worried and confused, he stepped quickly into the bedroom, to find it exactly as Nur had left it the day before, then roamed around the entire flat. Nur had not returned. Where, he wondered, could she have spent the night? What had prevented her return? And how long was he to be sentenced to this solitary confinement?

He was feeling distinct pangs of hunger now, despite his worries, and he went into the kitchen. On the unwashed plates there he found several scraps of bread, bits of meat sticking to bones, and some parsley. He consumed them all, ravenously gnawing on the bones like a dog, then spent the rest of the whole day wondering why she had not returned, wondering if she ever would. He would sit for a while, then wander about and sit again. His only distraction was gazing through the shutters out over the cemetery, watching the funerals and aimlessly counting the graves. Evening came, but Nur still had not returned.

There must be some sort of reason. Wherever could she be? He felt his worry, anger, and hunger tearing him apart. Nur was in trouble, there was no doubt of that, but somehow she simply had to free herself from her difficulty, whatever it was, and come back. Otherwise what would become of him?

After midnight he quietly left the flat and made his way over the waste ground to Tarzan's coffeehouse. He whistled three times when he arrived at the spot they'd agreed on and waited until Tarzan came out.

"Do be extremely careful," said Tarzan, shaking his hand, "there are agents watching everywhere."

"I need some food!"

"You don't say! You're hungry, then!"

"Yes. Nothing ever surprises you, does it?"

"I'll send the waiter to get you some cooked meat. But I'm telling you, it really is dangerous for you to go out."

"Oh, we had worse trouble in the old days, you and I."

"I don't think so. That last attack of yours has turned the whole world upside down on top of you."

"It's always been upside down."

"But it was disastrous of you to attack a man of importance!"

They parted and Said withdrew a little. After some time the food was brought to him and he gulped it down, sitting on the sand beneath a moon now really full. He looked over at the light coming from Tarzan's café on the little hill and imagined the customers sitting there in the room chatting. No, he really did not like being alone. When he was with others his stature seemed to grow giantlike: he had a talent for friendship, leadership, even heroism. Without all that there was simply no spice to life. But had Nur come back yet? Would she return at all? Would he go back to find her there or would there be more of that murderous loneliness?

At last he got up, brushed the sand and dust from his trousers, and walked off toward the grove, planning to go back to the flat by the path that wound around the south side of the Martyr's Tomb. Near the tip of the grove, at the spot where he'd waylaid Bayaza, the earth seemed to split open, emitting two figures who jumped out on either side of him.

"Stop where you are!" said one of them in a deep urbanized country accent.

"And let's see your identity card!" barked the other.

The former shone a flashlight into his face and Said lowered his head as though to protect his eyes, demanding angrily, "Who do you think you are? Come on, answer me!"

They were taken aback by his imperious tone; they'd now seen his uniform in the glow of the flashlight.

"I'm very sorry indeed, sir," the first man said. "In the shadow of the trees we couldn't see who you were."

"And who are you?" Said shouted, with even more anger in his voice.

"We're from the station at al-Waily, sir," they answered hastily.

The flashlight was turned off now, but Said had already seen something disturbing in the expression of the second man, who had been peering very quizzically at him, as though suddenly filled with doubt. Afraid he might lose control of the situation, Said moved decisively and with force, swinging a fist into both their bellies. They reeled back, and before they could recover he sent a hail of blows at chins and bellies until they were unconscious. Then he dashed away as fast as he could go. At the corner of Sharia Najm al-Din he stopped to make sure no one was following, then he continued along quietly to the flat.

Once there he found it as empty as when he'd left, with only more loneliness, boredom, and worry there to meet him. He took off his jacket and threw himself onto a sofa in the dark. His own sad voice came to him audibly: "Nur, where are you?"

All was not well with her, that was obvious. Had the police arrested her? Had some louts attacked her? She had to be in some sort of trouble. Emotions and instincts told him that much, and that he would never see Nur again. The thought choked him with despair, not merely because he would soon lose a safe hiding place but also because he knew he'd lost affection and companionship as well. He saw her there in the dark before him—Nur, with all her smiles and joking, her love and her unhappiness—and the terrible depression he felt made him aware that she had penetrated much deeper within him than he had imagined, that she had become a part of him, and that she should never have been separated from this life of his which was in shreds and tottering on the brink of an abyss. Closing his eyes in the darkness, he silently acknowledged that he did love her and that he would not hesitate to give his own life to bring her safely back. Then one thought made him growl in anger: "And yet would her demise cause so much as a single ripple anywhere?"

No, definitely not. Not even a pretense of grief would be made for the loss of Nur, who was only a woman with no protector, adrift on a sea of waves either indifferent or hostile. And Sana, too, might well find herself one day with no one to look after her. These thoughts scared and angered him and he gripped his gun and pointed it in front of him in the dark, as though warning the unknown. In deep despair, delirious in the silence and dark, he began to sob; and sobbed until late in the night sleep finally overcame him.

It was daylight when he next opened his eyes, aware that someone's knocking on the door had awakened him. He jumped up in alarm and tiptoed to the front door of the flat, the knocking continuing all the time.

"Madame Nur! Madame Nur!" a woman's voice shouted.

Who was the woman and what could she want? He got his revolver from the other room. Now he heard a man's voice: "Well, maybe she's gone out."

"No," he heard the woman reply, "at this time of day she's always home. And she's never been late with the rent before."

So it must be the landlady. The woman gave one last angry bang on the door and yelled: "Today's the fifth of the month and I'm not going to wait any longer!"

Then she and the man walked away, grumbling as they went.

Circumstances were after him now, as well as the police. The woman would certainly not wait long and would be sure to get into the flat by one means or another. The best thing for him was to get out as soon as he possibly could.

But where was he to go?

SEVENTEEN

Late in the afternoon and then again during the evening the landlady returned. "No, no, Madame Nur," she muttered as she finally left, "everything has to come to an end sometime, you know."

At midnight Said slipped out. Although his confidence in everything had gone, he was careful to walk very naturally and slowly, as if merely taking a stroll. More than once, when the thought struck him that people passing by or standing around might well be informers, he braced himself for one last desperate battle. After the encounter on the previous day, he had no doubts that the police would be in occupation of the whole area near Tarzan's café, so he moved off toward Jabal Road.

Hunger was tearing at his stomach now. On the road, it occurred to him that Sheikh Ali al-Junaydi's house might well provide a temporary place of refuge while he thought out his next moves. It was only as he slipped into the courtyard of the silent house that he realized that he had left his uniform in the sitting room of Nur's flat. Infuriated by his forgetfulness Said went on into the old man's room, where the lamplight showed the Sheikh sitting in the corner reserved for prayer, completely engrossed in a whispered monologue. Said walked over to the wall where he'd left his books and sat down, exhausted.

The Sheikh continued his quiet utterance until Said addressed him: "Good evening, then, Sheikh Ali."

The old man raised his hand to his head in response to the greeting, but did not break off his incantations.

"Sheikh, I'm really hungry," Said said.

The old man seemed to interrupt his chant, gazed at him vacantly, then nodded with his chin to a side table nearby where Said saw some bread and figs. He got up at once, went to the table, and ravenously consumed it all, then stood there looking at the Sheikh with unappeased eyes.

"Don't you have any money?" the Sheikh said quietly.

"Oh yes."

"Why not go and buy yourself something to eat?"

Said then made his way quietly back to his seat. The Sheikh sat contemplating him for a while, then said, "When are you going to settle down, do you think?"

"Not on the face of this earth."

"That's why you're hungry, even though you've got money."

"So be it, then."

"As for me," the Sheikh commented, "I was just reciting some verses about life's sorrows. I was reciting in a joyful frame of mind."

"Yes. Well, you're certainly a happy Sheikh," Said said. "The scoundrels have got away," he went on angrily. "How can I settle down after that?"

"How many of them are there?"

"Three."

"What joy for the world if its scoundrels number only three."

"No, there are very many more, but my enemies are only three."

"Well then, no one has 'got away.'"

"I'm not responsible for the world, you know."

"Oh yes. You're responsible for both this world and the next!" While Said puffed in exasperation, the Sheikh continued: "Patience is holy and through it things are blessed."

"But it's the guilty who succeed, while the innocent fail," Said commented glumly.

The Sheikh sighed. "When shall we succeed in achieving peace of mind under the rule of authority?"

"When authority becomes fair," Said replied.

"It is always fair."

Said shook his head angrily. "Yes," he muttered. "They've got away now, all right, damn it." The Sheikh merely smiled without speaking. Said's voice changed its tone as he tried to alter the course of the conversation. "I'm going to sleep with my face toward the wall. I don't want anyone who visits you to see me. I'm going to hide out here with you. Please protect me."

"Trusting God means entrusting one's lodging to God alone," the Sheikh said gently.

"Would you give me up?"

"Oh no, God forbid."

"Would it be in your power, with all the grace with which you're endowed, to save me, then?"

"You can save yourself, if you wish," came the Sheikh's reply.

"I will kill the others," Said whispered to himself, and

aloud said, "Are you capable of straightening the shadow of something crooked?"

"I do not concern myself with shadows," the Sheikh replied softly.

Silence followed and light from the moon streamed more strongly through the window onto the ceiling. In a whisper the Sheikh began reciting a mystic chant: "All beauty in creation stems from You."

Yes, Said told himself quietly, the Sheikh will always find something appropriate to say. *But this house of yours, dear sir, is not secure, though you yourself might be security personified. I've got to get away, no matter what the cost. And as for you, Nur, let's hope at least good luck will protect you, if you find neither justice nor mercy. But how did I forget that uniform? I wrapped it up, intending to take it with me. How could I have forgotten it at the last moment? I've lost my touch. From all this sleeplessness, loneliness, dark, and worry. They'll find that uniform. It might supply the first thread leading to you: they'll have dogs smelling it, fanning out in all directions to the very ends of the earth, sniffing and barking to complete a drama that will titillate newspaper readers.*

Suddenly the Sheikh spoke again in a melancholy tone of voice: "I asked you to raise up your face to the heavens, yet here you are announcing that you are going to turn it to the wall!"

"But don't you remember what I told you about the scoundrels?" Said demanded, gazing at him sadly.

"'Remember the name of your Lord, if you forget.'"

Said lowered his gaze, feeling troubled, then wondered again, as depression gripped him further, how he could have forgotten the uniform.

The Sheikh said suddenly, as if addressing someone else, "He was asked: 'Do you know of any incantation we can recite or potion we can use that might perhaps nullify a decree of God?' And he answered: 'Such would be a decree of God!'"

"What do you mean?" Said asked.

"Your father was never one to fail to understand my words," replied the old man, sighing sadly.

"Well," Said said irritably, "it is regrettable that I didn't find sufficient food in your home, just as it is unfortunate that I forgot the uniform. Also my mind does fail to comprehend you and I will turn my face to the wall. But I'm confident that I'm in the right."

Smiling sadly, the Sheikh said, "My Master stated: 'I gaze in the mirror many times each day fearing that my face might have turned black!'"

"You?!"

"No, my Master himself."

"How," Said asked scornfully, "could the scoundrels keep checking in the mirror every hour?"

The Sheikh bowed his head, reciting, "All beauty in creation stems from You."

Said closed his eyes, saying to himself, "I'm really tired, but I'll have no peace until I get that uniform back."

EIGHTEEN

At last exhaustion conquered his will. He forgot his determination to get the uniform and fell asleep, awaking a little before midday. Knowing he would have to wait until nightfall to move, he spent the time setting out a plan for his escape, fully aware that any major step would have to be put off for a while, until the police relaxed their surveillance of the area near Tarzan's café. Tarzan was the very pivot of the plan.

Sometime after midnight he entered Sharia Najm al-Din. There was light coming from a window of the flat. He stood staring up at it in amazement, and when he finally believed what he saw, his heart seemed to beat so loudly as almost to deafen him, while a wave of elation roared over him, sweeping him out of a nightmare world. Nur was in the flat! Where had she been? Why had she been away? At least she was back now. And she must be suffering the scorch of those same hellfires where he'd been burning, wondering where he was. He knew she was back by that instinct of his that had never deceived him, and the

272 / Naguib Mahfouz

strain of being on the run would now recede for a while, perhaps for good. He would hold her tight in his arms, pouring out his eternal love for her.

Intoxicated with joy and assured of success, he crept into the building and climbed the stairs, dreaming of one victory after another. There was no limit to what he could do. He would get away and settle down for a long time, then come back eventually and deal with those scoundrels.

A little out of breath, he came up to the door. *I love you, Nur. With all my heart I do love you, twice as much as you have loved me. In your breast I will bury all my misery, the treachery of those scoundrels and my daughter's alarm.* He knocked on the door.

It opened to reveal a man he had never seen before, a little man in his underclothes, who stared back at him in astonishment and said, "Yes; what can I do for you?"

The little man's look of inquiry soon gave way to one of confusion and then alarm. Dumbfounded, certain he'd recognized him, Said silenced him instantly, slamming one fist into his mouth and the other into his stomach. As he lowered the body quietly to the threshold, Said thought of entering to search for his uniform, but he couldn't be sure the flat was empty. Then from inside he heard a woman's voice calling, "Who was that at the door, dear?"

It was hopeless. Said turned and raced back down the stairs and out into the street, then made his way up Sharia Masani to Jabal Road, where he could see suspicious figures moving about. He crouched at the base of a wall, carefully recommencing his walk only when the street was entirely empty. It was a little before dawn when he once again slipped into the Sheikh's house. The old man was in his corner, awake and waiting for the coming call to prayer. Said took off his outer clothes and stretched out on the mat, turning his head to the wall though he had little hope of falling asleep.

"Go to sleep, for sleep is prayer for people like you," the Sheikh said.

Said made no reply. The Sheikh quickly chanted the name of God, "Allah."

When the dawn prayer was called Said was still awake and later he heard the milkman on his round. He knew he'd fallen asleep only when he was disturbed by a nightmare and opened his eyes to see light from the dim lamp spreading through the room like a fog, which made him suppose he'd slept for an hour at most. He turned toward the Sheikh's bed and found it empty, then noticed near his pile of books some cooked meat, figs, and a pitcher of water. He silently thanked the old man, wondering when he had brought the food.

Voices coming from outside the room surprised him. Creeping on all fours to the partly open door, he peeped through the crack and to his amazement saw a group of men who had come to pray, seated on mats, while a workman was busy lighting up a large oil lamp above the outer door. Suddenly he knew it was sunset, not dawn, as he had imagined. He had slept through the whole day without realizing it, a really deep sleep indeed.

He decided to put off any further thought until after eating. He consumed the food and drank his fill, then dressed in his outdoor clothes and sat on the floor with his back against his books and his legs stretched straight out in front of him. His thoughts turned immediately to the uniform he'd forgotten, to the man who had opened the flat door to him, to Sana and Nur and Rauf and Nabawiyya and Ilish, to the informers, to Tarzan, and to the car he would use to break through the cordon. His mind churned with agitation. Clearly neither further patience nor hesitation was now in his interests. No matter what the danger, he had to contact Tarzan that night, even if it meant crawling to him over the desert sands. Tomorrow the police would be busy everywhere and those scoundrels would be out of their wits with fright.

Outside he heard someone clap his hands. The men's voices were suddenly silent and no other sounds could be heard. Sheikh Ali al-Junaydi chanted the word "Allah" three times and the others repeated the call, with a melody that brought the memory of the notion of the mystic dance to his mind once more. "Allah . . . Allah . . . Allah." The chant increased in tempo and pitch like the sound of a train racing ahead, continuing without interruption for a considerable time. Then it began gradually to lose its power, its rhythm slowing, hesitating, and finally sinking into silence. At that point a full, fine voice arose in a chanted melody:

> *"My time in vain is gone*
> *And I have not succeeded.*
> *For a meeting how I long,*
> *But hope of peace is ended*
> *When life is two days long;*
> *One day of vexation*
> *And one of separation."*

Said could hear the other men murmuring sighs in appreciation all around, and then another voice began a melody:

> *"Love enough to lay me down enthralled:*
> *My passion before me, my fate behind."*

This song was followed by more sighs of delight and more singing, until someone clapped hands again and they all began repeating at length the name of God—Allah.

As he listened, Said allowed his mind to wander and the evening wore on. Memories came drifting by like clouds. He remembered how his father, Amm Mahran, had swayed with the chanters, while he, then a young boy, had sat near the palm tree observing the scene wide-eyed. From the shadows emerged fancies about the immortal soul, living under the protection of the Most Compassionate. Memories of hopes once bright shook off the dust of oblivion and flashed with life again: beneath that lone tree at the edge of the field tender words were whispered again in early-morning joy; little Sana sat again his arms, speaking her first wonderful baby words. Then hot winds blew from the depths of hell and a succession of blows were struck.

In the background the prayer leader's chant and the congregation's sighs wailed on. When would peace come, when his time had passed in futility, when he had failed and fate was on his trail? But that revolver of his lying ready in his pocket, that was something at least. It could still triumph over betrayal and corruption. For the first time the thief would give chase to the dogs.

Suddenly from beneath the window outside he heard an angry voice explode and a conversation:

"What a mess! Why, the whole quarter is blocked off!"

"It's worse than during the war!"

"That Said Mahran . . . !"

Said tensed, electrified, gripping the revolver so tightly that every muscle in his body strained. He stared in every direction. The area was crowded with people and was no doubt full of eager detectives. *I mustn't let things get ahead*

*of me. They must now be examining the uniform and the
dogs will be there too. And meanwhile here I am, exposed.
The desert road isn't safe, but the Valley of Death itself is
only a few steps away. I can fight them there to the death.*

He got up and moved decisively toward the door. They
were still engrossed in chanted prayers; the passage to the
outer door was clear. He crept out into the street, then
turned off to the left, walking with studied calm, moving
into the road to the cemetery.

The night was well advanced, but there was no moon
and the darkness made a black wall across his path. He
plunged off among the tombs, into the maze of ruins, with
nothing to guide him, stumbling as he walked, not knowing whether he was progressing forward or backward.
Though no spark of hope glimmered within him, he felt he
was bursting with incredible energy. The loud noises which
were brought to him now on the warm wind made him
wish he could hide inside a grave, but he knew he could
not stop. He feared the dogs, but there was nothing at all
he could do. There was nothing within his power to stop.

After some minutes he found himself at the last row of
graves in front of a familiar scene: the northern entrance to
the cemetery, connecting with Sharia Najm al-Din, which
he recognized, and there the only building on it, was Nur's
flat. He located the window. It was open and light was
streaming out. He focused his gaze on it and saw a woman
through the window. The features of her head were indis-
tinct, but the shape of the head reminded him of Nur. His
heart pumped hard at the thought. Had Nur returned,
then? Or were his eyes deceiving him now, as his emotions
had done before? The fact that he had become so completely deceived foretold that the end was near. If that was

Nur, he told himself, all he wanted was for her to care for Sana, if his time indeed had come. He decided to shout to her, disregarding the danger, to tell her what he wanted, but before a sound could emerge from his mouth he heard dogs beginning to bark in the distance, and the barking went on, breaking the silence like a series of explosive shots.

Said started back in fright, darting in again between the tombs as the barking grew louder. He pressed his back against a tomb and took out his gun, staring out into the darkness resignedly. There it was. The dogs had come at last and there was no hope left. The scoundrels were safe, if only for a while. His life had made its last utterance, saying that it had all been in vain.

It was impossible to tell precisely where the barking came from; it was carried in on the air from all around. It was hopeless now to think of fleeing from the dark by running away into the dark. The scoundrels had indeed got away with it; his life was a proven failure. The barking and the commotion were very close now, and soon, Said knew, all the malice and vengefulness he'd been running from would be breathed right into his face. He held his gun poised as the barking grew ever louder and closer. And suddenly there was blinding light over the whole area. He shut his eyes and crouched at the base of the tomb.

"Give yourself up," a triumphant voice shouted. "It's no use resisting."

The ground shook now with the thud of heavy feet surrounding him and the light spread all around, like the sun.

"Give yourself up, Said," the voice said firmly.

He crouched closer still to the tomb, ready to open fire, turning his head in all directions.

"Surrender," came another shout, confident, reassuring, and dignified, "and I promise you you'll be treated with all humanity."

Like the humanity of Rauf, Nabawiyya, Ilish, and the dogs no doubt? "You're surrounded on all sides. The whole cemetery is surrounded. Think it over carefully, Said. Give yourself up."

Sure that the enormous and irregular multitude of the tombs prevented them from actually seeing him, Said made no movement. He had decided on death.

"Can't you see there's no point in resistance?" the firm voice shouted.

It seemed to be nearer now than before, and Said shouted back warningly, "Any closer and I'll shoot!"

"Very well, then. What do you want to do? Make your choice between death and coming to justice."

"Justice indeed!" Said yelled scornfully.

"You're being very stubborn. You've got one minute more."

His fear-tortured eyes could see the phantom of death now, stalking through the dark.

Sana had turned away from him in alarm, hopelessly.

He sensed surreptitious movement nearby, flared with rage, and opened fire. The bullets showered in, their whistle filling his ears, chips flying from tombs all around. He fired again, oblivious to danger now, and more bullets pelted in. "You dogs, you!" he raved in a frenzy of rage, and more shots came in from all sides.

Suddenly the blinding light went out, and the firing stopped; there was darkness again and quiet fell. He wasn't firing anymore either. Slowly the silence was spreading, until all the world seemed gripped in a strange stupefaction. He wondered . . . ? But the question and even its subject seemed to dissolve, leaving no traces. Perhaps, he thought, they had retreated, slipped away into the night. Why, then, he must have won!

The darkness was thicker now and he could see nothing at all, not even the outlines of the tombs, as if nothing wished to be seen. He was slipping away into endless depths, not knowing either position, place, purpose. As hard as he could, he tried to gain control of something, no matter what. To exert one last act of resistance. To capture one last recalcitrant memory. But finally, because he had to succumb, and not caring, he surrendered. Not caring at all now.

Translated from the Arabic by
Trevor Le Gassick and M. M. Badawi.
Revised by John Rodenbeck.

Autumn Quail

FOREWORD

The stature which Naguib Mahfouz has earned as the Arab world's most illustrious novelist is well captured by 'Abd al-Rahman Yaghi when he entitles the fourth chapter of his book *Al-Juhad al-Riwa'iyya* (*Endeavors in the Novel*, 1972) "The Novel's Establishment Stage, in other words the Naguib Mahfouz Stage." Several studies of his works in English have by now been added to the myriad books, articles, and interviews on him which have appeared throughout the Arab world itself. While he is not yet as well known to Western readers as some other famous non-Western writers, several of his works are available in English.*

The word for "establishment" in Yaghi's title quoted above is *ta'sil,* which literally implies giving something roots. That describes very well the role which Mahfouz has played in the development of the modern Arabic novel.

---

*A listing of many of these works and translations into English can be found in my book *The Arabic Novel: An Historical and Critical Introduction* (Syracuse: Syracuse University Press, 1982).

Throughout a long career he has indeed laid the ground-work for the emergence of this most taxing and variegated genre and then proceeded to experiment with a number of forms and techniques. Some scholars have chosen to divide his works into "phases," each one with its specific charac-teristics; others have preferred to illustrate the continuum of themes which occupy the author's mind, pointing out at the same time that features of these "phases" will often have been presaged in earlier writings. In spite of the dif-ferences between these viewpoints, both acknowledge that Mahfouz has been constantly striving to find new ways to express his vision of Egypt's present and therefore its past and future. This remains as true of his most recent writ-ings, where, in addition to his continuing experiments with multi-sectional works and a variety of narrative voices, we find echoes of earlier Arabic literature, such as *The Thou-sand and One Nights* and the travels of Ibn Battuta.

During the 1960s, Mahfouz wrote a great deal: nov-els, short stories, and plays. Much of the inspiration for this outburst of creativity was certainly prompted by the wide success of his monumental three-part novel, *Al-Thulathiyya* (*The Trilogy,* 1956–57). And yet it is also abundantly clear from his writings in all the genres listed above that an equally cogent force impelling him to write was a deep disquiet with the course of the Egyptian revo-lution, a feeling which was to be vented at its fullest in *Miramar* (1967) and in works published after the June war of 1967. With that in mind it is of some interest to note that Mahfouz chose in the second of the novels of this decade, *Al-Summan wal-Kharif* (*Autumn Quail,* 1962) to indulge in a historical retrospect by placing the action of the novel during the Revolution of 1952 itself and the years immediately following. Thus, while this work may be something of an anomaly within the sequence of Mahfouz's works conceived and written during the 1960s, it surely works to treat the events of the Revolution itself within a fictional context.

The novel opens with a description of the famous Cairo fire which followed the massacre of Egyptian policemen at the Suez Canal by British soldiers in January 1952. It goes on to trace (often through the medium of radio broadcasts) the main events of the early stages of the Revolution—the purge of corrupt officials and the abolition of political parties, for example. It comes to an end sometime after the nationalization of the Suez Canal Company and the Tripartite (British, French, and Israeli) invasion of 1956. There is also a very concrete link to place in this work: to various districts of Cairo, each with its own memories and connotations; and to Alexandria, with its pounding winter seas, its foreign quarters, and its still much desired distance from the clamor of the capital city. Thus, of all the novels which Mahfouz published in the 1960s, *Autumn Quail* has the strongest connection with the realities of both time and place.

Against the backdrop of these places and events, the central character whose fall is portrayed in this novel is Isa ad-Dabbagh, a senior civil servant in the Egyptian government during the final days of the monarchy. He has just become engaged to Salwa, the beautiful and feckless daughter of Ali Bey Sulaiman, a justice and senior Palace official. Isa and his mother live in an opulent villa in Dokki, then as now a typical outward symbol of the *nouveau arrivé*. The graphic description of the Cairo fire— with its sinister symbols of smoke and fire—warns of dire things to come. Sure enough, after the revolution comes the Purge Committee. Isa's past willingness to accept

286 / Naguib Mahfouz

bribes catches up with him, and he is pensioned off. As a result of this loss of position and prestige his engagement to Salwa is abruptly terminated.

Isa is of course a symbol of all that the immediate past stands for. In his defense before the Purge Committee he excuses himself by pointing out that everyone behaved exactly as he did, and asks why it is that he is being singled out. However, in spite of Isa's rapid and heavy fall, the past which he symbolizes throughout the novel does manage to display positive characteristics as well. For, unlike his friend Ibrahim Khairat, who almost immediately sets about penning hypocritical articles in praise of the revolution, Isa remains stubbornly loyal to the old regime and adamantly refuses to consider accepting the offer of a job from his cousin Hasan, who has become an important figure because of the revolution. This positive aspect of Isa's character, his sense of loyalty and concern for his country, is perhaps best seen through his relationship with Qadriyya, the woman whom he eventually marries. At the onset Isa is aware that the marriage may not work and leaves himself an escape route by overlooking her previous marriages. But as the couple live together through the Suez Crisis of 1956, Isa is amazed by her total lack of concern with politics and the fate of Egypt. Qadriyya, the barren, overfed nonentity, brings out the positive side of Isa's attitude.

On the intellectual level Isa seems to become reconciled to the idea of accepting the revolution and the changes which it is bringing about. But on every occasion his basic emotional instincts hold him back, at least until the very end of the novel. He suffers an internal conflict between mind and emotion, and it is in the latter area that the women of the novel play such an important role. If the marriage to Qadriyya, with its literal and figurative barrenness, is doomed from the start, then the relationship with Riri, the Alexandrian prostitute, represents Isa's real fight with emotion, his total failure to meet his moral responsibilities, and his eventual realization through a very bitter lesson of what those responsibilities are. This relationship is as creative—literally—as that with Qadriyya is not. Isa's failure to regain his real family (as he comes to call it) symbolizes the failure of his emotions to react responsibly to the circumstances in which his own past has left him. As he realizes this bitter fact and its consequences for the future, his life with Qadriyya emerges as the sham which it really is and always has been; in his own words, he has no home with her.

The final pages bring Isa together with a young man whom he had imprisoned during his period as a powerful civil servant. By now, his emotions have been jolted into some kind of reality by the sight of his own daughter and by Riri's bitter words to him. Past and present encounter each other in the dark under the statue of Saad Zaghlul, the poignant symbol of the past mentioned several times in this book and with equal effect in *Miramar*. Isa is disturbed and troubled by the young man's friendly attitude and by his enthusiasm for the revolution. When the latter gives up hope of converting Isa and heads toward the city, Isa follows him. Since it is past midnight, this may perhaps be considered a move away from Saad Zaghlul's statue, out of the darkness toward some new dawn.

From an artistic point of view, this ending—with Isa running after the young man into an uncertain future—has been regarded as contrived. We have already noted that Isa had given several signs of a dispassionate *intellectual* acceptance of the revolution. The question to be posed in the current context thus concerns his stubborn adherence to his own past and his emotional attitudes. What is the role of his final encounters with Riri and his own daughter, Ni'mat, in this process? Has it shaken him into a sense of emotional and moral responsibility sufficient to justify his decision to run after the young man? Is the Indian palm reader's comment about "recovery from a serious illness" a forewarning of his eventual decision to follow the young man? I must leave it to the readers of *Autumn Quail* to make their own judgments on the *artistic* efficacy of the ending vis-à-vis these questions; I would merely comment that I find it less unconvincing than many of its critics do.

The long period of time (over four years) covered by this novel, the close linkage with the political events of the day, and the optimistic ending have all been criticized on artistic, if not political, grounds. It has been suggested that *Autumn Quail* represents a response on Mahfouz's part to critical reactions (including presumably those of "the official cultural sector" of which he himself was a part) to the subtly negative commentary on the Revolution to be found in *Al-Liss wal-Kilab* (*The Thief and the Dogs,* 1961), the first novel in the series of works published in the 1960s. In the latter work, a man who has been "framed" is released from prison and vows vengeance on his wife and her lover, who have tricked him. In trying to kill them, he mistakenly kills two other people and is then hunted (or hounded) down by the police as a homicidal maniac, meeting his death in a cemetery as the police dogs chase after him. *Autumn Quail* certainly represents—at least in the implications of its ending—a more "upbeat" view of Egyptian society than that. I would not wish to imply that Mahfouz felt himself to be under the same constraints as Dimitri Shostakovich, who prefaced his Fifth Symphony with the phrase "an artist's response to just criticism" in the wake of his ostracism from Russian cultural life (in turn a reaction to his Fourth Symphony). However, one may legitimately wonder whether the general intellectual atmosphere in Egypt during the early 1960s—a period about which many details concerning assaults on civil liberties have only recently come to light—did not suggest to Mahfouz that a retrospect with positive contemporary implications might be at least apropos.

Whatever the artistic and societal motivations may have been in writing *Autumn Quail,* Mahfouz decided to trace within a novelistic framework the relationship of past and present within the Egyptian Revolution and the possibilities of cooperation, or perhaps coexistence, in the future. It has to be admitted that the novel's narrative suffers from the extended time period. Bearing in mind Isa's frequent travel back and forth between Cairo and Alexandria, the links of time and place seem to be extended beyond endurance in a comparatively short novel (compared, for example, with *The Trilogy,* a huge societal canvas in which these two aspects can be more expansively and successfully managed).

All this said, *Autumn Quail* will provide the Western reader with insights and reflections on the Egyptian Revolution and its progress, put into the mouths of Egyptian characters from different backgrounds and with varying social and political attitudes. Indeed, several themes of this work—alienation, political downfall, moral responsibility, to name a few—transcend the boundaries of independent national literary traditions and are to be found in much of contemporary world fiction. As for the characters themselves (quite apart from the intrinsic interest of their comments about politics, religion, and the world situation), the symbolic mesh within which Mahfouz illustrates their relationships gives this work a peculiar fascination.

ROGER ALLEN

Autumn Quail

O N E

When the train drew to a halt, he could see no one waiting for him. Where was his secretary? Where were the
office staff and the messengers? He looked among the
people standing outside on the platform but failed to find
anyone he recognized. What had happened? At the Canal
the blow had been vicious, but was Cairo reeling as well?

He left his place in the front of the carriage and walked
toward the exit, briefcase in hand, feeling irritated and
tense, then worried, until, driven by some natural impulse,
he began to examine people's faces closely. They seemed to
mirror a terrifying anxiety. He himself felt apprehensive.
What was the cause? The massacre at the Canal the day
before or some new miseries on the way? Should he ask
people what was going on? No one had been waiting for
him; nobody from his office had taken the trouble to come
and meet him. Incredible behavior! These were strange
days indeed.

His mind still held the bloody scenes at the Canal, the
slaughtered policemen, their defenseless heroism. He still

heard the earsplitting shouts of the young commando: "Where are you people? Where's the government? Weren't you the ones who proclaimed the holy war?"

"Yes!" he'd replied in anguish. "That's why I'm standing here in the middle of nowhere."

The young man had turned on him. "What we need is weapons!" he'd shouted. "Why aren't you people providing them?"

"Money's tight and the government's position is precarious."

"What about us? And the people whose homes have been destroyed?"

"I'm well aware of that. We all are. Be patient. We'll do everything we can."

"Or is it enough for you just to watch?" What fury! Just like fire.

But what was going on in Cairo?

There was no car to take him anywhere. In the station square, people were walking in every direction, anger on their faces, heaping curses on the British. It was cold. The sky was hidden by ominous clouds; the wind was still and lifeless. Shops were closed as if for mourning, and thick smoke rose along on the skyline.

What was going on in Cairo?

Cautiously, he began to walk, then beckoned to a man coming toward him. "What's going on in town?" he asked.

"The last day's come," was the bewildered reply.

"What do you mean? Protest demonstrations?"

"Fire and destruction," the man yelled, moving on.

As he started walking again, slowly and cautiously, looking carefully at what was going on around him, he asked himself in bewilderment where the police and the Army were.

In Sharia Ibrahim, things looked even worse and showed clearly what was really happening: the whole square had been given over to angry people. Feelings from the depths of their subconscious had erupted like a volcano and they were shrieking, howling like dogs. Anyone standing on either side was seized; gasoline was flowing, fires were burning, doors were being knocked in, all kinds of merchandise was being strewn about, and water was gushing out in crashing waves. This insanity, uncontrolled, was Cairo in revolt, but revolting against itself, bringing on itself the very thing it wanted to bring on its enemies. It was suicide. And he asked himself in dismay what could be behind it all.

His instinct warned him of grave danger in the future. Tomorrow the true extent of the tragedy would become clear, and with it a real danger, threatening the very essence of our lives—threatening us, not the British, threatening Cairo, the course of battle at the Canal, and the stability of the government. Threatening him too in that he was considered a part of that government. This flood would uproot the government, the party, and himself. It was no good trying to squeeze the fear out of his mind or pretending—in the face of this swirling spirit of unreason that engulfed him on all sides, more powerful than madness, destruction, and fire—pretending to forget it. He trusted this instinct of his implicitly; it had been his harbinger in times of political crisis, warning him time after time on the eve of all those occasions when his party had been dismissed from office. Perhaps this was the end. If so, it would be a fatal one. And there would have been nothing like it before.

Feeling utterly bewildered, he kept walking toward the center of the city. He decided to find out all he could. After all, he was a responsible person, and even though his position was a minor one, relatively speaking, he was still responsible and should see everything for himself.

The din was unbearable, as though every atom on earth were yelling at once. Flames were spreading everywhere, dancing in windows, crackling on roofs, licking at walls, and flying up into the smoke that hung where the sky should have been. The burning smelled hellish, a concoction of wood, clothes, and different kinds of oil. Stifled cries could be heard coming out of the smoke. Young men and boys, in frenzied unconcern, were destroying everything, and walls kept collapsing with a rumble like thunder. Concealed anger, suppressed despair, unreleased tension, all the things people had been nursing inside them, had suddenly burst their bottle, exploding like some hurricane of demons.

Many things would be burned, he told himself, but not Cairo. You people don't know what you're doing. A whole division of British troops couldn't do a tenth of the damage you're doing here. The battle at the Canal is over. We lost. I've been through hardships before and my heart doesn't lie to me. The government has no soldiers and the fire is raging out of control. Is it to be allowed to consume this whole great city? Are three million people going to spend the night without any shelter? Are destruction, disease, and chaos going to spread, until the British come back to restore order again? Have people put aside independence, nationalism, and their greater aspirations merely to go through this ordeal of destruction? Creeping into his heart like an ant came a sense of despair and the world momentarily went black before his eyes, and his confidence disappeared.

Men on the street corners urged people on. "Burn! Destroy! Long live the homeland!" they yelled.

He looked at them with curious resentment and would have liked to be able to stop them, but the buffeting stream of people made it impossible even to pause. They were unknown faces to him; not from his party or any other, strangers, who seemed to exude the smell of treason, of which he imagined a putrid reek in the air even more gloomy than the smoke itself. Disconsolate and at a loss, he gave an angry sigh.

"Burn! Destroy! Long live the homeland!"

Miserable wretches! Had all that blood been wasted at the Canal? What about the dead policemen and their officers? Everything valuable, everything worthwhile, was going up in smoke. How could he get to the ministry and find the people in charge? The streets were full of smashed cars; the sky had turned a deep red color as the fires blazed away under their black cloud of smoke. What would the furious commando have to say if he could see this bloody spectacle of treason? What would he say if he could hear these shouts?

"Burn! Destroy! Long live the homeland!"

Fire, destruction, and smoke, the awful hallmarks of the day, made even worse by the air of conspiracy that lurked on street corners. Waves of berserk demonstrators kept crashing into him as if they didn't see him in his long gray coat. Swallowing hard, he said nothing, though he lost his balance, and the briefcase he was clutching knocked against his leg. All the details of the report he had to submit to the minister, describing the way the battle had gone and the commandos' requests, had gone right out of his mind and he thought only about the future, which seemed to loom before his eyes like the smoke of the city burning.

Heading toward a street where things seemed calmer and more quiet, he recalled the comment of a shaikh who was a member of Parliament on the subject of the annulment of the treaty, "It's the end for us," he'd said. "Now things are in God's hands."

He'd been sitting next to the shaikh at the club and had lost his temper at the time. "That's how you people in Parliament are," he had yelled. "You only care about your own interests!"

"This is the end," the shaikh had repeated with great emphasis, in a tone of voice not entirely devoid of irony. "Now it is in God's hands."

"In our entire glorious past," he had said enthusiastically, "there's never been a situation like this one!"

The shaikh had toyed with his mustache. "Oh yes there was," he had replied sadly. "Saad's* time, for example. But it's the end now!"

A seasoned old man might be justified in having put the age of enthusiasm behind him. But here was Cairo burning. And these traitors standing on the street corners—there were so many of them! Everything was quite obvious, but there was so little that could be done about it that the best plan seemed to be to get drunk on a cocktail of woes, to wallow in it until you drowned. The sky itself was strewn with blackened splinters from all the destruction, and a sense of grief seemed to materialize out of it as palpably as from an animal's dead carcass.

He felt tired and decided to head for home, imagining that, tortoiselike, he would have to spend a long time on the road before glimpsing the high parts of Dokki.

---

*An asterisk indicates that the name or term so denoted is explained in the Notes section at the end of the book.

TWO

Later, at nightfall, he went to Shukri Pasha* Abd al-Halim's palatial house, a quarter of an hour away from his own home in Dokki.* The Pasha received him in his study and they sat down facing each other. The Pasha's stubby form seemed almost lost in the big chair and his small, round, smooth-skinned face showed gloom wrapped in the tranquillity of old age. His gray English suit was extremely smart and he wore a red tarboosh on his babylike bald head. The greetings they exchanged were cursory, a sign of the critical nature of the situation. Isa felt awkward at first: the Pasha had had his eye on the ministerial position, but for a month or more Isa himself had hesitated about putting his name forward for the first cabinet reshuffle; and wondered what this old man would be thinking. He'd waited so long for a ministry. But the Pasha's energies for office work had sunk to their lowest ebb and he no longer had any real job except to serve on the Finance Committee in Parliament. Isa felt as sorry for him as he did for himself and looked at him diffidently, as though it were a kind of consolation. After a rest at home some of Isa's color had returned and he felt better as he sat there in the chair, while the Pasha kept turning the wedding ring on his finger. The worst kind of loss was one that affected both private and public life at the same time.

"We'll be dating things from today for a long time to come," the Pasha said.

"I saw some of it myself," Isa said, eager to hear any news. "What a black day!" He lowered his head—which looked large and elongated in the mirror across the room—until his black wavy hair came close to the Pasha's eyes. Then, frowning, he lifted it again so that he could look straight at the Pasha.

"So Cairo was burning when you came in?"

"Yes, Pasha. It was pure hell."

"How terrible! What were things like over at the Canal?"

"The young men were all full of enthusiasm, but they need weapons desperately. The massacre of the policemen shattered everyone."

"That was a criminal affair. A disaster."

"Yes," Isa replied angrily. "We're being pushed toward—" The rest of his sentence needed no saying and his words faded away. Their eyes met sadly.

"What are people saying about us?" the Pasha asked.

"Nationalist feelings are running very high. Our enemies are saying that we manufactured a battle to take people's minds off us." He lowered the corner of his mouth in contempt. "They'll always find something to say," he went on. "Miserable wretches—scoundrels!"

Between them was a table with a silver jug and a tray of biscuits on it. The Pasha motioned to Isa to pour out two glasses and they proceeded to drink although neither of them enjoyed it. During all this, Isa looked around at the picture of Saad Zaghlul* hanging on the wall above the huge desk to the right of where they were sitting.

"Would you believe, sir, that I haven't been able to contact my minister so far?" Isa asked.

The Pasha quietly stroked his silver-gray mustache. "I can't blame you for complaining these days," he said. "Where's the minister? No one knows. Where's the Army? No one knows. Where are the police? No one knows. The public security system has disappeared and meanwhile the devil's on a rampage."

"I wonder if the fire's still burning."

The Pasha stretched his legs till they reached around one of the ebony legs of the table. His black shoes shone more brightly in the gleam of the quadrangular crystal chandelier. Isa glanced at the heater mounted on the wall and was struck by the transparency of the flickering red flame; it made him think of the Magi and he began to enjoy the pleasant warmth it was giving out. His eyes glided over the classical-style furniture, which seemed to be shrouded in a kind of dignity and antique splendor, and at the same time to convey the sorrow of departure, which in turn made him think of Antony's funeral speech over the body of Caesar.

"The fire should be out by now," Shukri Pasha Abd al-Halim replied with careful indifference. That is, now that it has done its job!"

The young man's honey-brown eyes gleamed. He tried to draw some more out of the Pasha. "Maybe it was just reckless anger," he suggested tentatively.

The Pasha showed his teeth as he smiled. "It was anger

all right!" he replied. "But beyond that anger there was envy. Anger may be genuinely reckless, but envy always follows a distinct plan of action."

"How can this happen when we're in power?"

The Pasha gave a dry and abrupt laugh. "Today's like an overcast night," he replied. "Wait till we find out where the head and feet are."

Isa breathed in sharply and then sighed so hard that the fringe of the velvet tablecloth rustled. "What about the parties?" he muttered.

"They're too weak to organize anything at all!" the Pasha replied, both corners of his mouth curving down as a sign of contempt.

"Who then?" asked Isa with a clear look of doubt in his eyes.

"Things are not as obvious as you imagine," the Pasha replied. "It is possible that prearranged signals filtered through from the Palace; it is also possible that English spies are in high spirits over the havoc they have caused. But it seems to me that this deluge began quite naturally and then certain people took advantage of the situation."

Suddenly deep-seated anxieties stirred inside Isa's mind and his heart jumped. "But what about the battle?" he asked.

The Pasha slowly twisted his mustache and looked up at the ceiling, where lights hidden behind golden wings were gleaming in the four corners. Then he looked at the young man again, his eyes showing all the signs of his own uncertainty and depression without needing to say a word.

"Damn anyone who lets himself get talked into trifling with our struggle!" said Isa, trying to fend off his own apprehension.

No signs of cheerful optimism appeared on the Pasha's

face. He simply made do with replying, "Today will have grave consequences."

"For the second time today," said Isa, suddenly feeling listless and defeated, "I'm reminded of what Shaikh Abd at-Tawwab as-Salhubi said after the annulment of the treaty: 'It's the end for us. Now it's in God's hands.'"

The Pasha smiled. "It'll never be the end for us," he said. "We may fall but we'll come back even more powerful than before."

The telephone rang. It was the Pasha's wife calling from the top floor. He looked upset as he put the receiver back in its cradle.

"Martial law's been declared," he said.

They both sat for a while astonished, then Isa broke the silence. "Perhaps it's necessary," he muttered, "so that they can arrest the culprits." But then he noticed that the Pasha was lost in his own morose thoughts, and tried to make amends. "Martial law in our times!" he said. "What a terrible thing to happen!"

"It was not declared because of our times," the Pasha replied, frowning.

THREE

"A decree's been issued transferring me from my position in the minister's office to the archives."

His mother raised her head and looked at him. Her thin face was much like his own, especially in its triangular shape, but heavily wrinkled, with signs of age in her eyes, mouth, and jaw.

"It's not the first time," she said. "Don't worry, you'll get your old job back. Or maybe something even better. Our Lord will put things right."

The sitting room overlooked Sharia Halim in Dokki. The wide window of the balcony was closed as a protection against the cold and behind it willow branches rose and fell limply. Beyond them clouds stretched away into the distance, bunched together, foreboding. Like the political situation. The ministry had been dismissed, and the new minister had removed him from his job, along with many other people, especially anyone who had been connected with the battle at the Canal. But these things had happened so often that his mother had come to regard

them as almost normal. She had become quite used to seeing the most disastrous floods followed by a smooth ebb,
which always turned out to be in the best interests of her
beloved son. Though old and illiterate, she still followed
current events closely and kept up with whatever was
going on in politics, especially with matters that affected
Isa's life.

She was very proud of him and believed everything he
said. His success amazed her—it was so far beyond anything she had ever imagined—it had been beyond the
hopes of either her or his late father, who had spent his
entire life as an obscure minor civil servant. In spite of the
pitfalls and storms of politics, Isa had forged ahead, floun-
dering at times to such an extent that people gave him up
for lost, but then always rising again to achieve some new
level of seniority. This gorgeous house in Dokki was a sign
of his successful ambition, and its furniture was a delight
to behold. Pashas and ministers would frequently favor
him with visits.

His mother held a rosary from the Hijaz* in her gnarled
hands and used the beads in litanies to God. Would there
be an end to this situation, she asked herself, and would
everything turn out for the best? Were there complicated
factors involved which were difficult to comprehend or
was it just that the evil eye had struck?

"It's incredible," said Isa listlessly, "that we have hardly
settled into the business of running the government for a
year before we're thrown out again for four. We're the
legitimate rulers of this country and there are no others
besides us."

"Health and well-being are the important things," the
old lady said with firm conviction.

He smiled bitterly, but concealed his real feelings. "I

think it's important," he said, "that I take advantage of this period of retirement to attend to my personal affairs."

Her dim eyes flickered with interest and for the first time she spoke joyfully: "Oh, I'm delighted. It's about time you got married. The girl is waiting for you and her father has not withheld his consent."

"Wouldn't it be better," he asked with a laugh, "to get married when I'm enjoying a prestigious position in authority?"

She smiled and her teeth gleamed, like some forgotten sprig of jasmine in a garden where all the trees have been uprooted. "You've got a prestigious position now," she said. "People realize that you've been nominated for senior posts. Ali Bey* Sulaiman understands these things very well. And besides, he's your relative. He loved your late father more than anything else in the world."

All this was true. Ali Bey Sulaiman was his father's cousin, on a side of a family tree that was otherwise bare. Rich and from a rich background, he was also an influential justice, quite apart from the fact that he was a Palace man. Once Isa strengthened his position by becoming the Bey's son-in-law, he would be able to depend upon his father-in-law for a convenient harbor to shelter in whenever his boat was rocked by political storms—an important consideration since the losses he would suffer from remaining with the party seemed likely to outlast any possible gains. And besides, Salwa was really a marvelous girl. There was no comparison between her and his other cousin, whose family had been trying for ages to get him to marry her. Salwa's mother was a fine woman too; she tended to a conservatism rare among people of her class. Fortunately for Isa, she thought very well of his future prospects, to such an extent that she could envisage him as a minister even before he himself could: when he had broached the subject of asking for her daughter's hand, she had told him quite frankly that she was not interested in money but in status. And wasn't the second grade* a real sign of distinction for a young man in his thirties? She had a particular admiration for young men who had studied abroad, and even though he had not done so himself, he had still served for a year in the London embassy and traveled as an attaché with the secretariat of the delegation to the treaty negotiations. He liked to visualize Salwa's enticing beauty, her crème-Chantilly complexion. It was just as well for him that she was not a socialite, one of those girls who went to clubs or had taken up modern ideas.

"Do you realize," he asked his mother, "that I hadn't seen her since we were children?"

"That's your fault!" his mother retorted. "The fact that you were so involved in your work is no excuse either. Anyone with a relative like Ali Bey Sulaiman should have kept in as close contact as possible."

"I used to meet him abroad, but I wasn't thinking of marriage at that time."

When he'd asked her father for her hand he'd had only the vaguest picture in his mind of what she actually looked like. But he'd found her to be a real gem and had fallen in love with her with all his heart. He was in the process of choosing the appropriate words to express his new feelings to his mother when Umm Shalabi came in to announce that his cousin Hasan had come to pay him a visit. Still nursing defeat, Isa felt unready for this particular caller, and so it was annoyance that predominated over his other feelings.

Hasan Ali ad-Dabbagh came in beaming. Of medium height, well built, with a square face and deep-lined fea-

tures, he had a broad chin, and his clear intelligent eyes
and sharp-pointed nose were very distinctive. He kissed his
aunt's hand, shook Isa's warmly without managing to
lessen the latter's feelings of annoyance, then sat down
beside him and asked for some tea. He was almost the
same age as Isa but was still in the fifth grade, whereas politics had managed to push Isa up to the second. Though he
had a bachelor's degree in commerce, the only work he'd
been able to find was with the draft board.

"How are you?" Isa's mother asked.

"I'm fine," Hasan replied, "and my mother and sister
are well too."

Isa felt even more uncomfortable at the mention of his
sister; not because he disliked her but because she was the
sister of this old rival of his. They'd been competitors, in
close contact, and had once harbored harsh and painful
sentiments against each other. It was only politics that had
put an end to the causes of this contentiousness between
the two of them: politics had raised Isa to his important
position, while merely nudging Hasan on in slow stages
down a long, arduous road. Their relationship had flagged
somewhat, but feelings ran very deep, and Hasan had
never cut himself off from his cousin completely. Hasan
even wanted Isa to marry his sister and, amazingly enough,
had let it be known that he seriously contemplated going
to see Ali Bey Sulaiman to ask for his daughter's hand only
a few days after Isa had done so himself. Isa had laughed
in scorn when he'd heard the news and told himself that
God should have some mercy on a man who knows his
own worth. Nevertheless, even though he disliked Hasan,
Isa still reserved a certain admiration for him on account
of his strong personality and considerable intelligence.

"I heard you've been transferred to the archives,"

Hasan said. "Don't worry," he continued generously, "you're someone who was made to stand up to hardships."

Isa's mother entered the conversation. "There's nothing to be worried about," she said enthusiastically, "that's what I always say. Why do these people abandon their leaders and then take vengeance on their sons?"

Isa was a little nonplussed by Hasan's sympathy. "We're quite used to being imprisoned and beaten," he said proudly. "Today's afflictions are nothing . . ."

Hasan smiled and went on sipping his tea. "That's right," he said with traces of aggression in his voice, "you're imprisoned and beaten while the other people do a little bargaining."

Isa realized full well whom he meant by "other people" and got ready for battle, while his mother left the room to perform the sunset prayer. "You know very well what I think of the others personally," he said by way of warning, "so be careful!"

"Everything's collapsing so fast," said Hasan with a provocative grin. "It's best to let it happen. The old way of doing things must be torn up by the roots!"

"And what about the problems our nation faces?" Isa retorted. "Who'll be left to deal with them?"

"Do you think that those corrupt idiots in Parliament are the ones to solve them?"

"You don't see them as they really are."

"The truth is that I *do* see them as they really are."

"You keep on repeating exactly the things that the opposition press is saying!"

"I only believe in the truth," Hasan replied with a confidence that was exasperating. "Young people have to rely on themselves."

Isa stifled his own irritation. "A call for total destruction is very dangerous," he said. "If it weren't for this treachery, we could have kept the King within his constitutional limits and got our independence."

Hasan finished his glass and smiled, trying to clear the atmosphere. "You're a loyal man," he said amiably, "and that leads you to respect certain people who don't deserve it. There's widespread corruption, believe me. Nobody in a position of authority today thinks about anything but the rotten game of getting rich quick. We inhale corruption in the very air we breathe! How can any of our genuine hopes emerge from the quagmire?"

They could both hear the sound of Isa's mother praying. For the sake of hospitality, Isa controlled his temper. Nothing could make him admit that what his rival was saying was right: sheer obstinacy would hold him back. But he felt extremely depressed: the world was changing and his gods were crumbling before his very eyes. For his part, Hasan changed the subject and began talking about the property lost in the fire, the estimates of compensation, the position of the British, and the continual arrests. Before long, however, he came back to the point: "Just show me a single sector that doesn't ooze with corruption!"

What appalling notions! How impudent and thoroughly irritating he was! Just then, Isa remembered a totally unconnected event that had happened a long time ago. He had gone to visit Ali Bey Sulaiman's house with his father and found himself alone in the dining room, where he'd noticed a piece of chocolate in a half-opened drawer. He had slipped in his hand and taken it. That had happened almost a quarter of a century ago. What a memory! As always, Hasan kept up his attack—damn him!

"What is it you want?" Isa asked listlessly.

"Fresh clean blood."

"Where from?"

Hasan's pearly teeth gleamed as he laughed with health and well-being. "The country's not dead yet," he said.

"Show me a group of people apart from our party that deserves any confidence!" Isa demanded angrily.

Hasan glared back at him without saying a word. Outside, the old lady's voice could be heard in a flow of prayers.

"What's to be done then?" Isa resumed.

"We'll support the devil himself if he volunteers to save the ship."

"But the devil won't volunteer to save anything." Isa glared away, looking unconcernedly up at the pitch-black sky, trying to avoid Hasan's gaze for a while.

"The English, the King, and the parties, they'll all have to go," Hasan said. "Then we must start afresh."

Isa laughed bitterly. "The burning of Cairo has made it clear that treason is more powerful than the government and the people put together," he said.

His mother came back into the room. "Isn't there something else you can talk about?" she asked. Her cheeks looked flushed and puffy as she sat down in her old seat. "When are you going to get married?" she asked Hasan.

At that point Isa was reminded of Hasan's bold attempt to get engaged to Salwa and that made him even more annoyed. Hasan was poor but brash. It was obvious he was after her money, as a final way of getting himself out of his difficulties.

"Momentous events are happening so suddenly," Hasan replied with a laugh, "and without the slightest warning."

"When will you be seeing your mother to give her our greetings?"

"Your house is a long way from Rod al-Farag, but she'll definitely be coming to visit you." Hasan was on the point of standing up to leave. "Where are you going this evening?" he asked Isa.

"To the club," Isa replied defiantly but calmly.

Hasan got up. "Goodbye," he said, "till we meet again!"

The day the engagement was announced at Ali Bey
Sulaiman's mansion was one to remember. Men and
women were not really separated from each other; they
occupied two drawing rooms connected by a common
entrance which was considered a beautiful work of art in
its own right. Isa's mother and her sister-in-law, Hasan's
mother, were sitting among the female guests in the red
room, while Isa's close friends, Samir Abd al-Baqi, Abbas
Sadiq, Ibrahim Khairat, and his cousin Hasan, were all sitting in the green room among the family guests and rela-
tives. The important guests were being welcomed in the
large room adjoining the entrance. These included Ali Bey
Sulaiman's friends, all of them Palace men or people connected with the law, and party men who were acquaintances of Isa. Isa's mother and her sister-in-law withdrew
into themselves as they sat there in the glare of the brilliant
lights which were shining down on them. Neither of them
seemed to have any connection with the world around her.
Isa's mother was wearing an expensive dress and her age

gave her a certain dignity. Her senses were weak—especially her sight and hearing—and this made her less receptive to the festive atmosphere. She withdrew into herself and made no effort to give any kind of impression that might be considered appropriate for the future groom's mother.

Susan Hanem,* Ali Bey Sulaiman's wife, made a special effort to be nice to her so as to make her feel more at home. She had been fond of Isa's mother for a long time— at least since she had become Ali Bey Sulaiman's wife— and her affection for the old lady had been one of the reasons that had led her to agree to accept Isa as a future son-in-law. A chronic liver disease and a bad kidney condition had left Susan Hanem in her mid-fifties with only her height, proportions, and immutable grace to mark what had once been great beauty. "Don't forget you're in your own home," she told Isa's mother very kindly.

Hasan started a fierce argument about politics with Isa's friends even though he did not know them well. Isa listened to him for a while from a distance. He had thought that Hasan would not come to the reception and his behavior astonished him. Hasan could defy time itself if he wanted, Isa was convinced of that.

But Isa did not stay in one place for long, giving particular attention to his guests from the party. The atmosphere in the room was a little tense. The party men were all facing the Palace men, but even though they were bound together by old ties of friendship, the majority of each group was pretending not to know the other. In all this, Ali Bey Sulaiman was playing his role with unerring skill. He was greeting everyone on equal terms even though he was a Palace man himself. He had been an ordinary lawyer until the Palace had nominated him for the post of justice in one of the judicial reshuffles. Not recognized as having any particular political coloring, he had become a kind of political rainbow, then, just at the right moment, had joined the Unity Party, becoming attached to the King's retinue, from which he had risen to occupy the highest position in the judiciary. Though he was nearly sixty, he still enjoyed extraordinary good health and vigor. He was tall and had a marvelous athletic posture and his black eyes, which gleamed beneath bushy eyebrows, made him irresistibly attractive. Very early in his life he had given himself the valuable support of marrying into the Himmat family—Susan Hanem's family—and had then laid out his patch of earth and planted the aristocracy in his progeny.

He started laughing and joking with all his guests. "Happy occasions should bring together people who disagree about politics!" he said.

"Do you think," Shukri Pasha Abd al-Halim whispered in Isa's ear, "that your relative is acknowledging by that joke that the King's men—and consequently the King himself—aren't above the parties?"

Shaikh Abd as-Sattar as-Salhubi leaned over in their direction to hear what they were whispering and then laughed silently. "In that case," he whispered in turn, "the parties should be above the King!" He then looked anxiously at the picture of the King hanging on the central wall of the room.

Isa smiled. "Don't worry," he said. "People are heaping curses on him quite openly in cafés."

But as the party and the drinks proceeded, the bitterness of politics vanished. Even Isa, who was a political creature above all else, abandoned himself wholeheartedly to his feelings of sheer joy. He knew that he was immaculately dressed, that there was a glow on his triangular face, and that his round eyes looked serene and limpid. The happiness he felt at the thought of marrying into a wealthy and influential family was a mere trifle compared with his feelings about his bride-to-be and his sincere hopes for a really pleasant life, for a tomorrow packed with happiness, a future which would hold the promise of real prestige. He forgot about the burning of Cairo, his dismissal from the ministry and transfer to the archives, the depressing apathy that had dampened popular enthusiasm, the indolence that seemed to be endemic in official quarters, and the gloomy melancholy that, even while the glories of spring were giving physical life an intoxicating stimulus, tinged the horizon.

In his present excited state, Isa did not have to stay in one spot any longer than suited him. He went over to Susan Hanem and they took a final look at the buffet together; everything seemed to be there and it all looked very colorful. Then he made for the green room and sat down with his closest friends, where he would have liked to stay until he was called for the announcement of the engagement. Ibrahim Khairat was looking into the red room. "There's a whole lot of white flesh in there," he said. "It looks beautiful!"

"Do you mean al-Hajja,* Isa's mother?" Abbas Sadiq asked jokingly.

Isa looked at his mother in her expensive but modest gown and was happy that she looked more dignified than Hasan's mother in spite of the latter's beauty. Abbas Sadiq started to complain to him about Hasan. "Your cousin's fiercer than the Cairo fire itself!" he said. Hasan gave a long laugh and Abbas carried on in a cautionary tone. "Get married yourself and you'll be convinced that it isn't all that bad to belong to a party."

"Things are very confused at the moment," Samir Abd al-Baqi interjected.

They all realized that it was politics he was talking about.

"There's no question about that," Isa replied.

"But they're even more confused than is generally apparent," said Samir emphatically.

"May the good Lord honor you!" Hasan said sarcastically.

"They say the King is going to hire mercenaries. Because he doesn't trust anyone any longer!"

"Nothing shows more clearly how bad things are," Abbas Sadiq commented with a laugh, "than what one of the Liberal Constitutionalists said. He declared he'd rather have the Wafd* return to power than put up with the present chaotic state of affairs."

"May God increase the confusion and chaos!" Hasan replied with great emphasis.

Isa was called inside for the announcement of the engagement. Everyone was watching him and there was complete silence; for Hasan it was a very heavy silence. Then the shrill cries of joy echoing through every part of the mansion pierced the air.

Salwa stood with her mother on one side and Isa on the other. Then she walked around among the guests before taking her seat in the red room on a chair banked with roses. She looked really beautiful. She had inherited her mother's stature and long, thin neck, and had her father's eyes set in a face that seemed to have a white translucence like moonlight, but with a sweet gentle expression that showed not only a kindly temperament but also an almost total lack of intelligence or warmth. She looked at her mother continually, as if asking her guidance and help, fearful and insecure at the thought of separation. The guests discussed her dress at length.

As the party continued, the piles of food prepared for the buffet disappeared and guests started to leave, carrying souvenir tins of sweets with them. The engaged couple and Susan Hanem were finally left alone in the sitting room. Its huge veranda looked out onto Baron Street. Night was spreading through the pure spring air, and the full-grown trees around the garden, swimming in the brilliance of the electric lights, swayed from side to side in the gentle breeze, moist with refreshing coolness.

"Today I think I've reached the peak of happiness," Isa said.

"Thank you!" Salwa whispered with a bashful smile. "I hope I can tell you how I feel—when I find enough courage."

Susan Hanem watched them both happily. "When you are married in July, God willing," she said, "our happiness will be complete."

Isa wondered when he would be allowed to kiss Salwa. He was so drunk with happiness that it almost worried him. He would follow in Ali Bey's footsteps, he told himself, and eventually come to occupy the same kind of position. He had never tasted the feeling of love before, except once when he was in secondary school. He'd fallen in love with a nurse at the morning tram stop, and had plunged into the experience headlong—foolishly—but his father had eventually brought him under control again. Now here he was today, having gone through imprisonment, beatings, dismissal, promotion, and demotion, here he was engaged to a fiancée whom he hadn't seen in more than ten years. Now he knew about love and had already drunk from its nectar. He felt almost as if he was clutching guaranteed happiness with his hands. "You're the image of your mother, my beloved," he said, "so dazzling I can't conceive how happy I really am."

Susan Hanem laughed. "I hope you'll remember what you've just said in the future," she said. "People say that we mothers-in-law get to hear nice things like that only on this one occasion!"

Salwa gave a gentle laugh and Isa felt even happier. Suddenly he felt the urge to show off. "I wonder if you'll dislike living abroad," he asked, "if circumstances make it necessary in the future to work in the diplomatic service?"

"Salwa graduated from a German school," Susan Hanem replied for her daughter.

He smiled to show how pleased he was. "Let's hope our life will be happy," he murmured. "We've seen real suffering and I hope our happiness will be real too."

FIVE

"There's a secret in our life," Isa told Salwa, "which you ought to know." They were sitting together on the veranda, the scent of roses and carnations all around them. It was almost sunset; daylight had half-closed its eyelids and the sun was withdrawing its lashes from the mansion rooftops. Spring seemed to be breathing with the pure energy of youth. Susan Hanem had disappeared for a while and left them alone. They were drinking lemonade. A crystal decanter stood on a table of painted rattan.

"A secret?" Salwa whispered inquisitively.

He lifted himself, beginning with his eyebrows, something he always did when he was on the point of speaking. "Yes," he said. "You may think that I hadn't seen you before when I asked for your hand. But in fact I loved you tremendously ten years ago; you were ten and I was twenty. We were living in my mother's house in Al-Wayiliyya* and your family lived out by the Pyramids. Your father was a lawyer in those days and a close friend of my father and they used to visit each other a lot. You were very beautiful then, as you are now, and I fell in love with you. Don't you remember those days?"

She stifled a laugh by biting the inside of her lip. "Only a little," she replied. "I remember seeing rockets on the Prophet's birthday at your house once, but I don't remember anything about your loving me . . ."

He laughed, tossing his head back in a particular way, quite unwittingly copying one of the pashas in the party.

"No one remembers such things," he said. "But my late father had to restrain me once when I was looking at you in utter infatuation and on another occasion when I kissed you!"

"No!"

"Yes! A pure kiss to match your tender age."

"But you weren't a child."

"No, but you were! It doesn't matter anyway. Work hard and you'll marry her, my father told me at the time; make sure you turn out to be a young man who is worthy of her and I'll see you're married! I asked what degree of worthiness was required, and my father replied that Ali Bey Sulaiman was his relative and close friend but we needed Susan Hanem's approval. She was rich and not concerned with wealth; what she wanted for her daughter was a successful young man—a judge, for example. The fact of the matter is that my own rapid promotion has impressed a number of people. I've become an important civil servant—no, politician even—at a very early age. But no one knew what the real reasons were for this unusual energy on my part!"

With a graceful gesture, she opened an ivory fan. On its outer edge was a picture of a swimming duck. "All this, and yet you hadn't been to see me for ten years!" she said with mild irony.

"Don't forget," he said earnestly, "that your father was appointed a justice after that, that he worked for years plying between Asyut and Alexandria, and that I myself got heavily involved in politics."

"How were you to know that ten years hadn't turned me into something awful?" she asked with a coquettish smile.

"My heart! I trust its feelings. And when I saw you again my confidence in it was doubled. So our betrothal may seem traditional on the surface, but there's a real love story behind it even though it was all one-sided."

"Well, at any rate," she murmured, gazing into the distance, "it's not that way any longer."

He took her chin between his fingers, turned her head gently, leaned forward until his hungry mouth met her soft lips in a throbbing kiss, then drew his head back again, smiling with a sense of happiness so deep that as his eyes wandered over the collection of flowerpots on the veranda, they were misted with emotion like a fog-covered windowpane. The tale he'd told her was not a complete fabrication. Not all along the line, in any case. He had often admired her beauty in the past and he really loved her now, even if he'd forgotten her for ten years. So what harm was there in a little white lie, which was a shining example of good sense and which would give their relationship a magical beauty of its own?

His beloved was not ready, however, to be parted from her mother; it was almost as though the midwife had forgotten to sever the umbilical cord. This attachment worried him sometimes. He looked forward eagerly to the day when he would really have her completely as his own and was somewhat disturbed by the way she looked at her mother during breaks in conversation. But his happiness swept all misgivings away, just as a big wave will sweep away the flotsam from a beach and leave it smooth and clean, and he found delight in the fact that she had so appallingly little experience of life's normal happenings. Her innocence may in fact have flattered his own feelings by simply giving him a sense of superiority. He was also pleased at her love of music and her wide reading of travel literature.

"For me your love is a treasure without price," he said. "When I came to meet you for the first time, I asked God that I might make a good impression on you."

"I'd seen you before in the newspapers."

"If I'd known that at the time, I'd have taken more care getting ready for the photograph!" he replied delightedly.

"That doesn't matter. But I also heard about your misfortunes in politics."

As he laughed, he threw his head back once again like the pasha. "I wonder what you make of that?" he asked. "I'm an old friend of police truncheons and prison cells. I'm quite used to being dismissed and expelled. What do you think of that?"

She bit the inside of her lip once more. "Papa says . . ."

"There's no need to quote Papa on the subject," he interrupted quickly. "I know what he thinks already; he belongs to the other side. But don't you think about anything but music and travel books? From now on, you're going to have to prepare yourself for the role of a politician's wife—a politician in every sense of the word."

Susan Hanem came back into the room. "Everything is as you wish," she said, sounding like someone announcing that a project had been successfully concluded.

"Thank you, madame," Isa replied, standing there in his sharkskin suit. They both sat down. "The marriage will be in August, then," he continued, smoothing his trousers over his knees, "and afterwards we'll travel directly to Europe."

Their eyes met in delight. The last ray of the sun had disappeared. "I was telling Salwa that I've loved her for ten years!" he told Susan Hanem.

The lady raised her eyebrows in surprise. "Don't believe everything he tells you," she warned her daughter. "Your fiancé is a politician and I know all about these politicians!"

All three of them dissolved in laughter.

S I X

Isa was at breakfast on the morning of the twenty-third of July* when the radio interrupted its normal broadcast to announce the Army declaration. At first he did not fully comprehend what he was hearing. Then he leapt up and stared at the radio, listening dry-mouthed to these strange words which kept following each other, forming startling sentences. When he realized what he was hearing, his immediate reaction was dismay. He reeled, like someone suddenly coming out of darkness into brilliant light. What could it all mean?

He went into the sitting room and sat down next to his mother. "Very grave news," he said.

She raised her dim eyes in his direction.

"The Army's defying the King!" he said.

She found the news hard to digest. "Is it like the days of Urabi Pasha?"* she asked.

Ah! Why had that thought not occurred to him? He was really in a very agitated state. "Yes," he muttered, "like the days of Urabi."

"Will there be war?" she asked anxiously.

What would really happen? He couldn't get any more news now since there was no one left in Cairo to consult. The only reason why he himself was not on vacation was that he'd postponed it until the time for his trip abroad.

"No, no," he told his mother, "the Army's making some demands and they'll be met. That's all there is to it."

He traveled to Alexandria, mulling over what had happened en route. Here was the tyrant himself being dealt a blow of steel: it should match the brutality of his own tyranny and should be final—let him burn, in the contemplation of his own crimes. Just look at the consequences of your errors and stupidity! But where would this movement stop? What would be the party's role in it? At one moment, Isa would feel intoxicated by a sense of hope; at others, he would be overcome by a feeling much like the whimpering uneasiness dogs show immediately before an earthquake.

He found Abd al-Halim Pasha in Athenios* wearing a white suit of natural silk with a deep red rose in the buttonhole of the jacket. In the glass on the table in front of him, all that was left was the froth of a bottle of stout, looking as though it was stained with iodine. The Pasha narrowed his eyes languorously. "Forget about the Army's demands," he said. "The movement's bigger than that. The demands can be met today and the people who are putting them forward will hang tomorrow. No, no, my dear sir! But it's very difficult to judge what's behind it all."

"Haven't you any news, sir?"

"Things are moving too fast for news. Goodwin, the English journalist, was sitting where you are just an hour ago, and he assured me that the King's finished."

The shock was tremendous. It overwhelmed him for a

moment. "Don't we have any connection with what's going on?" he asked.

"One can't be sure about anything. Who are these officers? And don't forget that our leaders are abroad."

"Maybe their journey abroad has got something to do with the movement?" Isa suggested.

The Pasha's expression showed no signs of optimism. His only comment was a barely audible "Maybe."

They continued their conversation without saying anything new; this became an end in itself, providing a release for their anxieties.

He found Ali Bey Sulaiman in his villa at Sidi Bishr,* sitting in a bamboo rocking chair, his forehead contracted into a frown and looking haggard and sickly, all healthy good looks and innate haughtiness gone. When he looked up and saw Isa approaching, he gave him an anxious stare. "What news have you got?" he asked impatiently.

Isa sat down. He could feel the burden as the Bey, his wife, and his daughter looked at him. As he spoke, there was a superficial calm to his voice, concealing a certain pride at the new factor he was about to introduce to the situation. "The King's finished," he said.

The last gleam went out of the Bey's eyes. He threw a sickly glance through the balcony toward the pounding sea. "What about you? I mean you people. Do you approve?"

For a moment Isa enjoyed a sense of exultation, a moment that seemed itself to swing to and fro above a painful wound. "The King's our traditional enemy," he mumbled.

The Bey sat up straight in his chair. "Has the party got anything to do with what's happening?" he asked.

Isa would have loved to be able to give an affirmative

answer to these people who were looking at him. "I don't have any information about that," he replied, concealing his own chagrin.

"But you can find out, no doubt."

"No one whom I've met knows anything. Our leaders are abroad, as you know, sir."

The Bey snorted angrily. "We've forgotten the lesson of the Urabi revolt pretty quickly," he said. "The British will be marching in soon."

"Is there any news about that?" Isa asked anxiously.

The Bey gave an angry gesture with his hand.

"Wouldn't it be better for us to go to the estate?" Susan Hanem asked.

"No one knows what's best," he answered languidly.

Events moved on until the King left the country. Isa saw it in Alexandria. He also saw for himself the Army movements and the clamorous demonstrations. Conflicting emotions kept preying on his mind, sweeping him around in a never-ending whirlpool. The exhilaration he frequently felt was difficult to confirm, to define, or even to contemplate: though it cured the pains of his own resentment, it did not last, always collapsing against some dark cloud of other emotions. His pleasure was spoiled to a certain degree. Was this the natural reaction to the release of bitter feelings? Or was it the sort of pity that anyone might feel, standing secure over the corpse of a tyrannical rival? Perhaps when we achieve a major goal in our lives, we also lose a reason for our enthusiasm for living. Or could it be that he found it hard to acknowledge a great victory without his party taking the main credit for it?

This was the state of mind Isa was in when Abd al-Halim Pasha's visitors arrived at the latter's mansion in Zizinia.* Their feelings seemed very mixed; some of them were delighted, while others looked apprehensive and even worried.

"Glory to Him who never ceases," the Pasha said.

"Faruq's finished," Shaikh Abd as-Sattar as-Salhubi said in his oratorical manner, "but we need to reassure ourselves."

The ensuing wave of nervous chuckles was devoid of joy. Isa was sitting beside his friends, Samir Abd al-Baqi, Abbas Sadiq, and Ibrahim Khairat. "What about the future?" he asked.

"It will undoubtedly be better than the past!" Abd al-Halim Pasha replied, ignoring the point of the question.

"Maybe he's asking about our own future," Shaikh Abd as-Sattar as-Salhubi said to the Pasha.

"We'll have a role to play," the Pasha replied with an expressionless face, which suited an old politician. "There's no question of that."

Shaikh Abd as-Sattar trembled like a Qur'an reader steeling himself during interludes in recitation. "This movement isn't in our interests," he commented angrily. "I can smell danger thousands of miles away. On the day the treaty was annulled, we lost the King and the British, and now today we're going to lose everything."

"We're the last people who should have to worry about any danger. Or at least that's how it should be."

"We would have done exactly the same as what has happened today," Ibrahim Khairat said, "if only we'd had the strength."

"Yes, but we didn't, Sidi Umar!"* Shaikh as-Sattar retorted sarcastically.

With sudden, hammering violence, the past surged up in Isa's mind, crammed full now of glory and grief, a past, his heart told him, that was taking shape as a bubble about to burst, as a new kind of life from within revealed its outer surface bit by bit, a life charged with new and very strange notions. He could know this new way of life—he had already seen hints of it here and there—but how could it get to know him when he was still inside the bubble and it was about to burst?

His eyes rested on a picture hanging on the wall over the cold heater. It showed a black woman—thick lips and big eyes, not bad-looking. She was leering down at him with a saucy sensuality that spelled out enticement and seduction.

To Isa the atmosphere seemed to be weighed down with a variety of conflicting probabilities, which somehow combined to rob him of his peace of mind. He suffered through his life with his nerves on edge. The postponement of his marriage had become inevitable until such time as the earth had settled under his feet again and his father-in-law had become aware of reality again. Question marks kept springing up in front of his eyes and those of his friends like black flags on the beach when the sea is rough. They all chewed over rumors like colocynth.* Then he learned not only that his cousin Hasan had been selected for an important post but that the way was clear for him to be appointed to even more important and influential positions. As proof that Hasan belonged to the new world, this particular news stunned Isa even more than the events that had given that world birth. For a while, he did not know how to tell his mother about it, but the old lady did not understand how things really were. "Your turn will come," she said naïvely. "Don't be sad. You deserve all the best."

How nice it would be, he told himself, for a man to live far from the realm of his own consciousness. Then the purging statute was announced. He read it with a frenzied attentiveness and bitter despair: the destruction threatening the parties and leaders would destroy him as well; the roots that kept him fixed to the ground would be torn up one by one. What strange things were happening! Here was his friend Ibrahim Khairat, a lawyer and ex-member of Parliament, writing enthusiastically about the revolution in more than one newspaper, as though he were one of the officers himself! Attacking the parties—his own among them, of course—and the past era as though he himself had never been a part of it. Abbas Sadiq, calm and peaceful, a man who had not taken any notice of the events, had found a shield to protect him and had even continued his ambitious quest for promotion with greater hopes than he'd had before. Only Samir Abd al-Baqi, a thin, slender young man with a yellowish complexion and a dreamy look in his green eyes, had suffered the same fate as Isa and shared his own anxious fears. In him Isa found some consolation. "What will happen to us, do you think?" he asked.

"Dismissal is the least we can expect," Samir replied with a pallid smile.

"What should we do?" he asked with a dry throat.

"A worthless salary. But we might find a job with a company."

"I wonder if that could be arranged for us. Could we find the courage to start at the very beginning all over again?"

His friend shook his head. There were even a few gray hairs among the black.

"Maybe events will prove us wrong," Isa muttered spiritlessly.

Complaints piled up in the office of the Purge Committee like so much refuse. Isa gathered that most of them were aimed at him. This did not surprise him, however, in view of the nature of the situation. Of the people who now held senior positions in the ministry, more were his enemies than were his friends. To those he could add the spiteful and the jealous as well as others who would volunteer for any opportunity to inflict some damage. Some of these people defied him openly in the ministry for no particular reason and made sarcastic remarks about him to his face. Even a few of his subordinates considered themselves permitted to look on him with contempt. All this turned the ministry into a corner of hell itself.

Then he was summoned to appear before the Purge Committee. It was seated behind a green table that stretched across the room in the office of the legal adviser to the ministry. The secretariat occupied one end of the table; he was asked to sit down facing the members of the committee, who sat on the opposite side. On the wall behind them, he noticed that God's name in a frame had taken the place of the King's picture. When he looked at the faces of the people sitting in front of him, he recognized the representative of the State Council as an old colleague of his on the Students' Committee; they had both almost been killed one day during a demonstration in front of the parliament building—and his mouth felt a little less dry. The committee only looked at him gravely, however, or glanced into their dossiers. None of them gave the slightest indication of having worked with him, even though the personnel director and the director of the general administration

332 / Naguib Mahfouz

numbered among them. There'd been a time when he'd made several members of this committee tremble even when his party was not in power. But now a cold neutrality had taken the place of sympathy or cordiality: an icy terror pervaded the atmosphere of this big room with its high ceiling and dark walls, filled with the smell of stale cigarettes. Through the glass of the locked door, he saw a kite land on the outside balcony and then take off again at great speed, making a noise like a dirge.

The chairman stared at him for a long time through his dark blue gold-rimmed spectacles. "I hope you're completely convinced of our impartiality," he said. "We seek only justice."

"I've no doubts of that," Isa replied, a calm smile concealing his desperation.

"I want you to know that the purpose of the task with which we have been entrusted is to serve the public interest. There's no idea of revenge or any other motive . . ."

"I've no doubts about that either," Isa replied, sinking several levels further into the clutches of despair.

A gesture was made toward the secretariat and then the petitions were read out one after the other. Some of them came from civil servants, others from *umdas*.* The voice of the person who was reading them out became as monotonous as the *faqih** who intones advice to the dead at funerals. In an attempt to concentrate, Isa closed his eyes. All the accusations applied to the appointment of *umdas* on the basis of party bias and gifts, and, in the midst of so much repetition, his concentration lapsed, melting into the darkness he'd chosen by closing his eyes, which felt as if arrows were piercing them through a red fog. His efforts to regain his concentration were thwarted then by something he remembered from early childhood. It sprang up in his mind as fresh and vivid as some tender plant like youth itself: he was coming home from a game of football in the open country around Al-Wayiliyya, the rain was pouring down in torrents, and the only protection he could find was under a refuse cart. Asking himself what it meant, he opened his eyes and saw faces wavering up and down; it looked to him for an instant as though the left side of the legal adviser's mustache was connected to the right side of the State Council representative's. He was asked for his opinion. What opinion? "Rubbish! All of it!" he shouted in fury. "I would like to see one piece of proof." With this vigorous outburst, however, his energy was exhausted and he collapsed like a wilted leaf.

"The minister relied on your nominations," the chairman commented, "so you were primarily responsible."

"That was one of my duties and I carried it out in a way that satisfied my own conscience."

"Is there any other criterion—apart from party bias—to account for the appointment and dismissal of *umdas?*"

"Suppose party politics were the criterion," he replied, trying desperately to control his erratic breathing, his trembling. "Wasn't that one of the mainstays of our past life?"

"Are you satisfied with the propriety of your conduct?"

"I consider that it was quite normal."

"What about the gifts?" the chairman asked, playing with a Parker pen in his hand.

"I told you that was rubbish," Isa retorted angrily. "I'd like to see one piece of evidence."

The names of *umdas* themselves who were witnesses were read out.

"What's the point of this vulgar intrigue?" Isa yelled.

Afterward, civil servants who had worked with him for some time were called in to give testimony, then his own signatures were shown to him, on authorizations for promotion of civil servants in exceptional circumstances, orders for irrigation and farming services, and recommendations on behalf of provincial criminals connected to party hacks by patronage or kinship. As time dragged on, things began to lose their color.

"Show me a single government civil servant who deserves to stay on," he blurted out nervously, his voice too loud.

A member of the committee whom he did not know turned to him and gave him a stern lecture about a civil servant's duties toward the people. "The revolution is determined to purge the governmental machine of all kinds of corruption," he said. "I assure you that in the future no Egyptian will be deprived of his rights or gain any kind of benefit or concession for himself through belonging to any group, family, or organization."

Something deep inside Isa warned him not to argue with this member of the committee, and so he remained silent. The investigation went on until four o'clock in the afternoon and then he left the committee room, feeling like a dried-up twig snapped off and devoured by worms. Crossing town toward Dokki, he felt as if he were floating in some sort of Atlantis. The lifeless streets, their lengths and widths, the neighborhoods they intersected, seemed remote, submerged beneath the seething clash of his own self. All he could see, hear, or think about was this unrelenting anxiety that tormented him.

"Why don't you talk to your cousin about the situation?" his old mother asked. "He's one of them!"

Her advice stung him, and he was aware that an insane look of rage flashed in his eyes.

EIGHT

The personnel director called him in to tell him that the decision had been taken to pension him off, crediting him with a two-year addition to his period of service. This was the same director who had written the memoranda connected with Isa's advancement, through promotion by exceptional promotion, all the way up to the second grade; he might still have the draft memorandum about his promotion to the first grade which had been prepared for submission to the cabinet, Isa knew, one week before the treaty had been annulled—the promotion that, in the course of events that had followed the annulment of the treaty, there had been no chance to confirm. The director himself had no party affiliation. Isa did not doubt for a moment, however, that the man loathed him: they held the same rank, after all, despite the enormous difference in their ages. He seemed moved by the situation and took advantage of the fact that there was no one else in the room to say so. "God only knows, Isa," he said, "how really sorry I am!"

Isa thanked him. He knew perfectly well the man was lying. Eight years of dealing with civil servants was quite enough to make him expert at translating their stock phrases of courtesy into what they really meant. There was his file thrown down on the desk with his name written on the cover in Persian script: ISA IBRAHIM AD-DABBAGH. In his imagination, he pictured it being thrown into the Records Office, where it would be buried forever, along with old signatures that testified to his distinction and gave promise of a happier future. He asked the director how much his pension would be.

"Twelve pounds," he was told, "but you'll also receive your full salary for a period of two years."

He left the ministry building, his eyes fixed on something inside his head, resigned to the fact that he had been destined to live through one of those lurches in history when it makes some important leap forward but forgets about the people it bears on its back, not caring whether they manage to hang on or lose their balance and fall off.

He wandered aimlessly for a while in the sunlight, oblivious of the identity of the streets he walked along, then thought of his favorite café, El Bodega, and headed in that direction. As it was noon, there was no hope of finding any of his friends there, and so he sat down and ordered a tea by himself, with his own melancholy image in the polished mirrors to keep him amused. A group of backgammon players, hovering with bated breath over the next throw of the dice, provided an appropriate example of the total indifference with which the world regarded his troubles.

He turned away from them and from the other people there who were drowning themselves in *nargila** smoke. He stared at his own dismal reflection. If this image could speak, he thought, then I would really find a person who understood me. Tell me, what have you done? Why didn't you read the future when it was only a few hours away from you, you who can confirm things that happened on this earth millions of years ago? The face, with its big head and triangular shape, praised by a poet and likened to the Nile Delta; this face which had been a contestant for front-page coverage in the newspapers, how could it possibly fall into oblivion like some dinosaur? Or like the tea you are drinking which has been pulled out of the good earth in Ceylon to get stuck eventually in the Cairo sewers? If you go up several thousand feet into space, you cannot see anything living on the earth's surface or hear a single sound; everything fuses into a cosmic insignificance. All indications point to the fact that the mighty past which is still breathing around your face will dissolve in the near future and decay. All that will remain will be a foul smell.

"My heart told me I'd find you here," a raised voice said nervously. Samir Abd al-Baqi came up and sat down beside him. He looked haggard and dispirited, almost as though he were looking at him through bars. Isa was so delighted to see him that he shook his hand fiercely in a manner that seemed to be a plea for help as well.

"My heart told me I'd find you here!" Samir repeated with more assurance.

Isa laughed loudly, so loudly that the café owner behind the table blinked. "After today," he said, "this is the only place you'll find me."

Samir gave him a mortified look with his green eyes. "It's the same with me," he said. "I left the ministry for the last time today."

They looked at each other for a long while, each of them plunged in despair. Then Isa had a feeling of mirth;

it seemed strange and not really genuine, as though he had been drinking or taking drugs.

"What's to be done?" he asked.

"We've two years' grace on full salary."

"What about afterwards?"

"We may be able to find a job with a company."

"Which company will risk taking us on?" Isa asked doubtfully.

"There's a solution to every problem," Samir replied with a sigh.

Isa started on his way home. He looked at people with curiosity as though he were seeing them for the first time. They were strangers and had nothing to do with him; nor had he anything to do with them. He was an outcast in his own big city, banished without really being banished. He was amazed at the way the ground had suddenly collapsed under his feet like a puff of dust and how the pillars which had withstood fate for a quarter of a century had crumbled. When he got home, he looked at his mother's withered face and then sprang the news on her. She put her hand on the top of her head as though she were trying to stop the mounting pain. "Why are they doing that to you, my son?" she asked with a sigh.

Fortunately she did not know anything. Walking slowly around the house, he thought about how expensive it was. He couldn't possibly keep it now. Two years' salary, even added to what was left in the bank of the *umdas'* gifts, wouldn't last longer than two years. All those objects decorating the entrance, the reception room, and the library were "gifts" too. Certainly the crooks outnumbered the people who had been dismissed for crookedness. He was guilty, though, and so were his friends: what had happened to the good old days? Gifts were forbidden, after all, a mark of corruption. But this sudden loss of everything, just when he was on the very threshold of a senior position, which would have led to the minister's chair! How could you live in a world where people forgot or pretended to forget, where there were so many others who gloated over the whole thing with unfeeling malice, where hard-won honors were being stripped away and vices trundled out and exposed, unfurled like so many flags?

In the afternoon, he went to Ali Bey Sulaiman's villa. The sky was lined with clouds and a chill breeze stirred up the dust blowing like the khamsin* winds. As he climbed the broad marble steps, he thought to himself that if it were not for judicial immunity, Ali Bey Sulaiman would have been thrown into the street along with him. The Bey was outside, but Susan Hanem was in bed with a chill. Salwa appeared in a blue velvet dress. Her face gleamed out from the top of the dress like a beam of light—beautiful, but so expressionless that he could detect no reaction to recent events. His worried heart fluttered when he saw her and a spasm of love throbbed inside him like an escaped melody. He told himself she was the only thing of value he had left, and in the very next moment asked himself if she really belonged to him! "Salwa," he blurted out abruptly, anxious to put an end to any doubts, "they pensioned me off today."

Her beautiful, languid eyes blinked. "You?" she whispered in astonishment.

"Yes, me. The same thing is happening to many people these days," he said, entrusting things to fate.

"But you're not like the others!" she replied, staring at him.

Her words stabbed like a spear through the eye, and his mind reeled, his thoughts hanging suspended only by the gifts and the bank balance. "They're taking advantage of us in the name of the purge," he said.

Salwa glanced casually up at the bronze statue of a Maghrebi* horseman mounting his steed, as if asking it for an opinion. "What an insolent thing to do," she murmured.

"I'll find a better job than the one I've got at the moment," he went on, feeling encouraged.

She smiled at him as if to apologize for always seeming so listless. "Where?" she asked.

How much did she really love him? What new betrayals would the days ahead hold for him? A man's image suddenly intruded into his consciousness and under his breath he cursed the chairman of the Purge Committee. "With a company or else in some private-sector enterprise," he replied.

The tip of her tongue showed as she moistened her lips, an action so unstudied as to suggest that for a moment she had lost interest in the impression she was making. He was aware of how disappointed she must be. "Let me draw some strength from you," he said hopefully.

Only her mouth smiled. "I wish you success," she murmured.

He put his hand over hers on the arm of the chair. "Love," he said in something close to a whisper, "can scoff at problems like these quite easily."

"Yes, yes . . ."

She might have been a little phlegmatic by nature, but she undoubtedly loved him. Overwhelmed by an urge to clasp her, he leaned forward and put an arm around her. She gave him a velvety look, surrendered her body to his arm, and a spark of sudden lust shot out from deep down in his troubled soul. He lowered his eager lips against the softness of hers and released himself to a passionate craving for consolation. But she reached up a hand to stop him, turning her face away to escape from this frenzied onslaught; they drew apart, panting, then sat back in an awful silence, during which each read the thoughts in the other's eyes, reprimand on her part and apology on his. His voice emerged broken from the confusion. "Salwa," he said, "I love you. My entire life is embodied in one thing—you."

She patted his hand sympathetically.

"You should say something," he said.

She sighed deeply and seemed to regain composure. "We must face up to life," she said, "and everything in it."

He heard the sweet melody of her voice with a profound calm. He would have liked them to leave the world and go to some unknown place forever; a place where there were no politics, no jobs, no revolutions, and no past. "Will you give me your trust and encouragement?" he asked, the first signs of cheerfulness in his voice.

"You can have what you want and more," she replied, dabbing her lips with a handkerchief.

He wanted to embrace her again, but Ali Bey Sulaiman's voice was heard outside announcing that he was about to come in.

NINE

The Bey came toward them half smiling and stayed for a short while, then called Isa away for a talk in his study, a room set far back from the street and so dark that the Bey put on the lights. Isa looked at him anxiously and read a deep concern in his eyes. He asked himself whether it had anything to with him or was merely the result of recent events: looking up, he noticed that a picture of the Bey in his judicial uniform had taken the traditional place of the King.

"How are things?" the Bey asked.

"I'll start afresh," Isa replied, pretending to make light of things. He told the Bey about his unhappy situation, as he saw it.

The Bey thought for a while. "You won't find things easy," he said.

"I know that, but I'm not discouraged."

The Bey looked extremely serious. "To tell you the

truth," he confessed, "your news didn't come to me as a surprise."

"Did the chairman of the committee tell you, sir?"

"Yes."

"Wouldn't it have been possible . . ."

"Certainly not. It's true he's a friend, but the committee's more powerful than the chairman. And everyone's afraid."

"In any case," Isa said bitterly, "what's happened has happened. Let's think about the future."

"That's the best thing you can do."

"I've spoken to Salwa about it," said Isa, taking on the unknown.

"Salwa! Did you really tell her?"

"It was only natural."

"Everything?" the Bey asked after a pause.

Isa looked at him warily. "Of course!" he replied, rather unnerved.

"What did she say?"

"Exactly what I would have suspected," he replied, inwardly considering all the possible options. "She's with me at all times, good and bad."

The Bey drummed with his fingers on the glass-covered top of the desk. "I want to be perfectly frank with you," he said. "Marriage is now quite out of the question!"

"That's true at the moment, of course!"

The Bey shook his head, as though, in addition to what he had stated so frankly, there was something else, something that he was keeping hidden.

"I'm a political victim," Isa said, trying to probe deeper.

The Bey raised his bushy eyebrows without saying a word.

"It's often been my privilege to be in this situation," Isa continued, stung to anger.

"It wasn't just politics this time," the Bey retorted.

Their eyes met and they stared at each other uneasily, while a new wave of fury came over Isa. "Explain further, please," he asked in a quavering voice.

"You know what I mean, Isa," the Bey replied, in a voice filled with exasperation and sorrow.

"Have you any doubts about me?" Isa barked, in a tone that seemed to make even the corners of this sedate room sit up and listen.

"I didn't say that."

"Then what are you driving at?"

"All the evidence looks grave," the Bey replied, frowning at Isa's tone of voice.

"It's not just grave," Isa shouted. "It's despicable—so despicable that it takes a despicable mind to digest it!"

"Your nerves are obviously—"

"My nerves are like iron, and I mean every word I'm saying."

"If you make me angry, you will truly regret it!"

His chances of having Salwa had been reduced to a hundred to one. "I don't care how things are," he yelled, "or how grave the evidence is you've mentioned. I've never been an opportunist for a single day. And the ex-King had no—"

The Bey leapt to his feet, his face black with anger, and he pointed to the door with a quivering arm, wordless. Isa left the room.

In spite of this scene, Isa decided not to give in to despair before making one final effort to defend the sole corner of consolation that had not yet been destroyed for him: the last word had to come from Salwa and no one else. Neither the strength of her character nor the depth of her love gave him great expectations, but he phoned her next day in the afternoon. "Salwa," he pleaded, "I've got to see you immediately."

Back came her answer like a slap in the face.

T E N

"There must be a solution to every problem!" Ibrahim declared as they sat in their corner at El Bodega. Ibrahim was so small that for his feet to touch the floor he had to sit close to the edge of his chair, with the brow of his over-sized head furrowed to give him a stern and serious air and thus discourage any would-be jesters from poking fun at him. The four men had piled their coats on two adjacent chairs and sat there in the crowded, noisy café with their heads close together. Ibrahim Khairat could feel relaxed when talking about problems and how to solve them, Isa told himself; the recent earthquakes had not caused any losses in his world. He was a successful lawyer and a brilliant journalist. It was the same with Abbas Sadiq, who was secure in his job even though he'd been grabbing money from more people than Isa himself. There was no envy, resentment, or anger to disturb their firm friendship, however, or their long-standing political camaraderie.

Samir Abd al-Baqi took a handful of peanuts from a

heaped saucer. "That's all very well," he said. "But the days keep rolling by without our finding a real solution."

Isa looked through the window at the drizzle falling outside. "Do we start at the beginning of the road, on a typewriter?"

Abbas Sadiq began puffing at a *nargila* and blowing smoke, joining the orchestra of smokers already in the café. Smoke hung like fog around the lamps suspended from the ceiling. Isa surveyed the café, scrutinizing people's faces and their different expressions, the daydreamers looking drowsy, the people playing games with looks of fierce concentration. Why was it his fate, he asked himself in dismay, to swim against the current of history, which has been flowing for eternity? He looked out through the windowpane onto the street, inundated by rain and light, and examined with lust a woman hurrying for shelter in the dark entrance of a building. "Winter's beautiful," he said, "but Cairo isn't ready for it."

"Don't forget," Ibrahim Khairat said to Abbas Sadiq, "that our men are scattered around on the boards of directors of several companies."

Here he was talking about them and saying "our men" while at the same time writing articles attacking parties and partisanship and trying to rub out the old days altogether. Loathing reaches a very low ebb when it leads to utter disgust, but then disgust itself is an important element in loathing. The confusing exception was his own past life—and theirs—which had been marked by affection and magnanimity.

"Tell me what your feelings are," Isa asked, "when you read your articles in the newspapers?"

"I ask myself why God willed Adam to appear on the

earth!" Ibrahim Khairat answered quite calmly, ignoring everyone's grins.

Abbas Sadiq raised his head from the mouthpiece of the *nargila*. He was pudgy, white-faced, his protruding eyes gleamed like a symptom of disease, and he was completely bald, with an overall appearance that would have led you to believe he was at least ten years older than he actually was. "We'll all be unhappy," he said, "till we see you both installed in two important posts with a decent company."

Trying to penetrate into the minds of these people who were clustered for no apparent reason in this café, Isa let his own mind wander through past millennia, questioning their meaning, and was at first perplexed, then alarmed. He turned again toward the window. A beggar was standing outside, giving him an imploring look. The rain had stopped. "Just imagine," Isa said to his friends, "these human beings are originally descended from fish!"

"But aren't there still millions and millions of fish crowding the oceans?"

"That's the real cause of our tragedy," he replied firmly, dismissing the beggar with a wave of his hand. "Sometimes," he continued, "it gives me great comfort to see myself as a Messiah carrying the sins of a community of sinners."

"Are you sure of the historical facts?" Abbas Sadiq asked.

He'd been sure enough, he told himself, when that telephone was slammed down.

"This would be a good time for some brandy!" said Ibrahim Khairat.

With a little water, Samir Abd al-Baqi washed down a mouthful of peanuts. "Even supposing we did do wrong," he said, "Couldn't they find anything in our past records to compensate for our conduct?"

Isa closed his eyes to hear the past, its living heart-beats, the seemingly endless roar of glory, the rocket-like hiss and crack of soldiers' truncheons. There had been self-destructive enthusiasm, then sedition sapping at aspirations, with apathy creeping forward like a disease, followed by earthquakes without even the uneasy howl of a dog's warning. And the hollow-hearted search for consolation. And finally the buzz of the telephone line, the source of a void.

"We were the vanguard of a revolution," Samir Abd al-Baqi said, "and now we're the debris of one!"

"I say we should keep up with the procession," said Ibrahim Khairat, as though in a general way he was trying to justify his own position.

A sorrowful look appeared in Samir Abd al-Baqi's green eyes. "We're fated to die twice," he said.

"That's true," said Isa, endorsing his view, "and that's why we're fed on fish!"

They noticed the shoeshine man banging his box on the floor alongside them and resorted to silence till he had gone, when Samir Abd al-Baqi aroused their curiosity by laughing out loud. "I remember I once almost joined the military college!" he said.

They all laughed.

"How do you think I can feel so cheerful," quipped Ibrahim Khairat, "when things are getting darker and darker?"

Offering condolences, Isa told himself, is not the same thing as being bereaved yourself. Leaving the café at about ten in the evening, wrapping his coat around him, he looked up at the sky and saw thousands of stars; he could smell winter in the clear air after the rain. The pavement looked washed and gleamed with grayish reflection. An invigorating wind, as cold as a gibe, brushed his face in staccato gusts. He felt very strange again and kept himself calm with the thought of the two years' full salary and the remainder of the *umdas'* gifts in the bank.

In Groppi's,* he sat down alongside Abd al-Halim Shukri and Shaikh Abd as-Sattar as-Salhubi, who was in the process of whispering the latest joke. They both asked him, perfunctorily, about the latest news. He expected the Pasha to disclose the results of the efforts he'd made to find him a job.

"Are you still happy the treaty was annulled?" the Shaikh asked ironically.

He realized that the Shaikh had an obsession with the question of the annulled treaty. All the calamities that had fallen on them stemmed from it alone.

"Events are striking our colleagues down like thunderbolts," Abd al-Halim Shukri said, and then asked, "Is our turn coming?"

Isa sipped his tea and looked at the faces of people around him enjoying food and drink. Suddenly Abd al-Halim Shukri leaned toward him. "Anticipation is better than doubt," he said.

Furiously disappointed, Isa reminded himself that in the old days all these people had come to see him with some favor they wanted done. Why on earth were they snubbing him now? As he was leaving, foxy laughter burst from the mouth of a beautiful woman, as sexy as a suggestive song. In the street, the sorrows that had bent him double when the telephone was slammed down suddenly overwhelmed him again and, in spite of the cold, he almost melted away.

He had loved her without once doubting that she was worthy of his love. It was true that each had accepted the other at the very beginning on the basis of other attractions which had nothing to do with love, but he had loved her quite genuinely afterwards. She had been very quick to slam the phone down in his face. Perhaps he was lucky to have suffered this blow to the heart at the same time as the blow to his political career; it could not monopolize his feelings.

His anger over all this had begun to get so out of hand that there was no room in his mind for anything of value. How can you imagine, he asked himself, that you really want to work, as you've made these other people think? Work is the very last thing you want. Who cares if these drunkards know it? Why not tell them? But before you do that, at least start looking for distractions. Let yourself enjoy a lengthy convalescence—longer than death itself. And let whatever happens happen.

His cousin Hasan came to visit him. Isa told himself that no one doing well in the world ever comes to see someone who has been left behind. So why had Hasan come? At the thought of Hasan's sister anger rose up in him, but a supreme effort enabled him to be welcoming. Their relationship alone brought them together, and he wanted to hide like a criminal, but he succeeded in putting on a happy front in spite of his nervous exhaustion. Hasan's vitality, on the other hand, seemed at its peak, and his handsome, distinctive features were flushed with confidence and success. No longer the carping defeatist, he would soon, no doubt, be generously offering sympathy!

Some instinct in Isa's mother made her take an interest in Hasan's visit, and she stopped muttering her prayers so that she could hear every word being spoken. Hasan sipped his tea, smacking his lips, then asked Isa how things were. Isa answered by laughing, but said nothing. Hasan repeated his question.

"Can't you see," Isa replied, "that I'm living like a notable?*"

"It's time you got a job," Hasan said earnestly.

Isa's mother blinked and looked hopeful; she agreed with what Hasan was saying. Isa was annoyed at her hasty reaction and asked himself suspiciously what the real reason for the visit might be, vowing that he would never agree to marry Hasan's sister even if it meant dying of hunger. "I could find work if I wanted," he replied with a false air of confidence.

"Why don't you want to?" Hasan asked, with what seemed an air of brotherly concern.

"I want a long rest, something like two years or more."

"You're joking, of course!"

"No," Isa replied. "I see no need to hurry," he went on in an irate tone of voice, "especially as my engagement has been broken off."

Hasan looked at the tree standing motionless outside the window, avoiding his friend's gaze. He said nothing.

"Had you heard the news?" Isa asked anxiously.

"Yes," Hasan replied, in a voice that showed he did not like the subject. "I heard about it. During a conversation I had in passing with Ali Bey. A most regrettable situation!" The last words sounded critical.

"I taught him a lesson he won't forget!" Isa snapped.

"I gathered as much from our conversation, although the Bey didn't mention it in so many words. But let's change the subject. Maybe the best thing is to accept the choice God has made." He looked affectionately at Isa. "I've got a job for you with a respectable company," he said.

The sudden frown on Isa's face showed Hasan that something was troubling him.

354 / Naguib Mahfouz

"A company that produces and distributes films," Hasan continued. "I've been chosen as deputy director, but we need a qualified accounting supervisor."

"Hasan," Isa's mother exclaimed, "that's very good of you!"

Now the picture was becoming very clear, Isa told himself. I'm to be a civil servant with him as my boss, and a husband for his sister as well. If that's the case, then death take me whenever it wishes!

"I both congratulate and thank you!" he said carefully, and then smiled apologetically. "But I must decline."

Disappointment was written all over Hasan's face and seemed to dampen momentarily its overflowing vitality. "Won't you think about it?" he asked.

"I thank you once more, but no!"

Hasan looked at him and then at his stupefied mother. "It's a very respectable job," he said.

"I'm sure it is, but I'm determined to have a long vacation."

Hasan paused for a moment. "It's not just a job," he said. "It's also an opportunity to involve yourself in the new system. Our aim in creating this new company is to serve the government's interests."

"At the moment," Isa replied firmly, "rest is more important to me than any interest."

From junior civil servant to deputy director of a company! Isa's desire to boycott work entirely grew suddenly stronger. He knew it was insane, yet he felt even more self-destructive. He stood his ground resolutely while Hasan tried other ways to persuade him. Eventually he departed without any positive result, which left Isa with a feeling of blind joy over a momentary victory.

"I don't understand anything," his mother sighed.

"Nor do I," he replied sarcastically.

"You don't like your cousin Hasan, do you?" she asked.

"He doesn't like me either!"

"But he didn't forget his family ties at the right moment!"

"He didn't do it for nothing!"

"So what?" she retorted insistently. "His sister is better than Salwa. Have you forgotten? I wish you'd think about it."

Isa looked fixedly through the tree branches at the clouds bunched up on the horizon.

"I'm really thinking of leaving Cairo," he said vaguely.

TWELVE

For months he dithered.

"I'm thinking of going to Alexandria," he told his mother one day.

More accustomed to his strange way of speaking by now, she looked much thinner and had lost her color. "But the summer's over," she replied calmly.

"I intend to stay there, not just for the summer."

Her eyelids quivered anxiously.

"I mean for a period of time," he continued.

"But why?"

"I want to live somewhere no one knows me and I know no one."

"I'm not at all happy about your attitude," she said irritably. "A man should face up to difficulties in some other way. There's still an opening waiting for you with your cousin."

When she saw that he was determined to go, she called on his three sisters to help, and they came hurrying over to Dokki. They were all married and carried the family stamp on their faces, the triangular-shaped features and circular eyes. They all felt a real love for Isa, not just because he was a brilliant person of whom they could feel proud, but also because he was kind enough to arrange for promotions and raises for their husbands during his period of influence. They all agree that he should not go to Alexandria and that he should accept his cousin's proposition. "What's the point of staying in a town like a stranger?"

"Isn't it enough that I'll be able to get some rest?"

"What about your future?"

"My future's a thing of the past," he retorted.

"No, it isn't. Now you have an opportunity to recover everything you've lost!"

He raised his hand in a decisive gesture that told them to stop. "There's no point in going on like this," he said calmly. "What's new and important is the fact that I've decided to move out of this house!"

His mother's face turned pale.

"There's no sense in carrying its enormous costs any longer," he said apologetically.

"Is there any connection between that and your decision to leave?"

"No," he replied with a frown. "I regard the journey to Alexandria as a necessary cure."

"Don't let your enemies gloat over your situation," his mother pleaded. "You could certainly keep your beautiful house and your way of life if you accepted the job Hasan offered you."

He closed his eyes and said nothing; he refused to carry on a futile argument.

"You're my son," his mother continued bitterly, "and I know you. You're obstinate; you always were. You've chosen pride, however much it costs you. Well, your stubbornness has only encountered love and understanding from us here. But not everyone's like your mother and your sisters!"

He shrugged. "I'll pretend I didn't hear anything," he replied scornfully.

"You should follow God's command," she said even more pleadingly. "The power is His and He can do what He wishes; the future is in His hands. You can be happy without being an under secretary or a minister."

"Where would it be best for Mother to stay till I get back?" he said, looking at his sisters.

They kept out of the discussion. Each of them suggested that their mother should stay with her.

"I shall go back to the old house in Al-Wayiliyya," the old lady said.

"You'll never live by yourself," shouted Wahiba, the daughter most devoted to her mother.

"Umm Shalabi will never leave me," her mother replied. "I hope you'll come and visit me."

Isa remembered the old house, where they all had been born, and especially the wide courtyard with its dry, sandy floor. He did not know how to express his displeasure at his mother's idea. "Wouldn't it be best for you to stay with one of my sisters?" he asked.

"No," she replied nervously. "I'm stubborn too; it'll be better for everyone if I live in the old house."

All her daughters made it clear that they would be delighted if she would stay with them, but she paid no attention. Isa's thoughts were filled with his beautiful house. He looked at the trees outside the balcony, rustling gently against a white autumn sky that seemed to inspire a sense of melancholy. "Isn't God's curse on history?" he said to himself.

"The old house isn't suitable for someone who has been used to living here," Wahiba commented.

When Isa saw his mother's eyelids quivering, he thought she was on the point of crying. "It's perfectly suitable," she replied in a wavering voice. "We were all born there."

Everything seemed to promise a deathlike repose. Grief-stricken people are apt to welcome any kind of sedative, even if it is poison. This small, furnished flat showed that civilization was not entirely devoid of a little mercy at times. There was the sea stretching away into the distance till it sank over the horizon; from the mildness of October it derived a certain wisdom and tenderness. The walls of the flat were hung with pictures of the family of the Greek woman who owned it and every time you looked outside, you could see Greek faces on the balconies, at the windows, and in the street. He was a stranger in a district filled with strangers; that was the great merit of Al-Ibrahimiyya.* If you went out, the café with its tree-lined pavement, the vegetable market with its fresh colors, and the neat shops were also full of Greek faces and now at the end of the season you could hear the language being spoken everywhere. You could really imagine that you had gone abroad; the strangeness and unfamiliarity were intoxicating. These foreigners, of whom you had often thought badly, you had now learned to love even more than your fellow countrymen. You looked for consolation in their midst since you were all strangers in a strange country.

The choice of a flat on the eighth floor was another sign of your desire to treat the idea of traveling seriously: sections of neighboring buildings stretched as far as the Corniche,* and were low enough so that over them you could see the sea in the distance, where October had bewitched it, enchanting it into daydream. You could see the bevies of quail as well, swooping in to land exhausted at the end of their long, predestined, illusorily heroic flight. Cairo was now no more than a memory clouded by sadness, loneliness, the bitter experience you needed to keep from seeing the faces of people who would make you distressed and sleepless, or the signs of triumph that would arouse your sense of loss.

He experimented with solitude and its companions—a radio, books, and dreams. Is it possible, he wondered, to forget how to speak? Moments follow each other without any regulation, he thought; you don't know the time and hardly even remember what day it is. And so you look up bewildered at the sun's tranquil diamond disk appearing behind the light clouds of autumn, life flirting with you even though you are too morose to respond. It's as though you were seeing the world—and the people in it—for the first time after waking up from a fever, an illness by struggle and ambition, its essential values uncovered, revealing the brilliance of creation. Up till now, the sun's course has been merely a messenger, bearing news of the submission of a memorandum, the warning of a diplomatic reception.

Now that events have buried you alive, these troubles are no more than muddled dreams burning away inside your own decomposing head.

There was real loneliness in this Greek flat, and yearning in his heart. He missed the comfort of the corner in El Bodega, but his conflicting emotions connected with it seemed mean. I love Abbas Sadiq and Ibrahim Khairat, he thought, and yet at the same time I hate them! I love the part of them that was alive before the revolution, but I hate the way they've been able to live after it has taken place. Now I have an opportunity to clarify these vexing problems. Anxieties like mountains, the mind overwhelmed by rust, and the road to consolation, which is beset with folly, is paved and ready in the face of your ill-gotten gains and daydreams in which torture leads eventually to victory. A look from above at this boundless wilderness gives the soul a feeling of repose and an ability to rise above it all. O Lord, why don't You give us a gleam of inspiration about the meaning of this grueling journey stained with blood? Why doesn't the sea say something when it has seen the struggle going on since time immemorial? Why does this mother earth eat up its sons when evening comes? How is it that rocks, insects, and the condemned man in the mountain* have a role in the drama while I have none?

One morning he went to the Paradise Casino in Gleem* in response to a letter from Samir Abd al-Baqi. He hadn't seen Samir since coming to Alexandria in the middle of September and hadn't visited the Paradise Casino since the summer of 1951.There was no one on the beach and the casino itself was almost empty, as was usual during the final days of October. In the period of influence, Isa had gone to the Paradise with an arrogant air, and people would look at him with interest as he made his way between pashas—friends and enemies—to the table reserved for him in that ephemeral world. How could people forget the reception at the Paradise two years ago? The fabulous sound, the all-embracing magnificence of it all and the ringing shouts, and then his own arrival with an entourage to drink, have fun, and while away the evening. All he had seen on the horizon then were hopes that had held the promise of sure success.

He sat in his old place to the right of the inside entrance, among the empty seats. Some old pashas, who were hanging on till the last moment of the summer season, were sitting at scattered tables; two women sat by themselves, one old, the other middle-aged. A dreadful silence hung over the whole place. Isa stole a look at the old woman and told himself that Salwa would meet the same fate one day, going the way of all prestige and power, of all expectation. He took pleasure in looking at the expanse of sea, calm and pure blue, and at clouds, which looked as though they might be swollen with white rose water.

Samir Abd al-Baqi arrived on time and they embraced warmly. Samir looked even thinner than when he'd seen him last, but he was in better health and his eyes looked clearer. "My wife and I are here visiting her mother," he said. "We're going back tomorrow."

Isa asked about the corner in El Bodega and Samir replied that there was nothing new. "I've sold my share in an old house," he said, "and gone into partnership with an uncle who sells furniture. In fact, I'm his accounts manager and a junior partner."

Isa congratulated him and told him that he himself had no desire to work at the moment.

"Just look how empty Alexandria is!" Samir said, gazing around.

"The whole world's empty," Isa replied. "What's that you're holding?"

Samir handed him a book and he read the title *Ar-Risalat al-Qushairiyya*** on the cover. Isa looked inquiringly at him.

"Haven't you heard of mysticism?" Samir asked.

Isa laughed abruptly. "I never knew you were interested in it," he said.

"I wasn't, but then I heard Ahmad Pasha Zahran discussing it. He's given me some books on the subject at various times and recently I've found myself looking into them."

"Are you serious about it," Isa asked with some vestiges of laughter still visible on his face, "or is it just a question of amusement?"

Samir emptied a bottle of Coca-Cola into his glass. "It's more than just amusement," he replied. "It's a real source of relaxation." He drank half the glass and then continued. "The fact that you only look to it under the constraint of specific circumstances doesn't negate its qualities. We may only go to Aswan in winter to cure an illness, but that in itself doesn't discredit the benefits which Aswan can offer a whether we're sick or healthy."

"But there's obviously a difference," Isa said mockingly, "between turning to mysticism during a political crisis and doing so quite spontaneously when things are going well."

Samir smiled patiently, his green eyes glinting even more brightly than the candescent clouds. "Yes, there's a difference," he said, "but the lesson's in the consequences. Sometimes a disaster will hit us in such a way as to lead us unawares along the right path!"

"Suppose, for example, that the world . . ." Isa stopped speaking suddenly, as though he'd stumbled on silence, caught up in an exchange of glances with the middle-aged woman who was sitting next to the old one. Then he turned back to his friend, thinking that if things had gone as he'd wanted, Salwa would have been his wife now for at least a year. If only . . . ! "What is the mystical view of the particle 'if only'?" he asked.

Samir did not understand his point, so Isa gave the answer himself. "'If only' is the particle of anguish which has stupidly hankered after some illusory ability to change history."

"From the mystical point of view," Samir replied simply, "it represents a denial of God's manifest will in history. What it does is to imbue things with futility and irrationality."

Salwa has not budged from your heart, Isa thought to himself, even though you despise her character. The mind may formulate specifications for the ideal woman however it likes, but love is an essentially irrational proceeding— like death, fate, and chance. Salwa's behavior was typical of this world. You'll still need girls, though; they're wonderful tranquilizers for anxieties. Probably better than mysticism, he thought, remembering the question he'd broken off. "Suppose," he said, "the world promised us we'd be appointed to the ministry again! What would you do with mysticism?"

Samir laughed so hard that his teeth flashed. "It isn't difficult to do both at once," he replied. "That's what Almad Pasha Zahran used to do. Now you see me combining mysticism with commerce. It doesn't stifle your energies, but gets rid of flaws."

"It's better than suicide, at any rate," said Isa sadly.

The sun shone for a few seconds, then disappeared again. Samir asked him what he intended to do.

"Are we really finished?" Isa asked him in turn.

"Most probably," Samir replied, shaking his head in despair. "Things aren't as they were in previous revolutions."

Isa said nothing for a while, as though he were listening to the all-pervading silence. "We're just like the Alexandria beach in autumn," he said.

"That's why I'm saying you should get a job."

"We won't be working, whatever job we take," Isa replied, "because we've no role to play. That's why we feel excised and rejected like a removed appendix." He gave a smile, then continued. "I must confess that I have my own mystical beliefs. They keep me busy when I'm alone."

Samir looked concerned.

"I'm thinking of taking up crime," Isa said blandly.

Samir let out a long laugh. "That's a novel form of mysticism!" he said, still chuckling.

"But you don't kill your own body with it. Just other people's."

"I suppose you'll choose some kind of sex crime."

They both laughed.

"Thank God, there's still a world that can laugh," Samir said.

"We'll laugh a lot more every time we take a look at what's going on. It'll all be worked out for us. But we won't be participating in it. We'll be like eunuchs."

A gentle breeze blew. The pashas looked as though they were asleep. For no particular reason, Isa remembered the first speech he'd made in Parliament, when he was still a student at the university. "Our very history is threatened with extinction," he said sadly.

"History is very long-suffering. It'll defend itself when all the other combatants have disappeared."

The Greek proprietor walked over to them, smiled at Isa, and asked him how he was and how things were going. Isa recognized the political import of his question immediately. "Just as you see," he replied with a smile.

When he returned to his tall building near the tram stop, he was feeling depressed at saying farewell to Samir. As he walked through the high, dark entrance, he cursed Salwa, and as he entered the elevator, he told himself how much he needed a "tranquilizer."

FOURTEEN

He stood alone with his glass in the dimly lit corridor connecting the candy counter outside and the ballroom inside at the Petit Trianon. A big band was playing dance tunes, and couples clung to each other as they danced with light and elegant movements; in that way they could shrug off the discomforts of the sunlight. All these beautiful women belonged to houses now, not to the streets, as had been the case before and during the war. He'd begun to appreciate what was happening during his adolescence and early manhood. They'd made a lot of money during the war years and wouldn't stoop now to displaying themselves on the cheap any longer. They've disappeared from the square, leaving it vacant, Isa told himself, for people who wanted the job of making a quick profit from political outcasts! One tune made him sway and he longed to dance—something he did fairly well—but where was the beautiful partner? He took a drink of cognac, which he liked in moderation. He felt sheltered and that made him more relaxed. His little cache of money from the *umdas* would provide him with funds to indulge in some delightful escapades, he told himself. If it weren't for our morbid feelings about the future, nothing would ever bother us!

He did not enjoy his shelter alone for long. A voice caught him by surprise. "What do you think of the world?" it asked.

The shock made him shudder. He looked along the bending corridor but could not see anyone. The voice belonged to an old drunk, obviously spouting his quota of drivel. But where was he? The voice spoke again. "Do you want to know where I am?" it asked with a laugh. "Fine! I'm behind the tree."

At the bottom of the bend in the corridor that led to the candy counter was a half-grown tree—natural or artificial—in a huge pot; everything beyond the tree was total darkness, the candy counter having closed at eight in the evening. Isa deduced that the man had been sitting in the corridor and that for some reason he'd decided to move his seat into the dark to play his stupid game. He cursed the man under his breath and ignored him, but the latter began asking questions again without coming out into the dim light. "Have you ever tried drinking in the dark?" he inquired.

Isa said nothing, hoping he'd shut up.

"Drinking in the dark allows you to concentrate," the man went on. "That's why I'm thinking about the state of the world. Is it really going to ruin?"

Isa watched the dancing, half attentive, and took pleasure in the faces, breasts, and rosy complexions.

The drunk would not let go. "The question's really important to me," he said. "If it's moving to destruction, then I'll drink cognac. If there's any hope, I'd prefer whiskey. And therefore if I find myself in both situations,

I'll destroy myself, because I'll be struck by three momentous diseases at once—low blood pressure, cirrhosis, and hemorrhoids!"

Isa smiled in spite of himself. It was nice to be drunk, at any rate. The trials that have descended upon us are enough to break our hearts, he thought; enough to kill us. It's as if all the debris from the collapsed old world were piling on top of your head. And the worst thing of all is the knowledge that, even though you loathe the new era, you still cannot reject it in your mind. Neither you nor your cache of *umdas'* money!

"Destruction's nothing new in the world. If it's written on your forehead, then it's better for it to be quick."

"Why do you want it, provided it's quick?" Isa asked the man almost without realizing it.

"As the proverb goes," the man replied with a boisterous laugh, "the best charity comes quickest!"

Isa pitied the victims of history with a sigh in his heart, drained his glass, and left. He walked along Saad Zaghlul Street, his favorite street in Alexandria, particularly after the revolution; his own private street, in a way, and he liked walking along it, if only once a day in each direction, so that he could be alone with his flooding memories.

It was getting close to midnight and the air had become refreshingly cool. The whole area looked deserted. He glanced at the back of the statue gazing out to sea and tossed his head back like the pasha whom he had loved to imitate in times past.

He took the tram to Al-Ibrahimiyya and then went to the Corniche for a gentle walk along the seawall to calm his nerves. The salty air rose up around his head, which was reeling from the alcohol he had drunk. The stars were shining in the wide gaps between the clouds, and the sea was calm, like someone asleep in the dark. In the distance, the rows of lights attached to the fishing boats stretched out in a line. There was no one to be seen on the road. The sense of total abandonment came back again and he sat down on a stone bench to savor this feeling of silence and sympathy. He would not go back to his empty home till drowsiness persuaded him: since coming to Alexandria, he'd been living his own life, not following anyone's orders or conforming with any customs, satisfying his own whims in absolute freedom, going to sleep when he could not stay awake any longer, waking up when he got tired of sleeping, eating when he was hungry, and going out when he was bored. He'd never enjoyed freedom like this before.

Something to his left attracted his attention, as though some hidden temptation were trying to contact one or more of his senses—a figure coming toward him from a distance. When it came closer under the streetlight and the features became clear, he saw that it was a girl. The cheap cotton flannel dress, the defiant look untinged by reserve or haughtiness, and the very fact that she was walking alone at night, all these things showed that she was a Corniche girl. He examined her as she walked past him through the narrow space between his bench and the seawall. He could see she was young and had quite nice features, but her appearance was very common, and she had an air of ready response to some gesture that would take her in, like a stray dog looking for any passerby to follow. She walked past till she reached the next bench and sat down on it, eyes fixed in his direction. What a bunch of scavengers these whores are, Isa thought. But what else is there once the summer season is over and Alexandria folds up totally, looking as though its doors were locked in the face of strangers? Deep down inside he felt disgusted. But his pulse was throbbing insanely with desire. The director of the minister's office with designs on the minister's chair was dead and buried. That much was quite clear. All that was left of him at the moment was a drunkard alone in the dark whose desires were crawling all over like nocturnal insects. It was as though an irresistible impulse to wallow in the dust were blowing through his brain.

He signaled to her with as flirtatious a gesture as he could muster, and then repeated it. She got up and moved toward him till she stood at arm's length. He gestured to her to sit down, and she did so with a laugh as soft as the whisper of the waves that lapped below, at the foot of the seawall. He looked at her face and was shocked by its youth. "How old are you?" he asked.

She laughed without answering. He repeated the question anxiously.

"Guess!" she said.

"Maybe you're fifteen," he said.

"No," she replied proudly. "I'm not a minor, in any case, so relax."

A pale matte complexion, round face, full cheeks, small, full body, and short hair like a boy. She kept playing with her nails; the varnish on them had flaked away.

"Where did you come from at this hour of the night?"

"From the café," she replied, pointing back down the road behind her to a lighted door wrapped in darkness and silence.

"I didn't notice it as I was walking," he said.

"People heading there usually see it." She laughed. "Cigarette?"

They both lit cigarettes. He couldn't think of anything to say. "Let's go," he whispered.

They walked side by side along one of the roads leading off the Corniche. She took his arm and he winced, scowling, in the darkness, remembering Salwa. If they're sincere, he told himself, they should let free elections decide!

FIFTEEN

He woke up about noon and looked with curiosity at the naked girl sleeping next to him. Recollections of the previous night came back and he told himself that as long as oblivion and habit still existed, everything remained possible. As she lay there, almost completely uncovered, he examined her, coldly and calmly, contemptuous of everything. Her full lips were parted, revealing a neat set of teeth, but after a night's sleep her hair looked as it really was, dry, coarse, and unkempt. There was an odd physical inconsistency about her; her eyelashes were long and voluptuous, but her breasts looked chapped and flaky, like a pair of toads.

He got out of bed and went to the bathroom. When he came back, he found her sitting up in bed yawning. She lifted two beautiful, heavy eyes in his direction. He decided to get rid of her as soon as possible. "I've an appointment," he said. "I've got to go."

She looked at him, hesitated, and then left the room. He

opened the balcony door and a strong breeze blew in. It felt quite pleasant, full of the smell of the sea and the warmth of the sun, which was shining in the middle of the sky. As he dressed, he looked out to sea. There was an impetuous motion to it today; the whole surface was flecked with foam and the waves looked like mouths laughing. She was a long time in the bathroom, he thought, until he went into the lounge to turn on the radio and found her there, cleaning and putting things straight with great industriousness. "Thank you," he said, "but leave that for the *bawwab*.* It's time for me to go."

"Go ahead," she replied, without stopping what she was doing.

"But when are you going to get dressed?"

She sat on a big chair in the lounge and smiled.

"You may be able to dawdle," he said, "but I've got an appointment."

"Do you live alone?" she asked quietly.

"Yes . . . but come on!!"

She started combing her hair. "I told myself you might need someone as a companion and servant," she said, showing a genuine shyness for the first time.

"Thank you," he replied in astonishment, "but I don't need anything like that. Haven't you got a home?"

"No."

"Where are you living?"

"Sometimes with the woman who owns the café," she replied shamefully, "and other times I spend the night in the café! We don't find any work in the winter, and last summer was just like winter, in any case!"

"Whatever your problem is," he snapped, "you'll find the solution outside."

She stood up. "I didn't save anything for this winter," she said quietly, "and you need someone to serve you."

Her insistence only made him more obdurate. "Why don't you go to Cairo for the winter?" he said.

She looked at him in amazement, as though the idea would never have occurred to her. "But I'm from here," she answered simply.

"Haven't you got any family?"

"Of course, but I can't go back to them!"

"Aren't you afraid one of them might see you?"

"They're in Tanta.* That's where I come from."

"If you don't mind," he said, annoyed at having let the conversation go this far, "I'm in a hurry."

As she went into the other room to put her clothes on, he remarked to himself that they were very much alike—both disgraced outcasts. When the girl came back she seemed to have despaired of arousing his sympathy and tried being playful. "Is that your family?" she asked coyly, looking at the picture of the Greek family on the wall.

He laughed in spite of himself. "What a devil you are!"

Her laugh was unexpectedly merry. Then, more seriously, she asked him, "Are you from Alexandria?"

"No."

"Then you're here as a civil servant?"

"Almost."

"Almost?"

"You're like a district attorney!" he barked. "Come on!"

She asked to be paid and he gave it to her—much less than he'd expected. He felt sorry for her for the first time since he had woken up. They left the flat together and separated at the entrance to the building. He headed straight for a restaurant to satisfy his hunger, then killed the hours between three and six at the first cinema he came to. Afterwards, he sat in the Grand Trianon drinking coffee and reading the evening paper. Around nine o'clock he went to his dark seat in the Petit Trianon corridor and listened to the music, amusing himself by watching the dancers and swilling cognac. At one point he wished that the man who'd been behind the tree the night before would raise his voice again and pour abuses on the world.

"I'm a student of Sufism* as well," he said aloud, as though he were talking to Samir Abd al-Baqi. "You're not the only one." He smiled regretfully to himself. Don't think about the future, he told himself. That's right. You're still only at the honeymoon stage. What you need is a long unbroken vacation. Don't be upset by your own insignificance. It's a historical phenomenon.

He left the place a little before midnight. As he approached the entrance to his building, he was surprised to see the girl sitting in the Greek café on the chair nearest the doorway, her face smiling in welcome. She sprang up and ran to meet him in front of the entrance. He stopped in bewilderment.

"You weren't late for your appointment?" she said.

She went in first. He hesitated a moment and then followed her. "What are you doing?" he asked.

"I was waiting for you," she replied, taking him by the arm. "If he comes back alone, I told myself, I'll be in luck."

He was pleased by her flattery, even though he was painfully aware of the situation. "What's your name?" he asked her in the elevator.

"Riri," she replied.

"That's obviously a genuine Tanta name!" he retorted
with a laugh.

"It's the one I use in Alexandria."

There was a short pause.

"My heart tells me," she continued, "that you'll offer
me your hospitality."

SIXTEEN

He allowed her to stay in the flat as she wished. He made it clear to her from the very beginning that he was a free man, and that she had to keep within her bounds even if he brought a woman home every night; to all of which she agreed without question. Afterwards he could not deny that she gave the flat a friendly feeling and cleanliness that had been absent before and introduced a breath of warm air into its cold atmosphere. When she wore the new clothes he bought for her, she looked really presentable, and she always took particular care of her appearance. She played her role adroitly, something above that of a servant and yet below that of mistress of the house. She avoided getting on his nerves in any way whatsoever. She shared his food, cigarettes, and drink, but did not ask for a penny apart from that. He gave her no encouragement to get emotionally involved with him or use endearing words. "I'm a man who distrusts everything," he told her. "That's the way I am, so make sure you don't lead me to suspect you're lying."

When winter took over, the weather seemed to be as unsettled as the invisible world itself. He was forced to spend long nights in the flat with her. They would listen to the radio or else he would spend a few hours by himself reading or give his exhausted feelings some relief by listening to her silly chatter. The worst thing that would happen while he was living with her was that sometimes she would suddenly strike him as a symbol of the utter humiliation into which he had sunk. When that happened, he would keep out of her way and start insulting her at the first opportunity. Her full, round face would show a frown. He would be aware of the effort she was making to keep her temper under control and suppress a desire to give vent to her aggressive instincts, instincts that she had acquired through her life on the streets. All this involved an inner struggle, traces of which were clearly visible on her cheeks and lips and in her expression and the way her features altered. Even though she was illiterate, she was well educated in the cinema and radio. She could remember the names and pictures of the various stars as well as the films, songs, and programs, and she could never have enough of talking about them. "Don't you think," she asked him, "that I'm good enough for the cinema?"

He told her that he had no experience in that field. He was amazed at mankind's power of self-deception, more powerful than the atom itself. She told him stories about the stars, and he had no idea of where she got them from; this was all to convince him that she was worthy of the bright lights and that it was a question of luck—no more and no less!

"You should be looking for a producer's or director's flat," he told her with a laugh, "so that you can share it with him!"

Since the nights were so long and he refused to go to bed before dawn, she taught him various kinds of card games. She gambled with him a great deal and won some money from him, but this was the only money from him that she ever put in her pocket.

Once it occurred to him to ask her what she knew about politics, which had swallowed him as a hero and then spat him out as a corpse. So he asked her about some names and events, but she shrugged her shoulders and did not bother to answer. He was amazed that there could be a human being in existence who did not care about the world of politics. "What do you know about the constitution?" he asked mockingly.

Her eyes showed no signs of understanding.

"What are your views on independence?" he continued.

Her look did not change.

"I mean the departure of the English," he said by way of explanation.

"Oh!" she shouted. "Let them go if you want them to. But I've heard a lot about how good things were in their day. My mistress, the café proprietress, opened her café on their money!"

For her, he thought, real independence meant being rid of the need for me and others like me.

She opened her heart to him and told him about her past with an unusual frankness. "I have a mother, aunt, and sisters," she said. "The only male relative I have left is an uncle in his nineties. So I don't expect to be killed for honor's sake." She had been a devil since she was young. Her father had died when she was ten, and her mother had been unable to control or discipline her. She could not keep her daughter away from the boys and no amount of scolding or beating was of any use. "I loved a boy before I had even reach maturity and became proverbial in the village for that reason . . ." Then the inevitable thing had happened. "My mother hit me, then slapped her own cheeks until she fell to the ground as if she were dead." She had run away with the boy to Alexandria where he was going to finish his education. He got rid of her after a few months and she had found herself alone. It was then that she had begun this life.

"You're a small girl," he said with a smile, "but a big devil . . ."

"An old *khwaaga** in Al-Azarita* loved me," she said proudly, "and took me on, to stay as his servant. He had an old, bedridden wife."

"But you weren't as good at making good use of opportunities as your mistress, the café proprietress."

"I seek nothing but shelter," she replied simply.

He laughed loudly and told himself that it might be useful if we could find something to convince us that we are not the most miserable of all God's creatures. "What do you expect from the future?" he asked.

She raised her eyebrows for a few moments. "Our Lord is great," she mumbled.

"You sound religious!"

She smiled at the sarcastic tone in his voice and took refuge in silence.

"But you admit yourself that you're a devil, don't you?"

She laughed heartily. "The time for sleep came along," she said, "and that's better than wearing your head out for nothing."

He became increasingly convinced of similarities that joined him and this girl together. He conceded that she was absolutely necessary and indispensable to him in his loneliness, especially when things were really bad. The ax had fallen on the leaders and the hearings were over. He felt ill at ease, like a drug distributor when he hears all of a sudden that the big operators have been arrested. He denied the world and refused to acknowledge it any longer. He was not astonished anymore by the blustery days when the harbor was closed and the angry waves in the raging sea flew up in the air and battered the Corniche. The clouds were as dark as parts of night itself and the lightning flashed incredibly like rockets. The rain came down in torrents like little creatures running away from the wrath of the heavens. It seemed blind stupidity to stay in Alexandria, and he longed to be back in Cairo and the warm corner at El Bodega.

"I wonder where you are!" she said to him. "You're not with me and you're not anywhere in the world either!"

He came back down to earth again. His expression looked tired from all this wandering around in oblivion. He gave a weak smile but said nothing.

"You've been like this for days," she said.

"Yes, I have," he replied angrily. "All you listen to on the radio is the songs!"

"Are you a notable?" she asked, in an embarrassed tone.

"Or unemployed!" he said with a dry laugh.

"You? Oh no! But you certainly are a mystery."

"They unravel mysteries."

"Tell me, how long are you going to stay like this?"

"Let me ask you the same question."

"My life isn't in my hands."

"Nor mine." He continued with a smile. "When spring comes, we'll each be on our own way."

"I won't go," she said with an unexpected intensity, "until you have me thrown out."

Blasted emotions! Sincere or false, God damn them all! Her affection for him inspired exactly the opposite reaction in him—he became almost angry. He concentrated on the song that was being broadcast. Then a program on economics was announced: a group of economists were going to hold a discussion. When, listed among the participants, he heard the name Hasan ad-Dabbagh, he rushed over to the radio and turned it off. She asked him why he was annoyed.

"I said you only listen to the songs!" he replied angrily.

On the clear winter days, he wandered around the different places in Alexandria that he loved. He did not take her with him even once, but neither did he prevent her from exercising complete freedom to move around as she wished. In her eyes he could read a desire to go out with him, even if only for a short walk on the Corniche, but he hated the very idea.

"Don't you think," she said, "that you're treating me as though I were . . ."

"Stop looking for trouble," he interrupted firmly.

Her face flushed with obvious emotion. When he noticed it, he felt sorry for her and fondled her short hair. "Stop looking for trouble," he repeated tenderly.

She no longer expressed her feelings in words, but rather in the effort she made to serve him and tend to his comforts. He received these gestures with a gratitude mixed with distrust. Winter would soon be over, he told himself, and then he would be rid of this attachment that had infiltrated his flat. Even from his bitter experience with Salwa, there was only a surface wound left, and that may have been pride rather than love. He realized that the void which politics had left in his heart would have to be filled by some amorous escapades for a while and that might prove troublesome.

As the days passed, he was amazed to see the girl's health getting noticeably worse. She looked terrible: pale, weak, and exhausted. How could this happen when she was getting food and comfort which she had never even dreamed of? He thought she might have a cold, but none of the symptoms of a cold was apparent. The ailment stayed with her to a degree that both worried him and kept him occupied. "What's the matter with you?" he asked her. "Have you ever had anything like this before?"

She replied that she had not and kept moving away when he followed her, until suddenly she had to give up and lie down on the bed. He stood there looking at her, alarmed and angry. "I'll have to call a doctor," he said.

She gestured to him not to do that. "No," she said. "It's just that I'm exhausted by the humidity."

Tears were pouring down her face and she looked like an inexperienced child. Suddenly he felt fear gripping him for some unknown reason. "No doubt you've something to say," he said.

She shut her eyes in despair and pointed to her stomach without saying anything. His heart gave a violent thump, something it had done only during the terrible events that had finished him off. His fear turned to pure anger. Now it was quite clear what the sly little minx was after! "You poisonous little snake!" he yelled at her. "Is this how you pay me back for giving you a home?"

"I didn't realize it until some time had passed," she wailed.

"You little devil, are you pretending to be that naïve?"

"No, never," she replied, "but it happened in spite of all the precautions I took."

"You liar! Even if I believed you, why didn't you tell me?"

"I was afraid! I was so afraid, I couldn't!"

"Even devils are afraid of people like you!" he yelled. "What are you waiting for then? When are you going to do something about it?"

"I can still remember a friend of mine," she pleaded, sobbing as she did so, "who died while doing that. . . ."

"So?" His voice was blocked because he was so angry. "Well then," he yelled, "reveal your cunning plan! Now, just listen to me." Then, warning her with his index finger, he said, "Don't let me see your face from now on, or ever again!"

"You haven't wasted the opportunity to get rid of me now it's come," she pleaded, "but at least be kinder than that."

"From now on," he yelled like a demon, "I understand you! From now on! Never again."

SEVENTEEN

Loneliness began to weigh heavily on him. He could no longer bear returning to the flat before late at night. However, his fear of the girl was even greater than all the tortures he was going through. He started wondering whether she was going to create a public scandal. Would he soon be standing in disgrace in front of the public prosecutor? How the newspapers would relish the thought of exposing him! What a wonderful opportunity it would be to expose the others as well, and his entire era! These anxious thoughts preyed on his mind like mosquitoes in a swamp.

However, days went by without any of his fears being realized; nor did a bill for an abortion come from the girl. He knew he should return to Cairo, but for some incomprehensible reason he was determined to stay in Alexandria. Every time he felt safe as far as the girl was concerned, he clung still closer to his own sufferings. The storms no longer disturbed him so much as fascinated him, and loneliness worked its cryptic and deadly magic on him. The atmosphere of living among foreigners, with its own strange aroma, gave him dreams of emigrating forever to the mountaintops painted with green fields; there he could spend the rest of his life far away from anxieties.

He was very fond of Ramla Square;* it was a permanent stage for elegantly dressed women with golden tresses wrapped up in their raincoats. Every time a tram came, flocks of beautiful women would emerge; it made Isa feel more relaxed and almost drunk as their legs seemed to play all kinds of tunes to him. When a policeman noticed him staring at a gorgeous girl and getting ready to follow her, their eyes met, and the policeman smiled. Isa suddenly came to himself as he remembered the awe that he had inspired in all ranks of policemen in the old days. He took a seat behind the window in 'Ala Kaifak* which looked out onto the square, where streams of humanity kept crashing into each other. From his vantage point, he could live among them as he liked without getting tired. In his past life, weighed down by ambition, he had had no chance to sit down like this, even though all he was really doing now was sitting there like some discarded foam left behind on the beach by a wave for the municipal workers to come by and scoop up. Where were the key power figures who had been forced to go into hiding? When would people stop crying about them? These days, the game could only be undertaken on impulse, without relish or real human contact. When time did allow some human relationships to be formed, the hurricane would rage and everyone standing up would be blown away.

The sky was getting darker now. Some unknown force was swallowing up all the daylight; clouds were gathering, and human beings could be seen scurrying away like ghosts. Alexandria! Your winter is as fickle as a woman! The wind blew hard, like bad news. People wrapped their coats around themselves. Newspaper vendors closed up their stands; it became the ultimate in blessings to take refuge behind the window of 'Ala Kaifak and sip hot tea. The thunder rumbled, and people started. Down came the rain, but with a certain grace to it; the space between the sky and the earth seemed to be fixed to electric wires. The square was empty, and the people huddled together gave him a warm feeling; he felt relaxed and at ease.

He heard a slight cough and turned to his left. There was Riri, sitting at a table only one away from his! He quickly looked toward the square, but, in his churning thoughts, she was the only thing he could see, wearing that old orange coat of hers. She had only turned around for a moment, but her smiling eyes were full of tragedy. Was she following him on purpose, or had she simply wandered aimlessly across his path? Would it all end peaceably, or burst into a public scandal? Had she got rid of the thing, or was she still determined to keep it?

He decided to leave, but when he looked outside he saw that the storm was still raging, and resigned himself to remaining a prisoner inside the café. He resolved to leave Alexandria at the first opportunity, the next day if he could. Then he put on a careless air and rested his cheek on his fist as though he were pondering dreamily. Suddenly, he thought that her presence there might be part of a plan she had arranged with the police so as to arrest him, that now his name would be added to those of all the outstanding members of his generation who were being thrown outside the walls one after another. That might lead to something even worse too, for they would undoubtedly examine his bank account, and then they might start asking him where the money had come from. But before he realized it, the girl was sitting down at his table. "I thought I'd invite myself over," she said, "since he doesn't want to do it himself!"

He stared at her coldly so as to hide his alarm, and said nothing.

"Don't be afraid," she said. "We can sit together for a while, as old friends should."

This was the first step in the trap, he told himself; maybe the other people involved were watching too. He decided to defend himself to the death. "What are you talking about?" he said in a voice loud enough for the people who were sitting nearby to hear. "I don't understand a thing!"

His feigned ignorance surprised her, and the jovial look went out of her eyes. "Is that all you can say?" she muttered.

He stretched out his left hand in a display of bewilderment.

"Well, now," she said in amazement, "so you don't recognize me?"

"I'm sorry. Maybe you've mistaken me for someone else."

Her disappointment made her look sad. Then she closed her lips in anger, and her whole expression changed. She looked so threatening that he expected something terrible to happen in front of all the people sitting there. However, she simply got up.

"I suppose you're going to say God creates forty people who all look exactly alike, aren't you?" she said in a sarcastic and defiant tone.

He was so worked up that he felt giddy. He never thought it would end that way. Every time he remembered her changing expression, he shuddered, and felt sure that, under a happy girl's skin, a tigress was always lurking. He stayed in this daze for a long time; he had no idea how long. Eventually he noticed that the rain had stopped and a gap was opening up on the horizon. A ray of sunshine was bursting through, even though it looked thoroughly washed. He got up without delay, put his coat on, and left without looking in her direction.

It was after midnight when he got back to his building. He found a telegram waiting for him from the family saying that his mother had died.

The funeral would be held at Al-Qubbat al-Fidawiyya on the following afternoon. Isa got there early to welcome the mourners, and his arrival coincided with that of Hasan, his cousin, in his Mercedes. Naturally the car was no surprise to Isa, but the sight of it irritated him. He was amazed at the sudden and obvious improvement in his cousin's health; an air of superiority gave him an upright bearing, and his eyes had a look of authority in them. They shook hands and stood there waiting in the shade of a tree. Hasan started looking him over. "You don't look as healthy as I would have expected!" he said.

"Perhaps the weather doesn't agree with me," Isa replied, reviewing his sorrows in a single fleeting moment.

"That was a meaningless trip to Alexandria," the young man said in a decisive and official tone of voice, "but then, you're a stubborn man."

Hasan was still hanging on to his old dream, Isa thought, of marrying him off to his sister. Then Isa's friends, Samir Abd al-Baqi, Ibrahim Khairat, and Abbas

Sadiq, arrived with various former senators and representatives. Countless groups of people came to offer their condolences to Hasan, and the tent was crowded with them all, even though it was huge. There was an anxious moment when Ali Sulaiman got out of his car. Hasan welcomed him, and Isa saw no way out of greeting him too. They shook hands with each other and Isa accepted his condolences, but neither of them looked at the other once. The traditional stages in the ceremony followed, one after the other. Isa lost his composure only at the burial itself, when his eyes filled with tears in spite of the effort he made to control his emotions. He had supervised the entire proceedings himself. Unable to resist the eternal temptation, he looked at the grave pit for a long time. He wanted to be left alone to say some important things to her. He suddenly remembered the last time he had said goodbye to her in the old house. She had kissed him on the forehead. "Do whatever you want," she had said. "May the good Lord protect you wherever you are. I'll hold back my tears so that you can leave in peace!"

He could hardly remember the expression on her face because he had not been looking at her closely; but her hands had felt cold, lean, and trembling.

When the recitation started, he moved to one side, and more than once exchanged glances with his friends. He asked himself why they looked sadder than they needed to be. This, then, is the ultimate destination for everyone, he thought with a comforting enthusiasm and a certain amount of malice, for poor people and tyrants alike; yes, and tyrants too!

The condolences in the house that night were restricted to members of the family and his three friends. Ali Sulaiman did not come, and Isa avoided going to the harem so as not to see his uncle's family. Nevertheless, he wondered whether Susan Hanem and Salwa had come. The scene in the room where Samir, Abbas, Ibrahim, and Hasan were sitting with him was almost comical. None of his friends dared to express his political views in front of Hasan, and since the discussion of politics could not be avoided in any gathering, they saw no solution except to be hypocritical. So they started praising the startling historic actions of the revolution, the abolition of the monarchy, the end of feudalism, and the evacuation—especially the evacuation, that age-old dream. Isa contributed only a little to the conversation; he was exhausted and felt empty and sad. He concealed his sarcastic thoughts about the situation by pretending to listen to the Qur'an reciter, who was sitting in the lounge on the third floor. Hasan had become a key figure, he told himself, someone to really reckon with! Wasn't that laughable? He surrendered to the incredible notion that his mother had not really died, that she was still alive in some way, or that her spirit had not yet left the house. Then he recalled in amazement the old dream of the evacuation and how he had listened to the news of its announcement with a feeling of languid satisfaction mixed with anger merely because it was not his party that had brought it about. He could not help saying, "The fact is that the evacuation is really a fruit of the past!"

None of his friends said a word, but Hasan went to great efforts to prove that this theory was wrong.

"The truth is," Ibrahim Khairat said, "none of our old revolutions achieved any startling results. Now this revolution has come along to fulfill the missions of the old ones as well as achieve its own particular goals."

The conversation continued until the house was empty. When Isa went to see Hasan to the door, the latter stopped suddenly and smiled at him fondly. "Your trip was a mistake," he said. "You should examine your position again."

Isa smiled. He had not the least inclination to talk.

"Tell me one of your past hopes," Hasan continued, "which hasn't been achieved today. You should jump on the train and join the rest of us!"

Isa shook his head enigmatically. They shook hands.

"When you change your mind," Hasan said, "you'll find me at your beck and call."

Isa thanked him gratefully. In fact, he was greatly touched by his kindness, but he refused to think about moving that wall which kept them apart. He often admitted his adversary's logic and acknowledged his own secret defeat in front of him. But every time he seemed more convinced, he felt a bitter resentment building up inside him.

Afterwards, he sat down with Umm Shalabi, who greeted his arrival with a flood of tears over the death of his late mother. He waited till she quieted down. "How was she?" he asked.

"She didn't sleep for a single day."

"Suddenly then?"

"Yes, and, fortunately, in my arms."

"Was she alone in the house for a long time?"

"Never. One of your sisters came to see her every day."

"Didn't Susan Hanem come tonight?"

"Yes, sir, she did."

"And Salwa?" he asked after a short pause.

"No, sir, she didn't come." She blinked and then continued. "She's engaged to your cousin Hasan . . ."

His weary eyes leapt in a look of astonishment. "Salwa and Hasan?"

"Yes, sir."

"Since when?"

"Last month."

He stretched out his legs carelessly and leaned back against the headrest of his chair. He saw the old, faded ceiling resting on its horizontal pillars. His gaze settled on a large gecko at the top of the wall; it was so still that it seemed to be crucified there.

It was nice to sit on the El Bodega pavement in the warm June air, especially when the evening brought with it a gentle breeze. Silence prevailed when a pretty girl walked by, but Isa and his friends were by no means tired of talking about politics. Even though Abbas Sadiq had a position in the government, and Ibrahim Khairat worked as a lawyer and writer for the revolution, they still held the same views as Isa or Samir Abd al-Baqi, who tended to be reticent. Ibrahim summed up their general feelings. "It's right there in your hands, and then someone else gets it!" he said.

Signs of resignation were written all over their faces, but they still hoped for a miracle. Sometimes they would seize on the most trivial news, and a hidden flicker of life would rouse in the barren wasteland of their hearts. Incredibly enough, Ibrahim Khairat and Abbas Sadiq were even more disgruntled than Isa.

"One of you is an important writer," Isa told them with a laugh, "and the other is an important civil servant. So what do you want?"

"On a personal level," Abbas replied in his ringing and harmonious voice, his eyes flashing wide, "things may be reassuring; but that doesn't alter the general picture."

"The truth is," said Ibrahim Khairat, "no one has any value today, however senior his position may be. We're a country of bubbles."

"When I was only in the sixth grade," Abbas said, "I was as good as an entire ministry!"

"Nothing bothers me anymore," said Samir Abd al-Baqi with a soothing tone of resignation.

"But your position is at least as difficult as any of ours!"

Samir hurriedly revised his statement of his views. "I meant that I'm no longer troubled by regrets about the past. Sometimes I wish them success. My own dismissal doesn't bother me because I chose it."

"You mean, it was imposed on you," said Isa jokingly.

"But, at the same time, I chose it. May God's will be done."

Ibrahim Khairat rubbed Isa's shoulder. "Why aren't you saying anything?" he asked. "Haven't you any news?"

"A few days ago," Isa said simply, "I hung a 'For Sale' sign on my late mother's house."

"It's old, but at least it's land!"

"My share of it will enable me to live like a notable," Isa said joyfully, "and that's how I'll carry on for as long as possible."

"Do you think that's a decent way to live?"

"Maybe it'll cure me of my split personality."

"Is that some modern illness?" asked Abbas Sadiq.

"The truth is," replied Isa after thinking for a moment, "although my mind is sometimes convinced by the revolution, my heart is always with the past. I just don't know if there can be any settlement between the two."

"It isn't a question of principles to be convinced by,"

said Ibrahim Khairat. "The relationship between ruler and ruled is regulated secretly, just as in love. We can say that the ruler who will be most attractive to his subjects is the one who respects their humanity the most. Man shall not live by bread alone!"

"But that's why I should still be out of work, even if I got scores of jobs," Isa replied sadly.

"Is that your heart or your mind speaking?" Abbas Sadiq asked.

"The heart means totally different things to us," Samir Abd al-Baqi said with a smile.

"Why are we laughing," Isa asked, "when life is a tragedy in every sense of the word?"

"We think of death as the ultimate tragedy," said Ibrahim Khairat, "and yet the death of the living is infinitely worse than that of the dead."

Abbas Sadiq gave an explosive laugh. "Isn't it appropriate," he said, "that the conversation should take us from death to the atom!"

Isa had still not fully emerged from his sudden feeling of sorrow. "One of the things about using the atom as a threat," he said, "is that it lightens life's drudgery; I mean, our life . . ."

"What about modern civilization?" Abbas Sadiq asked sarcastically. "Aren't you worried about what may happen to it?"

"Fortunately for us, we haven't entered the world of modern civilization yet. So why should we be afraid of getting wet?"

"I hope it'll be an age like the flood," Ibrahim Khairat said. "Then the earth will be purified."

"Have you heard that from an official source?" Abbas Sadiq asked.

"Let's admit," said Samir Abd al-Baqi, "that if it weren't for death, our life wouldn't have any value at all."

"What a lot of talk about death!"

At that, Isa remembered his mother's death, Salwa's marriage to Hasan, and the harsh way he had treated Riri. How consoling it was, he thought, to be able to chat with these friends of his. Talking to Hasan only made his split personality even more acute. Samir leaned toward him. "Your problem's easy compared with the problems of the world," he said. "You need a job and a wife."

"That's why I like horror films," Isa replied with no obvious connection.

"The trouble with those films," Abbas Sadiq commented, "is that they're imaginary."

"On the contrary," Isa replied, "the trouble with them is that they're too realistic."

The air-raid siren went off by mistake and blared for half a minute. Isa thought that eventually he would find himself searching for a job and a woman. But that would not happen till he admitted defeat and made a final exit from history.

TWENTY

The pleasures of the night are very intense, but they do not last long; and besides, they cost too much. The Arizona was particularly beautiful at midnight; gorgeous girls of various nationalities were dancing around, and drinks were mingled with the early morning dew. You could make do with lies. In the back garden, it was all love and lovers, moonlight or starlight. Money had no value at all, and emotions spilled over unchecked. There's nothing new about the picture, Isa thought, but he was still maintaining the deceits of his daily life in a fearsomely dull atmosphere. Here, on the other hand, you could blend in with the singing in a joyful ambience. Salwa had known about luxury, but she had never really known joy. It occurred to him to ask his Italian companion in the garden a question. "You've been to a number of countries; what do you think of people?"

She was something for all five senses to enjoy. "They're usually looking for pleasure when I meet them," she replied, "so they're all very nice!"

"But that's all lies."

"At least they're genuine about wanting me!"

"That's just a passing emotion."

"Everything's like that!"

He laughed and paused for a moment. "Can't you find even that passing emotion in yourself?" he asked.

"So you don't believe I love you?" she asked jokingly.

"How is it," he asked her with interest, "that it doesn't occur to people like you to enjoy a little stability in your lives?"

She sang an Italian song, and for a moment he was impressed by her beauty. Then his own degradation made him feel sad. Everything of value except beauty comes to the same end, he thought; people barter shamelessly with freedom, humanity, and even religion, and they are all really a single tragedy. In the past, he himself had indulged in this futile pastime. He had stomached all kinds of corruption and taken part in it himself; his bank balance was still there to prove it. Why couldn't purity prevail? What was it that had prevented it for so many centuries? Was there a single man anywhere on the face of the earth living without fear or blemish?

He began to amuse himself by following girls in the Cairo streets, especially young ones; it was as though some force were pushing him toward the sources of innocence. But these were mysterious and fruitless trips which brought no results. Every time the political storms blew up, and some idea or person from his past was thrown out, he reeled under the impact of the blow. Eventually there came a time when he wished that the Egyptians— like some other peoples—had a colony, in South America perhaps, where they could emigrate. The Egyptians were reptiles, he told himself angrily, not birds. The dream of some radical change in his life attracted him, but everything he did was just a waste of time. When he complained to his friend, Samir Abd al-Baqi, his friend had replied, "Where's your sail? You're a boat drifting without a sail!"

One day at about four in the afternoon, the real estate agent came to say that some people wanted to look at the house. Two women appeared, an old lady in her seventies and her daughter—at least that was what he deduced from their resemblance—who was in her forties or slightly younger. He took them from one room to another and answered their questions. The old lady was thin, with a white complexion, gray eyes, and thick eyebrows, and her expression full of experience and self-confidence. Her daughter was of medium height and had a full figure and a round face; her eyes were like those of a cow and equally placid. He noticed the women's amazement at the obvious discrepancy between the old house and the magnificent, contemporary furniture. This irritated him. After they had looked at the large courtyard, he invited them to sit in the reception room and offered them some coffee. The agent joined the group, and in his white *gallabiyya** looked at everyone with his narrow eyes. "The house covers a large area," he said, "and one could add a building on two sides. The northwest corner is a magnificent site; the quarter around it is rapidly being modernized, as you've seen. Five new buildings are being erected at the same time, and that'll raise its value."

"But the house is old," said the daughter. Isa again

noticed her black eyes and elegant clothes. "It's not fit to live in."

"You're not buying a house to live in, of course," Isa said. "It's a site to build on, as Al-Hajj* Husain just pointed out. It's a good location, and the price is right. You can make your own inquiries and find out for yourself!"

"And that's just the present," Al-Hajj Husain continued. "The entire quarter's guaranteed for the future as well. There's no quarter in the world like this one; it's in a perfect location, there are so many people living here, and transportation is good—it's ideal."

The daughter asked Isa about the dimensions of the property. She had a guttural voice that was rounded like her face, but provocative at the same time. Her magnificent appearance indicated to him that she was a woman who deserved some respect; she might be quite desirable too, for a while.

"A thousand square meters," he replied. "Al-Hajj Husain may have told you the price I'm asking."

"Ten thousand pounds!" the old lady exclaimed. "Where will you find someone to pay that much?!"

"Here!" Isa replied, pointing at her with a laugh.

"It's the kind of opportunity the world doesn't offer twice," Al-Hajj Husain said emphatically. "God be my witness!"

Isa refused to consider lowering the price a single piaster. The bargaining went on interminably, but it foundered on his determination. During all this haggling Isa and the daughter exchanged probing glances which had nothing at all to do with business. He got the impression that she was not married, and told himself that she was rich and acceptable. She was not the type he liked, it

405 / Autumn Quail

was true, and they were not the same age, but she was wealthy, placid, and well mannered, as far as he could tell. These were just passing notions, but it struck him that the old lady was following his train of thought. The meeting came to an end without his changing his mind or the old lady accepting his price.

TWENTY-ONE

The agent advised him to do a bit of bargaining, but he felt a pressing need to make his future secure and so he refused. His share of the selling price of the house would enable him to maintain his present standard of living for ten years at least, and during that long period of time a suitable job might open up for him. None of his three sisters disagreed with the position he had taken, and he was given absolute freedom to accept or reject the offer.

Days went by and he began to get worried. Then the agent brought him the good news that the lady had accepted the quoted price. From the agent's chatter he gathered that Inayat Hanem was the widow of a police officer, but her money had been left to her by her father. Her daughter, Qadriyya, her only child, had been divorced five years earlier without ever having any children. Isa went to visit the lady at home in a building she owned in Sakakini Square.* The superb, classically styled furniture showed that the family had real prestige, and all the formalities of the sale were settled at a friendly session. Isa pointed to the picture of the lady's husband. "I knew your late husband," he said suavely. "When I first started working, I heard enough things about him to convince me that he was a respectable man and loved his homeland."

This had a very good effect on the two women. Inayat Hanem invited him to stay for a while, and before long the servant brought in some tea and splendid cakes. The old woman expressed her happiness at being able to serve as hostess to one of her late husband's admirers. However, Isa did not sense that his welcome was due to any generosity on her part, and guessed that the invitation was rather more for her daughter's benefit. Qadriyya was sitting quietly and filled up the empty chair very nicely; from time to time, she looked at him drowsily.

"Those days serving in the provinces were really unforgettable," Inayat Hanem said, "days full of goodness. My late husband earned Saad Zaghlul's esteem, and he was transferred to the Interior in 1924. But he was subjected to the worst kinds of treatment during the periods of revolution." She went on to praise his intuition. "When Qadriyya's husband came to ask for her hand," she told Isa to prove her point, "my late husband said he was not happy with him. But I insisted, and so I was responsible for my daughter's bad luck!"

Isa happily took his cue. "How was that, might I ask?"

"He was from a good family, but had a really depraved character. My daughter is a good girl; she looks after the house, and is of a generous disposition. By her very nature, she wasn't prepared when he turned her home into a tavern and gaming den!"

"What bad luck!" Isa said regretfully. "Our Lord will recompense her well for her patience."

A considerable amount of time passed in this heavily

loaded conversation. Isa asked himself how much he could enjoy a woman like Qadriyya; he could regard her as a kind of lifetime security, and she could undoubtedly be considered a stroke of good fortune when measured against the misfortunes he had suffered.

When he left the house, he was sure that he had made a considerable impression on the two women. Qadriyya needs a husband, he thought with a good deal of sorrow, and I need a wife. He decided to make a few of the usual inquiries, which established that she had been married three times, not just once. The first had lasted for only a month. She had been betrothed to a relative of her father's, and before the marriage was consummated, they had realized that he was after her money and was just taking advantage of her. Her father had forced him to divorce her. The second had lasted for four or five years. Her mother was not prepared to give her daughter any of her money, even though the husband had asked that she should and kept pressing her. She thought that he should be able to take care of his own responsibilities without any help from her, and that these requests were irresponsible and showed some sinister design on his part. The argument had ended in divorce. The third marriage had lasted for six years and seemed likely to last, especially since her mother had changed her policy and gave her enough money and more. But the husband had wanted children, and Qadriyya had given him none; and judging from her previous marriage, probably would never do so. The husband had married again in secret and then told her. This had caused a crisis which could not continue indefinitely and so she was divorced for the third time.

This, then, was Qadriyya's story. However, Isa did not

go into all the details in the corner at El Bodega. "A very presentable woman wants to marry me!" he said.

Their gazes fastened on him like compass needles attracted to a pole.

"She's from a very respectable and wealthy family," he said gleefully and with a touch of vanity.

"The last quality you mentioned is the one to look for!" said Abbas Sadiq with his ringing voice, as though he were announcing the news.

"I hope you'll be very happy," said Ibrahim Khairat, smiling to hide his jealous feelings. "We should see about repairing the house now that political hurricanes are about to knock it down!"

This bitter comment irritated him. "Particularly as I haven't got a pen to use to curry favor with my enemies!" he retorted.

They all laughed. He was inundated with questions and began to answer them cautiously until the lies were piling up. He only revealed his real feelings to Samir Abd al-Baqi as they were walking alone together down Sulaiman Pasha Street. He told him the whole, unadulterated truth.

"Aren't you concerned about having children?" Samir asked.

"I need to find a companion and put an end to my loneliness," Isa responded angrily. "This woman is quite respectable and she's prepared to take me with all my faults. So why shouldn't I accept her with hers? Where can I find a decent girl who'll accept me in my present circumstances?"

He went to see Inayat Hanem to ask for Qadriyya's hand, and found her quite prepared to accept his proposal. "I want to be honest with you," he said. "Lies are the enemy of marriage. I have a fair amount of money left in the bank, in addition to my share of the money on the sale of the house. I also have a small pension. At the moment, I haven't got a job, but it's possible that I'll find a decent job in the future. I was expelled from the government, not for reasons having to do with honor but because of blind political partisanship. It wasn't possible for the present regime to spare someone like me whom it regards as being very dangerous!"

"That's fine," the old lady replied. "We're not worried about money. We prefer work only because it's undesirable to be doing nothing. I've no doubts about your honor whatsoever; my late husband suffered just as you have. My heart tells me that you'll be the best husband for my daughter."

She did not tell him about her daughter's successive marriages or her sterility. That made him happy. He realized that, if he knew about the bride's faults in advance, later on he wouldn't be able to play the role of the faithful husband whose hopes have been dashed. And that was a very important role to leave open should he later have the chance to regain his influence and prestige!

TWENTY-TWO

He travelled to Ra's al-Barr* to spend his honeymoon in Inayat Hanem's chalet. Relations among the three of them grew in a way which augured well for the future. From the beginning, he wanted to be a man in every sense of the word. He did not give way on anything which he felt he might regret later on. For that reason, he refused to stay in her mother's house, even though she suggested it, and insisted on living with his wife far away in Dokki, that quarter with its unforgettable memories. He showed a strange courage in telling her quite frankly that they both—he and his wife, that is—had to enjoy her money while she was alive so that they could honestly wish her a long life! He was sticking to his demands till they were all met in full; the reason why the mighty party had been ruined, he told himself, was that it had been too tolerant toward the end of its life, a life which had otherwise been marked by an obstinate persistence.

He was seeing Ra's al-Barr for the first time in his life.

He was struck by its special character, the way it combined the beauties of the city, the countryside, and the shore. The place where the Nile and the sea came together fascinated him, and so did the all-embracing quiet, like some happy dream, the fresh faces, and the dry, gentle breeze which seemed somehow to infringe on the house's sanctity as it permeated the hospitable walls. He did not find any of his friends on a summer vacation, and so he devoted all his time to his family. He found his marriage a great success and felt he had a powerful influence over his wife. For the first time, he found it irksome to be idle once he discovered that life in the house was revolving around an axis other than his own. He found out that neither his personality nor his wife's love of him, nor the way in which his mother-in-law adapted to his wishes, could drive this painful feeling away. In the old days, he had openly lived like a notable with his money, but now everyone was looking at his wife and her money.

No one would believe that he could lead a life of luxury forever with his share from the sale of the house and his pension. He started hiding his thoughts behind loud laughter and a pretense of naïveté and trust. However, he was quite sure that his life would not go on like this for long, and that he had to arouse his dormant ambitions and embark upon some enterprise worthy of himself.

He learned everything about his wife by living with her. She emerged as a past master at cooking and making clothes. She filled him up with different kinds of food, especially sweetmeats, which she was particularly good at making. She was gluttonous and infected the people with whom she ate with the same vice. Her prowess at innocent games like backgammon and conquian* gave her a great deal of pleasure. She was a devotee of the cinema and the comic theater even though her primary education had been almost completely erased from her memory; all she retained of it was a meager ability to read and to write a poor letter. A woman in every sense of the word, she had a fiery temperament, allowing him no complaints on that score. However, he did worry about the way she jumped down his throat every time she could. It seemed that she had an unconscious desire to make a husband, father, and son out of him at one and the same time; this may have had something to do with her sad but overwhelming longing for children, and the way she expressed her suppressed emotions through worried looks and sudden nervous movements that did not suit her staid and ample person. Misery, Isa thought, seems to be the greatest common denominator among people everywhere; and then he thought how insignificant appearances really are. What could be the hidden reason for this absurdity? he wondered; it is fortunate that we can at least hide our thoughts from other people. I wonder what ideas about me are going around in that small head of hers covered with thick hair. Would she be upset, for example, if she knew the real reasons for my having to give up my post?

He thought of Salwa and the wound she had gouged in his heart, and felt even more unnerved. He thought of Riri as well; he frowned bitterly, and a black look came over his face. He was aware of his own limitless insignificance, and recalled how the ministry used to quake when he got out of his government Chevrolet in the morning. He also remembered a day when he had wanted to put himself forward as a candidate for the al-Wayiliyya district. But Abd al-Halim Pasha Shukri had advised him to hold off till the coming elections because he was sure that he would be nominated as under secretary in the ministry!

One day, the radio surprised him by announcing the nationalization of the Suez Canal Company. His interest rose to boiling point, and he started panting apprehensively as in the old days. Before long, he was immersed in the same enthusiasm which was engulfing everyone. He longed to see his absent friends so that he could discuss the situation with them. He acknowledged in a daze that it was something of almost unbelievable significance and importance, and there his mind stopped. His heart buried itself inside him like an invalid, and a feeling of jealousy gnawed away at him. He felt alarmed every time a peak was reached in the present which would compare with those peaks in history which served as the backcloth for his life's memories. He felt an intense pain as he experienced the tug-of-war between the two sides of his own split personality. He wondered what the consequences might be, and tried to ask himself what his stand was in relation to them. But he soon fled from this inner struggle by sharing the news with his wife and her mother. However, he found they had no reaction to the events, and he hurried to the refrigerator to get something to drink.

In the middle of September, he returned to Cairo with his senses bloated. He had noticeably gained weight. He walked past his old home on his way to his new house in Dokki, and sad memories came flooding back. All his friends now had young, educated wives, and he began to exchange visits with them. Qadriyya was especially admired because of her social standing and wealth. Samir Abd al-Baqi asked him how he liked married life.

"It's fine," he replied after a diplomatic pause, "but . . ."

"But?"

"I doubt if any man could stand it without a job or children."

The Jews attacked Sinai. The papers slapped that in his face one morning, and the news staggered him. He sat down by the radio and followed the news with dwindling attention; it had such an effect on him that he was almost babbling. Thoughts spun around inside his head till he felt dizzy. Yes indeed, he thought, the fate of the revolution is swaying in the balance. However, his own nationalist feelings burst out and overwhelmed everything else; he showed a rage worthy of an old nationalist almost overtaken by death, an old nationalist who was suffering even though he had been tarnished because of Egypt. His feet clung to the edge of the abyss which threatened to annihilate his own country. He pushed the revolution and its fate out of his mind so that he could keep his feelings completely responsive. Through the sheer force of his will, he eliminated those contradictory emotions which were spreading beneath the stream of his turbulent consciousness. Turning toward his wife, he was astonished to see how unconcerned she seemed and how completely she was bound up in the routine of her daily life. She only came out of it when she asked scornfully, "War and raids again?"

He treated the whole thing as a joke and teased her to calm his nerves. "You're very concerned about getting food ready," he said. "Tell me, how would the world be if everyone behaved like you?"

"Wars would stop!" she replied simply.

In spite of his anxiety, he managed to laugh. "Qadriyya, you're not worried about public affairs," he said, feeling the urge to make a joke. "I mean things involving the people and our country."

"It's enough for me to look after you and your home."

"Don't you love Egypt?"

"Of course!"

"Don't you want our Army to win?"

"Of course. Then we'll have some peace again."

"But don't you even want to think about it?"

"I've got quite enough to worry about."

"Tell me how you would feel if the Jews were trying to take over your mother's property!"

"What a terrible thought," she replied with a laugh. "Have we killed any of them?"

He found it all very amusing, and it helped to relieve his tense feelings. Even though the sky was very overcast, they went to visit Inayat Hanem in Sakakini and had lunch with her. They left before it got dark. They were standing in the square looking for a taxi when the siren went off. She gripped his arm. "Let's go back," she whispered in a shaky voice.

They returned to her mother's building. As they were climbing the stairs, an antiaircraft gun began firing. She shuddered and his heart jumped violently. They all gathered in a room with the blinds closed.

"From one war to the next," Inayat Hanem protested, "life is lost. Sirens, antiaircraft guns, bombs. Wouldn't it be a good idea for us to seek refuge in another country?"

They stayed there in the darkness with dry throats. Four guns boomed out in the distance.

"This generation will enter Paradise without any Day of Reckoning!" her mother continued.

How could the Jews dare to attack Egypt, Isa asked himself in despair, when she had prepared herself with such an army?

TWENTY-THREE

The next evening he rushed to El Bodega with his head full of comforting and encouraging news from the newspapers. The weather was really marvelous as they clustered together around the table on the pavement. A warm and powerful force drew them all together, a force restless with the combined feelings of danger and hope. Ibrahim Khairat drew his small frame up to its full height. "Do you think," he asked excitedly, "that Israel will just make this one move?"

They looked at one another in a strange way which expressed their inner feelings clearly, as though some kind of drunkenness had put them all into a daze.

"France, England, and America are all behind Israel," Ibrahim Khairat continued.

Isa wondered anxiously how he could define his own position in the midst of such turbulent thoughts and emotions as these.

"It looks as though our army will be finished," said Samir Abd al-Baqi, "before our allies declare themselves."

They all laughed. The evening brought with it a quiet and secrecy. Ibrahim Khairat lowered his voice. "Things are clear now," he said. "This is the end!"

They listened to him with a sense of nervous joy, and some of them even felt a little guilt. Abbas Sadiq raised his head from the *nargila*. His bulging eyes were gleaming brightly. "They have supporters behind them too," he said.

"No one could be so crazy," said Ibrahim Khairat scornfully, "as to think seriously that a world war is going to flare up over a spot which can hardly be seen on the world map."

Isa found that their feelings reflected some of what he himself was thinking. He decided, however, that the other side of it should be voiced. "Do you really want the Jews to defeat us?" he asked.

"There will be a superficial defeat," Ibrahim Khairat said, "which will rid us of the new occupation army. Then Israel will be forced to retreat and maybe even to be satisfied with taking over Sinai and making peace with the Arabs. England and France will intervene to settle the problems connected with the Near East and return things to normal in Egypt."

"Doesn't that mean a reversion to Western influence?" Isa asked.

"That's better than the present situation, at any rate."

"What a trap we've fallen into!" said Isa, as though he were talking to himself. "We stumble about, then we're torn to pieces, and finally we suffer terribly. We betray either our homeland or ourselves. However, from my point of view, a defeat in this particular war would be worse than death."

"You're very romantic," Abbas Sadiq said.

"Why should we be unhappy?" Ibrahim Khairat asked. "There's nothing left to be unhappy about, and, in a dead man's view, any kind of life is better than death."

"Sometimes," Isa replied, "I tell myself that death would be more bearable than going backwards, and at other times I tell myself that it would be better to remain without a role in a country which has one, rather than to have a role in a country which has none."

"By your own admission," said Ibrahim Khairat with a smile, "you've got a split personality. We're not concerned about the side of you which is talking; the opinion of the silent side is good enough for us!"

They all laughed loudly. It was getting dark. Ibrahim Khairat looked at Samir Abd al-Baqi as if to urge him to say something.

"I would like all our fellow citizens to live to enjoy human generosity," said Samir.

"So you agree with us, do you?" Ibrahim Khairat asked.

"My words have a more profound significance than that," Samir replied tersely.

"Are you opposed to our views then?"

"My words have a more profound significance than that," he repeated.

Isa was lost in his own troubled thoughts. The side of him which was speaking had to defeat the silent side. He had to help it out; he had to show his scorn for the assailant quite shamelessly and thereby show his scorn for the silent side of himself. What has led us to this really sorry state of affairs? he wondered. Was there no way to forget personal defeats? The disease was raging throughout the country.

The air-raid siren sounded like a wall collapsing on

them suddenly. All light left the world, and the street was filled with the sound of people running in the dark. Samir suggested they go inside the café, but the idea got no encouragement from anyone. Isa thought of his wife on her own in Dokki with Umm Shalabi and felt sorry for her. Suddenly they were frightened by the sound of distant explosions, coming one after another. They quickly hurried into the café to the corner where they sat in the winter. The distant blasts kept coming with a frightening regularity. People started guessing in what parts of town they were falling. Shubra? Heliopolis? Hulwan?

"Where did the Jews get such forces?"

"And where are our planes?"

The attack continued and was certainly severe enough to be termed a real raid. The country had probably seen nothing like it throughout the Second World War. Their nerves were really on edge. A man came rushing in from outside. "It's British planes that are dropping the bombs!" he said in a voice which the whole blacked-out café could hear.

"Impossible!" scores of people yelled.

"I heard it on the Near East station!" he replied to confirm the news.

Comments began to pour out like hallucinations. Then the bombing stopped. Minutes passed in an anxious silence, and then the all-clear siren sounded. They released themselves from the grip of tension, and as the lights came on, gazed at each other with the same look of bewilderment that covers your face when you wake up after a long sleep. They were deciding whether to go or stay when the air-raid siren sounded again. Before long the explosions started again.

"The end seems even nearer than we thought," Ibrahim Khairat whispered.

"Pray God we're not a part of it," Samir Abd al-Baqi whispered.

After an hour of torture, the all-clear siren sounded. They left the café quickly and got into Ibrahim Khairat's car. They had only just gotten to Abu Ala's bridge when the siren sounded for the third time. They stopped the car near the pavement. As there were no shelters nearby, they decided to stay in the car. "We've got to live!" Ibrahim Khairat said with a nervous laugh. "The price of stock in our lives keeps going up."

About an hour later, they heard the all-clear siren. The Ford sped across the bridge, and then crossed the Zamalek Bridge headed for Sharia an-Nil. Just at the start of it, the air-raid siren sounded for a fourth time. They stopped the car near an open space. The raid continued and the bombing was heavy.

"Maybe they're bombing particular targets," Isa said to calm himself.

"Maybe they're bombing at random," said Samir anxiously.

"Bombing civilians is a terrible responsibility in the face of world opinion," Abbas Sadiq said in a voice which sounded as though he had been hit by shrapnel himself.

"The best thing is to keep calm," Ibrahim Khairat said.

The all-clear siren sounded half an hour later. The car sped along at top speed to get them home before the air-raid siren came on again.

TWENTY-FOUR

The Cairo sky was crisscrossed with planes day and night. The incredible thing was that daily life in houses, offices, shops, and markets carried on as usual, even though planes were screaming incessantly overhead and explosions kept going off. People still thought that the bombs were not falling indiscriminately, but there were many rumors of casualties. They carried on as usual, but death was looking down at them from a nearby window; its harbingers flew into their ears and it intruded into their innermost thoughts. The city was turned into an army camp; convoys of armored vehicles and trucks moved along the streets, and normal life was drowned in a sea of thoughts and misgivings.

Inayat Hanem came to live with her daughter in Dokki till things settled down. At night, the world looked as it had before history. They gathered around the radio in the house; their mouths felt very dry and they hoped that listening to the voices of the announcers and the national songs would help to relieve the dryness.

The explosions and gunfire carried on like street vendors' cries. Eventually the old lady's eyes began to wander and lost their color. She clutched the rosary in her palm as though it were a lightning conductor. Qadriyya broke down as quickly as her mother, and her robustness was of no help to her. Her languid eyes lost their look of majestic apathy. The discussions at the United Nations emerged from the radio like air for a suffocating man. The tales from Port Said followed and they began to grieve.

"Can we stand up to the English and French?" Qadriyya asked in a moment of alarm.

"Port Said is fighting back," Isa replied anxiously, "and the world's in a state of revolution!"

"They're all talking, and we're being hit!"

"Yes. What can be done?"

"There has to be a solution," she shouted nervously, "any solution. If there isn't, my nerves will be destroyed."

His nerves were on the verge of collapse too. Sadness, darkness, and prison. The darkness inspired him to hope desperately for victory. Many things melted away in the darkness. He forgot about the past and the future, and focused on the desire for victory. Perhaps the fact that he could not leave the house gave him a better chance to think about the situation and become thoroughly aware of the danger, to yearn for victory and keep the hidden side of his own nature quiet. Deep down inside him, a well of enthusiasm began to move which almost pushed him toward self-sacrifice. As he dawdled around in the daytime, he could read in hundreds of other faces the same feelings which tied him to life in spite of all the dust, oblivion, and undercurrents of selfishness. He was like a drowning man, thinking only of saving himself. It seemed to him that the barrier which stood between him and the revolution was dissolving at a rate which he would never have thought possible before.

Ibrahim Khairat came to visit him one afternoon on his way to his office in the city. He seemed extremely self-confident and serious. "The whole tragedy will be over in a few hours," he said.

Isa looked at him in bewilderment with his big, round eyes.

"Some of our men are meeting the responsible authorities at this moment," said Ibrahim. He was frowning because he felt a sense of authority. "We're trying to persuade them to surrender so that we can save whatever can be saved!"

Isa got the impression that he was seeing the High Commissioner's procession just as he had done in the old days. "What's left to be saved?" he asked.

"Don't be overly pessimistic," Ibrahim retorted, and then continued angrily: "People who regard life and death as the same thing are really miserable creatures."

"It's like a nightmare," Isa said sorrowfully.

"With the state of mind we're in," said Ibrahim angrily, "defeat is easy to live with."

"We'd soon get tired if we started counting mankind's troubles. I'm asking myself whether life is really fit for human beings!"

Ibrahim Khairat shrugged his shoulders contemptuously.

"Maybe it's some sort of idiocy to hang on to life in spite of all its miseries," Isa continued. "But as long as we're alive, we should wage an unflagging war on all types of stupidity."

"Tell me," Ibrahim asked him, "have you really changed?"

Isa did not say a word, but his face contracted into an expression of utter disgust. However, when the crisis reached its peak, new factors came rushing into the whirlpool. The world gave its decision, the threats disappeared, and the enemy was forced to swallow its pride and submit to an unprecedented reality. Then there was an outburst of joy greater than any bomb.

Life returned to the corner in El Bodega, and the friends all met again. A faded smile, and a languid look which could not see into the future.

"There's some hope that we'll gain some weight," said Ibrahim Khairat mockingly, "like people who are condemned to death!"

Abbas Sadiq brandished the stem of his *nargila*. "This is a chance," he said, "which is a million times rarer than winning money at roulette."

Even Samir al-Baqi's green eyes showed signs of disappointment deep down. Even more remarkable was the fact that Isa himself—even after he had felt the taste of victory—rapidly sank into a profound lethargy like a pile of ash. His thoughts turned in on themselves and were buried in darkness once more.

TWENTY-FIVE

Everyone has a job, but he had none. Every wife has children, but she had none. Every citizen in a country has his own abode, but he was an exile in his own homeland. After the usual escapist roles, what was left? In the mornings, he dawdled from one café to another; in the evenings, he would mull over his sorrows at El Bodega and make boring visits within the family circle. After the usual escapist roles, what was left? He went through terrible agonies, and felt lonely and bored. How much longer can this miserable existence last? he asked himself.

There he was sitting by the windowpane, sunning himself in the bitter cold, jobless and hopeless. Qadriyya was concentrating on some crocheting. She no longer dispelled his feeling of loneliness. With her disheveled hair and swollen features, she showed all the signs of an all too common neglect. She had become fatter and fleshier, and her face showed clearly that in its natural state it was a complete stranger to the comeliness of youth.

He looked at her sorrowfully, and then turned away to

read the headlines in the papers; he no longer bothered to read the news. Then he gave up and started talking to himself; in recent years he had been doing a great deal of this. Qadriyya was not the wife he had been looking for, and he still felt bitterly sorry about Salwa, even though the love itself had died long since. If it had not been for the wine, he would not have been able to give himself up to Qadriyya's arms. Nor would he have tolerated the hints about her wealth, which she kept using to hem him in, if it were not for the utter despair he felt. It was pure agony for him every time he remembered that she was spending money on her home while he was not spending a penny of his pension, except that is, on himself. Even his bank balance did him no good at all in his family life. So what was the point of all this sponging?

One day, she proved to him that she too was thinking about other things besides mealtimes and crocheting. "Isa," she said, "you seem very distracted, and sometimes you look so miserable. It makes me very worried."

Isa said that he was sorry that she was worried. "I'm quite well," he continued, "so don't worry yourself about that."

"Some things can be harmful for a man."

"Such as?"

"Not working when he can."

He smiled even though he was really furious. "Maybe you're annoyed," he said, "to find your husband out of a job."

"It doesn't worry me at all," she replied emphatically, "apart from the effect which it has on you."

"What do you suggest I do?"

"You know best about that, my dear."

"There aren't any ministerial posts vacant at the moment," he replied simply.

They both laughed with no feeling at all. However, she carried on hopefully. "Think about it seriously," she said. "Please."

He told himself that she was right, and that she did occasionally have a sensible idea in that stupid head of hers. He himself was convinced that he needed to get a job, but why did his ambition let him down? Did his will have some kind of disease? Why didn't he open an office, or else join one?

He was thinking about a job, but living without one and without any serious initiative about taking the required steps. His bank balance gave him a certain amount of security, and this had been increased by his prosperous marriage. And apart from all that, his pension could cover his daily expenses. So he gave in to laziness and arrogance, and his eternal sense of alienation was too great to let him begin at the bottom of the ladder. He sought consolation in any way he could, at home or outside, in Ra's al-Barr* or Alexandria, without paying any attention to the passage of time.

"You're getting heavier all the time," Samir Abd al-Baqi told him. "You should look after yourself."

It was true that he was eating too much, sweets especially, and no meal went by without having a glass or two. "I'm quite aware of that," he replied. "People will say that my wife is fattening me up well."

"I was only thinking of your health," replied Samir timidly.

"Yes, I daresay," said Isa. "But sometimes I can read it in people's eyes."

"It's entirely your own fault," said Samir with a frown. "You're so lazy. I often wonder in amazement where that Isa who used to leave the ministry after midnight almost every day has disappeared to, to say nothing of the one who put so much into the party and the club."

One day, the radio announcer spoke about the space flight and the dawning of a new era. Isa woke up from his slumber, and a new interest intruded into his apathetic spirit. He started reading the papers avidly again and listening closely to the radio. The gathering at the corner in El Bodega found something else to do apart from talking about political misfortunes and chewing over rumors.

"Isn't it marvelous," Abbas Sadiq remarked, "to read the papers every morning with this feeling of excitement?"

"This marks the setting of the politicians' star," said Ibrahim Khairat maliciously. "Why don't they relinquish their positions to the *ulama** and then go to blazes?"

"Now we should start looking hopefully to the heavens again!" said Samir Abd al-Baqi.

Isa raised his eyes to the ceiling as though he were looking at the heavens, and pictured the stars and planets to himself with a childlike desire for some magical and imaginary means of escape. "How wonderful it would be to leave the earth forever," he muttered, and then continued complaining. "It's all become so boring it's like a disease!"

He wondered if it would be possible for him to establish his connection with mankind in general and to forget his compulsory affiliation with this country.

TWENTY-SIX

They all spent the summer at Ra's al-Barr, which was in itself unusual; even Abbas Sadiq, a devotee of Alexandria, was there. Ibrahim Khairat got a room ready in his chalet where they could play cards and drink, and they all went back there after their regular exercise on the banks of the Nile. Shaikh Abd at-Tawwab as-Salhubi was on vacation at the same time and joined up with them. Isa slid into poker with no trouble at all; the gambling and the fact that it kept him up till dawn led to his first serious quarrel with Qadriyya. When there was a quarrel, he found that she could be as stubborn as a mule. But he did not care and carried on scornfully in his own sweet way. When he took his place at the table, Ibrahim Khairat poured him out a glass of cognac and asked how things were going at home.

"Lousy," Isa replied tersely.

"Our wives are more tolerant than Qadriyya Hanem," commented Abbas Sadiq. "She shouldn't keep such a close watch on you in a beautiful haven like Ra's al-Barr."

Isa looked at his hand and was delighted to see he had

a pair of aces. He entered the round with high hopes, and then luck gave him a pair of eights. He won six piasters.

"Just look after your profits," said Shaikh As-Salhubi with a smile, "and things will get better at home!"

"His wife's not worried about money," Abbas Sadiq said to put things straight.

The remark was quite spontaneous, but it hurt Isa very much, particularly as he was usually unlucky at card games; so much so that he had had to withdraw a hundred pounds from the bank to cover his losses.

Ibrahim Khairat asked Shaikh As-Salhubi about Abd al-Halim Pasha Shukri.

"He went abroad at the right time," the Shaikh replied, "and with the appropriate excuse. He won't be coming back, of course."

"It's no better than it is here," said Samir Abd al-Baqi. "The foreign policy page reads like the obituaries!"

"Then the world really is threatened by total destruction," Abbas Sadiq said.

"It's threatened by destruction," said Isa as he dealt the hand, "whether it's war or peace!"

"You only philosophize when you're feeling in low spirits," Shaikh As-Salhubi said with a laugh. "Maybe your flood of good luck is drying up!"

Isa lost the round even though he had three tens. "One word from you," he told the Shaikh angrily, "would bring a whole town bad luck."

"Rubbish!" As-Salhubi replied with a laugh. "I've chased the present generation with my blessed words since the day it was born. And just look what's happened to it!"

Isa put his whole heart and soul into the game. He enjoyed the ardor, hope, enthusiasm, and absorption of it all with a languid vitality. Everything was forgotten, even history and the disasters which it had brought with it. He joined with pleasure in its crazy existence. There were at least seven pounds on the table. He pinned his hopes on a solitary ace and then drew a card. There was the ace smiling at him with its red face. But then Ibrahim threw down his flush like a thunderbolt. His nervous system leapt several times, just as it had done on the day when the dissolution of the political parties was announced. He wondered what his wife was doing at that moment; would she be talking to her mother? Maybe the old woman would be telling her that they had accepted their particular problem, but it did not seem to have accepted them. He's out of work, she would be saying, expelled because of his bad reputation; and he doesn't worship God either. Too bad for Qadriyya if she got in his way. She had been married several times and was barren, naturally barren, and she was at least ten years older than him too!

When he came to himself again, Shaikh As-Salhubi was carrying on with what he had been saying earlier. "That's why we're in the age of fundamental principles," he was saying, "just like the days when the great religions were in conflict with each other!"

"What hope have the small nations got in life," asked Samir Abd al-Baqi, "if the great nations don't disagree with each other?"

"The atom is the flood," Shaikh As-Salhubi said with conviction. "Either we turn in truth to Almighty God, or else there will be 'clear destruction'!"*

Isa tried hard to remember where he had come across that idea before, the idea of the flood. He forgot this philosophizing when he found four tens in his hand. He sprang into action so as to make up for his losses during the long night. He opened with twenty-five piasters to draw them into the round, but they all passed because they had such poor hands. His head was spinning. Then he showed his winning hand.

"Your luck's worse when you're winning than when you're losing!" shouted Ibrahim Khairat.

"You're undoubtedly lucky in love," Shaikh As-Salhubi remarked.

Isa was about to boil over. Gambling can eventually become a deadly disease, he told himself. He started to reckon up what kind of crisis was waiting for him at home. Everyone stopped playing just as dawn was about to appear.

Abbas Sadiq stood up. "What fun would there be at Ra's al-Barr," he said, "if it weren't for gambling?"

Isa went out into the street feeling like a candle with only the vestige of the wick left. Abbas Sadiq and Samir Abd al-Baqi walked one way, and he walked another with Shaikh As-Salhubi. A dewy breeze blew quietly, and the sounds of people sleeping happily resounded in a darkness broken only by the light of the stars and by the moon rising at the end of the month. From afar, the horizon echoed the roaring of the sea. Shaikh As-Salhubi yawned as he intoned the word "Allah." "How beautiful it is at this time of night," he murmured.

"Especially when you've won!" Isa replied with a laugh.

"I've left this evening session of ours with no wins or losses," the Shaikh said with a laugh. "Abbas Sadiq is God's own lighted fire." Then, after a pause: "Isa, you're a risky gambler, you know!"

"I lost," Isa replied with a tone full of meaning, "even though I had a pair of aces in my right hand."

The Shaikh realized what he meant. "That's the way the world is," he replied. "Do we deserve the things that happen to us? Let's admit that we do make mistakes, but then, who doesn't? How can this renegade nation have forgotten us? How can it forget the people who used to treat it as a sympathetic mother treats her only child?"

A feeling of sadness overwhelmed Isa and his willful pride softened. "We were a party with the very loftiest ideals," he said, responding to a sudden desire to make a confession, "a party of self-sacrifice and absolute integrity. In the face of all kinds of temptations and threats, we were the party which said, 'No, and no again.' We were like that before 1936. So how did our pure spirit get so senile? How did we sink little by little till we had lost all the good qualities we had? Now here we are turning up our hands in despair in the darkness, feeling sad and guilt-stricken. It's too bad."

"We were the best of them all," the Shaikh said insistently, "right up till the very last moment."

"That's a relative judgment," Isa replied in a bitter tone which was really aimed at himself. "It doesn't fit in with the nature of things, nor does it satisfy the people who are tackling life so enthusiastically. Too bad, then . . ."

Isa said good night to him at the end of the street. He watched him as he walked slowly away with the wind blowing in his loose-fitting *gallabiyya*. The Shaikh had started his life, Isa thought sadly, by being imprisoned in Tanta when the Australian soldiers had arrested him as he was shouting. "Long live the homeland . . . long live Saad." He had ended up in 1942 trading in vacant jobs, just as I finished up with bank account number 33123 at the Bank of Egypt.

He looked up at the universe. The rising moon was shining brightly, and the stars were gleaming, infinity overwhelming everything else. "What does it all mean?" he asked himself in an audible voice. "Tell me; my guide's all confused."

The doorbell rang loudly in the nocturnal silence when he pressed it. He waited for a while, then rang it again. He waited, and then rang again. He kept on pressing the bell, but there was no answer. She must have decided not to open the door! he thought. He stamped on the ground, then turned around and walked away.

TWENTY-SEVEN

He spent the night at Ibrahim Khairat's house. The next day he took a room in the Grand Hotel on the Nile. After a week he had to draw another hundred pounds to cover his never-ending losses and his daily expenses. Ibrahim's wife went to see Qadriyya at her husband's suggestion to apologize for the unintentional role which Ibrahim had played in her quarrel with her husband. Then she tried to bring about a reconciliation, but got no response. Isa kept on gambling without the slightest consideration of the consequences. Samir stopped coming to their evening sessions because he was so disgusted by the dissipation he could see in his friend. "You should really take a look at your entire situation," he told Isa one day.

They were sitting in the Soprano Casino overlooking the sea. It was noon, the time of day when he usually woke up. With his round eyes, Isa was following a group of swimming girls. He did not comment on his friend's remark, but continued enjoying the view. Samir repeated what he had said.

"I'd really like to try an experiment," Isa said, "one that has never been possible at the right time. I'd like to flirt with a pretty girl and get to know her, then propose to her. Meanwhile, we'd be exchanging presents, talking to each other, and making promises to each other over the telephone."

"Do you really want to get married again?" Samir asked him.

He looked up at a slow-moving cloud which had a shape like a camel. "Just look at that cloud," he said. "Tell me, is it possible that our life was created like that shape up there?"

"Even that fleeting shape is inevitable," Samir replied with a smile. "It's the result of hundreds of different factors of air and nature. But tell me, do you want to get married?"

Isa laughed and finished his Spatis.* Just a dream," he said. "Why do Sufis always believe everything?"

"Well, then," Samir said angrily, "let's discuss your situation."

"Just imagine," Isa replied in a similar tone, "as I was coming from the hotel, I met Sami Pasha Abd ar-Rahman, the old Free Constitutionalist. I felt rather attached to him personally because we both belonged to the past generation. We shook hands with each other and stood there talking. Strangely enough, if it hadn't been for Saad Zaghlul, we wouldn't have got into this situation!"

Samir laughed so loudly that lots of people sitting around stared at them.

"The biggest trick I let them pull on me was the dowry balance," Isa said in a different tone of voice. "The old woman's a farsighted old devil!"

"Qadriyya Hanem is a very reasonable woman, Isa," Samir said sorrowfully. "You're mad to be doing all this gambling."

Isa breathed in angrily. "It's boredom," he muttered.

"Work and work again," said Samir, patting his hand. "That's my first and last piece of advice to you."

Samir came in at the very beginning of the evening session, when Isa was concentrating on the game, and invited him to accompany him on some urgent and important business. Isa tried to ignore the invitation and continue playing, but Samir dragged him from the table in spite of his cries of protest and the silent protests of the people around him as well.

He found himself in Samir's chalet confronted by Ihsan, Samir's wife, and Qadriyya, his own wife, who was sitting on a large chair with her head lowered. Ihsan welcomed him and sat him down next to her on a long, ornate semi-circular sofa. "Thank you so much for coming," she said. She gestured at Qadriyya Hanem. "May I present to you a dear friend of mine. She's married to a fine man who's been lost in action."

Isa frowned and Qadriyya blushed. Her eyes moistened and Samir noticed it. "That's a good sign," he said. "What do you say?"

They did not stop speaking for a single moment. "Every problem can be solved without an argument," Ihsan said.

"Things can be put right again with a little kindness," Samir told Qadriyya with a smile. "Your husband is a stubborn man. In the past, he was subjected to all kinds of terror and torture without changing his mind."

"Are you happy with this situation?" Qadriyya asked. "Tell me."

A silver tray with *cassata* cakes and pastries from the local market was passed around. There was a pause while they ate.

"Humanity as a whole needs some doses of Sufism," Samir said. "Without it, life would lose it pleasure."

"We need to come back to life several times," said Isa, "till we perfect it."

Qadriyya now spoke to him for the first time. "I hope you're not holding back your kindness toward me till some other life, then," she said.

Samir had moistened the edge of his handkerchief with water and was using it to rub his trouser leg at the knee where a drop of strawberry juice had spilled. "Let's talk about the future," he suggested. "Please . . ."

"I'm quite sure," Qadriyya said, "that the only thing that could get him out of his difficulties is a job. I'll accept any sacrifice to achieve that much!"

"I completely agree with you," Samir said. "But he must move away from Ra's al-Barr so that that excellent idea can sink in. You've spent the month of August here; that's enough. Go to Alexandria and spend the rest of the summer there. That seems both essential and urgent."

"We'll leave tomorrow," Qadriyya said, "provided he agrees."

"You'll find ample time to think in Alexandria," Samir said as he led them to the outside door of the chalet. "When you get back to Cairo in October, you'll start work immediately."

They walked side by side in the street, which was almost empty. The half-moon was fixed above the horizon like a cosmic smile in a clear sky. He had a thought; all that beauty scattered around in such remarkable order was just some unknown, mocking force, compelling mankind to realize the intensity and chaos of its own misery.

"I've found out that I've got high blood pressure," Qadriyya muttered, "and you're the cause of it all!"

"Really?"

"Yes. The doctor examined me and gave me some medicine and put me on a diet."

"I hope you'll soon get better," he told her, stroking her back very gently. He felt he was not getting any further in his quest for happiness. A marriage with no love, a life without hope. Even if he did have some success with a job, he would still be out of work.

TWENTY-EIGHT

The two of them traveled to Alexandria alone, and her mother stayed on in Ra's al-Barr. They lived in the Louvre Hotel for a few days till Isa found a flat in Sidi Gaber on the seventh floor of a building overlooking the sea. The summer season was almost over; there was less noise to be heard from young people now, and the skies were welcoming masses of white clouds. The weather was conducive to peace and contemplation. Qadriyya seemed to be really happy even though she felt unwell. She stuck to her diet in spite of her fondness for food. If it took off some of her weight, she said, then so much the better. Isa grew fond of walking and avoided eating fatty foods as much as possible so that he could regain his slim appearance. They both agreed that he would start work as soon as he returned to Cairo. He had decided to open an office, although the idea did not seem to fill him with a great deal of pleasure. "I'd really like some other kind of life," he said.

She stared inquiringly into his face with her huge, cow-like eyes.

"Don't get worried," he resumed hurriedly. "That's just a dream. I'd like to live in the country, far away from Cairo; I'd only like to see it on special occasions. I'd like to spend the day working in the fields and the night on a balcony looking out on space and silence."

"But we've no connections with the countryside," she said in alarm.

"It's just a dream."

Days went by, and he felt exasperated. All he got from the almost deserted beaches was a lonely feeling, especially since Qadriyya preferred to stay in the house most of the time because of her health. He used to walk till his feet felt tired; when he sat down, it would be in the Gleem Paradise, where he could hang on to his memories. His own era was over, he told himself, and he wouldn't be able to merge into the same kind of life as he had had before. Here he was, tied to a woman in order to steal from her, not love her. He wondered when the world was going to be wiped out, and whether there wasn't some other kind of ideas which might give his heart some life again.

He found a palm reader in Indian dress standing in front of him, looking at him with gleaming eyes. He was sitting in his usual place in the Paradise. He stretched out his hand, and the man brought over a seat and sat down in front of him. He started concentrating immediately on the lines of his palm, while Isa waited patiently for the voice of the occult with a smile of resignation.

"You'll have a long life," the man said, "and you'll recover from a serious illness." He looked at his hand again. "You'll marry twice," he continued, "and have children."

Isa listened with interest. The man continued. "There are many upsets in your life," he said, "but you've nothing to fear because you have a will of iron. But you, you'll risk being drowned at sea!"

"At sea?"

"That's what your palm says. You're an ambitious man without any consideration for others. You'll always find an abundant means of support, but your nervousness often spoils your peace of mind."

The man stood up, bending his head in farewell as he did.

"What's the way out?" Isa asked him without thinking as he was about to leave.

The man looked at him inquisitively. Isa scoffed at himself and gave him a thankful gesture.

In the evening, he started walking along the Corniche till he reached Camp Cesare.* There was a row of cafés and shops which were bunched together on the pavement in a riot of lights, and it was there that his eyes fell on Riri! He stopped dead in his tracks on the Corniche. Fear gripped him as he looked again more carefully. Yes, it was definitely Riri, no one else. She was in a small place which sold ice cream and *ful** and *taamiyya** sandwiches, and was sitting behind the till on the chair belonging to either the manager or the owner. He rested his back on the seawall at a spot out of the light and scrutinized her face in amazement. When he recalled the way he had behaved, he felt very uncomfortable—he was shocked by how cruel and unpleasant he had been to her. Riri! It was Riri, no one else; but she was no longer a girl. Certainly not! She was a woman now in every sense of the word, and had a personality of her own—which the waiter who kept moving to and fro with orders between her and the customers obeyed to the full. A serious woman and a real manager. The incredible thing was that he had walked this way for twenty days in succession without looking at this small place. Now he read the name clearly: Take It and Thanks. On the few occasions when he had spent the summer in Alexandria, he had thought of her and been worried about the idea of meeting her either by himself or with his wife and friends. But he had found no sign of her. Eventually he had come to the conclusion that she had left town or maybe the world altogether. How had it come about that she was sitting in that seat? Were five years enough—without a world war—for her to reach this level? Her teacher in Al-Ibrahimiyya would undoubtedly be jealous of the rapid way she had advanced. Her colleagues would never have dreamed of it!

He stood there in the semi-darkness, not taking his eyes off her, and recalled their old relationship which was now forever lost in the recesses of oblivion. The superficiality of human relationships amazed him. Without realizing it, he thought, we're trying out death; we experiment with it time after time during our lives before death finally catches up with us. The whole scene with Riri sitting there in her place looked just like the Saadi Club when he used to walk in front of it, or like the House of Parliament. They were all lives destined to an early death, and the only things to benefit from them would be insects.

A woman in servant's clothes came into the place leading a little girl by the right hand. She went and spoke seriously to Riri. Meanwhile the little girl jumped onto Riri's lap and started playing lovingly and trustingly with the necklace she was wearing. At that moment, Isa had a thought that made his heart pound so much that it even covered the noise of the sea behind him. His whole body went rigid, and he looked closely at the little girl. He lost all consciousness of what was around him. But no . . . no! Why was his head spinning like this? What a stupid thought, and terrifying too! The little girl's face was turned toward her mother, so he could not see it. Things would pass quietly, he told himself, and then he would laugh at himself after it was all over. But the earth had already slipped and everything standing had been destroyed. Well, then, he should run, and never come back to Camp Cesare again, never return to Alexandria. He did not budge a single inch from the spot where he was standing. How had these idiotic ideas managed to take him by surprise?

Riri released herself from the little girl, kissed her, and then put her on the ground. The servant took hold of her hand and led her out of the café. She made for a side street that went inland from the shore. Instead of running away, he dashed across the road toward the side street and kept quickening his pace till he almost caught up with the two of them. He could hear the little girl piping up with some unintelligible words, almost all of them unintelligible except for "chocolate"; she sounded just like a chirping sparrow. They stopped in front of a shop on the corner of a cross street which sold sweets and games. He took up a position next to her in the gleaming light, and asked for a box of cigarettes. He began to scrutinize the girl's face with an avid curiosity. Did not her face have a triangular shape to it? And those circular eyes! The features of his mother and three sisters were all mingled in hers; they seemed to come and go. Was it just his imagination? Was it fear? Or was it the truth? He almost collapsed from sheer exhaustion. His heart was pounding fast, sending out continuous waves of amazement, disgust, panic, grief, longing, and desire for death.

The servant took her away to a building which faced the shop on the other side of the street. He gazed after them till they disappeared. Breathing heavily, he looked up at the sky, and then muttered, "Mercy . . . mercy . . ."

TWENTY-NINE

He sat down in the Eagle Café near Riri's place, to avoid
being seen by her. He was very sorry that he had not spoken to the servant or the little girl, and had not been able
for a single moment to shake himself out of the paralysis
which had gripped him. The girl was sweet, energetic, and
dainty; wasn't her age consistent with the whole sad epi-
sode? What could he do now? He could not postpone his
answer; the past was becoming more and more loathsome,
and the thought of going back to Qadriyya was too awful
to even be considered. He totally abandoned the idea of
running away; he had got used to running several times a
day, but he would not do so in the face of this new reality
which had stirred up the turgid marsh of his own life till it
burst out from free springs. Maybe it was a final despair-
ing invitation to a life with some meaning—a meaning he
had failed to find anywhere. No, this time he would not
run away; he could not do so. He would face reality defiantly, and at any price; yes, at any price at all. How he
would welcome it! Qadriyya would certainly be able to

find another man to live under her wing. She deserved affection, it was true, but the false life which he had lived with her did not merit it. It was futile to carry on with such a life, mulling over past fancies without any future. His heart never throbbed with love for anything, but now here was a golden opportunity for it to throb till he died. The little girl was his own daughter; in a few minutes he would know the truth. He would not condemn her to the same orphaned state which history had decreed for him. A veritable bomb would explode in his life because of her; remarks, rumors, and thoughts, all these things would make him the talk of the town. However, he would steel himself to the ordeal; he would suffer, make amends, and then he would live. Eventually he would find a meaning in life. If and when he could join up with his real family, he would stay in Alexandria, invest his money in this little place, and start a new life. He suppressed his shame, pride, and stubbornness, and faced life courageously.

He waited until it was past midnight. The Corniche was empty, or almost so. The people who were sitting around went away. He noticed people cleaning up in Riri's place, getting ready to close. He went over to the side street that went up into town; he stood at the corner facing the building. A figure appeared at the end of the street; it was Riri approaching. He moved forward a step till he was under the light so that she could make out his features. She came nearer, but did not pay any attention to him as he stood there. She did not bother with dawdlers anymore; that was very good.

"Riri," he said in a gentle, quavering voice as she was about to walk past him.

She stopped and looked at him. "Who are you?" she asked.

He moved a step closer. She stared at him without showing any signs of emotion, "I'm Isa," he replied.

She was looking really fit, coy, and attractive. There was little doubt that she remembered him; at least, the way in which she looked so shocked, then frowned, tightened her lips, and showed her disgust indicated that she did. She was about to move on, but he blocked her path.

"Who are you?" she yelled angrily. "What do you want?"

"I'm Isa, as you know very well!"

"I don't know you," she replied, her face betraying all kinds of different emotions.

"Of course you do," he replied ardently. "There's no reason for you to deny it! I don't expect you to accept excuses, but we've some things to talk about."

"I don't know you; let me pass."

"We must talk," he said desperately. "There's no other way, I'm much more miserable than you can possibly imagine!"

"Go away," she replied angrily, "get lost! That's the best thing you can do!"

"But I'm almost going out of my mind. Who's the little girl, Riri?"

"Which little girl?"

"The one who came and sat on your lap a few hours ago, and then came into this building with her nanny. I noticed you quite by chance, and then I saw her. I followed her until she went into the building. I'm more miserable than you can imagine, I assure you."

"I don't know what you're talking about," she replied emphatically. "Go away; that's the best thing you can do!"

"I'm almost going out of my mind. You must say something. She's my daughter, Riri. You must tell me."

"Get out of my sight," she yelled in the silent street. "You're both blind and mad! Get lost, will you!"

"But my heart has told me everything."

"It's a liar, like you! That's all there is to it."

"You must tell me. I'm going crazy. I realize I've been despicable, but you've got to tell me. Tell me the girl's my daughter."

"The only thing I've got to say to you is: Get lost!"

"I know I deserve to roast in hell, but now I've a chance to do something good. Please don't make me lose it!"

"Go away," she yelled in a voice like a hurricane, "and don't let me see your face again."

"Riri, listen to me. Can't you see that I'm asking you to say something? Even if I died . . ."

"Go to hell! I warn you; get out of my way!" She rushed past him and dashed toward the door of the building.

THIRTY

He returned home before dawn after spending ages wandering along the Corniche by himself. He did not hear the sound of the waves, nor did he notice a single star. He found Qadriyya still awake waiting for him. She looked extremely anxious and annoyed. He was on the point of confessing everything to her; had he noticed any sign of encouragement from his conversation with Riri, he would have done so. But all he could tell Qadriyya was that he had been trying to resist his bad habits and had felt the need to hang around on the Corniche till dawn. "Damn it all," he told himself as he flung himself on the bed, "I must pull this false life out by the roots. Either there's got to be a new life, or else there's no escape; it'll be back to the gambling, cognac, and old women's chatter in the corner of El Bodega."

He went begrudgingly with her to the Rio cinema the next day in the evening, and then they ate dinner in a tavern. Afterwards they went home, and he made to go out.

"Go to sleep, my dear," he told her, "sleep well and leave me to cure myself."

He hovered for a long time around Riri's place and in front of the building in case he might catch a glimpse of the little girl, but without success. He sat down in the Eagle Café. In spite of his failure the day before, there was still a vague hope that kept toying with him as though he were drunk. He believed that tonight all the world's problems would be solved without any trouble. He looked up at the sky, obscured by dark clouds, and told himself that autumn in Alexandria has a spirit of paradise about it to wash away all sorrows; they were merely illusions, and death was the guardian of eternal happiness. "How marvelous," he whispered to himself, "to be drunk without drinking any wine."

A bootblack was standing in front of him and giving him a pleading look. Isa noticed him and read more than one meaning in the look which the man was giving him. Isa gestured to him to sit down and then gave him his shoes to shine. He was eager to console himself by confirming his idea about this man. "Are there any vacant flats around?" he asked.

"At this time of year," the man replied with a smile, "there are more flats available than worries in a man's heart!"

"I'm really looking for a vacant room."

"In a pension?"

"I'd prefer a family!" Isa replied with a wink.

The man smiled and relaxed a little. "There are more families around too than worries in a man's heart!"

Isa laughed happily. Then he had a thought and pointed toward Riri's place. "What about the proprietress of Take It and Thanks?"

The man's expression changed. "No, no!" he replied earnestly. "She's a proper woman in every sense of the word."

Isa looked at him in a way that seemed to be telling him to continue.

"Don't waste your time," the man said. "I've nothing to do with her."

"You don't understand me," Isa replied. "One look at her is enough to confirm what you're saying. She has a lovely little girl."

"Yes, Ni'mat. She's her daughter and she's legitimate too!"

Isa smiled, trying to look unconcerned. "But you never see her father," he said. "Isn't she married?"

"Of course. Her husband owns the place."

"Why doesn't he run it himself?"

"He's in prison," the man replied after a moment's hesitation.

"What for?"

"Drugs! He's been done an injustice, I swear by God."

"May the good Lord release him! But are you sure he's the child's father?"

A cautious look flashed across the man's eyes. "Of course!" he replied.

"No, no!" Isa said with a brash confidence. "Either you know the truth and refuse to admit it," he continued with a laugh, "or else I know more than you do."

"What do you know?"

"I'd like to hear it from you. Otherwise, how can we do any business with one another if you start off by lying to me?"

The bootblack put polish on Isa's shoes. "They say," he

replied with resignation, "that the good man wrote his name on the birth certificate!"

"But why?"

"He's old and a good man. He had no children and loved the woman. So he married her in the proper way!"

"A good man indeed," Isa replied, finding it hard to swallow his saliva. "He doesn't deserve to be in prison."

"That's why she keeps the place going and waits for him patiently and loyally."

"He deserves that and more," said Isa. He gave the man ten piasters and wished him well for the future.

After midnight he waited under the lamp. She spotted him as she was approaching, frowned angrily, and moved away from where he was standing.

"I've been waiting," he pleaded. "It's been agony for me. We must talk."

She walked on without answering, and so he stood in her way. "She's my daughter," he said. "At least tell me that."

"I'll yell for the police," she said angrily.

"She's my daughter! I know the whole truth."

"I'll yell for the police. Aren't you listening?"

"You should yell mercy and forgiveness instead."

She cowed him with a flood of abuse. "Hellfire's what you deserve," she retorted, "not forgiveness."

"Let's look for a way to forget the past."

"I've forgotten it entirely. Now you disappear with it!"

"Listen, Riri. You're waiting in vain. You'll get your freedom and then . . ."

"What lousy wretch you are!" she interrupted furiously. "Just as you always were. Can't you ever imagine anything good?"

He screwed up his face in pain. "It really has been agony for me," he groaned.

"Your agonies are no business of mine," she replied bitterly.

"She's my daughter. She's got nothing to do with that man in prison."

Riri looked at him aghast but soon recovered her composure. "She's his daughter," she replied. "He adopted her because of his own ideas about what's right. She belongs to him forever and so do I."

He screwed up his face even more.

"Just make sure you don't meet me again after this," she said threateningly. "I'm warning you . . ."

"You're closing the door of mercy, Riri."

"You closed it yourself. So get lost."

"But my daughter . . ." he said tearfully.

"You're not a father," she retorted as she rushed on her way. "You're a coward; you could never be a father!"

He stood there hiding behind the side of a cabin on the beach at Camp Cesare, stealing furtive looks at them. Riri was sitting under an umbrella with her arms folded, and little Ni'mat was bending over the sand a few yards away, eagerly digging a pit. It was a clear morning, and the sun covered the meager gathering of people scattered over the beach; it was a gentle, kindly sun, brightened by an invigorating breeze. He kept out of her sight, so much so that no one would have realized he had come. His heart melted as he looked at the little girl and he wanted to kiss her and then disappear forever. Her body was tiny but well formed, a woman's shape in miniature. Her tanned legs, her thighs, her long hair wet at the ends, her uncovered sides, her orange bathing costume, and her total involvement in what she was doing, it was all incredible and marvelous; and she was really happy. There she was, the fruit of boredom on his part and fear on the part of her mother; and yet, from these two reprehensible qualities, life had created an attractive being, overflowing with health and happiness. The hidden power's will had decreed, and all obstacles had collapsed in the face of the eternal enigmatic awakening. This little girl was a sure sign of the idiocy of many fears, a token of nature showing us how it is possible to overcome corruption. Now, he thought, can't you imitate nature, just once? From your sorrows, losses, and defeats, can't you make a victory, even if it's just a modest one? It's nothing rare or new. The sea has kept its appearance for millions of years and seen countless examples of it, and so has the clear blue sky.

Finally he left his hiding place and moved toward the little girl without worrying about Riri, who was standing up to face him. He sank down on the sand beside the little girl. He was alarmed by the suddenness of it all, but even so he planted a long, warm kiss on her cheek. Then he muttered, "Farewell," and left without turning back.

When lunchtime came, he did not feel like going home, and so he ate at 'Ala Kaifak. At three o'clock, he went to the cinema and then at six to another one. Afterwards he went back to 'Ala Kaifak to have dinner and drink some cognac. He sat there for a long time; the wine seeped into his head and made him feel drunk. He felt comforted by the view and by his own dreams.

Just before midnight, he saw someone coming toward the restaurant who attracted his attention like an electric shock. It was a tall, muscular, dark young man, wearing gray trousers and a white short-sleeved shirt and carrying a red rose between the fingers of his left hand. He came up close to the restaurant with a strong, graceful stride. There was a bold, piercing look in his eyes and they exchanged glances as he entered the place. He stared at Isa intently, and Isa realized that he recognized him. Then with some-

459 / Autumn Quail

thing akin to a smile the man averted his face with its elongated features, and went to the fruit juice corner.

It was he and no one else. From the war days. One
night, he had arrested this young man, and until dawn he
had attended the inquest himself in his official and party
capacity. The young man had been bold and stubborn, and
the inquest had not found him guilty. He had been sent to
prison anyway and had stayed there till the ministry had
resigned. What could he be doing now? Had he secured a
senior position in the new regime? Or was he still a revolutionary? Why had he smiled? It was quite clear that he
remembered him; should he expect some sudden act of
violence? He decided to put the man out of his mind, but
some irresistible impulse made him turn toward the fruit
juice corner. He saw the man standing there facing toward
the inside of the place; he was holding a glass of mango
juice in his right hand and looking inquisitively in his
direction. His eyes seemed to smile sarcastically. Isa looked
outside again; he felt utterly depressed. It was as though,
with that look, the past were pursuing him.

Before long he got up and left the place. He headed
straight for the Corniche. It did not occur to him to go
home; indeed it seemed to him that he no longer had any
home at all. After walking a considerable way, he headed
toward the square and sat on a bench under Saad Zaghlul's statue. Most of the benches were empty. The cold
breeze blew gently around the wide square and toyed with
the palm trees. The stars were shining in the enormous
vault above him, and the night was as fixed as eternity
itself. He had not yet succeeded in erasing the memory of
the young man from his mind, but he resolved to devise a
plan for the future. However, he had hardly buried himself

in his own dreams when he was aware of someone sitting by his side. He looked around with a suppressed feeling of annoyance and saw the defiant young man. He started in alarm, thinking that he must have followed him every step of the way and was planning to do him harm. He sprang up to defend himself but at the same time felt ashamed at the thought of slinking away. Just then, the young man spoke to him in a throaty voice. "Good evening, Ustaz* Isa," he said kindly, "or rather, good morning; it's a few minutes past midnight."

Isa looked at him coldly in the gleam of a distant light. "Good morning," he replied. "Who are you?"

"You remember me, of course!"

"I'm very sorry," said Isa, feigning amazement, "who are you?"

The young man laughed as if to say, "You know, and so do I!" "Enemies are the very last people you forget!" he said.

"I don't understand what you're talking about."

"Yes, you do! You remember the inquest that went on till morning. Then I was sent to prison. Even you used to put free people in prison. Unfortunately . . ."

"I don't know precisely what you're talking about," Isa replied, retreating a little, "but I certainly remember the war days and the harsh circumstances which often forced us to do things we didn't like doing."

"That's the traditional excuse. Never mind! What's past is past."

Isa did not say a word, but looked straight ahead to make it clear that he wished to be left alone, in the hope that the other man would go away and leave him in peace. But he started talking again. "The world has changed," the man said gently. "Don't think I'm being malicious. I would never do a thing like that, I promise you. But I often feel sorry . . ."

"I don't need your sympathy," Isa interrupted somewhat angrily.

"Don't get angry and misunderstand my reasons for intruding on you. I would like to discuss things seriously with you."

"What?"

"The world around us!"

Isa realized that he was still drunk. "Nothing bothers me anymore," he said.

"It's quite the opposite with me," the young man replied. "Everything concerns me; I think about everything . . ."

"Then I hope the world turns out as you wish."

"Isn't that better than sitting in the dark under Saad Zaghlul's statue?"

"That's fine as far as I'm concerned. Don't bother about me."

"You haven't made up your mind to open your heart to me yet."

"Why should I? Don't you see that the whole world's a bore?"

"I haven't got time to be bored."

"What are you doing then?"

"I make a joke of the troubles I used to have, and look ahead with a smile. I smile in spite of everything; so much that you might think I was mad."

"What makes you smile?"

"Incredible dreams," the young man replied in a still more earnest tone. "Let's choose somewhere better to talk."

"I'm sorry," Isa replied quickly. "Actually I've already had two glasses of cognac and now I need some rest."

"You want me to sit in the dark under Saad Zaghlul's statue," the young man replied regretfully.

Isa did not say a word. The young man stood up to leave. "You don't want to talk to me," he said. "I shouldn't pester you anymore." He walked away in the direction of the city.

Isa watched him as he left. What an odd young man! I wonder what he's doing now, he thought. Had those troubles really taken pity on him? Why was he looking ahead with a smile? He kept watching the young man till he reached the edge of the square. He had not meant him any harm after all. Why didn't I encourage him to talk? Maybe I should ask him to help me overcome my boredom, even at this hour of the night. Our conversation might lead us into an adventure that would brighten up the night.

He saw the young man disappear in the direction of Safiyya Zaghlul Street. I could catch up with him, he thought, if I didn't waste any more time hesitating. He jumped to his feet in a sudden drunken spurt of enthusiasm and started after the young man with long strides, leaving the seat behind him sunk in solitude and darkness.

Translated from the Arabic by Roger Allen.
Revised by John Rodenbeck.

AUTUMN QUAIL NOTES

'Ala Kaifak: the name means "as you like" or "whatever you like," and may have some symbolic significance—perhaps suggesting Isa's nihilism.

Athenios: a café-restaurant in Alexandria.

Al-Azarita: a district of Alexandria, also known as Al-Mazarita.

bawwab: doorman.

Bey: title of respect for important men, from the Turkish; formerly the title of the governor of a small Ottoman province. Went out of official use in Egypt after the 1952 revolution, but continues as a polite mode of address and reference.

Camp Cesare: a district of Alexandria.

casino: not a place to gamble, but a teahouse or restaurant, especially one along the Corniche in Alexandria or along the river in Cairo. A local evolution from the European-style casinos established around Azbakiya in the nine-teenth century.

"clear destruction": the Arabic adjective *mubiin* (clear, obvious, self-evident) is used many times in the Qur'an, thus giving this phrase a "Qur'anic" flavor.

colocynth: a bitter fruit.

condemned man in the mountain: in Egyptian Arabic, the word for "mountain" is often used to mean "desert," "wasteland," or, to Nile Valley residents, far-off, isolated areas such as the desert oases. Egyptian regimes have at times sent some criminals to work in areas such as these; thus "the condemned man in the mountain" would be a man sentenced to labor in the far reaches of the country.

conquian: a card game similar to rummy.

Corniche: from the French, a road passing alongside water (i.e., in Cairo, along the Nile; in Alexandria, along the Mediterranean coast).

Dokki: an upper-middle-class district of Giza, across the river from Cairo; it was then, as it is now, associated with the *nouveau arrivé*.

faqih: a reader or reciter of the Qur'an.

ful: fava beans; one of the staples of the Egyptian diet.

gallabiyya: the ankle-length garment worn by men of the lower classes in Egypt.

Gleem: a district of Alexandria.

Groppi's: a famous café-restaurant in Cairo; its proprietors were European.

Al-Hajj(a): someone who has made the pilgrimage to Mecca (the "a" indicates a woman).

Hanem: a term of respect addressed to a woman, much as the terms Bey and Pasha are applied to a man.

Hijaz: The area of the Arabian peninsula, formerly a kingdom and now a viceroyalty, that includes Mecca and Medina. The sandalwood rosary is typical of the sort of souvenir brought back by pilgrims from the Holy Places.

Al-Ibrahimiyya: a district of Alexandria.

khamsin: the hot winds which blow off the desert in Egypt, carrying dense clouds of sand.

khwaaga: the colloquial Egyptian term for "foreigner."

Maghrebi: from the Maghreb, or northwestern Africa.

nargila: the hookah or hubble-bubble.

Notable (*a'yan*): a technical term used in Ottoman and later times to denote the local families of influence.

Pasha: title of high civil or military rank used in the Ottoman Empire and continuing in official use in Egypt until the 1952 revolution. Still in use as a polite or respectful term of address.

Ra's al-Barr: a small town in the Nile Delta.

Ramla Square: the square in central Alexandria from which the trains for Ramla leave and where the Trianon restaurant is located.

Ar-Risalat al-Qushairiyya: a treatise by the famous mystic Al Qushairi (d. 1072).

Saad: see Zaghlul.

Sakakini: a district of Cairo.

second grade: the second highest rank in the civil service; the next step would be an under-secretaryship.

Sharia: the Arabic word for "street."

Sidi Bishr: a resort district in Alexandria.

Sidi Umar: the second Caliph, renowned for his asceticism and astuteness.

Spatis: a popular Egyptian cordial.

Sufism: Islamic mysticism.

taamiyya: a pâté made from crushed beans, onions, garlic, and parsley.

Tanta: a town on the railway line midway between Cairo and Alexandria; a center of pilgrimage in Egypt.

twenty-third of July: 1952. The day on which the Army officers took over the government, disbanding Parliament and outlawing the parties.

ulama: religious scholars, particularly those who have studied at Al-Azhar, a mosque and university in Cairo which was long the center of the Islamic intellectual world.

umda: the head of the village community in Egypt, responsible for such things as tax collection and drafting villagers into the Army.

Urabi Pasha: the hero and martyr of nineteenth-century Egyptian nationalism of the 1880s, when the autonomy of the country was threatened by European concerns over investments. The nationalist movement was crushed, but never forgotten, in 1882, when British troops defeated the Egyptian Army. This uprising was also characterized by fires, as Alexandria was set ablaze by the fighting.

Ustaz: literally "professor," but used in Egyptian colloquial dialect to mean little more than "Mr."

Wafd: "delegation"; the name of the political party founded in 1919 by Saad Zaghlul which was the major political force in Egypt before the 1952 revolution.

Al-Wayiliyya: a district of Cairo.

Zaghlul, Saad: the famous Egyptian nationalist leader and Prime Minister, 1924–27; founder of the Wafd Party, to which Isa belonged.

Zizinia: a district of Alexandria.

READING LOG
